FALLING FROM THE GROUND

TONIO FAVETTA

Can't Put It Down Books

Falling From the Ground
By Tonio Favetta
Copyright 2017 by Tonio Favetta

ISBN: 978-0-9972024-3-4
Printed in the United States of America

This is a work of fiction. Names, characters, places and incidents are either a product of the author's imagination or are used fictitiously. Any resemblance to actual events, or persons or locales, living or dead, is purely coincidental.

Published by
Can't Put It Down Books
An imprint of
Open Door Publications
2113 Stackhouse Dr.
Yardley, PA 19067

Cover Design by Genevieve Lavo Cosdon, lavodesign.com

To my extraordinary wife, Julie, the world would be a better place if you were in charge of it.

And to my ingenious daughters, Anna and Rachel, the world is a better place because you're in it.

You're all the inspiration I ever need.

1 ROAD TRIP

The beige minivan twisted down the exit ramp, tires shrieking. Screams became laughter in the back seat when Alison turned to look at Olivia. "You didn't think my family vacation was going to be *this* exciting, did you?"

Alison noticed her mother, sitting like a statue, gripping the dashboard and the grab handle above the door. Mom snapped around to glare at Dad. "Mother of Pearl! Tommy, the brake's the one on the left."

Here we go again. Alison checked to see if Olivia was cringing or anything, but Olivia didn't seem bothered by Mom and Dad.

It felt like they'd been on the road for a hundred years. The night before, Olivia had slept over so they could leave on time. Dad's idea of on time turned out to be crazy, stupid, still-dark early. Alison had wanted to stay in her pajamas, but Olivia talked her into getting dressed.

They had made it as far as the end of their street when Alison realized that she had forgotten her phone. Dad said he wasn't going to turn around for that, but then Mom had freaked out and made him.

"Suppose she's dead in a ditch?"

"If she's dead she can't call." Michael had been slumped in the back row like a dead body. Even with his eyes closed he looked grumpy and annoyed. But Alison thought he looked like that most of the time, especially in the morning. It was kind of a miracle to see him before lunch. The Vampire, Dad called him.

It had taken Michael and Dad forever to jam in all the bags, sweatshirts, pillows and blankets until the big luggage carrier strapped to the roof rack bulged like an overstuffed burrito.

When Alison had found her phone in her backpack, she knew Dad was going to flip.

He did.

Then Mom did.

"That's what happens when you rush me," Alison snapped.

"If you packed last night when we told you to…" Mom had let the ending just hang there.

Back at the roller-coaster off-ramp, after Dad had practically flipped the car and killed them all, Alison watched Mom stop glaring at Dad so that she could turn around and start glaring at Michael instead.

"Michael, I know that you think you're all grown up now and leaving for college, but I'm still your mother, and I told you not to use that kind language, especially in front of the girls."

"I'm surprised Vampire is awake." Dad huffed.

"Even he couldn't sleep through your driving," Mom said.

"Relax, Mom. They can't hear me," Michael declared. He was sprawled out, apparently enjoying having the back bench all to himself. "They're wearing headphones."

Alison smiled across at Olivia, trouble bubbling up like a fountain inside her. "We can *so* hear you, Michael." She pulled off the headphones, but did not turn around. "You should watch your mouth around our delicate young ears."

"Shut up, Alison." She heard Michael scrambling to lean forward, putting his head between her and Olivia's. "And don't act like you and Olivia don't talk like that when Mom's not around."

"Exactly. *Not* around Mom. *I'm* not stupid."

"So you're saying I am?"

"I didn't say that." Michael was making it too easy.

"You implied it."

"Implied. That's a pretty big word for you."

Michael put his face up to Alison's ear and gritted his teeth. "Alison, I swear…"

"ENOUGH!" Dad thundered.

"You really shouldn't swear, Michael," Alison chided. She slipped the headphones back on and pretended not to hear the things Michael called her.

"If by some miracle your father's right and this place really exists, we're stopping for lunch now. So stop eating those chips," Mom barked. "Especially you, Alison. What would Dr. Pam say? No point in seeing a nutritionist if you ignore her." Alison handed the bag to Olivia so she could roll the top closed.

Thanks, Mom. That's not too humiliating.

Mom waved a finger. "And stop bothering your brother! We let Olivia come with us so you *wouldn't* bother Michael."

"Yeah. Great plan," Michael snorted. "Now they're *both* bothering me."

Looking stunned, Olivia put her hand to her chest. "What did *I* do?"

"Could everyone please stop yelling for one minute?" Dad clenched his teeth. "I'm trying to drive here."

"If that's what you want to call it," Mom said.

Dad scowled. "You don't like my driving? Fine. After lunch it's all you. If you hadn't been distracting me with your directions, I would have been in the right lane in the first place."

"Distracting you?" Mom cocked her head around and looked just as annoyed as Dad. "If I didn't say anything you would have blown right past the exit. You're the one who's dying to stop here. We all want to get to Cape November."

"You didn't stop at Irma's with your friends?" Dad laughed. That was half the reason me and my friends liked driving down the Cape.

Alison always liked it when Mom and Dad talked about the past. It wasn't just that they had probably been happier back then, but they seemed happier when they talked about it.

Mom shrugged. "We drove straight through. Anyway, this place has probably been shut down for years." Mom stared out her window.

"Great positive thinking there, hon." Dad huffed.

Mom snorted. "Aww, poor Tommy. Why don't you tell Nelson and the rest of your buddies the next time you play golf with them?"

Alison cringed as something squeezed her gut.

Dad looked angrily at Mom. "You're not really bringing that up now, are you?"

Alison dug her nails into her palms. Her chest felt tight.

"What? That all you ever do anymore is play golf or go fishing with *your* friends?"

"That's *not* all I do."

"Oh right. How could I forget poker night?" Mom spat.

"Maybe we don't have to talk about this right now." Alison caught Dad's glance in the rearview mirror. His voice was tense and tight.

"No, I suppose you're right." Mom gave a big sigh and looked out the window. "You can talk about it later. You can call up Gerry. Or Roberto."

Alison watched Dad's lips tighten over his teeth, but he didn't say anything.

"Are we stopping soon?" Michael groaned. "I gotta take a leak."

2 REST STOP

As the minivan crunched onto the gravel parking lot, Alison surveyed the long, low wooden building. It looked like an oversized log cabin. It didn't encourage her that their minivan was the only car in the lot, but she felt stiff and sore from sitting and was happy to get out. Even if it was at a place where no one else on the planet apparently wanted to go.

"Dad, this place is a pit." Michal squinted up at the sign.

"You don't know anything." Dad put the car in park. "We used to stop here all the time coming down the Cape. You're going to love it." A large wooden sign hanging over the door advertised *Irma's BBQ Station*. On the other side of the parking lot another sign was supposed to say the same thing, but some of the letters were missing so it said *I ma B ation*.

"Look," Olivia said, "I'm a bat ion."

Alison laughed. "What's that? A bat with a negative charge?"

That made Olivia laugh. Michael looked annoyed, only making it funnier.

"Bantam's Qi Bistro!" Olivia added.

"Game on!" Alison thought for a moment, rearranging letters in her mind. "Batman's Qi Bistro!" Alison replied.

"Iraq bombs a tint."

"We're using proper nouns now?" Alison said.

"You started. You used Batman."

Alison closed her eyes for a moment, "Tom's in Qatar bibs. That totally wins."

"Does not!"

"It's basically a real sentence."

"Barely." Olivia folded her arms across her chest. "What are Qatar bibs?"

"Bibs from Qatar. Duh!"

"Nerds?" Michael cooed. "Oh nerds? You can stop now."

Creaking and groaning, they unfolded themselves from their seats and stretched in the oppressive, soggy heat.

"It's gonna rain," Dad said.

"Yeah, you might actually have to sit and talk to me," Mom snapped. "What a bore."

Alison stopped rummaging for her phone and turned to watch her parents. Something heavy writhed inside her.

"Did I say that?" Dad protested.

"You were thinking it."

"So now you're a mind-reader?"

Mom seemed to soften. "You're right. Why am I being mean? You're allowed to play golf. It's your vacation, too."

Alison felt Olivia's shoulder brush against her own. She relaxed her fists enough so that her nails stopped digging into her palms.

"I wasn't even talking about golf. I don't care if I go golfing. If you don't want me to golf just say it. I'll call Nelson and tell him forget it."

"Hang on. He's actually down the Cape?" Mom sounded suspicious.

Her father chuckled and looked at the gravel. "He's not down the Cape; he's over at Friendly Point."

"That's only an hour from the Cape," Mom said coldly.

"It's a little over an hour, actually." Dad's half-smile deflated to a scowl. "Look, I mentioned we were coming down for the week, and he said he was going to be in Friendly Point for the weekend—just the weekend. We thought maybe we could sneak in a quick nine. There's this great course over in…"

"It's never a quick nine with Nelson." Alison watched the muscles tighten in Mom's cheeks. "Nine becomes eighteen and then thirty-six. Then you head to the clubhouse for drinks, and I don't see you all day. Why didn't you tell me?"

"I didn't think of it. Look, if you don't want me to, I won't go. It's no big deal."

Alison knew that wasn't true, but she bit her lip like she always did. Hard. Getting in the middle would set off World War III.

Mom looked at the gravel and then at Dad. She dropped her voice to just above a whisper but Alison heard her anyway. "It's not that I don't want you to play golf," Mom said. "I don't want you to want to play golf. I don't want to always be the nag who says you can't go."

Dad laughed unpleasantly. "I'm an adult, Sara. I can do what I want."

"I know." Mom sighed and looked across the parking lot. "But it would be nice if what you wanted to do was stay with me sometimes."

"Is it such a crime that I like golfing and fishing? You have your book club."

Mom's hands snapped to her hips. "We meet once a month at most."

Dad's mouth hung open for a long, silent moment, but no words crawled out. Cringing, Alison looked at Olivia who stared awkwardly at the little gift shop next to Irma's. She looked as if she wanted to be anywhere but in that parking lot. Not that Alison could blame her.

From the entrance to the restaurant, Michael's voice floated across the haze. "Are you people coming? It's hot and I'm starving and I need to take a leak."

Inside Irma's BBQ Station, Dad reminded them about a million times that this was the place where everyone used to stop on the way down the Cape. Alison didn't think it looked like anyone stopped there anymore. It was a dark, old restaurant that smelled like mildew. Soft, old-timey country music crackled out from hidden speakers.

"Well at least it's not crowded." Mom said it a little too cheerily.

"Sure," Dad grunted. "Nobody likes to stop at places like this anymore. They just hit the drive-through and get where they're going."

Alison knew that was aimed at her and Michael. Dad always took them on roads labeled *scenic* and stopped along the way. This drove Alison and Michael crazy most of the time, but sometimes he surprised them with oddball stuff that turned out to be cool.

Mom had a photo album of these trips. Alison would look at it with her sometimes. There were pictures of Alison and Michael petting Otto, the World's Largest Two-Headed Dog. He was stuffed, of course. According to the guy in the museum, Otto died in 1974. The museum was in the back of a tractor-trailer. At that same stop they also got to feed a sheep with five horns, and there was a skeleton of a so-called *real* mermaid. It was the size of a large cat, and the tail looked like it had been made out of salami. Alison asked the guy about it, and he said that the original skeleton had been damaged in a fire but that this was a *faithful reproduction based on DNA samples and archeological evidence.* Alison remembered being impressed, but she had been only seven at the time.

Then there was the time they stopped at the old tin works. The sign on the factory read *If we can't make it out of tin, you probably don't need it.* Alison had spent the whole time pointing out why the sign was wrong because she thought annoying the tour guide was hilarious. *How about food? How about clothes? How about soap?* Mom was so embarrassed that at the end of the tour she bought a set of tin coffee cups that they used on their one and only camping trip the next year. Camping had been a real disaster. Michael and Alison had begged their father to rent a camper, but he insisted, *If you want to camp, you sleep in a tent. Otherwise what's the point?*

Even sitting in a booth at Irma's so many years later, Alison's mother started to laugh as soon as Alison reminded her of that trip.

"Your father was so proud of that sad little tent," she laughed.

"Until it started to rain," Alison said.

Dad's mouth twisted into a scowl. "Yeah, and the sun was going down and your brother, the rocket scientist, wandered off."

"Really?" Olivia asked. Alison hadn't realized that Olivia had never heard this one.

"Oh yeah," Dad explained. "There was no sign of him. I tell you, Olivia, we're laughing about it now, but at the time…It's a feeling I would never wish on any parent."

"How long was he gone?"

"Like three hours," Dad said. "So Sara and Alison stayed in the car while this big thunderstorm rolls in. Lightning. Thunder. Wind. I knew it was only a matter of time before a big tree fell on us and killed us all. We had to get out of there, find a hotel or something, but we didn't have Michael."

"What did you do?" Olivia asked.

Dad said, "It was like the Apocalypse. The rain was coming down like a waterfall. The lightning and thunder was right on top of me. Branches—trees—everything was coming down, and I'm picturing my son dead someplace. And if he's alive, he's terrified."

"Tommy was out screaming his head off through the whole storm looking for Michael. I was beside myself. I wanted to look too, but I had to stay with Alison. It was totally dark, but at least the storm had blown over by the time Michael came back to our campsite. He was asking what was for dinner, totally dry, like nothing had happened. This was about nine o'clock at night. None of us had eaten."

"Where was he?" Olivia asked.

Dad scowled at Michael. "The rocket scientist found another kid. He went back to his camper to play video games."

Everybody started laughing, even Dad.

"Tommy came back bleeding, covered in scratches and soaked to the bone. But you should have seen the look on his face when he saw Michael sitting at the campsite with a flashlight, on a little folding chair, eating a peanut butter and jelly sandwich."

"I was ready to kill him right there."

"That's not true," Mom protested. "You gave him a big hug because you'd been so worried."

"Aww," Michael said. "You really care, Dad."

"To top it all off, the next day and for three weeks after, I was itching all over because I'd gone through some poison ivy."

3 FEEDING THE PYTHONS

At the table, Olivia swallowed her last bite of awesome cheeseburger. Mr. Nunios was right; the food was great. The old wood paneling made everything dark, but antique stained glass lamps, each one different, hung over the tables. In the yellow light of the lamps, Olivia saw dozens of black and white photographs stuck on the mirror. Many were of parties from long ago with people dancing in suits and dresses. In some they wore paper party hats like it was New Year's Eve or something. Some were close-ups, signed by people Olivia had never heard of, but who must have been famous once. She wondered if she signed a picture and hung it on the mirror, would some kid in fifty years think she had been a celebrity because she had a picture hanging on the wall.

The table was littered with their dirty plates. Everyone's antique map placemat was stained with ketchup and barbecue sauce except Mrs. Nunios's. Her map was still clean. Olivia could see the tentacles of a mythical sea monster just offshore near a finger of land labeled *Cape November*.

Feeling guilty for picking at her fries in front of Alison, Olivia covered her plate with her paper napkin like Alison had. That had been Alison's nutritionist's suggestion. If Alison finished all her fries, her mother would be all over her about it.

To distract herself from the fries, Olivia watched Michael tip back in his chair and pat his rock-hard abs. The terrifying boneyard in his plate used to be his Oink and Cluck Deluxe platter.

Mrs. Nunios called the pale, young waitress and politely asked her to wrap up her grilled chicken Caesar salad.

"You're taking that?" Mr. Nunios asked, sounding doubtful.

"It's a whole piece of chicken and a lot of salad."

"Who's gonna eat it?"

"I'll eat the chicken." Michael beamed.

"You'll eat anything," Alison pointed out.

"I gotta feed the pythons." While the waitress cleared their places, Michael grinned broadly and, leaning farther back in his chair, flexed his huge biceps in his red sleeveless tee shirt. It said Bulls Wrestling. The waitress was pretty, Olivia decided, in a washed-out kind of way. Not her type, but she could see where Michael would try to flirt with her.

Olivia had spent a lot of time in one gym or another, and as a swimmer, she had seen plenty of great bodies, both male and female. There was no denying that Michael was in impressive shape. Big, but not bulky. Solid as a rock. A lot of girls thought Michael was totally hot and, while he definitely wasn't her type, she understood the attraction. She considered for a moment what it would be like to be with Michael, but it was only a thought experiment. With his thick mop of curly black hair, he looked like a male version of Alison, except his eyes were blue like his dad and Alison's were brown like Mrs. Nunios. It wasn't like she never fantasized about being with Alison, but when the fantasy was over and reality returned, she felt dirty and guilty, so she rarely indulged in that daydream. There were plenty of other pretty girls to think about.

Olivia felt embarrassed and slightly violated when Michael's chair made a loud cracking noise, startling her out of her naughty thoughts. He flapped his arms like a bird to keep from falling over backwards. Olivia laughed out loud.

"Don't encourage him," Mrs. Nunios sighed.

"Did you just break the chair, Mikey?" Mr. Nunios snapped. "I swear if you busted that chair…"

Michael looked down and wiggled his weight around on it. "No. I saved it."

Olivia cracked up at Michael and then really lost it when she saw that Alison had snarfed club soda out of her nose. Michael was laughing, too.

The waitress looked more annoyed than amused, probably because she was the one cleaning up. The waitress scurried back into the kitchen to wrap the food for Michael's pythons. Watching her sway Olivia realized the waitress might have been more her type than she had first thought. Not that Olivia could do anything about it at the moment. She couldn't even flirt badly like Michael. Not unless she was ready to answer a bunch of uncomfortable questions. And she wasn't. *Story of my life.*

"She was checking me out, though, right?" Michael winked at Alison and Olivia with his twinkling blue eyes.

"I don't even think she speaks English," Alison pointed out.

"Even better," Michael grinned. "She can marry me for citizenship and we won't ever have to talk."

"You're disgusting," Alison sneered. "That girl is a human being with a job. She's not here to be your sick fantasy."

"Calm down. I'm just joking around." Michael waved his hand dismissively.

"Listen, Romeo," Dad growled, "the way you eat I can't afford to pay for new furniture, too."

"Don't worry," Michael replied. He repositioned his Bulls baseball cap on his moppy head. "I have cat-like reflexes."

Olivia and Alison looked at one another and rolled their eyes.

4 GIFT SHOP

"Gotta drain the lizard again before we hit the road."

"Michael, honestly." Mom sounded exhausted. "Are you going to say things like that in college?"

"Only when I gotta go," Michael tossed over his shoulder.

Alison didn't want to just sit there waiting for the check with her parents. It would only make her want to finish her fries, and that would set Mom off. Nobody had screamed at anybody in the last fifteen minutes. Alison was afraid she'd jinx it, but she wanted to check out the store before they got back in the car.

"Olivia and I are going to the gift shop."

"Don't buy any junk," her father warned.

"Leave them alone, Tommy. She's got babysitting money."

"You should be saving up for gas money. Don't you want to get your license next year?" Dad looked hopeful, like a little kid.

"It's not like you're going to buy me a car."

Alison breathed a little sigh of relief that her father didn't sound angry. "That's what I'm saying. You can save up for a car."

"It would take me ten years to afford a car."

That made Dad scowl. "So what? You might as well throw your money away on some piece of junk at a gift shop as soon as possible. And where are you gonna put it? We're packed to the gills already."

Alison thought of a place she'd like to put it, but she was not about to say that to her father.

The gift shop was part of the log cabin building, but it had its own entrance. Just like the restaurant, everything was made of old wood. The same creaky music was pumping quietly. It took a moment for Alison's eyes to adjust to the dark store.

An old woman watched them from her perch on a stool behind the front counter. She was round and flabby. Parts of her oozed over the side of the stool. Her face was red and rough. Above her scowl, her hair stuck up like wires.

Alison remembered what it felt like to be overweight, not that she'd ever been as big as the old woman. She wondered for a moment if that's what she would have eventually looked like if she hadn't started eating better and exercising more. If Olivia hadn't helped her. Alison felt kind of sorry for the old woman who had no Olivia in her life. Maybe she didn't have anyone in her life. Alison smiled at her, but the old woman just kept scowling. This annoyed Alison. *This is why I never bother to be nice to people.*

Even this far up the highway, there were Cape November postcards and magnets, picture frames and ashtrays. Some showed the beach or the ocean, but they could have been of any beach as far as Alison could tell. There were a few old-fashioned sepia pictures of old cars and men in suits with derby hats and women in long hoop skirts. A few faded postcards showed a lighthouse that looked like it was made of blue stone blocks.

But the place was more like an antiques store than a gift shop. There were sets of old dishes, racks of men's neckties, a whole row of used coffeemakers, all shoved next to each other with no order, just chaos.

As Alison moved farther in, the shelves became more cluttered and dusty. A black mug caught her eye. Examining it, she saw a dark sky over a stormy ocean. Huge octopus tentacles reached up out of the waves. Blue, dripping letters spelled, *Beware of Cappy*. Alison shivered slightly and set down the mug. The whole place was giving her the creeps, and she was sorry she'd come in. Alison glanced back at the old woman. Still scowling.

Alison found Olivia, moving from shelf to shelf, picking up a ratty old pocketbook and then a huge desktop lighter. She was fascinated by stuff like that. Olivia was curious about everything, like a little kid in some ways. Each new thing she would pick up and show Alison. They laughed together. It felt good.

They laughed like that the night before when they were packing. Alison had spent an hour giving Olivia a killer pedicure, and then she hid her toes inside her stupid running shoes. She had probably destroyed the pedicure, but Alison had learned a long time ago that it wasn't worth getting annoyed at Olivia for things like that. That was just Olivia. She was proud to be clueless about fashion.

The crazy part was, even standing in some dirty gift shop wearing a pair of boring khaki shorts and a plain blue tank top, Olivia still looked ridiculously, hopelessly beautiful. Everybody said she looked exotic, which drove Olivia completely insane. Olivia's mom was tall, blonde and fair-skinned. Her dad was also tall with dark skin. When he was younger, he had been a soccer star in Senegal. Olivia's parents were both workout nuts. They ran marathons and stuff. Not together. They had been divorced before Alison even met Olivia.

Olivia was tall like her parents, and she had gorgeous caramel skin. Her long, coppery hair had blonde streaks that got lighter in the summer. On rare occasions when she didn't pull it into a ponytail it fell in thick curls to her shoulders. If Alison didn't love Olivia so much, she would hate her for looking like that. A lot of girls did.

Alison watched Olivia examine things from the shelves. *This place is so weird*. There were mounds of souvenir key chains piled inside antique ashtrays that were jammed in next to old picture frames, some metal, some wood, some made of shells. And those were next to more old ashtrays and sets of wine and beer glasses and bottle openers. Some of the bottle openers had handles shaped like lobster claws or octopus arms. There was a row of small ceramic saints and angels and other figures that Alison could not even identify. They were sort of like white squids, but they were standing up like people. Looking at the little squid statues made Alison's skin slither under her hair at the back of her neck.

Alison picked up a corkscrew. It was white and shaped like a squid, or a possibly a jellyfish. It was hard to say. The two arms that pulled out the cork were made to look like long tentacles coming off a bulgy head. There were no eyes, but the opening at the top looked like a mouth full of teeth. The teeth could open a bottle cap. Just looking at the corkscrew made Alison feel a deep, creeping fear. *Who would buy this?*

Olivia suddenly giggled right beside her. It startled Alison, and she dropped the corkscrew noisily into a pile of assorted snow globes.

Up front, the woman gave a wet-sounding grunt.

"Liv, you gave me a heart attack." She breathed a sigh of relief that nothing had broken.

Olivia held up a wooden sign with a picture of a huge man standing over a toilet. He was missing completely. The large letters under the picture read: *We aim to please, so you aim too, please.*

Alison laughed and the slithery feeling went away.

Olivia grinned and showed Alison a second sign. "We should get this one for Doctor Farwen's math class." The ceramic plaque read: *Today's not your day and tomorrow ain't looking so good either.*

Alison picked up a round mirror with a magnetic backing. It had the words *You look awful!* across the top. Alison laughed, "This is perfect for my locker."

"Not funny." Olivia's mouth was an irritated slit.

One of the things Alison always found amazing, but kind of annoying, was the way Olivia rarely said anything bad about anyone, even about the jerks who were mean to her. Olivia certainly never let Alison say anything mean about herself. She was like the self-esteem police.

She's a nationally ranked swimmer, in a hundred times better shape than me, but she never, ever, makes me feel bad about myself.

Alison continued to look at her reflection in the mirror. "God, do I really have a double chin?" Alison worked hard to stay in shape. She tried to eat the healthy foods Dr. Pam told her to eat. She watched her portions. She avoided sugar and starch. She ran, rode her bike and tried to get to the gym at least four times a week. Alison had come a long way since her childhood as the class fat kid, but she felt like her body still clung stubbornly to her chubby childhood.

"Don't be stupid," Olivia snapped. "You don't have a double chin. It's just the way you're holding the mirror. Here." Olivia took Alison's hand and brought the mirror up so that it was level with Alison's face. "See? You look great."

Alison didn't think so, but she had to admit her chin looked okay once Olivia moved the mirror. Dad and Mom were both kind of short and loved cooking and wine way more than exercise. Alison knew she was never going to look like Olivia. That used to bother her, but she was becoming okay with it. She was becoming okay with herself.

Dr. Pam, the nutritionist her mother had been taking her to, looked like she never ate anything but kale, and it seemed like that was her plan for Alison, too. She had lost count of how many parties she went to and didn't eat any cake or ice cream or chips. All her friends ate whatever they wanted and no stupid nutritionist had to weigh them once a month to see how they were doing.

The thing that really helped Alison was Aristotle. Yes, *that* Aristotle. The Greek dude with the beard. Student of Plato, teacher of Alexander the Great. He gave Alison the first piece of useful diet advice anybody had ever given her—and he'd been dead for twenty-three hundred years.

Alison and Olivia had first met in the gifted and talented program at school where Mr. W. had them do a unit on philosophy and taught them that, for Aristotle, the right thing was always the middle ground between two extremes. Aristotle called this the Golden Mean. Like to really be successful at school, you can't be just a total nerd who never does anything fun and who just studies twenty-four-seven because you will eventually have a total mental breakdown from the pressure. Alison hoped Olivia wasn't heading that way, but if anybody would...

On the other hand, you can't be a total loser who never does any work and who cuts class all the time because you will keep failing everything and eventually you will just drop out of school and live in your parents' basement complaining about the government. Alison was pretty sure that if she were going to flame out, that would be her way to go. Just flop on the couch with Netflix and Cool-Ranch Doritos and never come up for air until her parents took down a wall and rolled her out of the house on a gurney.

Aristotle's Golden Mean was a balance. So Alison tried to eat healthy, but splurged once in a while. She ate chips in the car, so she didn't eat *that many* of her fries. *Whatever. The place we're staying at the Cape has bikes we can ride.*

Alison put down the mirror and sighed. "What am I going to do next year when I won't have you at school to talk me down?"

"I won't have you either," Olivia protested.

"Hey, I'm not the one that got recruited by some whoop-de-do academy."

"You think I want to spend my junior year getting bullied by a bunch of rich, stuck-up mean-girls? I *begged* my parents to let me stay at the high school with you."

"Yeah, but our team sucks and Ashton Academy is basically a feeder to Team USA. You'll be fine." Alison laughed sarcastically. "Anyway, you're too beautiful to get bullied."

"Yeah." Olivia smirked. "That's how it works."

Olivia was amazingly, stunningly, drop-dead-in-the-street-with-a-smile-on-your-face beautiful. Alison kept waiting for birds and bunnies to flock onto

Olivia's shoulders. Alison was pretty sure that if *she* looked like Olivia, she would be able to take over the world. But Olivia carried her looks like a disease.

Olivia once told Alison that the reason she loved swimming was because the whole race was underwater and nobody could see her. But it was hard to be a recluse and look like, or be as talented, as Olivia. All she ever wanted to do was to fit in, but people treated her like a statue in a museum. Teachers assumed she was dumb. Coaches just wanted her to win. Boys never heard a word she said—and she wasn't even into boys. And forget the girls. The girls were always so jealous, all they ever did was compare Olivia to each other and to celebrities. Olivia had no interest in any of that. *Hel-lo! Haven't any of these idiots noticed that the girl doesn't even wear make-up?*

"Seriously, Liv, you know you look like a model."

Olivia scowled, but only a little. "Don't you start that, too." She laughed then, but something sounded bitter in it. "It doesn't matter. I'll never be popular like you."

"Shut up!" But Olivia was right. Alison owned any room she was in. She had earned that right. Being the fat girl had often made Alison the center of attention whether she wanted to be or not. When Alison was younger and seriously overweight, kids were mean and teachers only made things worse when they tried to help. But being the fat girl who came home crying every day in elementary school had done a few good things for Alison.

She grew a thick skin, and she didn't care who liked her. Unlike a lot of her friends who tried to act a certain way to fit in, Alison never quite fit in, so she could be herself all the time. Once the novelty of making fun of her for being fat wore off, kids just liked her for her. In case anybody didn't get the hint, Alison also developed a flair for coming up with on-the-spot putdowns. Whenever a kid with his hat on sideways and his own YouTube channel took a swipe at Alison, he ended up red-faced and crying while the class pointed at him and laughed. Alison got hauled into the principal's office a lot, but kids stopped bothering her.

That was the third gift her fat childhood had given her. Alison could sense what people were thinking and feeling. Empathy, her guidance counselor back in fifth grade had called it. What she didn't tell her, but what Alison figured out on her own, was that empathy is just another name for knowing someone's weakness.

Sometimes Alison had fun twisting some wannabe bully's insecurities until he cried, but empathy also meant that a lot of kids called her *Mom* and told her their problems and cried on her shoulder. Alison didn't mind that, even though she thought a lot of the kids' problems were just a bunch of stupid drama.

Olivia's arm felt as firm as a bike tire when Alison squeezed it to comfort her. "Going to Ashton might suck for—like—the first month, but then it will be awesome."

"I won't know anyone, Alison. I'm not like you. I can't talk to strangers. I barely talk to the people I know."

Alison laughed. "So be a hermit. They gave you a full scholarship. Girls would kill for that. Last year half the graduating class from Ashton went to Ivy League schools."

Olivia squinted skeptically. "Are you making that up?"

Alison realized that her reputation was even worse than she thought if Olivia had to ask. "It says it in one of those brochures in your bag."

Olivia looked at her skeptically. "Why were you reading that?"

Feeling sheepish, Alison shrugged. "It was the first thing I grabbed. I needed something for the bathroom."

Olivia sighed heavily. "I know Ashton is supposed to be this amazing place and that it's this huge opportunity and all that, but I don't want to move to the ass-end of Pennsylvania."

"You'd rather stay in New Jersey?" Alison found that hilarious.

Olivia punched her playfully in the arm. "I love New Jersey."

Alison massaged her arm. "It will still be here." Alison would not let herself think about how bad school was going to suck without Olivia. She took Olivia by the shoulders and pressed their foreheads together. "And so will I."

Olivia smiled sadly and pulled Alison into a hug. "I know."

Alison couldn't take another second of sappiness. "Hey, this is vacation. Why are we acting like somebody died?" A tee shirt on the shelf caught her eye. It was a cartoon picture of a very curvy woman's body in a bikini. Alison put her head over the collar of the shirt, covering her body with the voluptuous cartoon. "You have to get a picture so I can post this!"

Olivia laughed. "My phone's in the car."

"We'll use mine." Alison fished for her phone in her bag.

"NO PICTURES!" Alison felt an electric shock to the heart when the old woman suddenly screeched from her perch. "Look, this ain't a hangout. You gonna buy something or ain't cha?" The woman scowled and the extra flesh on her red face jiggled.

"I'm looking," Alison explained, her heart still racing.

"So stop touchin' everything unless you're gonna buy it." The old woman scowled at them sternly. "You gotta leave. You gotta leave now."

"Why?" Annoyed, Alison crumpled up the shirt and dropped it on the floor.

"See whatchur doin' there with that shirt? That's why." The old woman oozed off the stool. She flowed like lava around the glass and wood counter. Off the stool, she was short and round. Turning redder, the old woman shouted and spit flew from her flabby lips. "You spoiled rich kids always come in here and mess up the place."

"Mess up *this* place? This place is a pit. I bet no one's been in here for twenty years. Where'd you get all this stuff? From your disgusting hoarder house? Do you use a bucket because you can't get to your toilet?" Alison felt her freckles catch fire. She was mad at herself for feeling any compassion for the woman earlier.

"Get out!" the old woman howled.

Alison suddenly hated the old woman. Disgust churned in the pit of her stomach. "And I *would* have folded it nicely, but you started screaming at us." She began to knock over piles of shirts, ashtrays, plaques, snow globes. Whatever she could get her hands on. "Good luck cleaning up now. Can you even bend over?"

"Alison, cut it out!" Olivia's voice cracked a little. She followed behind Alison, putting things back. She was such a goody-goody.

"That's enough!" Olivia's voice was sharp. "You don't need to be so mean to her."

Her heart hammered in Alison's chest. She could hear the blood flowing through her ears. She felt like a monster.

Angry and embarrassed, Alison just wanted to leave. She took one step toward the door when she saw something shiny on the shelf beside her. She had to see what it was.

"Alison, we should just go." Olivia's words made perfect sense, but that snow globe was nothing like any regular snow globe Alison had ever seen. It was more like looking into a movie. No matter how she turned it, she always seemed to have the same view.

In the dark-blue miniature ocean, two figurines sloshed around through the sparkly flecks of artificial snow. One figure appeared to be a white sperm whale. *Moby Dick?* Alison wondered.

The other white creature was some kind of…sea monster? It looked alien and unfamiliar. It was hard for Alison to understand what she saw. A giant squid? A jellyfish? A lobster?

When Alison moved the snow globe around, the ocean and the two figures stirred slowly, at their own pace. It was as if they weren't reacting to Alison's motion, but were motivated by something else entirely.

"How much is this?" Still looking into it, Alison held the snow globe up to show the old woman.

The old woman's voice screeched, "Put it down. It ain't for you. Just get out!" Alison looked up from the snow globe and saw the old woman shooing at the girls with her hands as if they were raccoons on her garbage cans. "I'm not selling you nothing."

"Why not?" Alison's anger roared back. She looked away from the strange snow globe. The woman waddled over.

Red-faced and puffing, the old woman rasped, "I'm runnin' a business here an' you're trespassers. And shoplifters."

"We are not! Are you ugly *and* deaf? I said I would *buy* this snow globe." Obviously the old bat had no idea who she was dealing with. Alison's rage bubbled down. This final insult made her laugh. "If I wanted to steal something it would have been gone before you knew it was missing."

5 SHOPLIFTERS

Alison's freckles were getting redder and her eyes narrowed to angry slits. Olivia had seen that look too many times. She had to take Alison outside before something bad happened.

"Okay. Sorry. We're going." Olivia said it as calmly as she could.

"No we're not!" Alison didn't take her eyes off the old woman. "We're not sorry and we're not going."

"Yes we are," Olivia said in a pleasant singsong. "Your father is going to want to get back on the road by now. You know how he is if you keep him waiting." Olivia put her arm gently around Alison's shoulder and led her out the door.

As soon as they were outside, Alison broke away from Olivia and sprinted through the hazy parking lot toward the minivan. Olivia hurried to keep up. "Where are you going?"

"Olivia, *hur-ry*!" Alison commanded in an urgent hiss. "I don't want my parents to see." When they were out beside the minivan, Alison stood on the side that faced away from the restaurant.

"See what?" Olivia asked suspiciously.

Alison reached into her purse and pulled out a softball-sized object.

"Is that the snow globe you wanted?" Olivia blinked until she could get her thoughts into focus. "You stole it?" She looked at the two figures. Some kind of monster and… "Is that Moby Dick?" Olivia couldn't keep her voice from rising. "You're going to jail for a stupid Moby Dick snow globe?"

Alison *shushed* her violently and looked nervously over her shoulder, whispering, "Geez, Liv, I don't think my parents heard you yet. Want to just post it?"

Olivia felt herself tighten. She hated getting into trouble almost as much as she hated when Alison was sarcastic. "You *promised* no trouble on this trip, Allie!" She didn't whisper.

"Olivia!" Alison hissed. "Seriously. Shut. Up." The mischievous smile spread across Alison's face. "She deserved it. She was ugly."

"You don't get to steal things because people are ugly. Stop being so mean."

"*She* was mean," Alison added. She held the snow globe up, watching the statuettes inside move and twitch around in the water, almost as if they were alive.

"Whatever," Olivia added more quietly. "You have to bring that back. Your parents will go full psycho!"

"What am I supposed to do, go back in and say, S*orry, I stole some crappy* *crap from your crappy crap store?*"

Olivia looked nervously over her shoulder for Alison's parents "You probably aren't going to want to say it like that."

Alison just rolled her eyes. "Forget it. Anyway, she shouldn't have called us shoplifters."

"Are you mental? Now we *are* shoplifters." *We.* Olivia knew that it had been all Alison and that she was totally innocent of any of it. But *we.*

"Oh well!" Alison proclaimed. Her eyes sparkled like diamonds and were just as hard.

"Did you take it before or after she called us shoplifters?"

Alison gave Olivia a look that said *seriously?*

"You stole it after? When? I didn't see."

Alison's next look said *duh.*

Alison was scary good at things like that. Once in the sixth grade, after Mr. Barnes gave her an F on a social studies quiz, Alison snuck his phone out of his jacket, found the principal's number and texted *You're a jackass and I like little boys.* This was all *during* class. It was really funny when Mr. Barnes got called into the office over the loudspeaker. He cleared it all up, obviously, but they never figured out who sent the text. *Mr. Barnes works in a middle school. He should have known better than to leave his phone laying around with no password.* That had been Alison's justification.

To steady her nerves, Olivia took a deep breath just like she did before swim meets. "Okay. You took it. Why?"

"I told you. She called us shoplifters."

Olivia closed her eyes. Alison could be so frustrating sometimes. "I mean what's that thing?"

Alison shrugged casually. "I like it. Look how cool it is." She held the snow globe out like some kind of deranged peace offering.

Olivia could not figure out why, of all the junk in that stupid gift shop... "What is that thing we're going to jail for anyway?"

Alison examined the snow globe more carefully. "Look at how the inside doesn't move right." Alison shook it.

"So you stole a *broken* snow globe?"

Alison groaned. "It's not broken. Just *look!*"

Olivia stared into the little ball. For a second, she thought the figures might be alive, but that was ridiculous. The whale and the other thing—the monster— did not look like they were just floating, but Olivia couldn't figure out how it worked. That bothered her. She usually could figure out how stuff worked right away. That was how she liked it.

"The water moves, but kind of on its own. And the little guys in there don't react when you move the snow globe around."

Olivia saw what Alison meant. The figures moved independently of the way the snow globe turned. "Maybe they're magnetized or something."

"No way. That's not how they're moving."

"Motors?"

Alison held it up to her ear. "I don't hear anything. Plus, wouldn't that need a battery?"

"Maybe it's solar." Olivia stared into the dark, sparkling water, but she didn't see anything that looked like a solar cell. "Those figures are so lifelike. They're kind of creepy. Especially that monster-thing. What is that supposed to even be?"

"Maybe we can show it to Mr. W. when we get home. He knows about all kinds of weird stuff."

"If he finds out you stole it..." Olivia could not keep the anger out of her voice if she wanted to. And she didn't really want to.

Alison glared. "Are *you* going to tell him?"

It stung Olivia. "Why would you even say that?"

"You know you're not good at keeping secrets." Alison was so matter-of-fact about it. Like it wasn't even important. That didn't just sting; it was like a slap.

Alison continued her own thoughts. "I'm taking American Lit next year. That's when you read *Moby Dick*."

"It's not that bad," Olivia said, moving on. "Parts are pretty cool."

"Oh yeah, I forgot your dad made you read it last summer."

Every summer, Olivia's father had been making her read *the classics* starting with *Little Women* in fourth grade. She had to sneak her science fiction novels in between Leo Tolstoy and Charles Dickens. "I skimmed a lot. Did Michael read it? He took American Lit, didn't he?"

"Read what?" Michael bounded up, causing them both to jump. Alison gave a small shriek that decayed into a giggle.

"*Moby Dick*." Olivia was so used to covering for Alison that it had become instinctive. She moved to block Michael's view while Alison stashed the snow globe in her purse.

"Hey, we already discussed your potty mouths today, ladies!" Michael's fake, authoritarian scowl bent into a smile. "Why are you so weird? Can't you ever just—like—chill?"

Alison had the snow globe tucked safely away. "So you never read it?"

"*Call me Ishmael!* Blah blah blah, *From hell's heart I spit at thee.* Yeah. I read it. Really long. Parts of it were really boring descriptions of whales and boats, but some of it was pretty cool. Like when the dude got stuck inside the dead whale's head that was hanging upside down and he had to get rescued. That was kinda sick."

Michael unlocked the car, bounded into the driver's seat and started the engine while Alison and Olivia climbed in. The air conditioner blasted hot, stale air into their faces. "Why are *you* two eggheads asking *me* about schoolwork? We're on vacation, and anyway, *you're* supposed to be the smart ones."

"We were just talking about things we did in school with Mr. W. in PEP class," Alison explained. Olivia never stopped being amazed at how smoothly Alison mixed fact and fabrication.

"That smarty-pants geek class you used to be in?" Michael adjusted the seat.

"PEP, Michael."

Olivia added, "The Program for Exceptional Performance."

"Yeah," Michael chuckled, "even the name is for dorks."

Alison snapped coldly at her brother, "Just 'cause you're too dumb to get in."

"Woe is me. Or is it I? I don't know! All I know is they didn't pick me for nerdapalooza!" Michael mimed a pout and shaped his fingers into a heart with his thumbs making the bottom point. Then he separated his fingers. "My heart is breaking because I was too busy having a life to get into PEP. I'm just sorry that I never got to wear a pocket protector."

"What are you doing up there anyway?" Alison nodded at the driver's seat.

Michael adjusted the backrest and then plugged his phone into the minivan's auxiliary jack. "Dad says I'm driving the rest of the way." A hypnotic dubstep beat pulsed from all the speakers.

"We're all gonna die." Olivia deadpanned.

6 STILL LEARNING TO DRIVE

Michael adjusted and readjusted his seat and all the mirrors. He checked that he had clear sightlines, just like he learned in Driver's Ed. Dad was finally taking him seriously, giving him a chance to drive the whole family. Michael knew he had to drive flawlessly or Dad was going to be all over him like his sister at a shoe sale.

Dad climbed into the front passenger seat, already grumbling. "I can't believe how much they charged us for lunch in that place. We're never stopping here again."

"You were the one who wanted to stop there. Besides, it's vacation." Mom tried to play it off like she always did. "Let's not worry about it."

Dad looked at her, his eyes popping wide. "Okay, Moneybags. I didn't realize we hit the lottery."

"It *was* your idea to stop there, Dad. I would have been fine with a drive-through and a Dollar Menu." Michael rarely got involved in these things, but he thought it was only fair to point it out for Mom's sake, before the fireworks started.

"That's not food, Mama's Boy. And turn the music off."

"What? Why?" This was exactly why Michael never got involved. It always backfired. Maybe driving wasn't such a great idea.

"I don't want you getting distracted," Dad said. "First you start boogalooin', next thing you drive head on into a school bus."

Here we go again. "I'm a twenty-first century kid, Dad. We don't boogaloo and we do multitask. I always focus better with music. And it's summer. There are no school buses."

Dad's barrel chest heaved up and down as he took a deep breath. "Just lower it, okay? Besides, that ain't exactly music. It sounds like the radio's busted. Don't you have anything with a sax? Or at least a guitar?"

"Just go with it, Pop. Aren't you the one always saying how important it is to try new things?" Michael dialed down the music. He was happy he could keep it on and surprised he'd won that round.

Mom climbed through the sliding door to her place in the middle row. She reached out to pull the lever and close the automatic door, but Michael said, "Mom, I've got this. I'm the driver." He pushed a button on the dashboard, and her door slid slowly closed. "Stow your personal belongings in the overhead bins, and make sure your tray tables are locked in the upright position. We're ready for takeoff."

"Let's try and keep all four wheels on the ground, okay, Mikey?"

In the rearview mirror, Michael saw the girls rolling their eyes. He dutifully ran through Mr. Murphy's Driver's Ed checklist in his mind. When he got up to number four, he leaned on the horn.

"What are you doing?" Dad snapped.

Michael grinned, "Mr. Murphy said that we should make sure the horn is in good working order before we pull out."

Dad scowled. "It works, okay? Take this seriously. A car isn't a toy."

"I'm just following the rules, Pop." Michael glanced in the rearview mirror. Alison and Olivia were cracking up. Michael always enjoyed an audience.

"Check all the mirrors again," Dad commanded. "That's more important than the horn."

"Aye-aye, captain." Michael dutifully checked the mirrors again. He gripped the lever, and the minivan clunked into gear. He looked behind him and tried to ignore the faces and gestures Alison and Olivia were making as he stepped on the gas pedal. The engine revved, but the car didn't move.

Michael hoped nobody noticed.

"The parking brake's still on, Ace," Dad said. "Maybe you should have checked that when you checked the horn."

Michael released the parking brake and looked in the mirror. The girls were silently hysterical. He turned around, determined to back out in one smooth motion. He stepped on the gas with authority. The van lurched forward with a metallic scrape. There was a grinding *thump* and a teeth-rattling jolt as the front wheels rolled over a large obstacle. There was also an immediate blare from the horn of the delivery truck pulling up to the restaurant. Michael, his heart thumping, jammed on the breaks, snapping everyone forward. Luggage and other loose items thudded all around.

"WHAT ARE YOU DOING? YOU JUST RAN OVER THE CHOCK!" his father screamed.

"No!" Michael insisted. He could feel himself sweating. "It was just that concrete thing at the end of the space."

He could hear Alison and Olivia's hysterical laughter behind him. "The concrete thing is the chock, genius." Alison said.

"Alison, not now." Dad spoke calmly, his jaw clenched like a vice. "Michael, you aren't taking this seriously. Lives are in your hands. Our lives. Don't think of this as a car. It's a dangerous weapon. Like a gun."

Michael looked over at his father who had turned an angry shade of purple-red, all the way up to the top of his shiny scalp inside the stubbled, gray-brown horseshoe of hair. At moments like this, when his father was seriously ticked off at him and glaring at him with those steel-blue eyes, Michael felt like a five-year-old.

"Are you sure you can do this?" Dad asked. "Just because you passed the test and got a license doesn't mean you're ready to drive." He was serious.

Michael was caught between choking down nervous laughter and jumping out the door, finding that waitress and running away from all of them. He knew that even if his father didn't kill him, his sister and Olivia were never going to let him live this one down. "Sorry. I thought…"

"You can't think when you're the driver. You have to *know*. You have to *know* if the parking brake's on. You have to *know* whether the car is in reverse or in drive."

"I know," Michael mumbled.

"Do you? Or do I need to keep driving?"

From behind him, he heard Mom offer, "I can drive." *Thanks, Mom. After I had your back and everything.*

"I got this!" Michael surprised himself by raising his voice back. "Look, if you don't want me to drive, then I won't. I just put it in the wrong gear, okay? It was a simple mistake."

"Tell it to the insurance company when you back over some kid."

"If he'd backed up we'd be fine," Alison chimed in.

"You keep out of this!" Dad scolded.

Really? She had to stick her nose in? Michael glared at his sister in the rearview mirror. "I don't see you driving."

"I don't see you driving either," Alison shot back.

"Knock it off!" Dad snapped. "Now let's focus."

Mom closed her eyes and put her hands in her lap. "Can we have five minutes when no one is yelling? Please?"

"Are you in reverse now?" Dad sounded way too calm. He wasn't even craning his neck to see the instruments on the dashboard.

"Yes, Dad."

"Are you sure?"

"Of course I'm sure. You don't think I'm going to do the same stupid thing twice, do you?"

Dad glared like he was he was daring Michael to ask that question again. Michael cringed at the high-pitched grinding sounds coming from under the minivan as he backed it up, scraping over the concrete chock.

Dad used a whiny imitation that was obviously supposed to be Mom. "Let's go on a family vacation. Who knows how many more we'll get." In his own voice he added, "Hopefully none."

Michael risked a glance in the rearview mirror when he heard his mother's frustrated sigh. She was staring out the window looking sad. He saw Alison turn silently to Olivia and shake her head. She looked sad, too. Michael resisted the urge to punch the steering wheel.

7 CRASH

As funny as it had been to watch Michael crash and burn in the parking lot, Olivia felt relieved when they were back on the highway without any more disasters. The low electronic beats of Michael's playlist and the quiet drone of the tires on the road were only interrupted by the occasional thump of a pothole or a seam in the pavement. Now and then Mr. Nunios cautioned his son to slow down. Or to check his mirrors again. Or to speed up. Or to stay in his lane. Or to slow down.

After one of these warnings, Michael said, "Dad, can you please chill? We haven't seen a car for—like—fifty miles."

"You didn't see the chock you ran over either." It was all Michael's father had to say. Michael was done. He talked a good game, but he always backed down. Not like Alison. Alison never backed down.

Olivia glanced up at Mrs. Nunios. She wasn't saying a word either. Not since they pulled out of the parking lot. Craning her neck a little, Olivia could see that Alison's mother was lost in her book and her mind was probably somewhere in Georgia with a group of middle-aged women, friends since childhood, who have to help each other cope with divorce and cancer and parenting. Alison's mother read a lot, and she'd raved about this book the whole way down. Olivia thought she probably wanted them to read it, too, so that she would have someone to talk about it with, like her book club, but Olivia didn't see that happening.

Alison was playing a game on her phone. Olivia was trying really hard to read Jane Austin's *Emma* since it was on Ashton Academy's Summer Reading List *and* a Dad-approved classic, but she just couldn't get into the love interests of Emma and Harriet and their intelligent gentleman-farmers and respectable vicars. *Now if Harriet started crushing on Emma…*

Laying her head against the seatback, Olivia closed her eyes for a bit. Her mother had reminded her at least a dozen times to be a good guest, to stay out of trouble, to keep Alison out of trouble, to be grateful, to be gracious—and most of all, to use good manners.

Mrs. Nunios seemed to be taking a break from the ladies in Georgia to stare out the window. Olivia could only imagine what thoughts were going through that woman's head. Sometimes Olivia felt sorry for her. Yes, she could be a little annoying, but she was a mom. *It kind of goes with the job.* She was about a million times cooler than her own mother. All *she* ever wanted to talk about was Olivia's future or her own job, talking about how hard it was for a woman to be a partner in a big law firm and the glass ceiling and all that.

All Mrs. Nunios ever really wanted was for everyone to get along and be happy, or at least act like they were happy and getting along. It seemed so simple, but it never worked out.

Olivia saw how much Mrs. Nunios did for her husband and her kids. It wasn't that Olivia's own mom didn't try to take care of her, but she worked long hours, especially if she was in a trial, and she expected Olivia to take care of herself. Mrs. Nunios worked a lot, too, selling real estate, but she seemed to want to take care of everybody. Was it such a crime that she liked it when her family noticed and appreciated it?

"I really appreciate your letting me come with you on this vacation, Mrs. Nunios. I've never been to Cape November."

Michael called back from the driver's seat, "That's because you probably go on vacation to real places like Grimmyland where there's actually stuff to do."

Michael's dad cut his eye across at his son, "I guess college is going to pay for itself? Look, if you want to take that wrestling scholarship at State and save me from paying for Cartesian University…"

"I'm ready to try other things, Dad."

"Beer and girls isn't a major, Mikey." Mr. Nunios chuckled like he got a big kick out of himself.

"Yeah, Dad, that's why I'm going to college. To drink beer and meet girls."

Dad shrugged and smiled sheepishly, "It's why I went."

"My guidance counselor said that the journalism program at Cartesian is way better than what they have at State."

"Then maybe your guidance counselor can pay for it. And how did you end up thinking you wanted to study journalism all of a sudden?"

"All of a sudden?" Michael sounded offended. "I took every journalism elective at the high school."

"What was that? Two?" Mr. Nunios asked dismissively.

"How about five?" Michael's voice cracked a little. "Intro to Journalism, Newspaper One and Two, and Broadcast One and Two. *And* I've been writing for the school paper since I was a freshman. *And* I joined the photography club so I can take all my own pictures. The Middle East. North Korea. Sudan. Who knows where I might end up."

"Just go somewhere safe, Michael." Mrs. Nunios sounded anxious.

"You really wanted to play the saxophone, too—for about eight months. It's been collecting dust in the attic for seven years. I swear if you don't use that fancy camera we bought you…"

"Dad, what are you talking about? Have you even looked at the pictures I showed you? My Tumblr picked up like eighty new followers since I started posting the pictures I took with that camera." There was an uncomfortable silence for a moment before Michael added, "Seriously. Thank you for the camera. I really appreciate it. It was an awesome graduation present, and I know it was expensive."

Olivia smiled as Mrs. Nunios did what she always did when the conversation fell down a rabbit hole: She tactfully changed the subject. "Cape November is beautiful, Olivia. Wait 'til you see it. It's got one of the best beaches around. We used to come here all the time when we were kids. A lot of us would get jobs down here at the boardwalk."

"There's a boardwalk?" Alison popped up suddenly from her phone.

Michael groaned, "Are you kidding? You can't even find a game of skeeball anymore. The place is wiped out."

"I'm sure there's skeeball." Mrs. Nunios tried to reassure them, but she didn't sound confident.

"Mom, this place was already a dump, and then it was hit by six major hurricanes and winter storms. There was flooding. Then all those fires. There's nothing left. I can't believe you're dragging us here."

"How do you know all that, Mikey?" Mr. Nunios sounded genuinely interested.

Michael sat a little taller in the driver's seat. "I'm a journalist, Pop."

Mr. Nunios chuckled. "Right. Just be a driver."

"It's a good thing we're going to help out their businesses, isn't it? If they had all that trouble?" Mrs. Nunios was challenging any of them to contradict her. At least it sounded that way to Olivia.

Olivia looked at Mr. Nunios. She was expecting one of his usual comebacks about wasting money saving the hopeless businesses of Cape November, but to her surprise, he just leaned back with a smile spreading over his face. "My friends and I used to come down the Cape because we couldn't afford to go anywhere else and you could make big bonfires on the beach. Not a lot of places allow that."

Alison's mom jumped in. "Oh yeah. Kids brought down their guitars and bongos and radios. It was a big party. I met your father at a party like that, on the beach. It was the summer between junior and senior year of college, right after finals. It was a warm year, but it gets chilly there at night. And the ocean was freezing, but a lot of us jumped in anyway. The boys would always scream that Cappy got them."

"Cappy?" Michael asked.

"Just drive," Mr. Nunios growled.

Mrs. Nunios laughed. "Tell me you never heard of Cappy! The Cape Captain? Captain of the Cape?"

Alison glanced across at Olivia. "It's this old legend about a sea monster, right, Mrs. Nunios? They've been telling it down there forever."

"Whenever there's a big storm, they say that Cappy's coming. Beware of Cappy! It's great!" Mom sighed "What *do* they teach you in school?"

"Just chemistry, physics, U.S. History, calculus," Michael said. "Nothing important like BS stories about sea monsters. And what kind of a stupid name for a monster is Cappy?"

"They should do a better job of teaching driving," Mr. Nunios growled. "You're swerving."

"I am not!"

"Just drive."

"Fine!" Michael snapped. "But Cappy's a dumb name."

"Who knows how these things get started." Mrs. Nunios sighed. "Anyway, we always used to try to scare each other telling Cappy stories down there. We would sit all damp and sandy from the ocean, dancing by the fire under a big, golden moon, freezing our butts off."

"Sure it was cold," Mr. Nunios laughed. "The glaciers had just retreated and dinosaurs roamed the earth." His wife reached forward and swatted him playfully on the back of the head with her book. "Ow!"

"Look, you got me smackin' you." Mrs. Nunios laughed. "It wasn't *that* long ago."

"What's that they say? It's not the years, babe; it's the mileage."

Babe? Olivia had never heard Mr. and Mrs. Nunios talk like that to each other. One glance at Alison showed that she was seeing something new also. Maybe Mrs. Nunios wasn't so crazy for planning her family getaway.

"Wait," Michael challenged, "I thought you guys met in college."

Mr. Nunios picked up the story, "Me and a bunch of guys—Nelson was there, and Gerry—we rented a beach house down the Cape, dirt cheap..."

"And we still overpaid," Mom said.

Alison looked up from her phone. "Why?"

Her mother laughed. "'Cause the place really was a true dump!"

Alison leaned forward. "Wait. Why were you at Dad's beach house if you hadn't met him yet?"

Mrs. Nunios seemed to chuckle at her younger self. "A group of us girls also rented the same house. It turns out the landlord double-booked the place."

Mr. Nunios shook his head. "Idiot!" Then he sat up straight like he just thought of something. "Wait. I bet he did it on purpose to double his money."

Mrs. Nunios leaned forward, "No way!"

Turning around to look at his wife, the middle-aged couple was magically twenty again, "Way!"

Mrs. Nunios laughed, "God knows how many health codes and fire codes we broke."

"What'd he care, as long as the checks cleared. And was a group of guys going to cancel their trip because the bungalow they rented was full of girls? I don't think so."

"The girls could have canceled," Olivia pointed out.

"We could have, but we didn't want to lose our trip either. We probably should have," Mrs. Nunios said, still laughing at the memories. "If my father knew that I was down there with a house full of boys..."

"Grampa would have definitely had a stroke," Michael said.

"Keep your eyes on the road before you give me a stroke," Mr. Nunios warned.

Alison looked so happy listening to her parents' story. "So there were—like—thirty people jammed into a beach house?"

"More like forty." Mrs. Nunios cocked her head, remembering.

Alison's father laughed again. "Felt like a hundred."

"That's only because Nelson was there. He could violate health codes by himself." Olivia was surprised Mrs. Nunios would even bring Nelson up. It usually led to an argument. But she obviously knew what she was doing because Mr. Nunios sat back and looked more relaxed than Olivia had ever seen him. "We had some good times, didn't we?"

"Lotta tequila," Mrs. Nunios added.

Alison cracked up and Michael turned around, looking totally stunned at his mother, "Mom!"

Olivia waited for the warning from Mr. Nunios, but it never came.

"What?" Mrs. Nunios shrugged innocently. "What happens down the Cape stays down the Cape," she laughed. "Besides, we were of legal drinking age, which back then I think was somewhere around twelve years old."

"Hey, we're sixteen," Alison offered, a wicked smile lighting up her face.

Her father growled, "Don't even think about it." Olivia noticed the sting starting to edge into his voice again. He must have been thinking about his little girl in a beach house full of boys.

"It was a simpler time." Mrs. Nunios tactfully changed the subject. "Anyway, Olivia, I'm glad that your first trip down the Cape is with us because this place is special to us."

"Me too, Mrs. Nunios," Olivia replied dutifully.

"I think you're going to like The Mansion. It's a charming place."

"Charming is code for old, right?" Michael asked.

"Just drive," his father growled.

Mrs. Nunios set her jaw. Clearly she wasn't about to let this vacation get ruined before it even started. "It looks lovely on the website," she said flatly.

Olivia quickly added, "I'm really excited to check out the foundation."

Alison groaned. "You would say something like that."

"Seriously. Not a lot of people know this, but The Mansion's foundation might be made of sapphire."

Michael laughed. "What dumbass website posted that?"

Olivia felt her face getting red. "Okay, so it hasn't been confirmed by a major lab like Rutgers or Cartesian or anything, but The Mansion's foundation is one of the oldest structures in the country. Archeologists can't even tell how old it really is. There's a lot of theories. One lady from Princeton—"

"That's fascinating." Alison's flat tone made Olivia want to curl up. *That's just Alison. She hates anything school related.*

"And by the way, geniuses, it's called Maggie's Mansion now," Michael said.

Mrs. Nunios continued, "Well, when your father and I were your age it was just The Mansion."

"Yeah, and A New Hope was just Star Wars," Michael scoffed.

"Hang on. You never stayed there?" Alison sounded worried.

"Great!" Michael groaned. "It's probably a dump."

"Drive," Mr. Nunios commanded.

"It is *not* a dump. It's a very fancy bed and breakfast," Mrs. Nunios explained. "We never stayed there because we never could have afforded it back then."

"We can't afford it now," Mr. Nunios muttered.

"Oh, be quiet, you. I'm talking to Olivia. She's the only one who isn't mean to me." Mrs. Nunios smiled. "We haven't been down the Cape in years. I think Michael might have been in diapers the last time, but then, he potty-trained late."

"Mom!" squeaked Michael.

Alison and Olivia could not contain themselves.

Mr. Nunios seemed like he'd had enough. "All right, you two, knock it off back there. And you keep your eye on the road, Mikey. You never know what can…"

A huge black shape exploded into the windshield. Michael leaned uselessly on the horn and jammed on the brakes. The minivan skidded and stopped. Olivia's heart was racing. Turning, she saw that Alison was pale and gripping the edges of the seat in front of her.

"Is everyone okay?" Mr. Nunios asked, looking around the car. Once it became clear that no one was hurt, he looked back at the windshield. A baseball could have easily passed through the hole in the middle and cracks threaded out from it like a spider's web.

"Great! Look at that!" Mr. Nunios brushed tiny cubes of broken safety glass off his lap. "You know how much this is going to cost to fix? Michael, why weren't you looking at the road?"

"I was! That bird came out of nowhere!"

"We hit a bird?" Alison asked. She sounded pretty suspicious.

"Must have been an ostrich," Olivia remarked.

"Ostriches don't fly, genius," Michael snapped.

"She knows that, Michael," Alison sneered. "It was a joke."

"Michael probably doesn't feel like joking right now." Mrs. Nunios's voice dripped with maternal concern. Olivia winced, feeling like an outsider.

"I'm fine. I can still take a joke, Mom." Michael stared straight ahead. He looked shaken up and had none of his usual swagger.

"This is no joke," Mr. Nunios growled. "You just wrecked our car."

"I didn't do anything wrong!"

"The car isn't wrecked. We can get the windshield fixed," Mrs. Nunios soothed. "As long as nobody got hurt."

Olivia looked at Alison's face, tense with worry. "Seriously, are you okay, Michael?" Alison asked.

"Of course." He wiped the backs of his hands roughly across his eyes and through his hair. "I'm fine. It was just a stupid bird."

"Take it easy, Michael," his mother tried to sound calm and reassuring.

"I'm fine, Mom." Michael shut the engine and fumbled for his seatbelt. "Can everyone please just *stop?* I'm fine, okay? Are you guys okay?" He managed to get his seatbelt off, and he stepped out of the minivan. His father was already walking around outside, checking the front.

Olivia pressed her face against the rear window. She knew they were somewhere near the Pine Barrens. Olivia used to want to be a researcher there. She tried to imagine what it must be like to be surrounded by more than a million acres of wilderness with no people around. Nothing but federally protected, coniferous forest. All those different kinds of animals. *How many new species are in there, just waiting to be discovered? What other mysteries besides the Jersey Devil?* But when Olivia had mentioned it to her mother, she laughed her off. There was no money in it.

The highway must have been close to the beach. The soil looked sandy. Purple and yellow wildflowers sprouted up in in the wide patch of grass between the gravel shoulder and the tall evergreen trees.

The minivan sat in the bright sun, so Olivia couldn't see farther than a few feet into the shadows under the sagging branches of the dark, droopy trees. Michael walked up to join his father who was already heading toward the trees.

In the still, summer air, Olivia could hear their voices coming vaguely over the grass. "What are you doing?" She didn't know if he meant it to, but Mr. Nunios's question came out as a gruff sneer. He quickly added, "You're sure you didn't get hurt?"

"I'm fine, Dad. Are you okay?"

It surprised Olivia when Mr. Nunios smiled back. "I'm good. Let's go check out what we hit."

Olivia watched them retrace the highway another twenty yards or so. Michael and his father both stopped suddenly. Mr. Nunios pointed at something near the edge of the forest.

8 ROAD KILL

On the grass, it looked like a big garbage bag lying where the shade of the trees met the bright sun. Following Dad, Michael kept his eye on the shadowy bulk, trying to process the lumps and bulges, eventually settling them into the misshapen body of a huge creature.

"Dad, are we sure that's a bird?" It didn't look like any bird he'd ever seen. Michael glanced back at the minivan where Mom had stepped out, craning her neck. Alison and Olivia stood like pirates on the sill of the sliding door, holding the mounded roof rack and shielding their eyes.

With his palm, Michael waved for them to stay back. Through the hazy air, Michael could hear the pulsing thump of his playlist, but it sounded small and far away. He realized that he had been clenching his fists since the bird hit the windshield.

The bird was as big as a barbecue grill. Its wings were crumpled, but stretched out they would have covered him. The bird was purplish-black with iridescent flecks that changed kaleidoscopically in the shifting sunlight. It didn't look like it had feathers. The scales, if that's what they were, glistened with velvet ooze. Dangerous-looking black talons stabbed out from under the broken heap of wings. "Dad, let me run back for my camera."

Michael's father grumbled. "Between the windshield and the insurance, because you know those crooks are gonna raise my rates, this thing is going to cost a fortune."

"Dad, this isn't just some regular bird. I have to take pictures."

"We gotta get moving."

"This is the Pine Barrens, it might be an endangered species."

"It's endangered now. If I ever see another one..."

Michael looked at the long, razor curve of its beak. "We should call animal control or the Audubon Society or something."

"Are you some kind of tree-hugger now? You can become a vegetarian at college. Right now, let's just get back in the car and get to our vacation before your mother has a nervous breakdown." Dad was already heading back to the car.

"Hang on. Something's moving." Michael strained to see into the shadows.

"Trust me. Its moving days are over."

"Not the bird, Dad. Something else." Michael blocked some of the glare with his hand. "Behind the bird. I think it's...bugs. Flies maybe?"

"Probably coming to eat the dead bird."

Michael watched a swarm of flies in a pulsing, buzzing cloud. "Let me grab my camera."

"Are you working for the Discovery Channel now? Let's go! Chop chop!"

"Dad, what if the insurance company doesn't believe that a bird hit the windshield. Shouldn't we take pictures?"

Dad turned around. The edges of his lips turned down thoughtfully. "You know, you might be right."

Michael knew that would work.

Moving closer, the stench of seaweed and rotten fish punched him in the face. It had just enough sweetness in it to make him gag on his ribs and chicken. Beyond the crumpled bird Michael spotted a huge, pulpy mound camouflaged in the spiky grass. Whatever the thing was, it seethed with flies, but Michael caught glimpses of pale white.

It had a long, thick middle and a large triangular form at one end. The opposite end separated into several long, snaky tendrils. Another long, twisting limb stretched away from the body at a weird angle. Michael tried to organize the shape in his mind. *It's kind of man-shaped, but bigger. Lying on its side maybe? Was this a hit and run? A suicide? Murder? But something is really wrong with that body.*

"Look at that." Dad's voice was barely a whisper.

Michael turned his face away in disgust. "Dad, this isn't a human."

Dad laughed. "Of course it's not. Why would you even think that? It's probably a deer."

"There is no way that's a deer!"

"Maybe you should get your camera. This might be something."

Michael started to make sense of what he saw. "It's a body, Dad. It's on its right side, facing the forest. Its right arm is tucked underneath. The left, the one sticking out...it's way too long. And all those legs, all bent and crooked, like they don't have any bones? They're tentacles."

"Tentacles?" Dad laughed. "Michael, take it easy. Hitting that bird has you all shook up."

Michael had gotten close enough to the dead thing that the flies began to buzz around him. They were larger than Michael's thumb. He flailed wildly when the first one landed on his arm. It hung on too long and came right back a moment later. But it wasn't a fly. More like some kind of dragonfly. *Long, black body. Nasty, shovel-shaped head. Double set of wings? Ten legs?*

The thing on his arm dipped its shovel-shaped head and bit him. Michael screamed and swatted the bug off.

"What happened?" Dad called. He had already started back for the car again.

The squawk overhead filled Michael's bones with ice. He barely saw the black bulk hurtling toward him out of the sky. Michael dove to the ground as the huge bird grazed him with its talons.

Michael sprinted toward his father who came back to help. "Just go!" Michael yelled. "Get to the car!"

"Ow!" His father swatted the back of his neck. "One of those bugs just bit me."

Michael slapped his neck as another bug bit him. "We have to get out of here, Dad!"

His father slapped and screamed as the flies swarmed. Michael looked around frantically for the live bird. It landed near the dead one and the other dead thing.

Michael screamed as more bugs bit. A shrieking squawk jerked him around. The bird was in the air again and flying straight at him, slashing with its deadly beak.

It landed, and Michael barely got his leg back before the bird chomped it off. He backpedaled as it snapped after him. The enormous wings carried the monster up to slash at his eyes with its talons. He could feel the pressure of the air from the flapping wings against his chest.

Flies tore his skin, but Michael couldn't look away from the purple eyes and slashing, relentless beak. He lost his footing. Flat on his back with the air knocked from his lungs, he swatted the bugs away long enough to catch a glimpse of the spread claws diving for his chest.

With a shrill cry, the bird disappeared in a wet explosion of oily, black scales. Still swatting the bugs, Michael staggered to his feet. His father brandished a large stick. The twisted bird thrashed its wings in the grass and rolled to its feet.

Another cry pierced him from above. And another.

"Michael, watch out!" His father's voice came from far away like a dream.

He lurched out of the way as massive black talons shredded the air where his face had been. Stinging black wingtips slapped the side of his head as the bird *thumped* to the ground. It wheeled, catching his father's stick in its beak. Dad grunted and the stick slipped, bitten in half like a cracker.

Thump. Thump.

Hissing and cawing to one another, all three birds closed in on Michael, snapping their beaks like shears.

Within the sickening bird cries, Michael heard the dull bleating of the minivan's horn. Mom drove across the grass, scattering the birds. Michael and Dad dove through the sliding door.

Stomping the gas pedal, Mom punched repeatedly at the sliding door control as the minivan skidded back onto the highway.

Inside, everyone yelled over each other. Michael sat in the middle seat and let the questions fall like hail. Dad sat in front, not commenting on Mom's driving. "They got some weird animals down here."

Michael couldn't believe his father had just said that. "Dad, those were not just regular animals!"

His father smiled gently. "Michael, I know they gave us a good scare, but they were just some kind of big crows or vultures."

"That was way too big to be a vulture," Alison pointed out. "It was the size of a pterodactyl."

"Pretty sure those are extinct," Olivia offered. "Just saying."

Michael felt like he'd been punched in the chest. "Are you kidding? They had scales instead of feathers. Didn't you see?"

"I didn't get a great look," Dad admitted, chuckling. He rubbed his temples with his fingers. "It happened so fast. Just try to calm down. You know, when people get excited, the imagination…"

Betrayal splashed like hot oil in Michael's face. "Are you serious? You're going to say those were ordinary animals and not some kind of…"

"What?" Dad said sharply. "Monsters? You think we saw monsters out there?" Dad looked out the window in disgust. "Grow up, Mikey."

She tried to be slick and use the mirror, but Michael noticed Mom trade worried scowls with Dad. "Michael, did you hit your head when you fell?" she asked, keeping her eyes stiffly on the road in front.

"I did *not* hit my head." He couldn't believe what he was hearing. "You didn't see them up close. Trust me. They were not regular birds."

"Maybe they were a mutation. Like a part of a secret government experiment that escaped. There's a military base down here somewhere," Olivia suggested. "I mean that would explain…"

"Olivia, honey, I know that you're trying to help, but let's just be reasonable now, okay?" Mom said.

Olivia pressed herself back into her seat and folded her arms across her chest.

"Mikey," Dad said gently, "we were both scared. Adrenaline starts pumping."

"And what? You start seeing things? Those…things had scales! I saw them!"

"Okay." Dad held his palms up and shook his head. "Whatever they were, they were just there to eat the deer on the side of the road."

Michael felt an angry fist in his gut, and he scratched at the stinging welts popping up on his arms. "How about the flies? You're going to tell me ordinary flies bite like this?"

"They were big," Dad rubbed at the welts on his own arm. "Probably greenheads. They got those down here. Nasty."

"Why were they attacking us?" Michael demanded.

Dad shrugged, smiling so gently it made Michael want to punch him. "Flies bite."

"Actually, Mr. Nunios, it's just females that need blood when they start to lay eggs," Olivia called from the back.

Michael spun around glaring. "What?"

Olivia shrugged meekly. "I'm just…uh…reminding everybody that biting flies or mosquitoes or really any insect looking for a blood meal, they're reproducing. Like those big greenhead flies that live in salt marshes? The males don't ever bite, and the females start out eating nectar. It's only after they lay eggs that they become aggressive because they need a mammal's blood to lay more eggs."

"Why are you telling us this?" Michael asked.

Olivia raised puzzled eyebrows. "You're talking about biting flies. Seemed like a good time."

"It isn't." Michael said.

"So there are going to be more of those fly things?" Alison asked.

Olivia nodded. "All living things reproduce."

"You guys can say whatever you want and treat me like an idiot but I *know* what I saw. Those were *not* regular birds, and they were *not* greenhead flies."

"I never said *those* were greenheads," Olivia said quietly. "I was just saying that greenheads…"

"It doesn't matter." Michael said it coldly because that was how he felt, and he didn't care if he hurt poor, weird little Olivia's feelings. *It's not like anybody ever worries about how I feel.* "And, Mom, I don't care what Dad says. The dead thing wasn't a deer. It had tentacles."

Dad laughed. "Tentacles? What was it? An octopus?"

"Whatever." Michael looked angrily at the dark trees hurtling past the window.

"Wait, Michael," Alison said, "Could it really have been an octopus or something?"

Something snarled inside Michael. "Alison, I'm not in the mood for…"

Mom called loudly, "Alison, your brother's been through enough. Let him just sit quietly and rest a minute."

Michael's already itchy skin started to crawl with humiliation. *Great. Mom's treating me like a two-year-old.* "I'm fine, Mom."

"I'm not messing with him," Alison continued. "In case you haven't noticed, Olivia and I are the only ones taking him seriously."

"Why?" Michael caught the weird look Alison gave Olivia in the back seat. Olivia looked all wide-eyed and worried. "What are you two up to? Seriously, Alison, I'm in no mood."

"She's not up to anything," Olivia sputtered. "It's just, back in the gift shop—ow!" Olivia looked sharply at Alison.

"What?" Michael demanded.

"What's going on back there?" Dad rumbled. "Look, nobody wants any shenanigans out of you, Alison."

"We're not up to anything, Dad," Alison replied. But Michael noticed that she was giving Olivia major stink-eye. "Back in the gift shop we saw some souvenirs with squids and stuff. No biggie."

Michael felt the tension blow out of him like a balloon. He flopped back into his seat. "Well, who would have guessed that in a gift shop by the beach they would ever sell crap with squids and octopuses and sh—"

"Language!" Mom singsonged.

Michael sighed "And *shtuff.*"

"Let's everybody just relax." Dad leaned back in his seat, eyes closed. "Who knows how long that dead thing's been there. It could have been a deer. Maybe a coyote or a bear. It got creamed by a truck and sat there rotting. Of course it looked weird when we found it; it was half rotten. Look, there was a lot of excitement. We were upset."

"Bears don't have tentacles, Dad." Michael felt like he was yelling into the wind.

"Maybe it was some frozen squid that fell off a seafood truck. That would have attracted birds and flies, right?" It sounded so reasonable when Mom said it.

"Sure," Dad said. "If there really were tentacles—although I'm sure there weren't—that would be it. We were a little excited and…"

"Really, Dad?" Michael could tell by the tone of his sister's voice that she was getting frustrated. She was super smart, and she ran out of patience pretty fast when somebody was being stupid. Especially Mom and Dad. "Did you see those things?" she snapped. "Birds like that don't live anywhere, except maybe in a movie."

"Alison, you never even got out of the car," Dad said chuckling gently.

"A blind person could see they weren't regular birds, Dad!"

Olivia added, "And I'm pretty sure they were trying to kill you. Regular birds don't do that either."

Dad turned and scowled impatiently at Olivia. "They were just birds. We're in the middle of the woods. We probably don't have birds like that up by us, so they looked a little strange. We were already upset from the accident. They were regular birds. Why is everybody acting crazy?"

Alison turned to Olivia like they were the only ones in the car. "Maybe the birds thought they were trying to take their food and that's why they went after them."

Olivia tilted her head. "Could have been a nest around, too. Birds can be aggressive. Some dive-bomb and poop on anybody who gets too near to their nesting areas," Olivia added.

"These things weren't pooping on us," Michael said.

Mom clucked her tongue. "Those vultures could kill somebody."

"Mom, they weren't vultures!"

"Michael, stop being dramatic. And watch your tone. I'm just glad there weren't children around." Shuddering a little, Mom shook her head. "We should call the police."

"Absolutely not." Dad sounded final. "We're trying to go on vacation here. Do you really want to spend an afternoon sitting in some jerkwater police station answering questions?"

"Somebody needs to do something about those birds," Mom insisted. "They're dangerous."

"You know what's dangerous? Getting mixed up in something like this when we're trying to get someplace."

"Please don't tell me that you're more concerned about meeting Nelson for some stupid golf game."

"It's not our problem, Sara. And suppose Michael is right and that really was a dead body. Do you want to get mixed up in something like that?"

Mom looked across at Dad. Her mouth made a horrified *O*. "My God, Tommy, was it? This could be something big. Suppose that's somebody's husband or wife back there. We can't just leave them there."

"Plus, you might get into more trouble if they find out you were there and didn't report it, Mr. Nunios." Olivia sounded worried.

"What are they going to do?" Dad scoffed, "Trace the tire tracks?"

"You never know," Mom said. "If it turns out to really be a murder? Suppose it's a mob hit and the FBI gets involved."

"Stop it, Sara," Dad sounded like he was talking to one of the kids, "it's not a murder."

"You just said..."

"Just get us down the Cape."

Michael looked back and forth between his parents for a tense eternity until Mom, keeping her eyes straight ahead, added, "I still say we need to call the police."

"I don't think that's going to be necessary, Mrs. Nunios," Olivia said quietly from the back. That's when Michael heard the siren.

9 BUSTED

Alison never remembered either of her parents getting pulled over before. Little old grandmas were always passing Mom on the highway. It was annoying.

So Michael finds something dead on the side of the road and two seconds later a cop shows up?

Alison didn't like it. She could always tell when some lame teacher was going to bust her for something. And weren't cops basically just teachers for adults, giving out tickets and jail instead of detentions and suspensions?

She glanced at Olivia, who bit her lip nervously and looked at Alison's bag. Her gut tightened as she felt for the stashed snow globe. Her heart thumped a little harder in her chest as she quietly rearranged her bag, stuffing the stolen snow globe under the other stuff.

Alison's mind raced. *I bet the old lady called the cops on us.* She closed her eyes and forced herself to think. *That old bat didn't notice. Even if she did, the police wouldn't chase us all the way down the highway for a three-dollar piece of junk.*

Gravel crunched under the tires as Mom pulled onto the shoulder. The police car pulled up behind them, its red and blue lights flashing. It reminded Alison of Nyla's end-of-the-year pool party. Alison had managed to get away when the cops showed up, but of course, her parents still found out and grounded the snot out of her.

It had been worth it, though. She'd hooked up with the beautiful Darren Walker. Olivia had been at a swim tournament, of course, and had missed the whole thing including the cute girls from Saint Catherine's who showed up and started hitting on all the girls at the party. One of them even hit on Alison. She was so pretty Alison might have let it happen except she already had her sights set on Darren that night. But for sure Olivia would have gotten lucky for once if she'd been there. Instead Olivia missed out again because she was swimming. At least she didn't get grounded.

The officer got out. He was super short and shaped like a volleyball with stubby little arms and legs sticking out of it. As he passed Alison's window, she could see more of his fleshy face. His lower lip was crazy thick. When Alison saw that, along with his bloated double chin and almost total lack of a neck, she leaned over to Olivia whispering, "He looks like a frog."

"What are they eating down here?" Olivia whispered back. "Haven't they heard of cardio?"

Absolutely bald under his patrol hat, the cop's skin was pale, splotchy and pockmarked. A pair of large mirrored sunglasses hid his eyes as he took the license and registration cards his mother had ready. Without saying a word to her, he waddled back to his cop car. The cards looked tiny in his puffy hands.

The officer sat in his car with Mom's license and registration pretty much forever. Mom kept the engine off, and it was getting hot. Alison could feel sweat on her neck under her hair. While they waited, nobody in the minivan said a word, but Alison's mind was racing.

Olivia, whatever happens, just shut up! Alison hoped that if she thought it hard enough, she could get the message to Olivia telepathically. She didn't have much hope for that, but it was all she had.

The officer waddled back to Mom's window. "You have a clean record, ma'am," he said in a thick, wet voice, "so I'm gonna knock you back to just five over the limit. Now about that windshield."

"That just happened, officer," Dad sputtered.

They're definitely going to blow this, Alison thought, *and we'll be dragged down to some inbred, hillbilly police station. Great vacation, Mom.*

The officer looked irritated. "Sir, I'm not done."

See?

"Sorry, officer."

The officer didn't say anything, but his mirrored lenses were fixed on Alison's parents for way too long. "Why don't you tell me what happened to the windshield."

"We hit a bird." *Michael?* Alison wouldn't have guessed that he'd open his big mouth. He hated talking to adults.

Michael must not have picked up her telepathic scolding either, because he kept sputtering to the cop. "I...I hit the bird, officer. I was the one driving at the time." Alison noticed that Michael's voice sounded about two octaves deeper than normal.

Stupid. Michael should have just kept his mouth shut. If he had to say something, he should have just lied. It would have been so easy to say that a big rock fell off a dump truck and broke the window. That happened to Andrew Choi's older brother. At least, that's what he told his parents, and they believed him. But my idiot brother is sticking with the bird story? I was there, and I don't even believe it.

The cop stood still and silent for another long moment. His mirrored lenses scanned their faces. "Must have been some bird to do that."

"It was pretty big. Some kind of vulture I think," Mom put in. "And so vicious."

"It survived?" the cop asked. "You interacted with the vulture?"

First Mom nodded like a bobblehead, but then shook no. "Not the one we hit. That one was dead. I think. But then other ones came. They attacked my son and my husband. You should have seen how vicious they were."

MOM! Alison screamed in her mind. *Bad move.*

The cop scowled with his fleshy lips. "You say these vultures *attacked* you?" He gave a wet chuckle.

Her father smiled like a typical teacher's pet. And Alison knew that if ever there was a group of people who sucked at getting themselves out of trouble once they were in, it was teacher's pets. They were good at not getting into trouble in the first place, or at getting teachers and principals to take pity on them, but if any of them ever did get caught doing something they shouldn't, total meltdown. Crying pitifully was usually their only defense when things went bad. And Alison really didn't need to see her parents start crying on this cop.

"Those birds were big, officer. And like my wife said, they were vicious."

"Vicious birds?" The officer almost sounded like he was playing with them, but Alison seemed to be the only one to notice. He leaned slightly toward the window, directing his mirrored lenses around the inside of the car.

Alison's father started pointing and waving with his hands, "If you go back up the highway about ten miles, there's a whole bunch of them eating some kind of road kill."

"Probably a deer." The police officer sounded pretty confident.

"To be honest, officer…"

No, Dad! Alison thought desperately. *Don't be honest. Lie!*

But Dad seemed determined to be an upstanding citizen. A total suck-up. "My son and I…we thought it might have been too big for a deer." Dad sounded so chipper about it, like he was doing a favor for his buddy, his new BFF, the cop who just pulled them over.

"How do you know?" Dad's new bromance asked from behind his mirrored cop glasses. His soggy-sounding voice seemed to catch in his throat. "You stopped and got out of your vehicle? Am I understanding you correctly?"

Wincing, Alison wished her father had never said anything. She had been on the wrong side of authority enough times to know when to shut up. Her father, being the responsible adult that he was, had no idea what he was doing. He was never in trouble with anybody, except Mom, of course.

Alison listened critically as Mom tried to dig them out with one of her classic subject changes. "We only stopped to check the windshield, officer, to make sure that we could drive with it. We thought we'd get it fixed when we get to Cape November."

Not bad.

"Cape November?" the cop gurgled. "Vacation?"

Maybe this would work.

"Yes, officer." Dad sounded like he might start to breathe again.

"I didn't think anybody still went there. Tourism kind of fizzled." The cop's wide mouth turned down slightly at each corner. "Back to that carcass you say wasn't a deer? What do you think it was?"

I knew it was too easy. Now he is going to ask all kinds of questions.

"We didn't really get a good look. Maybe you should check it out."

"Are you telling me my business?" There was a swampy menace in the officer's voice.

"Absolutely not, officer." Dad sounded panicky. "I was just reporting that there's something at the side of the road that might present a health hazard. There were a lot of flies and a bunch of those large birds like the one that we hit."

"But you didn't call it in." His thick lips lay flat across his face like two dead worms.

"Well...no." Dad sounded lost and terrified.

"So if I hadn't stopped you, you would not have taken it upon yourselves to report this incident. Am I understanding you correctly?"

"Well no, officer." Dad cleared his throat. "We would have, but like I said, it just occurred and we were all kind of upset because of all these birds."

"Flock," the cop said in his wet croak of a voice.

"Excuse me?" Alison's father sounded totally confused.

"A bunch of birds," the officer continued. "It's usually called a flock. Or maybe a gaggle if it's geese." Alison caught something mischievous, even menacing in his flabby smile. "Do you know what a group of crows is called?"

Like an unhappy teacher waiting for an answer he didn't expect to get, the cop focused his mirrored lenses on each one of them, until his silver stare closed on Alison.

She'd had plenty of those teachers and she always stared right back. "A murder," she said flatly. She heard them all gasp. Everybody but the cop. His mirrors held Alison as the moments toppled heavily, but Alison would not look away.

Finally, he turned the glare of his sunglasses back onto her parents. "You got a smart one back there." The dead worms came back to life as the cop's large lips broadened into a smile that showed his nubby, yellowed teeth. "You really have to watch the smart ones. They get themselves into all sorts of trouble." He made a gurgling sound in his throat that Alison took for laughter. The sound made her queasy.

At that moment an annoying, electronic, samba came sashaying out of her Dad's cell phone. He always set it to a simple beep, but Michael thought it was insanely funny to change the ringtone and then call Dad, like when he was at the office or during a movie since Dad always forgot to turn his phone off and he had no idea how to mute it.

The only way Dad could stop the samba music was to answer his phone. Alison had to admit that there had been times when it was hysterical, like last Christmas Eve when Mom had forced them all to go to Midnight Mass. With that weird cop standing there, though, it wasn't so funny. Michael was stunned pale. He hadn't called Dad's phone.

The samba ringtone went through two full cycles with everyone trying to ignore it like a fart in an elevator. The song seemed impossibly loud in the hot minivan at the side of the road with the police officer glowering them.

"You going to pick that up?" the officer asked. His round, pale face was totally expressionless.

"I can let it go to voice mail.'

"Pick it up." The cop didn't sound like this was just a suggestion.

Dad picked up his phone and checked the number. "It's not important. Just my friend Nelson."

"Answer it," the cop said calmly.

The samba stopped. Dad chuckled nervously. "I guess I missed him."

The samba started to groove again. Alison watched her father laugh nervously as he answered. "Hey, Nelson." There was a pause as he listened. "Uh, I don't know. We're running a little late. I know, I know, I can't help it though." Alison couldn't make out the words, but she could hear Nelson's loud, thinks-he's-funnier-and-more-charming-than-he-really-is voice coming through Dad's earpiece. "Look, can I call you back? I'm kind of in the middle of something. No. Hey! That's my wife you're taking about. No! We just got pulled over."

It was always painful to watch her parents operate just about anything electronic. Sometimes even the channel changer for their cable box stumped them, so it didn't surprise Alison when her twentieth-century father, nervous as he was and fumbling to find the end button on his twenty-first century phone, turned on the speaker. Nelson's booming voice came out tinny, but loud and clear. "Tell that fascist pig to catch some real criminals and stop bothering the taxpayers!" She could hear him guffawing through the little speaker.

Dad made a big, fake laugh, and then managed to shut the phone off. Alison figured that the only reason he didn't pitch it out the window was he was afraid of getting charged with littering. "Sorry about that," he said sheepishly.

The officer's voice stayed flat. "I'm going to write you taxpayers up for just five over the limit. And to show you how generous a fascist pig can be, I'll let you off with a warning about the windshield. Just see that it's fixed as soon as you get down the Cape. How long you down for?"

"One week," Mom replied all sunshine and summer breezes.

"Where you staying?"

"The Mansion—uh—Maggie's Mansion."

The faintest twitch of a smile tugged at the officer's large lips. "Make sure your windshield is fixed before you head home."

10 CAPE NOVEMBER

Darkness was swallowing the last dim gray glow of daylight as they rolled into Cape November. The thunderstorm sizzled and crashed all around them with a screaming wind. Rain smashed onto the minivan like nuts and bolts. Olivia usually loved thunderstorms, but not this one.

Every few minutes a small lake pooled on the dashboard under the hole in the windshield. When Mrs. Nunios took a turn, or hit a bump, the puddle would slosh into Mr. Nunios's lap and he would string together a chain of words so stunningly foul that his wife had no choice but to reprimand him for talking that way in front of the kids. The kids had no choice but to laugh uncontrollably. Olivia watched the puddle grow on the dashboard again.

"Why don't they mark these roads better?" Mr. Nunios groaned, slapping the water out from under himself. He squinted out the windshield as the GPS ordered them to turn left.

Mrs. Nunios started to turn, but the headlights lit up somebody's picket fence. Olivia figured it had probably been white once. Mrs. Nunios jerked the wheel, sending the new puddle into her husband's lap.

About a quarter mile farther along, Mr. Nunios finally stopped conducting his swearword symphony. Michael and Alison were cracking up, but Olivia could only muster up a small chuckle. It was full dark outside her window, except for the lightning. She hoped that Mrs. Nunios could see the road.

The meager headlights picked out a small space between the trees that was just big enough to be the road the GPS must have been talking about, but it was too dark and there was too much rain to know for sure.

The minivan turned off the main road and wound through streets lined with shaggy trees, weathered cottages and tangled gardens. Mr. Nunios shook his head. He sounded pretty disgusted, "I'm telling you, I haven't seen one road sign since we left the highway."

"It's a beach town," Alison's mother offered as an explanation, "There aren't that many roads."

Mr. Nunios turned his head for a better look at one especially run-down house. "I can see why tourism is down. All the tourists got lost."

Olivia knew how meticulous Mr. Nunios was about maintaining his house and yard. She also heard enough of his rants to know that he had no tolerance for homeowners who slacked off. As if on cue he began, "You know what I always say…"

"Unkempt means contempt," Michael, Alison and even Olivia all chanted dutifully.

Mr. Nunios looked surprised. "That's right. Contempt for yourself and contempt for your home and especially contempt for your neighbors who have to put up with your eyesore of a house."

"We know, Dad," Michael sighed. "It's a life lesson."

"Are you saying that to make fun of me?"

Olivia laughed quietly to herself at Michael's overstated sincerity. "No, Dad, of course not," he said, while also nodding his head with an exaggerated *yes* motion.

"In any case," Mr. Nunios continued, "this place sure fell apart."

"It's a dump, Dad," Michael said. "I tried to tell you guys that when you booked the trip. Nobody comes here anymore. We should have gone to Grimmyland like I said."

"Is Grimmyland free this week or something?" His father asked with heavy sarcasm. "Do you have any idea how much it costs to go there?"

"Do you?" Michael shot back.

Mr. Nunios turned down the corners of his mouth. "More than we got."

"Things will look a lot better in the sun, after we've had a nice dinner and a good night's sleep." Olivia smiled at Mrs. Nunios and her positive outlook. She really was a grand master of the tactful subject change.

According to the voice on the GPS, the address was coming up on the left, but all Olivia could see was a dense tangle of ancient trees and a thick overgrowth of wild underbrush.

"Wait. I think that's a driveway." Alison's father pointed to their left.

Olivia could make out a break in the trees that formed a natural arch. The minivan lurched, splashing through puddles in the unpaved driveway. Low branches of the huge old trees, heavy with rainwater, hung down scraping the roof and sides of the minivan. There was a sudden, *thwapping* crack.

"Now what?" Mr. Nunios moaned.

Hitting the brakes, Mrs. Nunios tried to look through the rain on the shattered windshield. "Antenna I think. Must've gotten caught on a branch and snapped off."

"Perfect." Alison's father leaned his head onto the headrest heavily. "Put it on the bill for this trip. Michael, don't say one word."

It was especially dark under the canopy of leaves. Olivia heard Alison's mom clicking the high beams, the low beams, the fog lights, but it was almost impossible to see. The knot of woods stretched back at least a hundred yards from the road until it thinned out to a weedy, overgrown lawn that Olivia could only see in pale, ghostly bursts with every flash of lightning. In between the flashes, the world disappeared.

A few old trees sat here and there around the lawn like old ladies feeding pigeons in the park. Olivia thought these trees probably would have decorated the lawn and added character once, but it had been so long since anyone had taken care of them, that they had grown into huge, bony fingers against the flashing sky.

The driveway opened to a gravel plaza that wound around a large, circular stone fountain. The headlights lit up a tower of three fish that stood in the middle of the fountain. Each crumbling fish jumped out of the mouth of the larger fish below it. Or maybe each larger fish was swallowing the smaller prey.

Big fish eats little fish? Olivia wondered. *Or little fish lives to swim another day? Hope or despair? She loves me. She loves me not. I would ask the artist about the theme, but he or she has probably been dead for fifty years. If not longer.*

The fish at the top looked like it used to spit out the water that made the fountain. But the only water in it now came from the rain. *Mosquitoes must love it. Zika virus, anyone?* But then, she reasoned, if there are mosquitoes, there must also be birds, dragonflies and bats to eat them.

How many microorganisms live in that water? A tiny ocean full of all kinds of creatures. I should have brought my microscope. I don't care how dorky Alison thinks it is. We could have seen dinoflagellates whipping around. Maybe some protozoa. Like a private zoo.

The minivan stopped. Wondering what the latest disaster was, Olivia leaned over to look out the window. Under the strobe lights of the storm Maggie's Mansion suddenly sprawled into view. A long, wide flight of steps led up from the gravel plaza to the wooden porch that stretched across the entire front of the building. A square, flat-roofed tower stretched up four stories taller than the square, flat-roofed shoulders of the three-story base.

Alison wrinkled up her nose, "Great! A haunted house!"

Clucking her tongue against the roof of her mouth in disgust, Alison's mother said sharply, "Stop being dramatic. It's charming. They don't build places like this anymore."

"Because they're creepy?" Alison asked. "Nice sign." She pointed to a large sign lit up in the beam of the headlights. The words *Maggie's Mansion* appeared in an elegant, but fading script. Painted above the name, a jagged, red proofreading caret indicated an insertion between the two words on the sign. Above that, in red, drippy letters, somebody had scrawled in the word *Haunted*.

"Great, Mom," Michael moaned. "You actually booked us at a haunted house."

Olivia laughed to herself. She didn't want to add to the tension by making Mrs. Nunios think she was piling on, too, but she had to admit, Michael was pretty funny sometimes. *And he had a point.* She turned to Alison, who looked miserable.

"Knock it off." Mr. Nunios sounded commanding and curt. "Don't everybody get excited because some knucklehead thought he was being funny and defacing private property. So let's everybody relax."

"I'm totally relaxed, Dad," Michael breezed. "I'm sure we'll sleep like the dead here."

"Enough with the smart remarks," his father warned. "It's just an old hotel."

"Yeah," Michael added, "it's not like any horror movies ever take place in old hotels."

"Shaddup, Mikey!" His father looked nervously at Mrs. Nunios while he scratched violently at the fly bites on his arms. "Geez this one's starting to bleed."

"If you scratch them, of course they're going to bleed," Mrs. Nunios scolded.

"They're itchy!" Mr. Nunios sighed heavily. "Look, we had a long, weird day. We're all tired and hungry. Let's just check in, okay? Then we can get something to eat."

"I think I have some cream for you and Michael in my bag," Mrs. Nunios added.

"I don't know," Alison said softly. If her family heard her, they didn't react at all, which was pretty unusual. Intense lightning and eruptions of thunder dared them to get out of the car. "I might be staying right here," Alison muttered.

"Well, I'm going in," Mrs. Nunios said coldly. Olivia swore the woman had ears like a hawk. Alison's mother snatched a magazine off the floor and held it over her head like a rain hat as she opened the door. She splashed out of the minivan and up the steps.

Mr. Nunios barked at Michael, "Okay, help me take some bags in, Hercules."

"We don't have a room yet, Dad," Michael protested. "We don't know where we're going."

"Whaddya mean? We know we're going in, right? Chop chop."

Scowling as he sloshed to the back of the minivan, Michael grabbed the two largest suitcases and squeezed two smaller bags under each arm.

"We've got the whole roof rack, too, Mikey. You're going to have to make a couple of trips!" Mr. Nunios warned. He was gathering phones and wallets and things from the seats to take in.

"It's raining! I want to make as few trips as I can." Michael called over his shoulder as he slogged toward the steps. On his way up one of the smaller bags slipped and tumbled back down into the large mud puddle at the bottom.

"For cryin' out loud, Mikey, that's *my* bag!" Mr. Nunios scowled out the window at his son.

"It's fine, Dad." Michael dropped off the other bags on top of the porch and jumped back down the stairs to pick up the bag that fell. "See," he called through the rain. "The bag's kind of waterproof."

Mr. Nunios yelled from his seat, "I hope your rear-end is kind of foot proof!" Normally this would have gotten big laughs from Alison and Olivia.

Olivia saw his blue eyes as Alison's father glanced into the mirror on his visor, like he was looking for a reaction from them. "Hey, you all right back there? I never heard you two this quiet."

"I don't like this place, Dad," Alison spoke with the calm of total certainty.

"Your mother picked it," her father smiled, "so I'm sure it's gonna be great. It'll probably stop raining soon. You'll be able to go to the beach. Maybe Mommy'll take you shopping. It'll be nice." He chuckled, "I might even be able to get a round in with Nelson tomorrow."

"It's golf, Dad, who cares?"

"Whaddaya mean?" Olivia thought he looked surprised, hurt even, as he turned to face Alison.

"You should spend time with us like Mom wants," Alison added. "With her."

In the dim light inside the minivan, Mr. Nunios cocked an eyebrow at his daughter. "Where's this coming from? Did your mother say something to you?"

"She doesn't have to say it, Dad. Can't you see it?" Olivia couldn't believe what Alison was saying. She grabbed her hand as the words seemed to tumble out. "Mom's lonely."

"She told you that?"

"She didn't have to." Alison sighed heavily. "She just wants us all to spend some time together. Especially you."

Mr. Nunios's voice sounded almost fragile. That made Olivia way more uncomfortable than his usual huffing and puffing. She could only imagine the effect it was having on Alison. "I spend lots of time with Mommy."

"Yeah, but not just to hang out and have fun like you do with your friends." She squeezed Olivia's hand a little harder. Alison never backed down. Not out of fear and not even out of pity. Not even when she should, like at that moment.

"You should have never told Nelson you'd meet him. You know what a big deal Mom's been making about this trip."

"Hey, I'm not the one talking about all this haunted house stuff. Besides…" Mr. Nunios looked around, almost like he was nervous. "What's the big deal? Nelson happened to be staying at Friendly Point with his girlfriend," her dad explained. "Mom and I might meet them together for dinner one night. *Together.* Like a double date."

"You mean that woman who wrecked Nelson's marriage?"

"Allie…" Olivia whispered, trying to hold her back. *This is going to be bad.*

"Who told you that? Did Mom say that?"

"Mom hates her. And in case you haven't noticed, she thinks Nelson is a creep, too."

Olivia had heard Alison butt heads with her parents, but never like this.

"Alison, what's gotten into you?" Her father's voice cut like a steel blade. "What your mother and I do and who we…And how dare you talk about my

47

friends? You don't get to talk about adults. Any adults. Ever. You're only a kid. What do you know?"

"I know Mom hates him," she spat. "Why don't *you* know that? Or do you just not care?"

Olivia could feel her knuckles cracking as Alison squeezed harder, but Olivia just winced silently, riding out the storm.

"Don't be disrespectful, Alison, I'm warning you…" That fuzzy feeling Alison had tapped into in her father was gone. Mr. Nunios was back. "What your mother and I do is none of your business." He folded his arms and faced the ruined windshield. The puddle continued to collect on the dashboard, slowly spilling onto the floor with a steady *drip…drip…drip*.

Alison's hand relaxed around Olivia. Alison looked smaller as she deflated back into her seat. Olivia stared at the rainwater washing inevitably down the windows.

"Come on, Olivia. We should help Michael with the bags." Alison opened the sliding door and stood in the rain. She didn't seem to care that the muddy puddles were overflowing her flip-flops and swamping her fresh pedicure. Grabbing her backpack and another small duffel bag, Alison headed up the steps.

Olivia smiled awkwardly at Alison's father, "I guess we'll give Michael a hand with the bags." She scampered out, grabbed her own backpack and duffel bag and followed Alison through the rain.

11 CHECKING IN

At the door to The Mansion Alison turned and watched Olivia jump the puddles, uselessly trying to keep her sneakers dry. With a sad creak the old glass and wood door opened, but only after Alison fussed with the knob. They stepped across the dark, wide-planked hardwood and onto the rich, red, Oriental rug spread across the large sitting room. Alison resisted the urge to kick off her flip-flops and feel the warm carpet under her bare, wet feet.

In the vast, dim space, she shivered, listening to the storm claw at the walls and windows. Shadows flickered between orange and yellow candlelight and caught in the nooks and grooves of the embossed tin ceiling. It shimmered on the paneled walls, the pale portraits and marble sculptures, fading finally down the hallways stretching from both sides of the lobby.

"Well," Olivia whispered, "it's a lot nicer inside than it looked from out there."

"A cave would be better than out there." Alison shrugged and sighed. "But you're right. Mom wasn't completely tripping when she booked this place."

Careful not to bump anything with their bags, Alison followed the path of trembling candles and hissing oil lanterns, set like beacons on the small wood and marble tables. There were old clocks, white marble statues, colorful ceramic leopards and elephants. Crossing the lobby, it reminded Alison of the gift shop, except everything looked clean, organized and expensive.

A baby grand piano braved one lonely corner. Shelves crammed with books stood around it. Overstuffed leather sofas and armchairs lounged next to tall, droopy plants and dwarf trees in ceramic pots.

"When the power comes back we should come here and read at night," Olivia whispered. "This place must look amazing when the lights are on. Check out all the old lamps."

Across the foyer, Alison saw her mother standing next to Michael at a long, wooden bar. Michael was sipping a soda from an old-fashioned glass bottle. Standing behind the bar in front of a scratched and cloudy mirror lined with shelves of colorful bottles, a woman in a business suit pushed her glasses up onto her nose as she leaned over a ledger. With her blonde hair pulled back it was hard to tell, but she looked younger than Mom. *Pretty, but not glamorous*, Alison decided.

"Hi," she said cheerfully as Alison approached. "Welcome to Maggie's Mansion. I'm Penny. You must be Alison and Olivia." Penny grinned and held out her hand for them each to shake. It surprised Alison. Adults didn't usually go out of their way to introduce themselves personally. Penny looked them each over quickly, not in a way that made Alison feel like she was being judged or studied, though. Penny's face was alert and curious. Alison waited for Penny to make the usual comment about Olivia being a model. "Your mom says you will be sharing one of the rooms." Penny handed Michael a flashlight from behind the bar. "Why don't you give the girls a hand?"

He took the flashlight and turned it on. The beam landed squarely on Alison's face.

"Michael!" Alison yelped and dropped the bags. One landed on Olivia's toe. "Ow!"

They both started laughing.

Michael quickly pointed the beam at the carpet in front of the girls. "Sorry." He shrugged.

"Please try not to embarrass me," Mom pleaded. "This is a nice place."

When she noticed Penny laughing, too, but covering it with her hand, Alison decided that she approved of her. Penny was okay.

"I'm really sorry about the lights." Penny made an adjustment on the lantern at the bar, and it burned a little brighter. "The power went out about two hours ago. It's all over the Cape I think. Pretty bad out there, huh?"

"It's like a monsoon," Mom said.

"We needed the rain. We've had a drought for months. I'm glad you made it, though. Roads flood down here a lot." Penny moved comfortably and quickly behind the bar. She smiled at Alison and then Olivia, but it looked kind and not patronizing. Alison liked that. "I can only imagine how this old place must look to you right now. Like Castle Dracula, am I right? But I promise you, when the sun comes out, you're going to love it here."

"Have you worked here long?" Alison asked.

Penny laughed. "This old place has been in my family a long time. I practically grew up here. Now I own it." She sounded apologetic about it, Alison thought.

Alison watched the candlelight dance on Penny's glasses as she wrote things down and found their room keys in a cabinet behind the bar. Penny's funky, green frames looked designer, and had probably been expensive, but they were scratched and banged up. Her clothes were well cared for, but a little worn, and the style was a little dated.

The key made a rasping sound on the bar as Penny slid it to Alison. "You girls are in room eleven." She smiled warmly. "Your parents will be on one side in room ten, and your big brother here will be all on his own in room twelve. You girls will be safe and sound in the middle, but try to look after the big guy." She pointed at Michael with her pen. Alison wondered if Penny was like this with everybody. She seemed to be making a point to talk to her and Olivia in particular. She wondered if Mom had told Penny that they were scared or something. She hoped not. That would have been so embarrassing.

Penny continued brightly, "The bad news is that I have to go out of town for a couple of days to take care of a few things. The good news is that my niece, Maggie, should be getting here in a little while. She runs this old place better than I do."

"*The* Maggie? Like...the place is named after *her*?" Michael asked.

"I know, right? Practically a celebrity." Penny gave him a theatrical wink. "She's cute, too. If you play your cards right, she might even give you a *personal* tour."

Alison thought it was hysterical how Michael made a few nervous, blubbering sounds, but apparently could not come up with any words.

Penny spread her hands flat on the bar. "The other good news for you is that no one else is scheduled to be here this week, so you'll have the place to yourselves, and you'll have Maggie's undivided attention."

"That's not good news for you, though, is it?" Mom asked.

Penny laughed awkwardly. The keys clacked as she placed them on the bar and passed them to Mom and Michael.

"Real keys." Mom picked up a key on its white plastic fob and looked at it. "I haven't seen those in while. So many hotels use those cards now."

From behind the desk, Penny sighed, "Yeah. My boyfriend was pretty handy. He was going to install a card system, but he never got around to it."

Alison wanted to ask what happened, but decided it was too personal.

"Well, real keys have so much charm," Mom said cheerily. "And my husband always loses the cards anyway. And speak of the devil!"

The door banged open. Dripping with rain and carrying an armload of luggage, Dad lumbered up to the desk and glowered at Michael. "You never came back. We still got the roof rack."

This can play out a lot of ways. Alison thought nervously.

"Sorry." Michael sounded sheepish and set down the bottle of soda.

The tiniest of smiles curled at the corner of Dad's mouth as he shook his head. "College boy." He shook his head slightly. "Would you please help me get the bags *now*?"

Alison felt the fist in her chest loosen its grip.

Dad smiled politely as Mom introduced Penny. He kept smiling politely when Penny apologized for the power failure, and he continued to smile politely when she apologized for not having anyone there to help them with their bags. She began to pick up the bags herself. "I'll show you upstairs to your rooms."

"You don't have to take those!" Dad protested. "Michael, don't make the lady carry the bags. Where are you manners?"

"But it's her job," Michael whined.

"Michael," Dad growled.

"I know, Dad. It was a joke. Don't get your boxers in a knot. Should I get the stuff from the car first or carry everybody's crap up the stairs first?"

"I don't care. Just help. You lift all those weights for nothing? Chop chop!"

Michael sighed and looked at the floor. "Why do you always say *chop chop*? It's stupid."

"Because it's what I'm going to do to your head if you don't move your butt."

Shrugging his broad shoulders, Michael wrangled the luggage up the stairs.

"You'd think we were moving in," Dad remarked as Penny led them with a flashlight back across the foyer and down the dark hallway.

"Oh you should see what some people bring in. Sorry again about the lights," Penny said. "There are some oil lamps on the nightstands in each room. I'll help you set that all up once we're upstairs."

Alison thought about a hotel that kept oil lamps in the rooms. She worked it over in her mind for a moment as she climbed the stairs with her bags. "I guess you lose power a lot."

Penny laughed. "Look at little Miss Sherlock here. All the electrical down here is old, even the town's grid is dated."

Up ahead, right behind Penny, Michael lugged his armload of suitcases and bags. "Isn't it a violation of fire codes to use open flames in an old wooden place like this, especially a hotel?"

"You'll have to excuse him." Mom sounded irritated. "My son wants to be a journalist so he thinks he can ask people rude questions."

Penny stopped at the door on the second floor landing and tilted her head at Michael like he was some kind of strange, amusing bug. "Inquiring minds want to know, huh? We keep the lamps there for decoration. You can write that in your story. See, normally they're empty, but since the power's out I filled the ones in your rooms earlier. They were good enough for the pioneers, and they're safer than candles. Unless you'd rather unpack in the dark. Is that okay with you, Smokey the Bear?"

"Technically, it's just Smokey Bear," Olivia pointed out.

"What?" Penny asked. Alison couldn't tell if Penny was starting to get annoyed. She was still smiling.

"His name is Smoky Bear." Olivia said it like it was important. *That's just Olivia trying to be more social.* "Like Mickey Mouse. It's not Mickey the Mouse, right?" Olivia chuckled nervously.

Her parents and Penny looked puzzled at Alison who smiled apologetically. "She spends way too much time on the Internet."

Penny laughed. "No, no. That's really good information. I'll have to remember that." Turning to Michael, she added, "There are fire extinguishers in all the closets, too, by the way, so if you want to take one to bed with you, go for it. Anyway, here are your rooms."

Penny stopped at the first door on the right. "This is your room, big guy. A corner suite. Ocean views on two sides."

Michael unlocked his door. Since they only had the one flashlight, Penny helped him get in and light the oil lamp that was on the small table near the rear wall of windows. Once the flame was sputtering inside its glass cover, Alison and the others stepped in, too.

Alison was anxious about what the rooms would be like. A massive, intricately carved four-poster bed stood out from the wall on the right side. A stone fireplace that could have easily swallowed a couch took up most of the opposite wall. Everything was old wood and marble with a heavy feel. It reminded Alison of an ancient castle that used to be posh, but now was more like a museum.

The back wall was made of wood-framed glass panels. Michael pressed his face against the glass and wood door in the middle. "Hey cool, there's a deck out here. Can we go out there?"

"You might want to wait 'til the storm's over," Penny suggested wryly. "Tomorrow morning, hopefully the storm'll pass and you'll be able to watch the sunrise on the ocean."

"He's not really a morning person," Mom announced. "The lazy thing."

"Hey, if you can't sleep late on vacation…" Penny said cheerfully. "Just pull those curtains if you want to keep it dark, big guy."

Near the corner where the wardrobe cabinet stood beside the fireplace, there was another door that led to an old marble bathroom with antique brass fixtures including a box-on-a-pole-style toilet with a brass pull chain and a cast-iron ceramic tub that stood on four brass claws.

Alison noticed that the bathroom had another door on the opposite side. "What's through there?"

"That's your room," Penny explained.

Alison, Olivia and Michael all made the same wounded groan at exactly the same time.

"Double jinx?" Olivia said weakly.

"That's how they built 'em in the old days," Mom proclaimed. "People just had to share and get along."

"I'm glad I don't live in the old days," Alison grumbled. She had her own bathroom at home. The last thing she wanted to do was share a bathroom with her brother on vacation.

"It's only for a week," Olivia said brightly.

Leaving Michael in his room, Penny opened the next door for Alison and Olivia. Once their lamp was glowing, she moved on with Mom and Dad.

Alison and Olivia's room was the mirror image of Michael's, except they only had one set of windows. That was fine by Alison. At home she always kept the curtains closed. Windows creeped her out at night.

"It's funny that we have to sleep next to a giant wall of glass. With a balcony." Olivia closed the thick drapes.

"Hilarious." Alison was feeling more sour by the minute. "Do *not* say anything about it or my idiot brother will climb onto the balcony and try to scare us on purpose."

Alison opened the bathroom door and saw her brother, shirtless, moving around his room, and felt her usual sense of violation at seeing any part of him unclothed. "*Uch!* Bad enough *I* have to see you, but Olivia's here, too. Keep your door closed at all times!" She slammed his door and leaned against it. "Sharing a bathroom with my brother is even scarier than the windows."

He yelled something back, but Alison couldn't hear him through the door.

"Oh I don't know," Olivia mused. "I feel a little safer with the big gorilla right next door."

Michael suddenly burst through the bathroom door into Alison and Olivia's room. "Hey, where's Mom and Dad? I'm starving."

"Not cool, Michael. You can't just barge in here whenever you feel like it. And keep a shirt on at all times! We discussed this."

"We didn't discuss it. You told me what to do, and I ignored you." Michael laughed and flexed, making his chest muscles pop independently of each other. Alison threw a pillow at him. "Seriously. I'm going to eat my own arm. And these bites are killing me. You got any cream or anything?"

It was like lifting a child, but Alison hauled one of Michael's big arms up to her face. "Have you been scratching?"

"Of course I've been scratching. I just told you, they itch like crazy."

"You're going to get an infection," Olivia warned. She was over by the wardrobe, stuffing socks into a drawer.

There was a knock at the door, and Mom poked her head in, grinning. "How are we doing? Isn't this place dope?"

Michael looked at Mom sternly. "Never say *dope* again."

"What else is she supposed to call you?" Alison was pleased she got that in. "Mom, tell this big *dope* that he can't just come into our room whenever he feels like it! And he has to keep his shirt on," Alison demanded. "And he needs something for these bites. They look terrible."

"I know," Mom sighed. "Dad's are all red, too, and some of them are bleeding because he keeps scratching. Michael, knock first. Suppose the girls were changing or something?"

"I'd need therapy."

"Not as much as we would," Alison replied.

What's for dinner?" Michael asked.

"Penny said that with the power out we should probably eat in town. There's a great place called Olga's."

"What's Olga's?" Michael asked.

"You'll love it," Mom beamed. "They've got brick oven pizza and Italian food. Penny says it's great."

Dad appeared in the hallway behind Mom carrying the last of the luggage. "I ran into Penny. Get this! She says Olga's is still in business and they're probably still open tonight!" Alison was surprised to hear Dad sounding so enthusiastic. "I used to go there all the time when we came here back in the day. Olga's is the best."

"I'm in," Michael said. "But never say *back in the day* again either."

Dad scowled, "I'm gonna knock you back in the day."

12 STRANGERS ON THE ROAD

Olivia tried to see through the fog muffling the lake-sized puddles. Mr. Nunios had gotten clear plastic bags and duct tape from Penny to slow the leak. It almost worked. The good thing was, there were only pockets of rain and the rumblings of high, distant thunder were less frequent.

Driving to dinner felt so normal after everything the day had brought. It was finally starting to feel like a family vacation. The Nunioses were her family, more or less. Olivia didn't really remember any of her own family vacations back from when her parents were still together. She had seen pictures. They looked happy.

"I bet this would be a beautiful bike ride on a nice day," Mrs. Nunios offered cheerfully as the minivan rode through the dark.

Leaning forward, Mr. Nunios seemed to be struggling to see into the shadows. Olivia noticed that Mr. Nunios and Michael were still scratching the angry welts the flies had left.

"Yeah," Mr. Nunios said. "You could just take this up to the boardwalk and ride out to Central Avenue and then up to The Boulevard. Shouldn't take more than an hour." He laughed sarcastically, "Mikey, wanna take a ride into town?"

Michael boasted, fussing with his own bites, "You mean I don't have to spend any more time trapped in this car? Let me out right here."

"I wouldn't want to be riding tonight," Alison said quietly. Olivia saw her give a small shiver as she stared out into the night. She leaned her lips close to Olivia's ear. "I really hate this place. It's spooky."

Olivia shrugged and nodded her chin toward Mrs. Nunios.

Alison's lips twisted into a scowl. "Trust me. She hates it, too," Alison hissed into Olivia's ear. "But she knows that if she says anything, then everyone else will start in." Alison sighed heavily "It'll just be a big fight."

"You girls sure unpacked quick," Mrs. Nunios said brightly.

Olivia wondered whether she had heard Alison's whispering. *Ears like a hawk.*

"Olivia did," Alison said without missing a beat.

"I'm sorry to say that your daughter is planning on living out of her suitcase," Olivia reported dutifully. Olivia was an admitted neat freak, so it pained her that while she'd been folding and tucking her things into drawers and draping them on hangers, Alison had kicked off her flip-flops, sprawled across the comforter and played a game on her phone. She would have updated her status and texted all their friends, her friends, really, but there wasn't any phone service. The storm had knocked it out.

"Don't worry, Mom," Alison called, "Olivia left me some space in the drawers. She's planning on secretly unpacking me later. For my own good."

"Alison," her mother said sharply, "Olivia's not your maid. Don't let her do that. You unpack your own stuff!"

"I don't need to unpack. What's the difference?" Alison asked.

"How do you find anything?" Olivia asked.

Alison shrugged, still staring out the window. She seemed to only be half-listening.

Olivia laughed. "Organizing your daughter is my personal mission."

Mrs. Nunios clucked her tongue, "Seriously, I don't know where Alison would be without you."

Olivia stared out the window and thought back. After her parents divorced, Olivia and her mom moved to a new town, so she had to change schools in the fourth grade. In her old school, she could get an A on any test without studying at all, but she always studied anyway because she was afraid of getting a B.

Just before school started, Olivia's mom got a letter saying Olivia was invited to participate in the Program for Exceptional Performance. Olivia's parents both had to have a meeting with all of these people from the school district. She was worried that they wouldn't be able to go to the meeting together, because sometimes, after the divorce, they didn't like going to the same places. But they both seemed happy to go, even together.

The last thing Olivia wanted was to go to a new school and wind up in a special class. She just wanted to be in regular classes with regular kids. Her mother wouldn't even listen. *Olivia, we are not going to waste your abilities. You are going into that gifted class and that's final.*

The amazing thing for Olivia was not that her mother said these words. She had expected that. It was that her father then said the exact same words in the exact same tone that weekend when Olivia asked *him* if she could just be in regular classes. Sending Olivia to the PEP class was the only thing her parents had agreed on in years. That and refined sugar was undermining the country.

During those first two weeks of PEP, Olivia came home every day and cried. She begged her mother to take her out of the program. She tried to explain how mean and stuck-up the other kids were, but her mother would just tell her that she was being too sensitive and she needed to toughen up.

On the first Monday of her third week everything changed. A chubby fireball of a girl with freckles and thick, black hair burst into the classroom.

"Hey now, Mrs. Kingsley! Did you miss me?"

The class swarmed around Alison, and it took Mrs. Kingsley ten minutes to get things back under control. Alison wasn't allowed to talk about why she had been suspended. So she waited until lunch.

Olivia stood quietly on the fringe of a large circle of kids while Alison explained how a bunch of kids had been waiting at the bus stop when Milton

Carlisle started in with Alison…again. Besides bragging about the new tablet computer he'd gotten for making the honor roll, Milton threw in a few of his usual fat jokes that were not directed at Alison, but clearly intended for her. When Milton was distracted, talking to James and Roberta, Alison had slipped Milton's brand new lunch bag out of his backpack and put it under the back wheels of the school bus.

When it pulled away, the bus crushed Milton's thermos, his organic, non-GMO chicken salad sandwich on whole grain cibatta, his two organic apples and his brand-new tablet computer. Alison said that the funniest part was that Milton didn't even realize it was missing until lunchtime. And then he totally freaked out and started crying like a baby. Alison probably would have never gotten caught, but she straight up bragged about it. She wanted everyone to know. She was sending a message.

During Alison's first week back, their teacher paired Alison with Olivia to work on a project. Olivia remembered how they had sat together whispering and scheming to put together a rap to go with their diorama about Edgar Allan Poe. The other kids couldn't hear what Alison and Olivia talked about, and Olivia made sure to laugh extra loud.

After an hour or so, the class got to take a short break. Olivia went to the bathroom. Walking back, she heard Jessica Bundy.

"You got stuck with Minibrain?" Jessica sounded annoyed. She always sounded annoyed.

"Minibrain?" Alison asked.

"Yeah, Alison," Tyler Jones agreed. "You're going to catch stupid from her."

"I don't even know who let her in." Alexa Chua clucked her tongue. "My mom says they have to stop lowering the standards and watering down PEP."

Olivia could feel the tears stinging her eyes.

"Her name is Olivia," Alison said evenly.

"Doesn't she seem a little…not smart to you?" Tyler asked.

"You seem not smart, Tyler," Alison snapped. "You seem like a moron."

"She's not smart enough to be here," Jessica insisted. "That's why she never talks."

Alison said lightly, "She's just a little shy."

"Booor-ing!" Alexa chanted.

Alison's voice rose. "She's a champion swimmer with—like—a zillion trophies and medals and stuff."

"So?" Alexa laughed. "Who cares about swimming? That won't get you a seven-figure job."

"Who cares about swimming? Who cares about the cello?" Alison snapped. "Your mother makes you practice like what? Eighty-five-million-hours a day and you still suck, and then you spend another million hours doing math problems with your tutor. If your mother didn't make you do all that stuff, you wouldn't even be in PEP."

"I'M TELLING MS. KINGSLEY!" Alexa's shriek faded as she ran away.

Alison made a disgusted grunt and came out into the hall where she found Olivia crying.

In the back of the minivan, Alison turned and caught Olivia staring at her. Olivia could feel the heat in her cheeks just from the old memory. She was glad it was dark.

"What?" Alison sounded suspicious. "My hair's a mess. I know. It's all the rain."

"Your hair looks fine." Olivia shook her head. She didn't realize she'd been staring at Alison. "I was just thinking about fourth grade."

"Ugh! I was so fat."

"Come on," Olivia said firmly. They'd been over this too many times.

"Those kids were sooo annoying," Alison insisted. Her evil smile suddenly lit up her face. "Remember Milton Carlisle?"

"Remember him?" Mr. Nunios called from the front, "I had to pay six hundred bucks thanks to your shenanigans."

"Sorry, Dad, but he had it coming."

"Couldn't you have just punched him in the face?" Michael said. "It would have been cheaper."

"There's no point going over all that again," Mrs. Nunios urged them. "Olivia, you're going to meet some wonderful new girls at Ashton Academy. It's so prestigious."

"I'm sure you're right, Mrs. Nunios." Olivia was sure she was wrong, but it was pointless to argue. It was easier just to keep staring out the window.

As the minivan continued to slosh through the puddles and floods along the fringe of Cape November, Olivia noticed that the houses were mostly big and old, with a few smaller cottages or bungalows mixed in. She thought it was a little creepy to be driving past so many dark buildings. It was hard to tell which were dark from the blackout and which were just abandoned. Only a few scattered windows flickered with the orange light of candles or the white glow of flashlights.

At the first working traffic light, Mr. Nunios stopped. They were near a ragged cluster of two-story apartments with sagging balconies.

"Look at this," Mr. Nunios grumbled. "Some crooked real estate developer puts up a bunch of cheap apartments and then when nobody buys them, he declares bankruptcy and lets them go to pot." Mr. Nunios sighed and shook his head sadly. "That's what's wrong with this country."

"Really, Dad?" Michael scoffed. "*That's* what's wrong? Do you even watch the news?"

Mr. Nunios wrinkled up his face. "Okay, Walter Cronkite, maybe there's a few other things, too."

"Walter who?"

Mr. Nunios laughed. "And you want to be a journalist?"

"You know," Alison said, "it's kind of weird how this traffic light is red, but there's no power anywhere else around here." She squinted out the window. "Look how dark it is out there."

Looking out the window, Olivia noticed three large men in long, hooded ponchos coming out of one of the nasty, broken-down apartment buildings. They seemed to be heading toward the minivan. All she could see under the hoods were thin, pale chins.

"This light is taking forever," Michael complained. "I'm starving."

"What else is new?" Alison drawled.

"Where's that leftover chicken?" Michael asked.

"I had to toss it." Mrs. Nunios shook her head. "There's no fridge and it's been out since lunch."

"I'd have eaten it," Michael said. "How long is this light? We've been here forever."

"The light is probably busted," Mr. Nunios suggested. "You know, from the storm."

Olivia was only half-listening to their conversation. She could not take her eyes off the three large men walking straight toward the minivan. They moved slowly, hobbling with a strange, rippling rhythm.

"This light is definitely broken," Michael declared. "You should just run it, Dad."

"With the broken windshield and the speeding ticket?" his father said in disbelief. "If a cop sees us my insurance will go through the roof."

Olivia's heart beat faster as she watched the men shamble purposefully toward the minivan. She couldn't see their faces under their hoods. Little bubbles of fear gurgled in her stomach. *Run it, Mr. Nunios.*

"There're no cops here, Dad. The light is broken," Michael insisted. "I'm telling you. Just run it."

The three men got closer to the window, and Olivia could see how big they were. Michael was about six feet tall, and these men would tower over him. And they were freakishly wide. Like professional wrestlers. Olivia still couldn't see their faces under their hoods. *Please run it, Mr. Nunios.*

"That's a bad idea," Mr. Nunios insisted. "I'm not doing it."

"Will you just run it already, Tommy?" Mrs. Nunios insisted. "It's broken. You said so yourself."

"I said it was *probably* busted," Mr. Nunios explained.

Alison finally joined in. "We have been here forever, Dad."

Olivia swallowed hard and clawed Alison's thigh as the three men lunged toward the back of the minivan.

"OW!" Alison yelped. "Liv-i!"

"Fine!" Mr. Nunios gunned the engine, and the minivan lurched through the intersection.

Olivia looked out the rear window at the three men fading into the damp darkness. "Did you see them?" she whispered.

"Who?" Alison mouthed back

"Those three huge creeps."

Alison twisted in the seat to look out the back, but the minivan was too far away. Even Olivia couldn't even see the men anymore.

Olivia slumped heavily. "I...I guess it was nothing. I just thought that those three guys were—like—after us."

Alison laughed and put her arm around Olivia. "Why would anybody be after *us*?" she whispered. Her eyebrows were scrunched up with concern. "You're just freaked out. Trust me, I've been freaked out since we got here."

Olivia laughed, too, "Yeah. You're right. Sorry. Is your leg okay?"

Alison nodded, "A few stitches and I'll be good as new."

"Are you two okay back there?" Mrs. Nunios asked. "You're whispering. You know I don't like whispering."

"Sorry, Mom," Alison called innocently. "Olivia thought some people were coming after the car."

Olivia slapped Alison's thigh. "Throw me under the bus much?"

Alison yelped and laughed. "It's what you said."

"Just because somebody lives in a poor neighborhood doesn't mean they're a criminal," Mrs. Nunios scolded. "Olivia, I'm surprised at you."

"Yeah. It was probably just the cops coming for Dad for running that light," Michael offered.

"Shaddup, Mikey," his father growled.

13 OLGA'S

Michael couldn't wait to get out of the car and get some food. The minivan had barely come to a full stop in the empty parking lot when he yanked the door open and jumped out. The overhead lights made the lot look like daylight compared to the blackout everywhere else.

"Look at that." Mom sounded so happy. "The lights are back on."

"This place might be on a different grid." Dad closed the door and looked around while he waited for the girls to climb out of the back. "Maybe they have a generator just for The Boulevard, you know? Because of the tourists?"

"Yeah, Mom," Michael loaded the sarcasm. "I'm sure glad we drove all the way down here to admire the streetlights." What was wrong with his parents? Was he the only one who realized that they hadn't eaten in seven thousand hours? "I think I speak for everybody when I say, who cares about the lights? We're starving."

It was a short walk from the parking lot to Olga's Osteria. They passed a lot of dark storefronts. Michael wasn't sure whether they were closed for the night, closed because of the storm or closed for good. He did not see any other people or even cars.

"Anagrams!" Alison shouted as the sign for Olga's Osteria came into view on the large window next to the front door. "Goalie Roasts."

"A goalie sorts," Olivia replied.

"Go lose tiaras."

"Lost Asia ogre!" Olivia grinned.

Just to get Alison and Olivia to stop their annoying game, Michael almost asked what an Osteria was, but he didn't want everybody jumping down his throat for not knowing. He could just hear his father, *You want to be a journalist in East Nowhersicstan, but you don't even know what an osteria is?* Michael didn't need that aggravation, so he kept quiet and figured he could find out what an Osteria was later.

"Hang on," Alison asked suddenly, "What is an Osteria?"

"Great question, Alison," Mom said. "Michael, why don't you ever ask questions like that?"

"What kind of reporter doesn't ask questions?" Dad said.

Michael just gritted his teeth while Mom explained that an Osteria was an Italian word for a restaurant or a tavern.

"So…it's just a pretentious way to say *restaurant* in a foreign language? Boy! Am I glad we cleared that up! Great question, Allie. Really hard hitting."

"I'll show you hard hitting, Mikey." Dad held the door, and Michael entered

Olga's Osteria. It was a lot smaller than Michael had imagined. Olga's was in a small, two-story building with narrow alleys on both sides. The restaurant was tidy, and the small lamps hanging from the ceiling gave warm light. There were little candles and vases of flowers on the empty tables. In the back corner, the steps leading upstairs had a little rope across it. The sign on the rope read *staff only*.

A man folded his newspaper and stood. He was average height, late middle-aged with a fringe of salt-and-pepper hair and a thick moustache. It took three tries before he managed to get his reading glasses into his shirt pocket, and then he smiled warmly at them. "How you doin'? Wet out there, huh? Can we getcha fixed up with a nice, hot meal or are yous just lookin' for directions to the freeway like the last *googootz* that came in here?"

Michael surprised them all by taking the lead. "Hello, yes. Table for five, please."

The man with the moustache looked Michael up and down and turned down the corners of his mouth like he was impressed. "Very good, *signore*. Right this way."

"*Grazee*." Michael used the one word of Italian that he had picked up from watching old mobster movies.

An old woman peeked her head around a door at the back of the room. She was rail thin with high, bony cheeks and jet-black hair. Her tight scowl relaxed into a smile when she saw the family. "*Si* yes. *Prego*, sit. Sal, *subito!* Not there!" Her Italian accent was heavy. "Give the big table. Nah! What's a matter for you? The big one!"

"Right this way, ladies and gents." Sal took menus from a shelf in the front, but then put them back. "You ain't gonna need menus. We'll take care-ah-youz. *Fuhgettaboutit*." He winked like he was letting them in on a secret, then called toward the kitchen. "Hey Vin, *un po' di pane qui*."

They weren't even sitting yet when a man only slightly older than Michael came out of the back door with a huge, round loaf of fresh bread on a wooden board and a tray piled high with Italian cold cuts, cheeses, olives and roasted vegetables. He was lean with perfect hair, a neat goatee, a black shirt, gray vest and small, black-framed glasses.

Not long after the bread, the food just kept coming, and it was all incredible. Michael didn't know what half the stuff was, even though Olga personally explained every item on every dish. But he didn't care. He just knew it was awesome.

They crunched on fried calamari, slurped up savory mussels in garlic. The pizza came out of a coal oven and had this amazing smoky crust. There were huge platters of pasta in shapes Michael never knew existed topped with all different sauces. Sometimes red. Sometimes green. A few were pink. He tried to post a picture of the food for his friends and followers, but, of course, he wasn't getting any service.

"Don't even bother, cuz," Vinnie said, setting down a platter of sausage and peppers. "It's been outta whack all day."

They dug into a huge platter of something Olga called *polenta con polpetta e salsiccia,* which was sort of like lasagna with meatballs and sausage in it, except that instead of lasagna noodles, the layers were made of polenta, a dense, spongy stuff that tasted a little like cornbread.

"See," Mom said, wiping her mouth with a cloth napkin. "It's like I always tell you kids. There's more to life than food courts and drive-through."

As Vinnie poured the wine for Michael's parents, Olga insisted that Michael have a glass, too.

"Isn't that illegal?" Mom asked.

"*Beh!*" Olga gave an amused look.

"I don't know…" Mom said.

"Come on, Sara." Dad said. "You think he's not going to have a drink at Cartesian? It's only a month away."

Michael certainly didn't want to argue with Olga, and he felt proud that Olga *and Dad!* were treating him like an adult. Finally, a little respect.

By the time they finished all the courses, even Michael was too full to eat another bite. While Sal poured tiny cups of espresso, Olga disappeared into the kitchen and came back leading a thick, middle-aged man with curly hair and a moustache. He was untying his apron as she introduced another nephew, Tony.

"So Vinnie's your brother?" Michael asked, eager to show his parents his investigative skills.

Tony laughed. "No. I'm Sal's brother. Vinnie's my son."

Olga scowled and chuckled at the same time. "Vinnie is my *gram*-nephew."

Vinnie laughed. "Not *gram, Zi-Zi.* I'm your great-nephew."

"*Beh!*" Olga said.

Michael stood up and crossed the table, sweeping the surprised chef up in a bear hug. "That was the best meal I ever had! I mean it."

Michael could hear the horror in his mother's voice, "Michael, put that man down before you hurt him."

Alison and Olivia laughed hysterically.

"Actually," Tony said, straightening his clothes and pulling a chair up to their table, "You'd be surprised how often I get that reaction."

"No," Michael insisted, "I wouldn't be surprised at all. Not the way you cook. I'm serious."

"Take it easy, Mikey," his father laughed. "How much of that wine did you get?"

"Like…less than half a glass." *Two glasses. But who's counting?*

Tony and Sal laughed as they sat with them at the table, sipping espresso and telling funny stories about the restaurant in the old days, like the time a professional football team moved all the tables aside after dinner and started dancing with the other customers.

Sighing, Tony said, "It's been tough here the last couple of years. We just don't get the customers like we used to."

"Why not?" Michael asked.

Sal set his espresso cup down. "Things just ain't been good. The people here…"

"Things just aren't like they used to be," Tony said.

Sal nodded grimly and lowered his voice. "How long you in town for?"

"A week," Mom said.

"Where you stayin'?" Sal asked.

"The Mansion." Dad took a sip of his own espresso.

Tony and Sal's face brightened. "With Penny?"

"She's away. Maggie's taking care of us," Mom said.

A sad, dark expression crossed Sal's face. "She's a great kid."

Tony was shaking his head. "She's had some bad breaks, but she's good people."

Sal shrugged. "Still, things being how they are, you might think about leaving a little sooner."

Tony scowled at his brother. "Sal, you gonna take food outta Penny's mouth? They're her customers."

Sal shook his head, "I know, but you know how things been, Tone."

"How have things been?" Dad sounded suspicious and even a little angry. He glanced at Mom.

Tony and Sal smiled.

"Look, this is a great town," Tony said. "See all these lamps?"

"There were lamps like it in The Mansion." Alison smiled impishly at Michael, like she'd just gotten something over on him. "And even at that place up the highway where we stopped. Irma's."

Sal squinted his eyes at Alison. "Irma's? I can't believe that place is still open."

Dad sat a little taller. He looked a little defensive. "You have to stop there when you're driving down the Cape from up north. It's part of the experience. The food was still great."

"And they had lamps like these there, too," Alison said.

"They used to make them right here in town, these lamps." Tony sighed. "But that place closed down years ago."

Sal added. "It's not going great right now is the thing."

"What are you saying?" Mom asked. Michael noticed the way her fingers curled the tablecloth.

"You know what," Sal smiled. "I don't even know what I'm saying." He finished a glass of wine and poured himself another from the jug. "Wine makes me sentimental for the old days when this place was really something and business was a little better."

"Vin!" Tony called, and then he whistled loudly.

Vinnie popped his head out of the kitchen. "Ho? Whaddaya want?"

"Bring out the accordion," Tony said.

Vinnie tilted his head. "Really?"

"It's been a great night. Let's show these nice people how this place used to be."

Sal strapped on the accordion. In a big opera voice, Tony began to sing these old Italian songs. When Sal took a break, Tony sang songs from real operas right off the top of his head.

Alison leaned over to Olivia, and Michael heard her whisper, "I feel like we're in a movie."

"You're so good." Michael's mother gushed as Tony finished a song. She announced to the rest of them, "When he sang *Mamma* I cried." She teasingly smacked Michael in the arm, "Why don't you sing for me like that?"

"Ow!" Michael complained. "You know I can't sing like that."

"You can't sing at all," Alison said.

"Everybody can sing!" Tony corrected.

Sal quickly added, "Most people just can't sing good."

Olga and Vinnie arrived from the kitchen with a huge tray of pastries. Michael recognized the little tubes of crispy dough filled with cream as cannoli. There was another type of pastry on the tray that Michael had never seen before. He ended up liking it even better than the cannoli. It was shaped sort of like a seashell, but it was made of about a dozen layers of thin, crispy dough that was filled with a sweet cream. Olga said they were called *sfogliatelle*. She made Michael repeat it until he could make the *s-f* sound correctly.

Vinnie carried out a glass jug wrapped in a straw basket along with a handful of small glasses. Olga looked pleased. In her thick accent, she said, "You know what make Tony sing so good? He drink this." Olga began pouring the bright green liquid out of the jug.

"What is it?" Michael's mother asked.

Michael took a sniff of the glass in front of him. It smelled spicy and strong. On the side of the bottle, Michael read the name, *Centerbe*.

"It means one hundred herbs," Vinnie explained.

Michael tried to pronounce it, but Tony had to correct him. "It's like a *ch* sound."

"So like *chent-urb-ay*?" Olivia asked.

Olga's face lit up, "*Quanto sei bella!*"

Sal smiled warmly at Olivia and Alison. "That means, *How beautiful you are.*"

Alison cocked her head to the side. "You'd be surprised how often she gets that reaction."

Olga held up her glass of bright green liquid. "From Abruzzo," Olga explained. "Is good when you eat a lot. It help you digest."

"Wait," Michael asked, "Are you telling me to do a shot?"

Olga clucked her tongue and swatted him sharply in the back of the head. It didn't hurt, but it got them all laughing.

"Welcome to the family," Vinnie said.

"*Mannagia!* No shot! This...*non è tequila*, eh! Is only for digest a food."

"You should just sip it," Tony instructed.

"All of us?" Alison asked uncertainly, sniffing the spicy green liquid.

Tony smiled. "That's up to your parents."

"I don't think that's a good idea." Mom sounded worried.

Dad shrugged. "Let 'em taste it. When in Rome, right? And this is as close to Rome as we're going to get."

Olga scowled again. "No *Roma. Abruzzo!*"

"Come on, Mom," Michael urged. "It's family vacation, right?" He thought of exactly how to seal the deal. "What happens down the Cape stays down the Cape, right?"

His mother glowered hard at Michael, but she couldn't keep it up and they all started laughing.

It was a strange flavor, Michael thought, sipping. Sort of like medicine, but also like fresh herbs. It felt like hot sandpaper in his mouth and throat and all the way down. He could literally feel it travel all the way into his stomach. Miraculously, while he still felt full and satisfied, he no longer felt uncomfortable. Michael watched his father who seemed to be enjoying his *Centerbe*. His mother was sniffing and wrinkling her nose and sipping like a hummingbird. Just allowing the *Centerbe* to touch their lips was enough to convince Olivia that she probably should wait until her next trip down the Cape to try it, but Alison sipped hers. This seemed to make Olga and her nephews happy.

14 STRANGERS IN THE PARKING LOT

Olivia felt full and relaxed as they said goodbye to Olga and her nephews. Olga had kissed each of them and pinched Alison's cheeks until she yelped.

"See?" Vinnie tilted his head to show off the handsome creases in his face. "These aren't dimples. These are Zi-Zi's thumbprints."

Mr. and Mrs. Nunios promised they would come back again while they were in Cape November. Michael suggested they come back every night.

Outside, the rain had stopped but the fog still swirled around the streetlights. Full of good food, good wine and *Centerbe*, Mr. and Mrs. Nunios seemed happy as they strolled back to the minivan. Olivia could hardly believe it when Mr. Nunios took Mrs. Nunios's hand. The events of the day seemed to have finally been put behind them. If Michael and Mr. Nunios had been scratching, Olivia hadn't noticed.

"Mikey, here," Mr. Nunios said. He held out the keys to the minivan.

Olivia saw by the look on his face that Michael was stunned. "Are you sure?" If he had been trying to hide the fact that he was nervous, Olivia thought he was doing a pretty lousy job of it.

"Of course I'm sure," his father insisted. "I had all that wine and that green stuff. You're the designated driver."

"Since when?" Michael asked. He looked nervous.

His father grinned. "Since I designated you."

"But I had a few glasses, too," Michael sounded worried.

"How many is a few?" Mrs. Nunios sounded all business. "I said you could have a taste, not drink a whole bottle."

Michael sighed out an annoyed puff of air. "I never said I drank a bottle."

"Lighten up, Mom," Alison said. "Michael's built like an ox."

Michael turned on his sister so suddenly it startled her. His eyes flashed with anger. "Why do you have to always butt into everybody's business?"

Alison looked hurt. "Sorry. I was just trying to help."

"Well don't." Michael seemed caught off guard.

"It's no big deal." Mrs. Nunios' lips were as tight at her voice. "Like Dad said, he's old enough to make his own decisions. Next year it's up to him to make good decisions. Anyway, I didn't drink. I can drive us home."

"That meal was spectacular." Olivia wasn't sure whether Mr. Nunios was trying for a subject change or if he had missed the whole thing between his wife and kids. "And I can't believe how cheap it was. A meal like that would have cost three times as much at home."

"And it wouldn't have been half as good," Mrs. Nunios added, smiling.

"Who would have thought that our kids would eat squid?"

"Wait." Michael stopped short and spun to face his parents. "We ate squid?"

"Calamari is squid, genius," Alison said.

"Hang on. You're saying calamari really is squid?"

His father chuckled. "Yeah, they're little, cut up squids."

"Stop messing with me. They don't even look like squid. A squid is like…"

"A long, skinny octopus," Alison explained.

"Right," Michael said as they approached the minivan in the parking lot. "But calamari is like onion rings. Where are all the legs?"

"They cut them up," Mr. Nunios laughed. "All those little things."

"The things you said looked like little spiders," Mom added.

"Those were legs?" Michael sounded panicked. "Come on, stop!"

"I'm serious," his father insisted.

Michael looked suddenly ill. "That's gross."

"Look, if you're going to puke, don't get in the car," Michael's father warned him.

Mrs. Nunios nodded. "Really, Michael, the poor car's had enough for one day."

"Don't be stupid!" Alison huffed. "You already ate them. You said they were great!"

"You did eat about ten pounds," Mrs. Nunios laughed.

Olivia thought Michael looked a little green. "I thought they were some kind of Italian onion rings!"

"Sure," Mr. Nunios said, laughing. "Except instead of being made of onions, they're made of squid."

Sometimes Olivia felt like they picked on Michael a little more than he deserved, although she had to admit that he deserved a lot. Maybe it was just because he wasn't her brother. Either way, teasing him wasn't quite the art form for Olivia that it seemed to be for his own family, so she wasn't giving it her full attention.

While Michael was getting his usual share of abuse, Olivia glanced across the parking lot and her breath caught in her throat. The creepy-looking men from earlier huddled at the far side, just outside of the glow of the streetlight, merging with the foggy shadows.

Still laughing and joking, Alison, Michael and their parents walked to the car. The three men began to shuffle out of the shadows toward them with their strange, limping movements. Olivia could just make out what looked like long, pale chins sticking out from under their hoods.

Olivia reached out to grab Alison's arm just as Alison said, "Let's listen to my iPod on the way back." Alison fumbled her purse, dumping everything inside.

Olivia saw the snow globe topple out. Alison reached for it, but it rolled across her hand and tumbled over and over in the air toward the damp pavement. It landed with a solid *thud* that Olivia could feel in her feet. Olivia looked up at Alison. Her eyes were wide. Olivia knew that she felt it, too.

Olivia felt herself breathing hard as she scanned the parking lot. The three men stopped. One of them held up his baggy sleeve as if he were shielding himself. He looked like Dracula in an old movie. They scuttled back into the shadows and were gone.

"What is that thing?" Alison's father demanded.

"It's a snow globe."

"Snow globe?" Alison's father sounded skeptical. "I thought it was a bowling ball."

Olivia continued to look around the parking lot for the big men. She was hoping not to see them, but in a way, not knowing where they were was even worse.

"It's not heavy at all," Alison said. She sounded puzzled as she leaned down to pick up her souvenir.

"Sounded like it weighs a ton," Mr. Nunios said.

"Did it break, sweetheart?" her mother asked sympathetically.

"No." Alison held it up to the light and turned it in her hands, checking for cracks and leaks."

Her father frowned at it, "Where'd you get it?"

"Back at the barbecue place. In the gift shop." Alison knelt down and started scooping everything else back into her purse.

Reluctantly, Olivia decided that the men really were gone. Needing anything that felt normal, she helped Alison clean up her bag.

Alison's father stuck out his hand. Dutifully, Alison stood up and handed the snow globe over. "It's so light," he remarked. "When it fell I really thought you were carrying a bowling ball."

"Why would she be carrying a bowling ball?" Mrs. Nunios's tone sounded like this was the dumbest thing Mr. Nunios had ever said.

"I don't know why she does anything. She's a kid." Mr. Nunios held the snow globe up so that the streetlight cast shimmery, blue reflections through the glittering water. He gave it a twirl. "That's really weird. It moves, but not like a regular snow globe. And what is that in there?" Mr. Nunios wrinkled his face. "That monster looks like some kind of nightmare. And what's that other thing in there? A whale?"

Michael laughed. "So that's why you two nerds were talking about *Moby Dick*."

Mrs. Nunios smacked her son on the arm. "Watch your mouth."

"OW! I didn't name it. Blame Herman Melville!"

"His mother should have smacked him too!"

"Well, it *is* a book about a sperm whale," Michael grinned.

"Do I need to smack you again?"

Mr. Nunios turned the snow globe around and held it up to the light. "Why do the little guys move around like that? Is it like a computer or something?"

Michael laughed. "Dad, not everything you don't understand is a computer."

He shrugged and handed the snow globe back to Alison. "I can't believe you wasted good money on this piece of junk."

She stuffed it quickly back in her bag.

"She didn't waste money." Olivia cringed and felt like someone had shoved a hot bone down her throat.

Alison glared, but nobody else caught it. Like a circus performer, teetering on the razor's edge that separated fact from fiction, she smiled cheerfully. "I really like it, so it's not a waste."

"It's a gift for Mr. W.," Olivia offered. Right on schedule Alison shot her an irritated look. Olivia knew Alison hated it when she tried to help get them out of trouble. Alison said she always made it worse.

"Oh." Mr. Nunios rolled his eyes. "I'm sure *he'll* love this wack-a-doo thing." Mr. Nunios grumbled something about his tax dollars going to pay the salaries of lunatics.

Nervous and jittery, Olivia looked around one more time, but she didn't see anyone else in the parking lot.

15 WHISPERING

Sitting close together, Olivia whispered, "Alison, I'm telling you, the same three guys that chased the car at the light followed us to the parking lot."

Alison felt tired and grumpy, and she didn't need anything else to freak her out, but she noticed that Olivia had been acting even more nervous since they had gotten back to the car.

"It's a small town, Liv. It probably was the same guys, but that doesn't mean they were after us."

"But why were they there?" Olivia sounded intense. Alison knew that when Olivia latched on to an idea she could be like a pit bull.

Alison sighed heavily. "Maybe they were going to eat at Olga's."

Olivia shook her head. "You didn't see the way they lunged after the car."

"In the parking lot?"

Olivia clucked her teeth and rasped into Alison's ear, "No! At the traffic light. Are you even listening?"

"It's a crappy area. Maybe they were muggers."

"I don't think so," Olivia said. "These guys…there was something weird about them. They moved funny. And the snow globe…"

Alison groaned. "You love to keep talking about that in front of my parents. Nice job back there by the way."

"I know. Sorry. It slipped." Olivia looked so sad and guilty that Alison immediately felt like a jerk for bringing it up.

"Everything okay back there?" Mom asked. "I hear a lot of whispering. You know I don't like whispering."

"Olivia's having boy trouble," Alison said.

"Oh these boys!" Mom said.

"Don't date 'til college," Mr. Nunios offered.

"Do I need to kick somebody's ass?"

"Michael!" Mom warned sharply.

"No. Everything's fine." Olivia leaned close to hiss into Alison's ear. "Boy trouble? Really?"

Alison *knew* that was going to tick Olivia off, but she didn't have a lot of options. "It worked, didn't it? What was I supposed to say, girl trouble?"

"It would have been more honest," Olivia hissed. Her eyebrows knitted together.

"I was already lying. What difference does it make?"

"Sure. What's another lie?" Olivia scolded her with her eyes. "Anyway, I'm not ashamed of who I am. If your parents can't handle my being a lesbian, too bad."

Alison really didn't want to have this conversation whispered in the back of the car. It seemed like every time her sexuality came up Olivia got defensive.

Alison sighed. "I'm not ashamed of who you are either, but my parents don't even *know* you're gay. You never came out to them, and I'm not going to out you. Do you want to have *that* whole conversation right now? Besides, if they knew, they might not let us sleep together, and there's no *way* I'm sleeping down here alone."

Olivia's eyes narrowed. "Hang on. What would my being gay have to do with us sleeping together? Just because I'm gay doesn't mean we're going to do the nasty. *You're* not gay. You can't *catch* gay. Gay girls can have sleepovers with their friends just like anybody else."

"There is too much whispering, ladies. That's impolite." Mom clucked her tongue. "Save your girl talk for your room." Alison watched Olivia take in Mom's statement and work things out in her head.

A moment later, Olivia smiled and the fire went out of her face. "I guess I see what you mean." She pointed to Alison's bag. Alison was happy to change the subject. "Did you notice how when the snow globe fell, it sounded heavy? And right after that, the creeps left. Like they were scared of it. Do you really think that's a coincidence?"

Alison sighed. "I didn't pick up on any of that. Maybe you should lay off the sci-fi for awhile."

"I don't see what that has to do with anything, Allie."

"Can we talk about this later?" They were pulling up to The Mansion and Alison noticed it was still dark. Since there was power on in town, she'd hoped it was back on at The Mansion, too, but of course it wasn't.

Using the flashlights Penny had loaned them, they bumbled their way up to their room and said goodnight to Michael, Mom and Dad.

The curtains were still closed nice and tight the third time Olivia checked them, but she didn't seem to relax until they started trying to light the lantern the way Penny had showed them. They laughed and argued and knocked into things, trying to see through the dark with just their phone flashlights. About a dozen matches later, Alison realized that they both sucked at lighting matches, but the little lantern was sputtering and hissing pleasantly at the center of a warm glow.

They shut their phones off to save what little was left of their batteries since they wouldn't be able to charge them until the power came back—*and who knows how long that will be?*

The lantern sat on Alison's nightstand, a fragile, little oasis of pale orange light in the middle of the big, dark room. Olivia agreed that it was better to risk burning down The Mansion than blow out the lantern at any point during the night.

They searched the whole room, but couldn't find any extra oil. At least they could confirm one more time that the curtains were still closed and the wardrobe still only hid Olivia's clothes. They weren't sure how long the oil in the lantern would hold out. Olivia said that if they kept the wick short it would use less fuel. Of course, it would also make less light, but Alison thought there was no point stating the obvious.

"What if we fall asleep and it burns out?" Olivia sounded really nervous.

Alison shrugged. "We use our phones until they run out." She studied the little number next to the battery icon. "I charged it in the car, but I'm only at thirty-three percent."

"Where's the snow globe?" Olivia asked.

"It's in my suitcase, safe and sound. I already dropped it once tonight. Why?"

"Alison, in the parking lot—"

Alison realized that she needed to take this more seriously. Olivia wasn't letting it go. "Olivia, I'm sure you saw something. But it's just a snow globe."

"It's not *just* a snow globe. There's something weird about it. *You* showed *me* that when you stole it. Or did you forget that part."

Alison looked hard at her. They had been up early, and it had been a long day. "Liv, nobody's after us. Nobody even knows us here."

"I hope that lantern stays lit." Olivia scanned the shadows again. "It'll be really freaky to wake up and it's totally dark."

Alison noticed Olivia's sudden change of topics, but decided it was better to go with it. "Hopefully we'll just sleep 'til morning."

"When I have to go to swim meets out of town and I have to sleep in a hotel? Forget it. And those are just regular hotels." Alison watched Olivia's eyes dart again to the curtains. "I can never sleep in a strange place."

"Me neither." Alison pulled off her shorts and sat in underwear on the edge of the bed. "And it doesn't get stranger than this."

Olivia pushed some damp hair off her face. "And it's so hot."

Alison laughed. "I asked my mom if this place has air-conditioning. Know what she said?"

"It doesn't." Olivia chuckled as she pulled off her sneakers and socks and padded to the wardrobe. "It says that on the website."

"Yeah," Alison looked around the dark room and then at the curtains. "But my mother actually said that we should open a window and let in the sea breeze."

Olivia turned and raised both eyebrows. "I'll kill you."

Alison laughed, "Are you crazy? You couldn't pay me enough to sleep with the windows open in this dump."

"You shouldn't say that. The place itself is fine and Penny was super nice to us downstairs. And Olga's was awesome. I feel sorry for these people. This place is their home and it's falling apart." Standing in front of the open wardrobe, Olivia peeled off her damp clothes and stuffed them in the mesh laundry bag she had stashed neatly in the corner. She took a light blue nightgown off its hanger and slipped it over her head. "You should have let me tell your parents about the guys we saw."

"The guys *you* saw," Alison corrected her.

Olivia snapped around. "You really don't believe me?" She sounded offended.

"Of course I believe you saw them," Alison tried to be reassuring, "But there's no way they were coming after us."

"Allie, in the parking lot, the same huge, creepy-looking guys were there that I saw at the traffic light. Maybe it doesn't mean anything, but I'm *positive* it was the same guys. And then, when you dropped your bag and the snow globe hit the ground like a shot put…"

Alison puzzled that over in her mind. "It must have been something else. My phone is pretty heavy since my dad makes me keep it in that ugly case."

"You broke eight phones since middle school. Can you really blame him? But your phone wouldn't have sounded like that."

"If it hit just right, maybe?" Alison ran her hands through her damp hair. She studied Olivia's face. *Has she gone totally crazy?* "Let me make sure I got this. Three guys try to jump us all—my whole family *in a van*—at a traffic light. And then they follow us to Olga's, but then they run away from a snow globe?"

Olivia looked annoyed. "Okay, I admit it sounds crazy, but then why did the snow globe get so heavy?"

"It wasn't heavy!" Alison was too hot to think. "Can we worry about it tomorrow?"

"Fine." Olivia sighed.

Alison looked at Olivia's nightgown. It was a pale blue with tiny lace trim. "That's really nice. Is that new?"

"You're just changing the subject like your mother." Olivia smiled and looked shyly down at herself. "But yeah. It's new."

"It's really pretty."

Olivia fidgeted with the position of the nightgown and smoothed the fabric. "I needed something lightweight. I knew there wasn't going to be any air-conditioning here."

Alison watched as Olivia the neat freak took her toiletry bag out of the top drawer of the dresser. She plucked out her toothbrush and toothpaste, took the flashlight and headed for the bathroom. "Do you really think it was a coincidence that the first people we see—I see—down here are three big thugs?"

"Thugs?" Alison knew exactly how to rile Olivia. "Were they beating up an old lady? Why are they thugs? Just because somebody looks a certain way…"

Olivia put her hands on her hips, cocked her head. "Really? I'm mixed-race and you're going to lecture me from those lame diversity assemblies we have to sit through every year?" Olivia's smile cracked and she started over. "The facts are that the three large *individuals* who approached the back of your father's vehicle when it stopped for a red light happened to show up again in the parking lot where we parked. And then they suddenly ran away when you dropped your snow globe."

"They didn't run away."

"How do you know? You didn't even see them."

Alison threw herself hard back on the sticky pillows. "Because people don't run away from snow globes, Olivia."

Olivia looked at Alison for a moment and then sighed. "Whatever. I just think we should mention something to your parents. But if you don't trust me enough…" Olivia walked into the bathroom, shut the door, and shrieked.

Alison jumped out of bed with her heart crashing in her chest just as Olivia came out of the bathroom. She slammed the door behind her and leaned against it, laughing hysterically.

"What?" She laughed timidly, but Alison's heart still thudded like a hammer.

"Your brother was on the toilet."

"Eew!" Alison stomped over to the door and banged on it. "Next time lock our side, too, you moron!"

Michael's voice came muffled through the wooden door. "Doesn't anybody knock?"

"Hurry up, Michael," Alison said. "We need the bathroom, too. And don't stink it up!"

"No promises," came Michael's muffled voice.

"At least spray some of your cheap cologne or something!" Groaning, Alison sat on back the edge of the bed. She could feel sweat beading up on her scalp and trickling down her neck. She got up off the bed and rummaged in her own bag, which was sprawled against the wall, open and still unpacked. She eyed the snow globe tucked in the corner of the bag. Olivia's weird story ran through her head again like an earworm. She felt a little guilty.

"Liv, if you think something is going on, then it probably is." Alison doubted that. "You're the smartest person I know, and I trust you with my life." That part was true. "It's just that it would be hard to explain to my parents why three guys are following us in the first place, forget about convincing them that they got scared off by a snow globe."

"We don't have to tell them about the snow globe."

"My parents will still say we're nuts and you *know* it would set off my mother and then there will be a big fight." Alison rummaged through her bag, but didn't find what she wanted. She stood up feeling hot and annoyed. "I *didn't* check the website so the only lightweight thing I can sleep in is my underwear. I hope you're not offended."

Heading back to the bathroom, Olivia asked, "Offended by which part? The trust thing or the underwear?" Before closing the door, Olivia called over her shoulder, "If you haven't offended me by now..."

"Good," Alison called through the door. She smiled knowing that the almost fight between her and Olivia never happened. She was glad she had been able to steer them around that iceberg.

16 MAMMOTHS AND MASTODONS

Alison crossed back to her suitcase and scattered her clothes around until she found her own toiletry bag and her toothbrush. *Toothpaste?* Alison called through the door, "Can I borrow your toothpaste? I forgot to pack that, too."

The door opened a crack. Olivia's face wrinkled into a half-scowl, half-smile. "You forgot pajamas and your toothpaste. Did you pack anything?"

"I brought some awesome foundation and a few really good eyeliners."

"Because eyeliner works great on gingivitis." Olivia handed Alison the toothpaste as they passed each other in the bathroom door.

"I'm going to take a shower," Alison felt sticky and sweaty and miserable. And it didn't help when she noticed that the air still stank from her brother.

"In the dark?"

"I'm just so hot. I think a shower will cool me off so I can at least sleep. And hand me my perfume. It stinks in here." Olivia handed her the bottle, and Alison closed the bathroom door.

The spray helped a little. There wasn't much hot water, probably because the power had been out for so long. Alison didn't really miss it. The cool water running down her body helped her not think. The flashlight from her phone, lying on the antique, marble counter, looked like a fuzzy ball through the frosted glass of the shower door. The loud knock startled her.

"Allie, hurry up." It was Michael.

"Again?" Annoyed, Alison finished up and pulled on clean underwear and a pink tank top.

When she came out, Olivia was lying on the bed with the covers kicked off. She had moved the lamp to her nightstand and was reading a large coffee table-type picture book.

Alison tilted her head to read the title in the dim lamplight. "*A Picture History of Cape November?* Where'd you get that?"

"I found it in my nightstand when we were looking for the lamp oil," Olivia said without looking up. "Remember how I told you about the foundation here?"

"That it's made of gold or something?"

Olivia sighed impatiently "Sapphire. Maybe. And anyway, that's just one of about a dozen theories. The magazine, *Weird New Jersey*, published six articles about this place."

"Good, because I was worried that nobody actually cared." She flopped heavily onto the bed.

Olivia rolled her eyes and turned the page. "But did you also know that Ocean Boulevard is one of the oldest roads in North America?"

Alison was always amazed at the kind of stuff Olivia found interesting. And she had always been a little jealous of how fast she could read. Olivia could get homework done in half the time it took Alison.

"Ocean Boulevard? You mean over by Olga's with all the shops and stuff?" Alison blew a damp curl off her forehead. The shower had cooled her, but it was still stupid hot.

"Yeah." Olivia absently flipped the page. "It used to be a serious tourist attraction back at the turn of the century."

"Two thousand?" Alison asked.

Olivia laughed and shook her head. "Twentieth. Starting around nineteen hundred, but it was pretty popular until the nineteen-eighties."

"That's about when my parents were coming down."

"Yeah, but things started getting bad in the nineties and then when those hurricanes and fires and stuff started happening, the whole place fell apart. Businesses shut down. Tourists stopped coming." She turned to look at Alison with her eyes sparkling. She was the only person Alison knew who could get so excited about learning something so totally pointless.

"Historians say that Ocean Boulevard, the road itself I mean, goes all the way back to the Stone Age. The Lenape used it to get to the ocean to fish and catch clams and mussels and stuff."

"The Lenape?" Alison leaned across the bed to see the color sketches of Native Americans carrying buckets of seafood.

"They were also called the Delaware. You know, like the Delaware River? I guess down this far they would have technically been the Unalachtigo, or possibly the Unami. But they all spoke Lenape. In the seventeen hundreds, European settlers drove them out. They either had to assimilate or move to Oklahoma. A lot of people think the Lenape are extinct, but it says here that about eleven thousand Lenape still live in Oklahoma. Until recently, they were classified as Algonquin. Anyway, the Lenape lived here for thousands of years before European settlers came. And the road we call The Boulevard now used to be a major game trail."

"Monopoly?" Alison joked.

Olivia gave Alison a mock stern look. "Wooly mammoths and mastodons."

Alison shut her eyes for a moment and briefly considered cutting off all her hair. "Aren't they the same thing? Big, fuzzy elephants?"

"No." Olivia laughed. "Mastodons were around about twenty-eight million years ago, but mammoths only go back about four million years. And mastodons also have shorter tusks."

"Forget the game trail; you should go on a game show." Alison blew out a long, hot sigh. She could feel herself sticking to the sheets.

"Are you okay?" Olivia turned away from the book.

"I'm just really hot," Alison knew she was whining. She didn't care. "The shower didn't do a thing. Plus, Michael started banging on the door. He ate enough for six normal people. He probably needed to take another dump."

"Okay, there's an image I didn't need again. Are you *trying* to give me nightmares?" Olivia closed her eyes and gave a little shiver. "Anyway, it looks like it might be nice tomorrow," she added cheerfully. "Maybe we can go to the beach."

"It's so…empty here. It's creepy and kind of depressing. And did you hear the way Olga's nephews were talking in the restaurant? Something isn't right."

"Don't tell me you're starting to believe me?" Olivia laughed. "Besides Olga and her family, the only other people we've seen are the *gentlemen* who were *not* following us and who showed up twice *by coincidence,* and then left when your snow globe fell *way too loudly,* which was yet another *coincidence.* Yeah." Olivia turned the page noisily.

Alison felt a small throb in her temples. She would *not* have this argument. "I'm sure you saw the three guys and all, and they looked scary. It was dark and raining and foggy and all that weird stuff happened on the highway and all that. All I'm saying is that you don't know that they were coming after *us.* This place is freaking me out too, but…"

Olivia put up her hand in a *stop* gesture. "Whatever. Don't believe me, but when we get killed by three freaks…"

"That is *not* funny. Don't even joke around about that. Anyway, it's way too hot, and I really want to sleep."

"I thought you couldn't sleep."

"I can't. But I want to." Alison sighed in frustration. "I don't know what my mother was thinking. You're sorry you came, right?"

Olivia looked a little sad for a second. "We're going to different schools in the fall, Allie. I don't care where we are. I'm really just happy to hang out with you for a week with nothing to do and nobody to bug us," Olivia smiled. "Except for three—"

"Don't even say it." Alison held up her finger. She banged her head back against the soft pillow. "I swear, between this weird place and my psycho family…"

Olivia wrinkled her forehead and played gently with Alison's hair. It felt soothing. "You're still worried about your parents? I thought they did a little better today. I saw them holding hands after dinner."

"I'm not worried." Alison was lying, and she knew Olivia knew she was lying, but she didn't feel much like talking about it.

"You shouldn't worry so much about your parents. They aren't going to split up."

"How do you know?" Alison hated talking about this with anyone. Even Olivia.

Alison continued to stare at the ceiling, but Olivia's fingertips moved down her arm. It felt nice. It was a great distraction from her own irritating thoughts.

Olivia spoke gently, just above a whisper. "Look, just because my parents split up doesn't mean yours will."

"But I don't think my parents are happy."

"They're old. Old people are never happy." Alison could feel Olivia's body bounce with her nearly silent chuckle.

"They're not *that* old." Alison nestled a little closer to Olivia. It was hot, but it felt good to be cared for. To feel protected and safe. Even if it *was* just a feeling.

"They're not *that* unhappy."

"You know what I mean," Alison rolled over to face Olivia. "They don't seem happy with each other. I don't think they love each other anymore."

Olivia smiled. "Yes they do...I guess. I mean who can tell with parents? Would you rather have them kissing all the time like a couple of teenagers?"

"Uch! Please! Was that payback for the Michael thing? Because yours was way worse."

"I don't know," Olivia laughed, "Michael taking a dump was pretty disturbing."

"My parents making out? I might puke." Alison rolled back the other way. "I guess my parents love each other, but I don't think they like each other." She could feel Olivia's fingers tracing gentle paths up and down her arms and over her shoulder and through her hair, soothing her. Alison closed her eyes.

***

Sometime later, Alison awoke. She didn't know how long she'd slept. The lamp was still burning. The room had cooled off, and she felt a little chilly. She wanted to reach for her phone to check the time, but Olivia was spooned against her back. The gentle rhythm of Olivia's body, rising and falling, felt comfortably warm. Olivia's breath made a warm breeze over her neck, like a sleeping cat, purring with the gusts outside their window.

After a few quiet moments, Olivia whispered, "You awake?"

"Yeah. I thought you were asleep, though."

"I was."

"Sorry." Alison was, but she was also happy for the company.

"It's fine."

Alison pulled up the sheet and rolled onto her stomach. She turned her head to face Olivia.

"What you said before about me being worried about my parents...I worry all the time that they're going to split up. It scares me."

Olivia chuckled. "That's probably the only thing that does."

"You've already been through it with your parents, so what scares you?" Alison asked.

Olivia took so long to reply that Alison thought she had fallen back asleep.

Then she whispered, "Us not being friends anymore."

Alison felt a little sting in her chest. "Why would you even say that? Just because we're going to different schools?"

Olivia smiled weakly, curling and uncurling Alison's hair around her fingers. "Things change."

Alison closed her eyes. "So we just change with them. Together. Like always."

Alison felt Olivia's fingers playing gently with her hair. "I hope so. But things are going to be *so* different. I'm *moving away*. It's not just like I'm going to a different school and we can see each other at night and on weekends. This is a boarding school in Pennsylvania. And with this new swim team, I'm going to be travelling a lot." Olivia sighed tragically. "I'm going to have no life. I'll have no friends outside of swimming."

"It's not like you have a lot of friends now."

Olivia looked hurt, and Alison regretted saying it.

"You're right, though, Allie. I spend all my time with you."

"So are you saying it's good for you to move?"

"No!" Olivia laughed, but looked like she was on the verge of tears. "We're never going to see each other."

Alison felt them in her eyes, too, but she did not want to let this turn into a sappy cry fest. "We would have to deal with this in two years anyway, when we're both in college." Alison *really* didn't want to talk about this. She hated thinking about it. "Come on, this vacation is our chance to hang out together. We shouldn't ruin it by talking about this and getting all depressed. Anyway, what are we supposed to do about it?"

"I just won't go."

Alison's eyes popped open, and she propped herself up on one elbow to glare at Olivia. "Don't even say that."

Olivia shrugged. "I don't want to go. It's pointless. Who changes schools in their junior year?"

"Lots of people. And it isn't pointless, Olivia. It's a huge deal. Nobody gets a scholarship to Ashton like this."

"Maybe if I were a freshman, but what's the point now?"

"Better exposure on a better team? College recruiters? Team USA? Are you kidding me?" Alison traced her finger along the delicate bones of Olivia's perfect face where a tear made a wet trail to the pillow.

"Things change." Olivia's voice sounded thick. Abruptly, she turned her head toward the ceiling. "Remember Katie Anderson and Kyle Rodriguez?" Olivia asked. "They were best friends all through elementary school, and now they don't even talk anymore."

"Yeah, but that's a totally different situation. They started dating in ninth grade and it was bad when they broke up."

Olivia laughed. "Remember when we tried dating?"

Alison felt a hot gush of embarrassment mixed with nostalgia. "I wouldn't call it dating."

"Friends with benefits?" Olivia smirked.

"Eew! At no time were we friends with benefits. I'm not gay, remember?"

"You were a good kisser."

"Okay that was one short…dangerous…" Alison mushed Olivia's face with a pillow. "I'm still a good kisser."

Under the pillow, Olivia laughed and wrenched Alison's wrist away, but then she pulled the pillow back to her face with both hands. Her voice came muffled. "Smother me! Then I won't have to go to Ashhole Academy."

Alison pulled the pillow away. "We still won't be able to hang out if you're dead."

"I'll haunt you everywhere you go." Olivia sat up, slightly breathless from laughing under the pillow. Snatching it, she wound up to whack Alison.

The room suddenly became totally, impenetrably dark. Far off, someone screamed.

17 SCREAMS IN THE DARK

"Great job, Liv, you broke the lamp!" Alison scolded.

Turning gingerly on the bed, Olivia reached out and felt the lantern still on the nightstand. She kept blinking her eyes, hoping they would adjust, then realized there was just no adjusting to darkness like that.

"Who screamed?" Olivia did not raise her own voice above a whisper.

"How should I know?" Alison's whisper sounded annoyed. "Is there glass everywhere?"

"I didn't touch the lamp," Olivia protested. "It must have gone out." Olivia kept blinking and opening her eyes wide, but it was total darkness. She could feel Alison still up against her. The warm, solid weight of her body was Olivia's only life raft in that vast ocean of darkness. "Allie?"

"I haven't gone anywhere." Alison said it a little too sarcastically, Olivia thought.

"What should we do?"

Through the mattress, Olivia felt the vibrations of Alison's laughter as much as heard it. "We should just go back to sleep until the sun comes up. If it ever does here. What time is it?"

"I have no idea." Olivia felt like it was hard to breathe as ghostly images of strange men with long chins floated somewhere between her imagination and her eyes. "What about the screaming?"

"You heard that, too?"

"Yeah." Olivia was afraid to admit it. Like saying it made it real.

"Something outside maybe?" In the absolute blackness, Olivia clung to the thin wisp of Alison's voice and the solid reassurance of her body.

"I don't know...I think it came from above us." Olivia could feel herself start to shiver not from the chilly air.

Alison sounded as calm as ever. "I'm sure nobody died."

Olivia's stomach suddenly had a roller coaster in it when she heard a loud *thump* and an *Ow!* from Michael's room. "They got Michael!" Olivia could not keep her voice steady.

"Who?" Alison's voice sounded so calm it was comforting and frustrating at the same time.

Even the free-flowing F-bombs coming from Michael's room were reassuring. Olivia's racing heart slowed. Then the door to the bathroom was framed in white, quivering light. Olivia held her breath and listened to the thumping footsteps coming through the bathroom. She jumped at the loud *clunk* at the door.

"Seriously?" Michael complained. "Thanks a lot. I just smacked my head on your door."

"Oops," Alison said, giggling quietly. "I guess I locked it after my shower." She called louder to Michael, "What do you want?"

Michael's voice came muffled through the thick old wood, "Are you guys all right?"

"Yeah," Alison called back. "Are you?"

"Besides my head, I think I broke my shin against the stupid bed. Other than that, I'm fine. Let me in." His knocking sounded urgent.

Olivia hated the lonely feeling of Alison pulling away. She heard her move through the dark. There was a clunk and Alison grunted in pain.

"Now what?" Olivia asked. Her heart felt quick and shaky.

The flashlight came on blinding. "I dropped my stupid phone on my toe." Alison shined the light down toward her feet. "Aww, man! I chipped my pedicure."

Michael knocked again.

Stamping angrily toward the bathroom door, Alison's bare footfalls sounded like someone was punching meat. She slid the bolt. "What do you want?"

Michael stepped in wearing black boxers covered with yellow, skull-shaped happy faces. In one hand he carried a flashlight. In the other hand, he held a fireplace poker like a sword.

Olivia gave a small squeak and ducked under the covers.

"Where did you get that flashlight?" Alison demanded. "Did Penny give *you* a flashlight?"

"No. I packed it." His smiled beamed brighter than the light. "*Semper paratis.*"

"Did you join the Coast Guard or something?" Olivia wasn't used to Michael quoting Latin sayings.

Michael looked confused. "Huh? It's from Sharknado. It means always prepared." Michael shined his light around their room like a detective. "What are you guys doing in here, anyway?"

"Nothing," Alison sounded annoyed. "Our lamp burned out," Alison explained. "It just scared us."

Olivia called from under the covers, "But your underwear is scaring us more." Olivia peeked out. Alison stood angrily with one hand on her hip, tapping her toes.

"The rule, Michael!" she snapped. "A shirt at all times!"

"Hey, I was just trying to help you," Michael sounded dejected. "You *were* screaming." He turned to leave. "And by the way, *you're* in your underwear, too."

"It's *our* room. And we didn't scream," Alison said.

"So who did?" Michael stepped back in, bringing the little circle of pale light with him.

"How should I know?" Alison said testily. "Maybe it was a raccoon."

Michael shook his head and looked at Alison like she was an idiot. "It was definitely a scream. A *human* scream. And it came from inside."

"We're the only ones here, Michael."

"Didn't Penny say her niece was here?" Olivia said.

"Yeah. What was her name?" Michael snapped his fingers. "Millie? Michelle?"

"Maggie, genius." Alison said. "As in Maggie's Mansion. Don't act like you don't know."

Michael grinned. "The lady also said she was cute." Michael gave the girls an exaggerated wink. "I'm going to check it out."

"You're going to knock on a strange girl's door in the middle of the night? That's your plan to get a date?" Alison taunted.

"What are you going to say?" Olivia asked. "*Hi, I heard you screaming, so I thought I'd stop by in my underwear?*"

"I'm not an idiot," Michael scoffed. "I'm going to put some pants on first."

"Great plan." Alison pointed to the door.

"Did it ever occur to you two *geniuses* that if she was the one who screamed, she might actually *need* help?"

"From you?" Alison laughed.

"Yes, from me." Olivia noticed the way Michael's superhero posture deflated a little.

"Don't be stupid," Alison said.

"Maybe we should wake up your parents." The whole situation was giving Olivia the willies. "How can they even sleep with all this noise?" As she stepped out of bed, she quickly adjusted her nightgown to make sure Michael wasn't seeing more than he was supposed to.

"My mother has one of those white-noise machines," Michael explained. "Runs it all night."

"But the power's out," Olivia observed.

"Batteries." Alison shrugged. "She can't sleep without it."

"They haven't heard a thing." Michael bobbed his eyebrows like a dare.

"You can't go, Michael." It surprised Olivia. Alison sounded genuinely worried about her brother.

"Somebody screamed. We can't just ignore it," Michael said, turning to go back to his own room.

"We?" Alison asked.

Michael shrugged his big shoulders, "Do whatever you want. I'm checking it out."

"What are you, Batman?" Olivia asked, laughing.

"Yes," he said, faking a gruff, raspy growl. "I'm Batman."

"If you're that worried, you can just wake up your parents." Olivia felt a bundle of nerves bunch up in her gut.

"And you can grab a honey badger by the nutsack, but I wouldn't recommend it," Michael shot back.

"Liv, my parents freak out if you wake them up. You know this. Mom's first question is *who's bleeding* and then Dad says *somebody better be dead*." Alison's high-pitched imitation of her mother and her low, grunting caveman impression of her dad made Olivia laugh.

But the strange men from earlier lurked in her memory, and Olivia's stomach muscles tightened. "What if somebody really is hurt or something?"

Michael and Alison traded looks in some secret sibling code. "We're not involving Mom and Dad. Besides, what makes you think I can't handle it?"

"For one thing, we don't even know what *it* is," Olivia said.

A long, low, desperate moan seemed to float through the walls. Olivia felt the hairs creep up the back of her neck. She scampered across the room to stand near Alison and Michael. "I think the sound is coming through the fireplace. The stone chimneys really carry the sound."

Another long, low moan hung in the air.

"Okay, that was just creepy," Alison said, grabbing Olivia's hand.

Michael headed back for his room. Alison ran for her suitcase, dragging Olivia with her.

"Whoa, where are we going?" Olivia asked. She suddenly felt like things were falling through her fingers.

"Get dressed, Olivia." Alison pulled on her gym shorts and stepped into her sneakers. "We have to go with him."

"We do?"

"I'm not staying here without him. I mean sure, girl power and all that, but he benches like two-eighty."

"Two-eighty-five." Michael flexed in a body-builder pose, and then retreated into his own room.

Olivia couldn't believe they were serious. She called after him. "Great. You must be so proud. But see, *you* shouldn't be going either."

But Alison was getting dressed, and Olivia was *not* about to get left in the room alone. Scurrying to the closet, Olivia pulled off her nightgown and paused. She held the hanger, but when Alison hissed, *Hurry, Liv!* she chucked it into the closet and pulled on her shorts, tee shirt and sneakers.

"So you're coming?" Michael sounded shocked when they showed up in his room. And possibly disappointed. He had already put on his own sneakers, shorts and a tank top and was about to go out the door with his flashlight and the fireplace poker. There was another scary sounding scream.

Outside the room, Olivia felt the darkness thick around her like something alive. Down the creaky hallway, they huddled behind the silver shaft of Michael's flashlight until they came to the stairwell door. Michael looked back at the girls. "You should probably go back," he whispered.

"And let you chase down the Hound of the Baskervilles by yourself?" Olivia scoffed sarcastically.

"I don't need a wingman."

"Are you going to help her or hit on her?" Alison sneered.

Michael smiled guiltily.

"Maybe *I'll* hit on her," Olivia quipped. She saw the disbelieving looks on her friends' faces. "You never know."

"If that happens I'm staying to watch," Michael grinned.

"You're disgusting!" Olivia punched him in the arm. It was like punching frozen beef.

Michael looked more serious. "Look, this is all probably nothing, but just in case it isn't, maybe you should wait here."

Olivia felt her heart racing. She kept picturing three large men in hoods coming up the stairs behind them. "Explain to me again why we're not getting your parents? Or the cops?"

"Like that psycho from the highway?" Alison asked. "I don't think so."

"No phones anyway." Michael opened the door. Olivia thought it sounded only slightly louder than a truck. Cringing, he whispered, "I checked before."

"Michael, seriously, back in town, I saw these big, scary looking guys." Olivia didn't care what Alison thought. Michael needed to know. In case. "I really think they were coming after us. Allie doesn't believe me"

"I never said I didn't believe you." Alison sounded annoyed.

"You think they're here?" Michael asked. "In The Mansion?"

"Calm down," Alison scolded. "We don't even know if they're—"

"Real?" Olivia was furious.

Alison's eyebrows knitted together. Worried? Annoyed? Olivia couldn't tell. "I was going to say *involved*."

Not knowing what to say to that, Olivia looked from Alison's face to Michael's. He looked grim and held up the fireplace poker. "Let them come."

"This is serious, Michael," Alison scolded. "She really saw these guys."

"So you do believe me?"

Alison huffed. "I never said I didn't believe you."

Michael waved the whole thing off and headed up the stairwell.

She called after him. "These guys were huge, Michael. And weird-looking." Olivia couldn't tell if he didn't believe her either or if he thought he could fight off three gigantic axe-murderers with just a fireplace poker.

Olivia's eyes moved from Michael's broad shoulders, down his chiseled back to watch his powerful calves contract as he climbed the stairs. *Maybe he could.*

With her eyes, Alison seemed to ask Olivia what to do. Olivia shrugged and headed up after Michael with Alison right behind her.

18 HEROICS

A memory muscled its way into Michael's brain. Coach Collins called it Fun and Games. Everybody piggybacked a partner from the basement wrestling room up to the third floor. Then they'd sprint down the hall past the science labs, making as much noise as they could to annoy the nerds in Chemistry Club. Finally, they came running down the back stairs to the wrestling room where they'd switch. Michael always ended up with his buddy 'Bama, a gigantic offensive lineman who only wrestled because his football coach said he'd never make the Crimson Tide if he didn't get in better shape. Three times a week, Michael had to carry 'Bama up four flights of stairs.

In The Mansion, in the dark, walking up those creaky stairs with his sister and Olivia right behind him, Michael felt as if he were still carrying 'Bama. He knew he should have made the girls stay in their room. Not that anybody could tell Alison to do anything. And if Olivia was right and some dudes were looking for trouble, Michael was ready for that, too. He squeezed the handle of the poker a little tighter.

The stairway to the tower was in the middle of the top floor. They had to pass a lot of closed doors and silent rooms to reach it. Michael kept waiting for something to pop out of one. He only felt slightly better when they got to the stairway. The sign on the door to the tower read *Staff Only*. Michael opened the door, and another scream came down the empty stairwell, followed by more low moans. Tiny pins and needles skulked up his back. Turning, he saw that Alison and Olivia looked terrified.

Go back, he mouthed.

With her forehead creased stubbornly, Alison shook her head.

The staircase rose in a series of tight squares around a straight, narrow shaft. On each landing a pointy window overlooked the front courtyard with its weird fountain. On the opposite side, there was a door to a room. The spooky moans and scary screams seemed to be getting louder and more frequent.

"We shouldn't be here, Michael." Alison sounded pretty worried as they reached the top landing. Low, desperate groans and thrashing sounds floated through the darkness.

Michael took a deep breath. "She's in here." He put his hand flat on the door. "You should go back."

Alison looked at Olivia and seemed to read something in her eyes that Michael couldn't see. She turned back and shook her head.

Michael shrugged. He knew he wasn't going to win this one. Behind the door, a sad, desperate voice was begging, almost crying.

Pressing the girls back with his arm, Michael dropped his shoulder and rammed the door. The door didn't budge, and his shoulder hurt, but he wasn't going to stop now with Alison and Olivia looking at him like he was a moron.

He backed up across the landing and ran into the door with a rattling impact. The door made slight cracking sound, but otherwise it didn't seem to notice Michael. He could feel the bruise that was going to show up on his shoulder and elbow, though.

From inside, a young woman's voice sounded startled and afraid, "Leave me alone!" Then she demanded in a much firmer voice, "Who's there?"

"Are you okay?" Alison asked.

Annoyed, Michael looked at her. Mouthing, *I got this*, he put his face up to the door. It smelled of old wood and varnish. "We heard screaming. Do you need help?" He tried to sound bigger, older and more authoritative than he actually felt. He didn't think it was working, judging by the faces Alison and Olivia made.

There was movement inside. Someone walked toward the door. Michael put his arms up like a crossing guard and backed Olivia and Alison away.

The lock clicked and the door creaked slowly inward. Michael could feel all his muscles coil like springs. He raised the fireplace poker.

A tall, slightly disheveled, dark-haired young woman stepped into the doorway and squinted in the harsh flashlight beam. "Whoa, watch where you're aiming that thing," she croaked sleepily.

Michael guessed they were about the same age. She was in a short, blue, silk robe with white dragons on the sleeves. The room behind her was utterly dark. She studied Michael for a moment and arched one eyebrow. "Nice poker."

Michael attempted to smile back smoothly, but he felt his face go red. If this was Maggie, Penny had gotten it wrong. She was more than just cute.

She smiled and seemed to relax a little. "I'm fine," she said gently. "Just a nightmare. Sorry if I woke you up."

"Are you sure?"

"Am I sure I'm sorry? No, I love to wake up the paying customers. It's really great for business." She looked up and down at Alison and Olivia. "Look, you guys are sweet to worry, and I really am sorry I woke you up." She held her hand out for Michael to shake. "I'm Maggie."

"Michael." He handed the poker off to Alison so he could shake Maggie's hand.

"You're Maggie?" Alison asked, leaning the poker against the wall next to the door. "You're—like—*the* Maggie? Legit?"

"Yep. Maggie's Mansion. That's me. Legit."

Michael noticed that she didn't sound all that happy about being *the* legit Maggie of Maggie's Mansion. Like it kind of sucked being *the* legit Maggie of Maggie's Mansion. "Do you know what time it is?"

Michael lowered the flashlight so that he could see the large, glowing dial of the stainless steel sports watch that had been on his wrist since his grandparents gave it to him on graduation day. "A little after five."

"*Whoof*! Bright and early." Maggie sighed and ran her hand through her long hair. "Well, I don't know about you, but I'm never getting back to sleep now." She sounded tired and maybe even a little frustrated. Michael wondered how often things went some way other than hers. "Might as well get up and get breakfast started. I assume you people are going to want to eat at some point."

"Well we—" Michael didn't get to the end of the sentence.

"Hand me your light." It didn't sound like a request, so Michael handed it over. The last thing he wanted to do was argue with Maggie.

Nimbly, Maggie took the flashlight from Michael and headed back into her room. The white dragon swooped across the back of her robe when she turned and bent over her nightstand. In a moment, an oil lamp flared to life.

Michael looked at the girls. If Alison or Olivia knew what to do next, they weren't saying, and he certainly had no idea.

"Are you coming in?" Maggie called from inside her room. "You'll break your neck if you try to go back downstairs without your flashlight. I can give it back to you in a second and you can go if you're in a hurry."

"We're not in any hurry," Michael added. He grinned at Alison and Olivia, and it didn't even bother him when they rolled their eyes.

"Look," Maggie said, "it was really great that you guys came to check on me, but I'm fine. Really. Do you want to come in? It'll only take me a minute to pull myself together and then we can all go down together."

She stepped back into the room and Michael followed, careful not to bang his shin on another bed. The large room had windows on three sides. The front was a wall of glass overlooking the inky ocean. The sky was starting to go from black to gray, and he had a clear view of the jetty and the lighthouse tower, its stones pale and ghostly under the starscape. Out to the right, the buildings of Cape November squatted in shadow. To the left, smaller windows showed more of the beach and the dark tops of the trees that surrounded The Mansion that sat just outside of town.

Michael jumped when Maggie crept up next to him. "Great views here. Wait 'til the sun comes up in a bit." Maggie sighed. "I can't even imagine what The Mansion must look like to someone who's never been here, especially in a blackout, but I promise it really is a great old place. I love it here. The nightmares…that's just my own issue. That's why I started staying way up here on the top floor. I wake up fewer people up here."

"So you have nightmares all the time?" Alison asked, taking a step into the room.

Michael decided that Alison sucked as a wingman. *Seriously?* He mouthed at her.

Alison tilted her head to the side. "No offense. I was just curious."

"No worries," Maggie reassured them. Then she laughed. "I just hope your rates are cheaper than my therapist's."

"Look," Michael said. He was getting more and more uncomfortable with the conversation. "We don't want to be all nosy."

"I don't mind nosy," Maggie said cheerfully. "I just don't like people who are all judgmental."

"Oh, trust me," Olivia said.

"Good." Maggie nodded. "Then since you asked, I have nightmares a lot, and it's usually worse when I come down the Cape." She sighed. "It's gotten even worse than usual in the last couple of years."

"Is that why they say this place is haunted?" Alison asked with alarming bluntness. "Is it? Haunted, I mean? Is that why you have nightmares here?"

"Wow," Michael said, glaring at his sister, but forcing a casual laugh. "What is this? Truth or dare?"

Maggie turned on Alison quickly with her eyes narrowed. "What would make you say that?"

Alison's lip sneered with contempt. If Maggie was looking to intimidate his sister, Michael knew she picked the wrong person. He cringed, waiting for this to go horribly wrong. "Why did kids write it on your sign?"

Michael recognized the cold tone in Alison's voice. She was ready to throw down with Maggie. His head filled with regret for letting her come. He tried to catch her eye, but she kept staring coolly at Maggie.

Maggie laughed lightly, as if Alison had told her a joke, and then she turned and walked with the flashlight past the smaller windows, down a short, dark hallway to another part of her room. "I'm going to take a quick shower," she called over her shoulder. "Hang out. Make yourselves at home." Maggie closed the door.

19 PERCEPTION IS REALITY

Feeling a little stupid for barging in to save Maggie when she obviously didn't need saving, Michael slumped into a leather chair. He wondered whether he still had a shot with the girl or if he'd ever had a shot in the first place. For all he knew, Maggie was more interested in Olivia. He noticed the mural behind the four-poster bed. A huge, white dragon soared over the ocean at night. The colors were rich and deep. Michael had a fluttering feeling that he'd just seen a dragon somewhere else, but he couldn't remember where.

Distracting him, Olivia stepped past, straight to the huge bookcase built into the wall next to the windows. The way Olivia was practically bouncing reminded Michael of himself, back in middle school when Mom took him to the video game store. Books didn't get him so excited. He didn't think they'd get anybody that excited. Anybody except Olivia.

Alison sidled up next to Olivia. "Look at all these!" The old, polished wood reflected the lamplight like a mirror, and the shelves were stuffed with hundreds of books, right up to the ceiling.

Michael chuckled to himself at how excited Olivia sounded. "Her library is amazing. She's got collections of mythology, folk tales, fairy tales from all over the world. They don't have stuff this good at the school library. Look! A whole shelf on the Lenape."

"The what?" Michael asked. He felt bored and irritated and sorry that he'd bothered coming up here.

"Native Americans who lived in New Jersey. You know, the Delaware?" Alison sounded as if Michael were the biggest idiot on the planet. He was starting to think that maybe he was, for bringing the nerd twins with him as his wingmen.

"To be fair, Allie, you didn't know who they were either," Olivia pointed out.

Alison shushed Olivia by closing her thumb and fingertips like a bird's beak.

Just sitting there, listening to Olivia and Alison, was making him feel tired. Michael thought about how little he'd slept and wondered whether he should just go back to his room. This had all been a big mistake.

Olivia didn't seem bored at all. "Look at these. Quantum mechanics! Wormholes!" Olivia sighed. "I could spend my vacation right in here."

"Vacation in a library," Michael deadpanned. "Yipee."

"Look at all these philosophy books!" Alison sounded like she was looking at old pictures. "It's all the stuff we studied with Mr. W., remember? Plato,

Aristotle, Descartes, Hume, Berkeley…"

"I loved that Berkeley unit!" Olivia said. "Remember? For our project we posted that awesome music video? With the puppets?"

"Puppets?" Everything was getting on his nerves.

"We made these puppets," Alison explained. "Then we used them to explain one of the weirdest ideas in philosophy."

"Which is?" Michael asked. Not that he cared, but what else was there to do?

"To exist is to be perceived," Alison recited.

Michael hated these little nerd bombs that went off from time to time, but he was waiting for Maggie to finish her shower, so he decided to take his sister's bait just to pass the time. "What?"

"To exist is to be perceived. It means that the only things that really exist are ideas, and ideas only exist when somebody thinks about them."

"That's what they taught you in Nerdapalooza?" Michael laughed. "I thought they taught you smart stuff. That is the stupidest thing I ever heard." He knocked on the wall with his knuckles. "Hear that? It exists."

"Okay, Michael," Alison grinned in that way he hated. "How much?"

"How much what?" He knew she was up to one of her dumb tricks.

"How much do you want to bet that I can prove to you that the world is only made of ideas?"

Alison was always showing off how smart she was and, more important, making Michael feel stupid. Riddles, puzzles, brain-teasers, that annoying anagram game she played with Olivia. Michael wasn't an idiot. He got into a good college. "Okay. I'll take your money. Five bucks?"

Alison turned to Olivia, "You're a witness. Five bucks if I prove that only ideas are real."

"Which you won't. Look." Michael stood up and knocked his hand against the marble top of the dresser. "What am I hitting?"

"An idea," Alison said plainly.

Michael shook his head. "This is a dresser. It's hard. It's cold. The top's made of marble, I think."

Alison said. "You did say that the dresser felt hard and cold, right?"

"So?"

"So you're not really feeling the dresser. You're feeling hardness. Coldness. Smoothness. All those things you feel." Alison talked slowly, like she was talking to a puppy. It was infuriating. "Let's start with cold. Is coldness something real in the world or is it just in your head?"

"It's real. How else can I feel it? Ice is cold. Snow is cold. That's not in my head. I can measure temperature with a thermometer. People can freeze to death. Pay up."

"Take it easy. I'm not done yet." Alison said calmly. "What's more real, the cold in a refreshingly cool glass of lemonade or the cold in a frozen metal flagpole?"

"They're both the same amount of...real-ness or whatever. The frozen flagpole is more cold than the lemonade. But they're both real. It's like, I weigh more than you, but we're both here in the room."

"So you would drink the lemonade, but you wouldn't lick the flagpole, right?" Alison asked.

Michael scoffed. "I've seen that Christmas movie too many times."

"Focus, Michael. Why wouldn't you lick the frozen flagpole?"

"Duh! I'd get stuck, and it would hurt."

"So when you feel something extremely cold, cold enough to hurt you, do you feel the cold and the pain separately or do you just feel pain?"

"I would just feel pain." Michael knew Alison was setting him up, but he couldn't tell how yet.

Alison smiled wider. "Does the frozen flagpole feel the same pain you feel?"

Michael laughed. "Look, if you're going to say rocks and junk feel pain, forget it. Carrots don't scream when you pull them out of the ground. I might not be in Mr. W.'s super genius class, but I know that to feel anything you need a brain and a central nervous system and a flagpole doesn't have that, so there the flagpole doesn't feel pain."

"But the flagpole is cold, right?" Alison asked.

"Yes," Michael groaned. Little teeth of frustration nibbled the backs of his eyes. Where was Maggie? "Is this what you do in super nerd class? You talk about the same dumb thing until somebody drops dead from boredom? For the last time, the flagpole is cold but it doesn't feel pain."

"But you just said when you feel extreme cold, you only feel pain?"

"So?"

Alison laughed and held out her hand.

"What?"

"You just lost the bet." Olivia announced. She was laughing, too.

Michael didn't see it. They were so annoying. Alison was always trying to trick him like he was stupid. Not this time. "No way. I knew you'd cheat. I'm not paying anything. She didn't prove squat!"

"Yes, she did," Olivia said. "You said pain and extreme cold are the same thing, but when you lick a flagpole, you only feel pain, not cold and pain. The flagpole doesn't feel pain. So, the pain is only in *your* mind. There is no pain in the flagpole. If the pain is only in your mind, and the extreme cold and the pain are the same thing when you feel it, then the cold is only in your mind, too. It's not in the flagpole."

Alison nodded, grinning. "You also said that extreme, painful cold and ordinary, refreshing cool are both equally real. So, if the cold that hurts only exists in your mind, then refreshingly cool is only in your mind. If it's true for cold, it's true for everything: heat, cold, sweet. Everything. You only touch that dresser in your mind." Alison held out her hand. "It's all just in your head. Now pay up."

"Knock it off," Michael said. "You're not tricking me. You didn't prove anything. You know the flagpole really is cold."

"I know the flagpole feels cold when I touch it, but that feeling is only in my mind. In reality, there's no such thing as cold. It's only an idea."

"Sorry, Michael, she proved it." Olivia sounded sincere. That was worse than Alison's smug little smile."

"Would you look at that! I don't have my wallet on me," Michael said. "Anyway, it doesn't matter since money doesn't exist either, right?" He grunted his disgust. "I can't believe you guys waste your time arguing about stuff that doesn't even matter."

"Doesn't matter?" Alison asked, sounding disgusted herself. "You don't think it matters whether things are real or not?"

"It only matters in a classroom or in a book. In the real world, you have to deal with real things. See this dresser?" Michael knocked against it again with his knuckles. "You know how I know it's real? Because Mom and Dad are always volunteering me to help people move heavy dressers and couches and crap like that." Michael made his voice into a falsetto whine. *"Call Michael. He's strong. He can help."*

"They pay you for that?" Olivia asked.

Michael shrugged. "Usually they slip me a few bucks. Except Nelson. Dad made me help him move a treadmill out of his basement."

"Nelson does not look like he uses a treadmill." Alison pointed out.

Michael nodded. "That's why we were moving it. And it weighed about eight thousand pounds. It took me, Nelson and Dad two hours because the staircase was so narrow. Instead of paying me, he gave me a box of golf tees and leftover pizza. The point is, no matter what you say, this dresser is heavy and hard. It would be a hassle to lug it up the stairs, and if I dropped it, I'd break my foot. That's real enough for me."

Alison laughed. "Fine. It's a draw."

"Really?" Olivia asked, sounding surprised.

Michael was stunned. "Seriously, Al, this is not like you."

Alison smiled. "I'm getting more generous in my old age."

Michael crossed to the big wall of glass and wood. The velvety ocean rippled under crystal, snowflake stars. A thin band of orange and pink appeared just at the edge of the horizon like God's thumbnail.

"Hey!" Michael called to his sister who had moved to the corner of the window next to a stack of paintings and blank canvasses. "Be careful. We don't even know her. What are you stepping on over there?"

Alison stood on a large sheet stained with drops and slashes of color. An old metal coffee can bristled with brushes soaking in paint thinner. Tubes of paint stood at attention under the splotched easel that held a large canvass. "Whoa!" Alison tilted the canvas to get a better look.

Michael crossed over to look at Maggie's painting. He recognized the view. Glancing out the window, he could make out the silhouettes of the jetty and the lighthouse, dark and dense, just like in the painting. The canvas ocean was iridescent with dark swirls of black and deep blues, swept with lines of soft gray waves. A pale moon leered crookedly from the upper corner. It took a moment for Michael to figure out that Maggie must have intentionally blurred the moon so it would look like it was behind the smoke that poured from the top of the lighthouse that was clutched in a red and orange claw of fire. The flames dripped down the tower like wax from a giant candle until they faded with pale, blue tendrils of light that disappeared under the jetty. The painting gave Michael a weird prickle on the back of his neck.

"We should ask her about this," Alison said.

"No way!" Michael rasped. He felt a little panic rising. The whole point of this was that Michael wanted to hit on her. Especially now that he saw how hot she was. "I'm the one that wanted to come up here and meet her. I don't need you tripping me up."

"I thought you wanted to rescue her?" Alison said coldly.

"That was before I knew she was hot." Michael shrugged.

"You're disgusting," Alison said.

Olivia shrugged. "She is kinda hot."

Michael held up his fist and bumped with Olivia. "But I have dibs, okay?"

Olivia laughed. "I'd say that's up to her."

"She's a person. Not a piece of meat." Grunting her annoyance, Alison turned her back on them to look at the painting again.

The bathroom doorknob clicked. They all bounced back from the painting as Maggie followed the bobbing beam of her flashlight. She set the flashlight down on the edge of her dresser and dried her face and hair on a fluffy, white towel. She wore her robe, and Michael recognized the white dragon he couldn't place earlier.

"Like it?" Maggie asked, indicating the painting with a nod of her chin. Michael couldn't tell if she was mad at them.

"Is it yours?" Michael asked.

"I didn't steal it," Maggie drawled.

Michael laughed nervously. "Right, but you painted it?"

"Yes." Maggie ran her fingers through her hair, untangling it.

"It's cool." Michael hoped it sounded less awkward than he felt.

"Yeah, thanks. It's just something I...uh..."

Michael thought maybe he could rescue her after all. At least in conversation. "That dragon is really cool. I guess you're into dragons, huh?"

Maggie laughed. "Yeah. I like to think that if I have a guardian angel, he's a big white dragon."

"Until that dragon shows up, I guess you'll have to settle for me," Michael hoped that he was flashing his most charming smile. He ignored the eye rolls from Alison and Olivia.

Maggie rolled her eyes too, but laughed a little. Michael took it as a win.

"Is that what your nightmares are about? The lighthouse blowing up?" Alison's question hit Michael like a gut punch. He winced and wished again that she'd stayed downstairs.

But Maggie smiled. "Pretty obvious, huh?"

Michael didn't think so, but his sister and Olivia were acting like Maggie was holding a sign or something.

"It's good that you can paint about it," Olivia said.

"So is that what you were you dreaming about just now? The lighthouse blowing up?" Alison just wasn't going to let this go, no matter how much Michael wished she would.

Maggie sounded tired. "Not exactly, but it's always the same kinds of things, more or less."

"Why?" Alison asked.

Maggie laughed. "What do you mean why? It's a dream. You can't pick your dreams."

"But it's such a specific dream, and if you have the same dream a lot, you gotta have some idea why."

Maggie leaned against the edge of the dresser, looking up at them. Michael understood that Maggie was done talking about her dreams. He hoped the girls were too. "Yeah, look, we just met you. Nobody wants to get in your business or anything."

"I don't mind talking about it," Maggie said. "Just not right now. Maybe after some coffee."

"Cool," Michael said. "I got you. Alison, Olivia, let's give Maggie a little space." He tried to sound authoritative. Adult.

"You painted the sign, didn't you?" Alison said. "The sign out front? There weren't any kids, right? That was you."

So much for giving her space, Michael thought.

Maggie broke into a guilty smile. She looked up at Michael, "She always like this?"

Michael groaned and felt like smothering Alison with a pillow. "You have no idea."

Maggie turned back to Alison. Her voice came muffled because she was bent far over, wrapping her hair in a towel. "In college I took a marketing class, and it made me realize that this place needed a gimmick if we were going to stay in business. The Mansion already looks a little spooky, so I thought I could use that."

"And something here haunts you?" Alison said it quietly.

Olivia added, "And that's why you have bad dreams."

Maggie's eyes narrowed and she glanced back and forth between Alison and Olivia, but Michael couldn't figure out what Maggie's face was saying. She looked a little sad and maybe a little pissed and possibly impressed with them. He could relate to that. Olivia and Alison made him feel like that a lot of the time.

"I thought maybe we could start running some specials on Halloween. Put some coupons online or something. There are a lot of people who like the whole haunted house thing."

"We don't," Alison said flatly.

"Alison, stop messing around," Michael said, laughing uncomfortably. "She's just messing with you. This is a great place. We love it here."

"I'm being honest," Alison said, looking steadily at Maggie. This time, Michael couldn't read Alison's narrowed eyes.

"They say it's the best policy. Although I'm partial to an iron clad No Refunds policy myself." Maggie padded back into the bathroom. She called brightly, "The Mansion really is a nice old place."

"Except for the screaming," Alison said.

"You're hilarious," Maggie replied sarcastically. Michael could hear her in the next room opening drawers and closet doors. He smacked Alison gently on the shoulder.

Alison didn't even flinch. "My mom booked this trip," she explained. "We're staying here because it's ch—"

"Reasonably priced." Michael cut in. He glared at Alison. He wasn't ready to be quite that honest.

"You can say cheap," Maggie said breezily. "It wouldn't bother me, but the term we prefer to describe our price point is economical. It's how business people say cheap."

"Are you a business major?" Michael let his usual swagger speak for him. It wasn't like he didn't know how to pick up a chick. If Alison would just stop tripping him up.

Maggie poked her head around the door with her eyebrow cocked again. Michael thought it was cool the way she could do that. "I double major in comparative folklore and art history. I sort of dabble in philosophy, too."

"With all these science books," Olivia called, "I thought maybe you studied theoretical physics." Olivia sounded disappointed.

"Not me. My grandfather. I'm not nearly smart enough. Those are his books." Maggie's voice floated from the other room.

Olivia gushed, "We love your books."

Maggie called, "Yeah, it's kind of my thing. Collecting books. I'm basically a nerd."

"Us, too!" Olivia said.

"Yeah," Michael said. "I love me some science!" He scowled menacingly at Alison and Olivia, daring them to say something.

"So what made you major in folktales and all that?" Michael called to Maggie through the bathroom.

"Folklore," Maggie corrected him. "And why not? It's what I like."

"But what can you do with it?" Michael asked.

"Run a bed and breakfast." Maggie's voice was a little fainter, like she had gone into a closet or something. "What's your major? Let me guess, something really practical you can use to land a job like marketing or accounting."

Michael hesitated, but, of course, his little sister was all over it. "He just graduated from high school so he doesn't study anything yet. But he's going to study journalism." Alison grinned at her brother like she just won another bet.

"Journalism?" Maggie called from the other room. "And you think folklore is useless? Have you heard of a little thing called the Internet? All the newspapers are all closing down."

Michael felt like he was talking to his father. "That doesn't mean that we don't need journalists! A free press is the cornerstone of democracy."

"Yikes! What textbook did you steal that from?" Maggie poked her head and bare shoulders around the corner. "I'm just messing with you. Take it easy."

Maggie disappeared for a moment and then came back through the bathroom. Michael drank in the way her athletic curves filled out her white, cotton dress as she walked. When she stepped into a pair of sandals, she reminded Michael of a Greek goddess. Penny's description of her niece as cute was like calling a hurricane a little rain. Maggie looked like a force of nature. "Want to join me for an early breakfast?" the hurricane asked. "I make fantastic crepes."

"What's crepes?" Michael asked.

Alison, Olivia and Maggie chuckled, and Michael felt like a moron.

20 THE ART OF BREAKFAST

Alison sat on a high-backed barstool at a polished counter that had been built under three wide arches. Through the arches, Alison watched Maggie move around the kitchen like the unholy love child of a ballerina and a tornado.

Occasionally, Alison would take a break from watching Maggie's cooking circus to spin her stool and check out the fancy dining room behind them. Through the back wall of windows, the ocean twinkled with sunlight that warmed the polished wood of the tables and floor and the bright, butter-colored walls.

Maggie had been right. The Mansion looked a lot better in the daylight. But Alison had some questions about Maggie, too. Having recurring nightmares wasn't so weird. It just meant Maggie had anxiety issues. But dreaming about the lighthouse blowing up. There was more to that story. Maggie was hiding something.

One thing was sure: Since they met Maggie things felt a little more normal. Alison wondered how much of the creepy stuff from yesterday really had been in their heads.

"Did you paint all of these, too?" Michael asked, gesturing to the paintings around the dining room. "They're awesome."

Maggie smiled as she worked on a batter. "Yeah. Painting helps me relax."

Alison made up titles in her head. Fruit in a Bowl. Colorful Bottles. A Platter of Crabs. Shops on The Boulevard. Olga's Restaurant. Fishing Boats. Sail Boats. Sunrise. How could someone with such terrible dreams make such cheerful paintings? She studied Maggie again.

Setting her large mixing bowl down, Maggie hunched beside a humongous stove. The gas hissed loudly, and she held a match to one of the many burners. "Okay. Power's out so I have to go old school. Hopefully I won't blow us all up. Once I almost burned off my eyebrows, but I think I got the hang of it now."

There was a whoosh, and one burner blossomed into sharp, blue needles of flame. Maggie took a small bow when she blew out the match, and with much less drama, lit three more burners. "There used to be a whole team of professional chefs here, but that was before my time. Nowadays I handle most of the cooking whenever I come down. Who's up for crepes? I can do chocolate or Nutella, even better. I also have tons of fruit. Or you can have eggs, cheese, ham, bacon. It's going to take a little while to make the bacon, though."

"You mean eggs and bacon? Or eggs and bacon crepes?" Michael asked.

She is so out of Michael's league. Alison thought this as Maggie scowled playfully at Michael. Olivia might actually have a better shot.

"I could make you bacon and eggs," Maggie said, "but if somebody offers you fresh crepes, take them."

Soon Alison was inhaling the fluffy, sweet smell of frying crepes along with chocolate and fruit. She ate slowly, like Dr. Pam taught her, so she was still on her first crepe while a second—or was it a third now?—chocolate crepe gently hissed in the pan for Michael.

Maggie nibbled at the crepe she had made for herself. She closed her eyes and looked happy when she bit into it. Alison never saw anyone look so happy when they ate. Stupid Dr. Pam said that had been one of Alison's problems, eating mechanically, which was nutritionist-ese for stop shoving food in your face.

Watching Maggie savor every bite made Alison slow down her own chewing even more. Alison focused on the sweet gush of melted chocolate. The tender crunch of the crepe. She tasted butter. If Berkeley was right, all those flavors and textures might have only been in her head and not in the crepe, but they were still amazing. But if Berkeley was right and it was in her head, why couldn't she get celery to taste like pizza?

"What kind are you having?" Michael asked.

Maggie held up her finger. Chewed. Swallowed. And then said, "I call it a blintz crepe because it reminds me of the blintzes I get at my favorite diner in New York City."

"What's a blintz?" Michael asked.

Maggie smiled. "You've never had blintzes? They're the best. It's a little dumpling made out of layers of super thin dough. It's filled with a sweet cheese and topped with fruit, usually blueberries or strawberries. Mine's blueberry. It's good, but it's a crepe, not a blintz. For a real blintz, you need to go to New York."

Alison savored. Swallowed. "We've never been to New York." She suddenly felt a little embarrassed like she just crawled out from under a rock.

"Hey, speak for yourself," Michael quickly put in. "I've been to New York."

Alison challenged him. "When?"

"I went on that tour of Cartesian University last spring. Remember? You stayed with Olivia."

Alison knew that her brother was trying to show off for Maggie. A perfect target. "That was for about five minutes, Michael. And you were on a college tour with Mom and Dad."

"So?" Michael sounded a little annoyed.

"Did you eat a blintz?" Olivia asked.

Perfect, Olivia. Alison chuckled to herself. Olivia wasn't even trying to sink Michael. She was just asking an innocent Olivia-type question.

"No," Michael admitted. Alison caught him scowling at Olivia. Olivia shrugged. She had no idea what she'd just done. Hilarious.

"There you go," Alison said.

"How did you like Cartesian?" Maggie asked, apparently not noticing or not caring about Alison's little game.

"Loved it. I'm going there this fall."

"Go Spirits!" Maggie put her hand up for a fist bump. When Michael bumped, Maggie said, "That's where I go."

"Really?"

Alison chuckled to herself when Michael's voice cracked. In a deeper tone he asked, "That's cool. So how do you like it?"

"Sometimes it's hard to get a spot in the library because of all the premeds, but it's a great school and I love being in the city. Now…taste." She slid her plate across the counter. "It's not actually a blintz, remember. The dough on a blintz is totally different, but at least this will give you an idea of the flavors."

Olivia and Alison both leaned in with their forks, but Michael pulled the plate in front of him and finished it in one savage bite.

"I was still eating that," Maggie said, scowling a little.

"And we didn't even get to taste it," Alison complained. "You shouldn't eat mechanically, Michael."

"What does that even mean?" he asked through a mouthful.

"It means don't shove food in your face." Alison shook her head. He was hopeless, but what did it matter? It wasn't like he had to watch his weight.

Smiling hospitably, Maggie reached for the batter. "I'll make a few more."

"Could I try one with ham and cheese now? Or that bacon and egg situation you mentioned." Michael leaned back, grinning.

"He needs meat," Olivia explained.

Alison added, "He's gotta feed the pythons."

"The what?" Maggie's aristocratic features were tangled up in curiosity.

Michael laughed casually. "It's a joke. My arms…You know. Pythons." He flexed his big arms.

"Why?" Maggie's face was blank.

Alison watched Michael squirming. Hilarious.

Michael's arms deflated limp to his sides. "Because, you know, because my arms are…I'm just messing around."

"Big?" Maggie said flatly.

Michael laughed awkwardly, but Alison and Olivia just laughed. He waited until Maggie wasn't looking, then he glared at Alison and Olivia.

Alison could not resist. "Tell her about your rule, Michael," she said brightly.

"What rule?" Michael held up his fist, but dropped it quickly when Maggie turned back around. "I don't have a rule."

"He's got this rule," Alison explained. "If it's not hot meat, it's only a snack."

Maggie tilted her head and squinted slightly at Michael. "How about pizza?"

"I'd love some," Michael beamed.

Maggie closed her eyes, smiled gently and shook her head. "Funny. No. I mean does pizza count as a meal or a snack? And what's with the schmutz?" She took a cloth napkin and playfully wiped the corner of his mouth for him. "Try not to eat like a cave man."

Cave man? That's good. Funny. Maggie's funny.

"Sausage counts," Michael offered, totally serious. "And meatballs. Possibly pepperoni if there's a lot. Plain or anything with just vegetables, that's always a snack. Not broccoli. Only an idiot ruins pizza with broccoli. And forget mushrooms. I don't eat fungus."

"I love broccoli on my pizza," Maggie said defiantly.

"I…uh…"

Alison tried not to howl with laughter.

"How about a sandwich?" Maggie shot back.

Alison loved the way that Maggie was grilling Michael about his meat thing. She couldn't tell if Maggie was seriously interested or just giving him a hard time. She was a little tough to read. This surprised Alison, who prided herself on reading people quickly. She tried to get Olivia's attention, but Olivia was really in the zone with her strawberry crepe.

"In an emergency," Michael explained. "I guess I could count a cold sandwich, but it would have to have a lot of meat and cheese. Really, though, it should be a hot sandwich like a cheese steak or a chicken parm."

After she slid Michael his plate, Maggie rotated a tall metal pot that was on a back burner. "With the power out I can't use the coffeemaker. I haven't used this old-fashioned one in ages." Maggie inspected the coffee bubbling up into the glass cap. "It's probably dark enough. I hate weak coffee."

"Me, too," Michael said.

"Like you even know," Alison teased.

Michael flexed his huge arm and shoulder muscles and said in an extra deep voice, "I hate weak anything." He grinned at Maggie.

Maggie, Alison and Olivia all laughed and groaned at him while Maggie poured herself an oversized mug. She lifted it with both hands and sipped with her eyes closed, looking satisfied. Savoring. "I forgot how much I like percolator coffee. The electric is convenient, but this just tastes better. More character, you know?" Maggie set down the mug, "I'm sorry, where are my manners. You guys want some coffee?"

"Sure," Michael replied with his mouth full.

"You don't drink coffee," Alison laughed. Michael was really going for it. Alison considered letting him get away with it, but decided that torturing him was more fun.

Michael again scowled covertly at his sister. "You don't eat crepes," he said breezily. "That's why we go on vacation, right? To try new stuff."

"When I go on vacation—which is rare," Maggie said, "I just want to sit on my butt and read."

"That sounds awesome," Olivia said between bites.

"Nerd," Alison said, gently elbowing her.

Maggie filled up a mug of coffee for Michael. "How do you take it?"

"Take what?" Michael asked.

Alison and Olivia both cracked up. "He has no idea," Alison said.

After a moment of blank staring, Michael asked Maggie, "How do you take it?"

"Milk and two sugars."

"Hook me up."

Sliding the milk and sugar to Michael, Maggie turned to Alison and Olivia. "If you don't want coffee, how about some hot chocolate?"

"Yeah," Michael sneered playfully. "If coffee is too fancy for your young taste buds."

"Be quiet, Michael," Alison scolded. Alison thought that hot chocolate sounded really good, but she didn't want to feel like a little kid in front of Maggie, and she knew that Michael was going to make a big deal out of it. Payback.

"Before you decide," Maggie said, "you ought to know that I don't even have any of that powder stuff."

"How else do you make hot chocolate?" Alison asked.

Maggie's face lit up. "You have to try my hot chocolate. I make it from scratch, and it will change your life. If you say no, you'll hurt my feelings." Maggie winked at Alison.

She knows. She's giving us an excuse to have hot chocolate without Michael giving us a hard time about it. Alison decided that maybe Maggie was okay after all.

All tornado and ballerina again, Maggie moved around her kitchen, pouring and measuring. She pulled a huge brick of chocolate out of the dead refrigerator and chiseled off a sizable chunk that clunked into one of the pots. Then she clattered some more, stirring and whisking.

"Tell me that's not a bug," Michael said.

"This?" Maggie smiled and held up the large, brown string bean-looking thing. "It's a vanilla bean. It's the key to this whole thing. You'll see."

After another couple of minutes of whisking and mixing, Maggie slid two large mugs of hot chocolate across the counter.

Blowing the thick, sweet steam away from the mug, Alison tried to calculate in her head how many calories were in that homemade hot chocolate.

Too many. But I'm on vacation and this will be worth it and I only had one crepe.

If Aristotle had tasted Maggie's hot chocolate—if Dr. Pam had tasted it—they would have agreed with Alison. It was like no hot chocolate Alison had ever tasted. She slid her mug toward Michael. "Taste this. You're going to be sorry you picked coffee."

Alison's mother startled all of them. "Good morning, sunshine! Something smells really good."

Dad was right behind. "What are you guys doing up?"

"I think I woke them," Maggie confessed, "I'm kind of a noisy sleeper. I'm Maggie, your hostess until Aunt Penny comes back." She extended her hand and shook with Mom and Dad.

"Yes, your aunt mentioned that you would be taking care of us. I hope these guys aren't giving you too much trouble." Mom scowled in mock threat at the three of them.

"Not at all. Well, maybe him." Maggie joked.

Just to be sure, Mom smacked Michael's arm.

"Geez, Mom, that really hurt," Michael said sarcastically.

"I can get the tire iron out of the car," Dad offered.

"Maybe later when he really deserves it," Mom replied.

Mom and Dad sat at one of the tables, and Maggie brought a tray with coffee and the extra crepes she had made. "They're still hot, but I'll make you some fresh ones. Just tell me what you like."

Mom and Dad were both smiling, obviously surprised. "It's so nice to have somebody else do the cooking for a change," Mom said. "And crepes! We never get to have those."

Dad took a bite of a pear crepe. "Wow!" His eyes were two big moons. Alison was happy to see him so happy about something. "This is amazing."

Mom looked happy, too, as she looked out at the sun over the ocean. "It is just so beautiful here. See?" Turning back to Maggie, she said, "Everyone was so worried when we came in last night because of the storm and all, but I knew this place would be great."

"You were right, Mom," Alison agreed. "This place is awesome." Mom gave her a big hug. It wasn't even embarrassing.

21 SECRETS

With breakfast done, Maggie slowed down and puttered around the kitchen, making small talk with Mom and Dad. Michael watched her. The shine of her eyes. The curve of her hips. The dark flow of her hair. Her easy laugh. All of it made his chest feel warm and full.

"I'm so glad you like it here, Sara," said Maggie. Michael felt a little awkward about it, but Mom had insisted that Maggie call her and Dad by their first names. "I really wish I could have seen it fifty or sixty years ago."

"Yes, I remember when I was a kid, this was the place everyone wanted to go." Mom said. She turned to Michael and Alison. "Did you know Grandma and Grandpa almost came here on their honeymoon?"

Michael didn't know. That was kind of cool, he supposed.

Maggie talked with enthusiasm. Energy. "You know that plain, white oval with letters in the middle? People put stickers on their cars and all that? That started here with a B for The Boulevard. Ocean Boulevard. Cape November used to be the place everyone, seriously everyone, wanted to spend summer vacation."

"Tourists come down and have a good time and spend money. So everybody's happy." Dad liked to be an expert in everything. "And these crepes are fantastic."

"Thanks," Maggie said. "Family recipe."

Dad sounded like he understood exactly what Maggie was talking about, but Michael could tell there was something else that Maggie was trying to say. "It was more than just the tourists, though. Right, Maggie?"

Maggie looked at Michael. Her eyes looked a little surprised and grateful. She nodded vigorously. "Oh yeah. The biggest name musicians, actors, professional athletes," she looked at Michael. "Famous journalists—everybody used to mingle here. A struggling guitar player could sit in on a jam session with a rock legend. Writers and poets hung out at Olga's and gave readings. It was that kind of place."

"I didn't realize it was like that," Michael's mother said dreamily. Then she seemed to snap to attention and smacked Michael on the arm, "See? You said this place was a dump."

"Ow!" Michael could feel his face getting redder as he looked up at Maggie. "I never said it was a dump."

Olivia looked up. "That's exactly what you said. In the car, remember?" She had no idea she was wrecking him.

Alison laughed. She knew exactly what she was doing. "You wanted to go to Grimmyland."

"So did you!" Michael felt panic clawing at his throat. Worst wingman EVER! "But now that I see how cool The Mansion is, I love it here." He smiled weakly at Maggie.

"Whatever he said, Michael has a point." Dad gave Michael a knowing wink and casually added, "When Mom and I were kids, the Cape had already started going downhill. No offense, Maggie. The Mansion was always a nice place, but that's why we started coming down the Cape in college. It was cheaper than a lot of other places."

I never thought Dad would be my wingman.

"Business people say economical, Dad," Alison pointed out, giving Maggie a goofy grin.

Maggie shrugged. "That's fair." She sighed, and it hurt Michael's chest. She looked so sad. He just wanted to wrap her in his arms and protect her from whatever it was that was making her sound like that. "A lot of beach towns sprung up that had imitations of The Boulevard. They weren't as good, but they were closer to the big cities so people didn't have to travel all the way down the Cape. Then came the superstorms. Hurricanes, nor'easters. Always there was a storm surge and flooding. And then the fires. Year after year. Eventually, people gave up trying to rebuild." Maggie gave another one of those sighs that just about broke Michael.

Michael noticed the sad way her voice trailed off as she looked away from them. He wanted to help her. Like when she had the bad dreams.

"Weren't there some mass murders here or something?" Michael couldn't believe the way Dad asked it so casually, the way he might have asked for milk for his coffee. This was Maggie's home.

Worst wingman ever.

Maggie looked up with so much fire it startled Michael. "There were no murders, Tom," she snapped coldly. Then her features softened, but there was hurt in her eyes and her lips wrinkled slightly like she was annoyed. "Absolutely nothing like that has ever happened here at The Mansion." Maggie seemed to lose some of her height for a moment. In a gentler tone she continued, "There have been some unsolved missing persons cases, but the water can be rough around the Cape. Riptides. Sudden squalls. I hate to say it, but tourists who don't know what they're doing get drunk and go out too far, swimming or in boats they can't handle. They get lost. Drown probably. If their body doesn't wash up, they stay missing." Maggie shrugged.

Michael felt an uneasy twinge in his gut. The way she dropped her voice and downplayed the whole thing. The shrug. In his journalism classes, Mr. Rajai always said those were red flags in an interview.

Calm down. She's probably just being protective. It is her place. She'll never get any business if people are scared off. But what if it's really not safe here? Michael glanced at his family. For the first time in a while, the bite on his arms started itching. He'd been so distracted he'd almost forgotten the birds, the bugs and the dead thing on the side of the road.

It was probably normal stuff. I was just scared. What was it Alison said about Berkeley? The fear was in my head. They must have been normal birds. I'm just remembering it wrong.

He had to talk to Maggie. Alone. Not such a sacrifice. Her face looked more relaxed again. Like before. He was going to learn the truth about Cape November. And about her.

22 MAKING A MESS

Alison looked at her parents eating crepes and drinking coffee. They seemed happy. Nobody was yelling. It was nice. Maybe Olivia was right. Maybe her parents were fine. Maybe it was just in her own head. *I really hate George Berkeley sometimes.*

Mom smiled at Maggie. "I didn't know that much about the history of this place."

Maggie smiled and looked down like she was embarrassed. "Sorry. I know I go on and on and get emotional sometimes." Maggie came around the counter and collected the dirty plates. "This area is so old, and there are so many stories. It's how I got interested in folklore. That's my major."

"What kind of a job can you get with that?" Alison cringed a little when her father asked.

Maggie smiled. "I think I'm doing it. Anyway, it's a beautiful day. You should get out there and enjoy it. Me and my folklore will stay here and clean up."

Alison's father looked at his watch and clapped his hands together. "I'm... uh... teeing off with Nelson pretty soon."

Alison felt everything inside her fall through the floor. Her breath came in short, panting bursts.

"Now?" Mom sounded stunned.

Dad shrugged. "I thought I'd squeeze in a quick round."

"When were you going to tell me?" Alison heard the emotion in her mother's voice. *It's just in your head, huh? Bite me, Berkeley.*

"I need permission to play golf now?" Dad's voice got sharper.

"Not my permission, but it would be nice to know your plans."

Everything had been so good. Alison looked through the arches. Maggie kept herself busy in the kitchen. She didn't have to notice or care. It wasn't Maggie's family falling apart. Olivia shut down like she always did when Mom and Dad went at it. Alison dug her nails into her palms to keep from screaming at them all.

"My plans are I'm going golfing and I'll be back later." Dad could be so stupid. So selfish. Alison looked over to her brother for help, but he was focused on his crepe. He probably didn't even notice.

Mom said quietly. "I thought we were going to the beach together."

"The beach isn't going anywhere," Dad said casually.

"What am I supposed to do while you're golfing?"

Dad shrugged like it was the dumbest question he'd ever heard. Alison felt her face get hot. Under her hair her scalp was on fire. She felt as if she could slap her father at that moment. That thought scared her.

"You can go to the beach without me, can't you?" Dad said it like he was dismissing her. "Do whatever you want."

Mom's sarcastic laugh chilled Alison. "That's what you always do. What I want is to spend time with my husband on vacation." Alison saw her mom's face get red, her eyes narrow angrily and then she jabbed with her fork at her half-eaten crepe.

Anger and fear made Alison's hands shake and her stomach flutter. Michael pushed his giant, stupid meat-crepe around in his plate. Olivia stirred her hot chocolate; the spoon never touched the mug.

Mom stood so suddenly Alison jumped. She stalked away from the table without saying anything. The flapping of her beach shoes faded. In the heavy silence, Dad looked awkwardly at Alison. His eyebrows and mouth fluttered, like a bird trying to decide whether to land on sadness, anger, pain or humiliation. "We're going out to dinner later," he explained quietly. "Just the two of us."

"Why are you telling me?" Alison tried to keep her voice neutral.

Dad's eyes narrowed. "In the car last night you seemed pretty interested."

Alison's memory came crashing back, the angry words she traded with Dad when they had arrived at The Mansion. So many other things had happened, it felt like a million years ago.

Is he still angry about that or does he feel guilty? Is he yelling at me or apologizing? Alison shrugged. "I'm not the boss of you. I'm just a kid, remember? I don't have an opinion." Neutral tone. Quiet voice. She glanced over at Olivia who made no eye contact with her, apparently fascinated with Maggie's painting of a bowl of fruit.

Alison faced her father again. He kept looking like he was going to say something, but then changed his mind.

"What?" Alison asked. She could hear her anger escaping even though she tried to keep it in.

"I'll be on my cell phone." Dad said it abruptly. Alison's heart did a little skip in her chest. He stomped heavily out of the dining room.

"Pop, hang on," Michael said lamely, his voice cracking again.

Dad paused at the doorway and turned to face them. He made a mean little laugh. "You know why they call it a cell phone? 'Cause people can always keep track of you. Just like in jail."

Alison stared down the dark hallway where he had gone. The same way Mom had gone. Alison swallowed down everything that threatened to come out of her. She could hear Maggie quietly going about her business somewhere far away in the kitchen.

"Michael," Alison said quietly, "we have to do something."

His mouth opened stupidly. "About what?"

Alison's chest felt tight. "Don't be an idiot."

"I'm not an idiot!" Michael slammed his fist down hard on the counter, shaking the cups and dishes.

Sometimes she forgot how strong he was. The sudden violence of it made Alison's breath catch in her throat. "Then don't act like one. You know Mom and Dad are having problems." She knew where this was heading. She was ready for it. She wanted it.

"No. I don't know that. Neither do you. Even if they are, what are we supposed to do? You always make drama. Just mind your own business."

"They're our parents, Michael." Alison's heart hammered her chest. She could feel the heat of it erupting from under her scalp. "They are my business. They should be your business."

"People fight, Alison." Michael said.

"You really don't see it, Michael?" Alison kept her voice low to keep from screaming. "Maybe it's because you don't want to, or maybe you really are the dumb jock you pretend to be, but Mom and Dad—"

"Cut it out!" Michael slammed his palms flat against the countertop again. It threatened to crack, but this time Alison didn't jump.

"Why? You can't face the truth? Is it too scary for the big, tough wrestler?"

Michael popped out of his stool. It tumbled noisily to the floor.

Alison felt her breath coming faster. Michael's face carried a darkness Alison rarely saw. His huge muscles knotted with tension. Veins bulged in his neck and shoulders.

"Michael," Olivia said gently.

"Stay out of this, Olivia. You don't know anything about this."

"Doesn't she? Her parents have been divorced for years." Fire burned through Alison. It grew with every beat of her heart. She glanced at Olivia and saw her crying. Alison felt like someone crammed cement down her throat. "Olivia…"

Olivia looked up with red eyes. "Don't say anything else."

"What's happening out here?" The authority in Maggie's voice snapped Alison out of her rage.

"Sorry," Alison said. "Michael and I were just…uh..."

"Having a moment?" Maggie offered.

Alison nodded, but she kept watching Michael. He closed his eyes, and his big chest swelled as he took a huge breath. Alison watched him breathe in and out, and his shoulders lost their rigid tension. His arms unflexed. His fists unfurled. He kept his eyes closed, and in a calm, quiet voice, Michael said, "I worry about them, too, Alison."

Alison felt her own breath slowing down.

"Sorry I knocked over your stool, Maggie." Alison watched Michael gently pick up the overturned barstool, and she felt something warm for her brother. For maybe the first time ever. The idea exploded in her mind like an electric shock, and all at once she understood. Michael was terrified, too. He was more worried than she was, but he was even more afraid to admit it. The weight of that settled on her slowly at first, and then like an avalanche.

"It's okay to be scared, Michael," Alison said quietly.

"I'm not scared." A cocky sneer edged Michael's voice. "Scared of what?" He looked over at Maggie, but Alison saw that Maggie didn't return Michael's fake smile.

Maggie looked sad. "Look, you guys, if you need a little space…"

"We're fine" Michael said.

"We're not fine, Michael!" Alison hissed. "We're a mess."

Michael's eyes had something pleading in them. "Alison, we don't have to talk about this now."

Alison felt the heat building up in her chest again. "Why? Are you embarrassed to talk about it in front of Maggie? She's not deaf. She heard them fighting."

"So what if they fight? It doesn't mean anything."

"How do you know? They could be splitting up. This could be…you know…one more vacation together to try and fix everything, but it's not going work. Dad's ignoring the whole thing. Just like you."

"There is no thing."

"Haven't you been paying attention?"

"Yeah, and all I see is you constantly causing trouble and making drama. Why can't you leave them alone and just let them figure it out?"

"Because I don't want to lose my family. Olivia did, and it could happen to us. I don't want to deal with all the stuff she deals with."

Alison saw Olivia look up from her cold cup, her eyes round with shock and red with angry sadness. Alison hated the tears burning her eyes. She hated Michael for seeing her cry. She hated herself for what she had just said about Olivia. Alison hated words. All the words. All the stupid words that made people feel all these stupid feelings.

The enormous dining room felt claustrophobic. When she saw Olivia trying not to look like she was crying, Alison felt a hot gush of guilt and shame. She had to run out.

23 CLEANING UP

Michael felt guilty for fighting with his sister. He felt embarrassed for his whole stupid family and their stupid drama. Just thinking about it made his stomach tense and his fists clench, and then he felt hot shame for losing his temper and knocking over Maggie's stool. But he was so sick of Alison always treating him like an idiot, on top of all her drama about Mom and Dad. Okay, so they fought; that didn't mean anything. Nobody was hitting anybody. And even if Alison were right, and Michael seriously doubted that, what could Alison do about it? What could anybody do if two people just didn't love each other and were sick of being together? People can't make each other fall in and out of love by magic. By trying to help and always making such a big deal out of everything, Alison always made things worse. He looked at Olivia staring at the floor. Michael supposed she and Alison had their own problems now. But he couldn't leave things like this. He got up to go after his sister.

Maggie gently held him back with a hand on his forearm, her touch warm and vivid. Maggie seemed to look right down into him. It made him feel exposed. It was scary and thrilling.

"I realize you barely know me," Maggie said quietly, "but I think your sister needs a little space right now. No offense."

Michael was too stunned to be offended. "So what should I do?"

"You don't have to do anything. At least not right now." Maggie looked at Olivia, staring awkwardly into her mug. "Are you okay?"

Olivia shrugged, twirling her spoon and staring into her cup. "She's been worried about her parents forever. I guess I never realized that it's because of me."

"You?" Michael didn't understand. Olivia never talked about herself, not to him anyway.

"She always hears me complaining about having to split my time between my mom and my dad. Every holiday I have to work out a schedule. Sometimes they argue about whose weekend it is or whose turn for a vacation." Olivia laughed dry and hard. "To get to come here I had a big fight with both of them because it was supposed to be Mom's turn so she asked Dad to switch, but Dad had planned on taking me to Martha's Vineyard during his week. But he's going with his girlfriend and her two little boys. They just want me to babysit. For free." Olivia sighed heavily, and Michael felt sorry for her. "The point is I think I made Alison really scared of having divorced parents because having divorced parents kind of sucks sometimes. At least for me." Olivia smiled weakly. "Sorry I ruined your family's vacation, Michael."

Michael had no idea what to say to her. She looked like this broken doll, like a sad little kid. "It's not your fault, Olivia. Alison loves you."

Olivia laughed and sniffed back tears.

Michael didn't understand. "I'm serious."

"We're going through a…a thing I guess. Because I'm moving." Olivia shook her head sadly.

"You better not be fighting, too," Michael tried to sound light. "I'm pretty sure that's a sign of the Apocalypse." Olivia wasn't the most upbeat kid, but he'd never seen her look this down. And never when it came to anything about Alison. The thought of refereeing a fight between Alison and Olivia gave him a spinning, helpless feeling. "You know what a big mouth Alison has."

Olivia laughed weakly. "It's fine. I'm not even mad at her."

"Go find her," Maggie said. "Go out to the stable. Take a couple of bikes. Go for a long ride. Talk. It'll do you both some good."

Olivia looked up at Maggie. Her eyes were full of tears she wasn't letting out. "Thanks," she said weakly.

"For what?" Maggie smiled and put one hand on her hip and her finger pointing out the door. In a fake, commanding voice, she said, "Go." Michael thought it was exactly the way she might have said "Off with his head!"

When everyone else was gone, Michael looked awkwardly at Maggie. "So what'm I supposed to do now?"

She raised her palms toward him. "It's your vacation."

He decided to go for it. "What are you doing now?"

She smiled, and it broke into laughter. "I'm working. I'm not on vacation."

"Can I help you?"

Her amazing eyebrow popped up again in a puzzled arch that tugged at Michael's insides. "You want to spend your vacation doing dishes?" Her laughter was so easy and fun that he had to laugh with her.

"I'll do them if you're doing them," Michael said.

"Usually we only make people do dishes when they can't pay their bill."

"I don't care how economical your price point is. If my parents just ditched me, I can't pay my bill."

Maggie's voice was a suggestive purr. "So you're saying I should make you work it off? I might have to make you my slave."

Michael felt everything inside him light up. And then a damp dishrag flopped over Michael's face.

"You wash; I'll dry and put away."

Peeling back the towel, Michael looked warily at the stack of dirty dishes and gloppy pots and pans. He wondered whether this would all be worth it. Another glance at Maggie's cotton dress hugging her curves and he decided it was. "Don't you have a dishwasher in this place?"

"We do now!" Maggie grinned.

"I mean like a real dishwasher, you know, where you just shove the dishes in and they come out clean?"

"We're in a power failure here, remember? Besides, would you want me to run a whole commercial dishwasher just for a family's breakfast dishes? That's a total waste. Why not just run up to the arctic and start clubbing the baby polar bears? It'll be faster."

"Okay, okay. Calm down, tree-hugger." Michael rinsed a plate.

"Tell you what," Maggie suggested, "let's finish these up, and then I'll take you snorkeling down by the lighthouse."

Michael looked at her. At the mention of the lighthouse he felt uneasy. He thought about her painting. Her secrets.

She must have noticed because she smiled at him. He couldn't tell if she was amused or annoyed. "Dude, are you scared? There's nothing wrong with the lighthouse. It's just my issue, okay?"

He felt like a jerk. "No, it's cool. I wasn't even thinking about your painting or any of that."

"Liar." Maggie laughed and snapped his butt with the towel. It stung. "Anyway we call it the lighthouse, and it was used as a lighthouse a long time ago, but it's not a regular lighthouse. When it was built, there were no ships here yet."

"When was it built?" Normally, Michael thought history was about as interesting as listening to Alison and Olivia play their stupid anagrams game, but the lighthouse was interesting. And Maggie was interesting. He had to admit that when he could get his mind off how hot she was, he did like talking with her. So, he tried to think like a journalist and follow the story.

Maggie shrugged. "No one really knows when or why it was built or even who built it. Like The Mansion."

Michael looked around. "You don't know who built this?"

"The Mansion part we do. It was built right after the Civil War by a Confederate officer on the run from the Union Army. He and a few guys in his platoon who stayed loyal to him drove the slaves and the prisoners up here all the way from South Carolina. He used the slaves and the Union POWs to build The Mansion on top of the foundation. The interesting thing is that the foundation had been here a long, long time before that, along with the jetty and the lighthouse."

"The lighthouse that isn't really a lighthouse." Michael looked out from the kitchen at the spacious dining room and tried to imagine the man that built it.

"It's kind of like a Stonehenge, Easter Island thing. The lighthouse sits on this underwater mountain, and there's really cool fish out there. It's fun."

"I thought you said it was dangerous."

Maggie lowered her voice to a whisper, "That's what makes it fun." Her eyes looked like hot invitations. She laughed so abruptly it startled him. "Why are you so uptight? Look, if you don't know what you're doing out there, of course it's dangerous. But I grew up here."

"And the sharks are vegans now?" Michael laughed nervously. He didn't want her to think he was afraid.

"I wouldn't say vegans, but you literally have a better chance of being hit by lightning than you do of getting attacked by a shark." Maggie grinned. "Tell you what. Let's finish these up and then you can see for yourself."

"I've never been snorkeling." Michael said. He really wanted to go with her but his guts were a nervous tangle.

"You never tried crepes or coffee either." Maggie smiled.

He laughed nervously. "Yeah. The coffee probably made me a little jittery."

"That's not the coffee. That's me." Maggie winked, then laughed like there was something crazy and fun just around the corner. "Okay. Now less talking and more scrubbing. I love a man with dishpan hands."

24 SAPPHIRES

Olivia found Alison sitting on the front porch steps with her head flopped forward onto her knees and her hair tumbling down her legs.

Silently, Olivia sat next to her.

"I'm really sorry," Alison said into her knees.

Olivia put her arm around Alison and took a deep breath of the cool shade. She forced herself to listen as the seabirds cried in the distance and the humming bees visited the flowers around the porch. She was afraid to speak, to break the spell, but she had to let it out. "It's not that horrible being me."

Alison's body bounced under Olivia's hands as she laughed, but then she turned her face into Olivia's neck, and Olivia felt warm tears. It freaked Olivia out. Alison was supposed to be invincible. Indestructible. "Hey, come on. It's okay."

Muffled in Olivia's neck, Alison said, "I admire you, Olivia. Really. I can't believe how strong you are." She pulled away and looked at Olivia. Her eyes were red and puffy. "I'm not as strong as you."

Her own tears trickled out. "I'm not strong," Olivia sighed, stroking Alison's hair. "It's just…it's my life, you know? It's not like I have a choice. My parents don't live together, but so what? Lots of kids' parents are divorced. I know they love me, just not each other." Olivia stroked Alison's back. She wanted to tell her it would all be okay, but doubts stabbed at her gut. She swallowed down everything else until all she had left to say was, "You're my best friend. We're there for each other."

"I was never there for you." Alison sat up. Her eyes looked red. Exhausted. They hadn't slept much, but Olivia knew that wasn't it. Alison's voice was small and fragile. "When you were going through everything with your parents, I wasn't there."

"You didn't know me or you would have been." Olivia knew this to be true. She felt it in her skin and hair. "You would have been there for me then just like you are now."

"What about now? You're leaving me, Liv." Alison caught Olivia's eyes, and suddenly it felt like someone turned on a blender inside her. *She's been downplaying it the whole time.* Olivia didn't think it was a big deal to Alison, but then Olivia could have kicked herself for being such an idiot. Of course Alison downplayed it. She was protecting Olivia. But now the truth was out. "I'm scared to lose you, too, Liv."

Olivia had a peculiar feeling of being made of falling sand, and then Alison stood up and hauled Olivia to her feet. She sniffed and laughed and squeezed Olivia's hands. "For right now, let's just enjoy what we've got. Okay?"

"Okay." Olivia hated the way she kept repeating that word. She was not okay about leaving. She was not okay with her parents not giving her a choice.

Alison nodded toward the beach. "Let's ride some bikes into the ocean."

Olivia laughed. "Let's start with just riding some bikes. Come on."

She tugged Alison by the hand toward the stable. As they rounded the corner, Olivia looked at the massive blocks of blue stones. They really were amazing. Even Alison had to see that. Keeping Alison in tow, Olivia veered off the path toward the foundation. The grass tickled her thighs as they pushed through the chaotic shrubs.

"We're going to get poison ivy," Alison groaned

Olivia surveyed the foliage. "These are just regular garden plants that have grown out of control. I don't see anything bad. Maggie needs to hire a groundskeeper."

"Yeah? You tell her." Alison looked at her legs uneasily. "What about ticks? I don't need Lyme disease."

"We can check each other for ticks as soon as we're out of the grass."

"Ooh, tick check," Alison grumbled. "And I thought coming here would be boring."

"Hey, none of your sass. Now check these out." Olivia ran her hands along the uneven blocks. They felt bumpy, but her hand slid easily across the surface. "It feels almost soapy."

"Is that from the wind and storms and stuff?" Alison nodded down to the beach. "We are at the ocean."

"Maybe." Olivia felt the ridges in the stone. They were almost glassy. "Do you think these are natural stones?"

Alison chuckled. "You think somebody made these? Each one's the size of a truck."

Olivia rested her palms flat against the warm, uneven surface. "It's not ordinary rock."

"I'm not a geologist." Alison swatted some bugs from her face and huffed. "Are we going biking or not?"

Olivia's mind whirled, bouncing from articles she had read to websites she had visited. "Sapphires are just aluminum oxide, right? Somebody could have made them. They make synthetic gemstones."

"Yep. Somebody made gigantic sapphires and used them to build this place." Alison grabbed Olivia's shoulders and steered her back toward the path. "I don't want to pee in your ice cream or anything, but if this building is prehistoric, nobody was making rubies in a lab."

"Sapphires," Olivia only half-listened. She kept looking over her shoulder at the foundation of The Mansion, trying to figure out how and why somebody would make synthetic sapphires the size of railroad cars and then use them like building blocks.

Alison stepped around Olivia and led her more forcefully by the hand. "With the right pressure and temperature, giant sapphires could form in an asteroid. Then if that asteroid hit the Earth and people found it, cut it. I mean, it's possible."

"If an asteroid that big hit the Earth, wouldn't we find evidence or something?"

"Not if the crater got washed out by the ocean." Olivia liked the way her theory was taking shape.

"Okay, so a giant sapphire comes from an asteroid, and somehow ancient Native Americans figure out how to cut it up and build with it."

"Hey, ancient people built all kinds of stuff. Nobody knows who built Teotihuacán or Stonehenge. The pyramids, the Parthenon, all of it was built with no modern technology, but they have a mathematical precision that…"

"Again I ask: So?" Alison blew a hair off her face.

"So why did they do it? And why here? What was this place? A temple? A tomb? Before Colonel Coombs built The Mansion, what was this place?"

"Who's Colonel Coombs?" Alison stopped and turned to look at Olivia.

"The Confederate officer who fled the Union army. The guy Maggie was talking about. I read about him in the book last night while you were in the shower. Colonel Coombs used slaves and Union prisoners to build The Mansion, but the foundation was already here."

"Maybe it was aliens," Alison suggested.

"What?"

"It's like that show with that guy with the crazy hair. Every time there's any kind of mystery like how did they ever build the Hanging Temples of Babaganoosh or whatever, the guy always says aliens did it."

"Be serious!" Olivia laughed and stopped walking. "I'm just saying that suppose those blocks really are sapphires."

"They're not sapphires." Laughing, Alison dragged Olivia's wrist like a stubborn dog on a leash toward the stable.

"But suppose they are. Just ask yourself. Why would somebody go to the trouble of building something this big out of sapphires?"

"Maybe aliens buried a pharaoh here," Alison offered testily. Clearly she was getting bored. "Or maybe it's a temple to honor a god. No wait! They hid a spaceship!"

Olivia laughed. "Okay. Just forget it."

Alison let go of her wrist but kept walking toward the stable. "If I promise to keep talking about the alien sapphires, can we go biking?"

"No aliens."

"Hang on," Alison stopped. "You think that those blocks are giant sapphires that came from an asteroid."

"It's just my working hypothesis until I get better data." Olivia couldn't see how this wasn't obvious to Alison.

"So why not aliens?" Alison's hands were on her hips. She wanted an answer.

"You really should read Stephen Hawking."

"Don't give me that. Just tell me why you're allowed to believe in space sapphires, but I can't believe in aliens."

Olivia had to think about how she could take everything Stephen Hawking said and condense it into something she could explain before Alison lost interest. "Stephen Hawking says that first, if aliens really did visit Earth, it would be a lot like what happened when Columbus visited the Native Americans. The Americas were never the same after the Europeans came here, and it didn't turn out so good for the natives. So, if an advanced civilization found us, the chances are pretty good that we'd all know about it, and we would not be happy."

Alison stood there a moment with her face scrunched up thinking. "Okay, but what if they came here a long time ago and only found slime and bacteria or whatever. They thought the planet was basically empty, so they build the thing over there out of sapphires and left and just forgot about it." Her eyes opened wider. "Or maybe they're coming back for it someday. Maybe it's a monitoring system. Or a fuel station. Or a bathroom."

"Don't you think an advanced alien spaceship would have a bathroom on it?" Olivia laughed when she realized Alison was just busting her chops. But whether she knew it or not, Alison did have a fair point. "Okay. I admit that it's possible that aliens might have come a long time ago and thought this was an empty planet. But there are other reasons why aliens are unlikely." She started walking again toward the stable.

"I'm listening," Alison called from behind her.

Olivia was a little surprised that Alison wanted to talk about something so academic on vacation. Usually she was pretty firm about not mixing work and play. "For starters, there is absolutely no evidence to suggest that life is common; for all we know, the odds against life forming are so low, Earth might be the only planet in the whole galaxy, maybe even in the universe, that has any life on it at all. But even if life forms in other places, it's really unlikely for that life to evolve into something capable of space travel."

"Why?" Alison sounded impatient. Annoyed even.

"Because it takes so long for life to become intelligent. It took billions of years just to get multicellular organisms here on Earth. And billions more before there was anything close to intelligent life. And planets have a finite lifespan. And so many things can go wrong. And then, before a so-called intelligent life can figure out how to leave its home planet, there's a good chance it will destroy itself either through war or disease or pollution. We're not able to visit planets right in our own solar system. Do you know what it takes to go outside our solar system?"

"Who says we're that smart. Look around. People are basically morons. Maybe compared to intelligent aliens we're like monkeys. Or worms even."

Olivia laughed. "I guess you're right. Even if it's unlikely that aliens built the foundation of The Mansion, it's not technically impossible."

"This is it." It was an ordinary-looking concrete and wood barn. Alison stopped at the large, wooden double doors. They were probably white once, but the paint was faded and peeling. Everything looked old, but not as old as The Mansion. "I don't think it's made of sapphires."

"Funny," Olivia said, not laughing. She had been expecting Alison to say something like that.

The doors weren't locked. This surprised Olivia. They creaked as they swung outward. This didn't surprise her at all. Only a little dim light filtered in through the dirty windows, set high up in the walls. Concrete stalls lined both sides of the old building. She was distracted by the chittering and scratching of field mice all around them. At least Olivia hoped it was field mice. They stepped farther into the old stable. Little dust galaxies swirled in the blades of yellow light that sliced the shadows.

"Look," Alison called, laughing and moving wide-eyed from stall to stall checking out the bikes in each one. The first stall was filled with small tricycles for young children. The next one had antique velocipedes with giant front wheels.

"This is amazing," Olivia whispered. Biking was one thing she always looked forward to doing with her dad. He would have loved this place. "It's like a bicycle museum."

"Or a graveyard," Alison said. She suddenly sounded less enthusiastic, gesturing toward the dusty racing bikes covered in cobwebs. "Look at these bikes. We're not going to be able to ride anything in here." Alison put her hands on her hips. "Look how janky these are."

Olivia led the way to the next stall. Racing bikes were not going to be comfortable if they just wanted to ride around for fun. "They're just dusty, and they need a little maintenance."

"The tires are all flat." Alison pushed a bike away in disgust.

Kneeling to check the tire, Olivia didn't see any damage and the rubber looked okay. "Tires lose air after awhile. It's probably been years since anybody touched these. Help me find a pump." Olivia walked back toward the long, wooden worktable near the door. The tool rack was well stocked and there were tons of spare parts in the drawers and on the shelves. "These are great tools. We can get anything we want here. Trust me."

"I think this pump works," Alison said, coughing in the dust she blew off the pump in her hand.

"Perfect," Olivia said. She could feel her confidence swelling. "While you're there, check that cabinet for some chain lube. And something to dust them."

Rummaging through drawers, Alison screamed, "Eew! Big spider! Big spider! Big, nasty spider!" Olivia laughed as Alison thumped and swatted the big, nasty spider away with a cloth. "You can really get these working?" Alison asked. She sounded doubtful "I know you fix tires and chains and stuff, but these look pretty bad."

"They're not that bad, and anyway I can fix just about anything with the stuff they have in here. My dad showed me." Olivia felt so happy that Alison was impressed. She made a mental note to thank her father the next time she saw him. "Let's find some bikes."

25 HEALING

Working together it didn't take long to clean up from breakfast. If Michael had been doing the dishes with Mom or Alison, it would have been torture, but not with Maggie.

"Are you okay?" Maggie finished drying the coffee pot and placed it into a cabinet.

She had caught him off guard. "Huh? Yeah, why?"

"You keep scratching." Little worry lines creased her forehead.

Reflexively, he moved his hands to his sides. The bites were gross, and he'd hoped she wouldn't notice. He must have been scratching them without realizing it.

"Are those bug bites? They look bad."

"They're all right." Michael felt like he was under a microscope. "They itch a lot, but not all the time. It comes and goes. I'm fine."

Great. Now she probably thinks I'm a dirty, hippie, emo punk with herpes.

"I've got a really good lotion upstairs." Maggie lowered her voice. Her eyes sparkled. "Secret recipe."

That wasn't what the girls he knew at school would have said. They would have just been grossed out. Maggie made his insides wiggle. "I'm okay. Really."

Smiling, she patted his shoulder. "I know you're a big tough guy, but it's just a little lotion to help with the itching. I promise not to give you a facial or a mani-pedi. But I might have to pluck your eyebrows a little."

"What's wrong with my eyebrows?" Michael squirmed, feeling sheepish and self-conscious.

Maggie laughed, and then wrinkled her forehead again as she examined the bites on his arm more closely. "You got eaten alive. Where were you?"

By the time they got back to Maggie's room, Michael had finished the whole epic of the bird and the windshield. He left out any details he figured would make her think he was nuts. Still, when he mentioned the huge bird he got a weird look on her face, almost like she was afraid—maybe of him. Maybe she thought he was crazy. So, when he moved on to talk about the road kill he didn't mention the tentacles.

"I don't know. It was all decomposed and nasty. Probably just a deer. Maybe a bear. It was pretty big." Michael did not think he needed to elaborate. The more he thought about it, the more convinced he was that Dad was right. Too much adrenaline. Monster birds and bugs? How stupid! But even if Alison was right about perception creating reality or whatever it was she'd been babbling about, he still wasn't paying her.

Leading him into her bathroom, Maggie puckered her lips with a puzzled smile and arched her eyebrow in that way that Michael was starting to find irresistible. "I still don't understand. Why did your father get out of the car in the first place?"

"Because he's nuts?" Michael felt warm when Maggie laughed. He hated girls who never laughed. But he had to make sure she knew he was a man's man. "It wasn't all my dad. I wanted to check out the bird, too. You should have seen the hole it made in the windshield. I had to know what did it, right?"

Maggie talked into the large medicine cabinet. "Birds have hollow bones to help them fly. I can't believe a bird could put a hole in the windshield of a car. Was the windshield cracked before?"

Michael hadn't thought of that. It cast even more doubts onto his jumbled memory. "I don't think so."

"So did you ever figure out what kind of bird it was?"

Maybe she thought he was just trying to impress her. He really wanted to keep the conversation going, but he couldn't think of anything to say that wouldn't sound psycho. "What am I a birdologist? It was like some kind of vulture I guess. Condor maybe?"

"Ornithologist."

"What?"

"Forget it. We don't have condors in Cape November."

Michael took a page from Mom's playbook. "Hey, cool cabinet." It was old, but well cared for. Michael admired the hundreds of seashells of various shapes, colors and sizes stuck to the edges.

Maggie scowled, "It's so cheesy. I made it when I was little. It helped me get over...it was a craft project I did when I was sick."

"What'd you have mono or something?"

Maggie sighed heavily and studied Michael's face for a long moment. "It was after my parents died." Maggie tightened her lips and opened the cabinet. "I had a lot of anxiety and stuff."

The nightmares. Michael could tell that this was difficult for her. He didn't want to push her, but he had to say something. "I'm sorry about your parents. I didn't know."

Maggie looked at him and smiled weakly. "How could you? It's not like I wear a sign that says Dead Parents."

"Right." Michael forced a chuckle, but he felt embarrassed and uncomfortable. He ran his hand over the bumps of the shells on the side of the cabinet. A small, round shell broke off in his fingers, and Michael felt like the floor dropped out from under him. "Oh crap. I'm really sorry."

Maggie laughed and set the shell on the counter. "No worries. They come off all the time. I told you, I was little when I made it."

"It must have taken forever to glue all these shells on."

"Uncle Max took this cabinet off the wall and brought it to the hospital. He came to visit me all the time, and he brought tools so we could refinish it. It was a mess. After we stained it, he brought me a hot glue gun and my whole shell collection in all these boxes. I had a huge shell collection when I was a kid." Maggie smiled a little. "The staff didn't like it, but you don't argue with Uncle Max."

"Who's Uncle Max?"

"Yeah." Maggie's shoulders rocked a little as she laughed. "He's not really my uncle. I just called him that. He was my Aunt Penny's boyfriend. They took care of me after the accident. After my parents…" Her body seemed to wilt a little.

In the mirror, Michael found her eyes. He felt lost. He was curious about her and he wanted her to know that he cared, but he also did not want to push her. "So they…broke up? Your Uncle Max and Aunt Penny."

"It's not that simple." Penny said.

Michael sensed a change in Maggie. She slumped. Defeated. "You liked him, huh?"

"I loved him. I still do." Sighing impatiently, Maggie said, "I'm sorry. I don't like to talk about it." Her voice sounded hard. Final.

"Sure. No problem." Michael felt her words as if she'd physically pushed him back. "Look, you're probably busy." He started to back out of the bathroom. "Don't even worry about the cream. The bites are fine. Really."

He felt an excited flutter when she turned from the cabinet to look at him. "Just because I don't want to talk about all that stuff that makes me sad doesn't mean I don't want to keep talking to you." Her eyes sparkled and her lips looked soft and inviting.

Usually, Michael avoided talking about anything serious, especially to girls he was trying to pick up. But Maggie made his insides flutter. "I like talking to you, too."

"Good." She smiled and motioned for him to come back to the sink.

The wooden shelves inside the cabinet were also encrusted with thousands of tiny seashells. Michael marveled at the time and patience it must have taken to glue every one into place.

Maggie snatched up one small tube from a crowded shelf. "You don't have oily skin, do you?"

"Uh…not as far as *you* know." Jokes are good. Familiar ground.

Maggie put the tube back and continued rummaging, calling out the items in a quiet singsong. "These are for my anxiety. Ingrown toenail—yuck. This is a great moisturizer. Want me to do a quick mud mask on you?"

"No thanks. I'm trying to quit."

She laughed again. *Doing great. Keep it going.*

Snatching up a prescription bottle, Maggie looked at it like something alien.

126

"I thought I threw out all my ziprasidone a long time ago."

Craning his neck to see, Michael read the label. "What's it for?"

"Don't ask." She tossed the bottle into the small wicker trash beside the toilet and pulled a small glass jar off a shelf. "Here's the cream." Unscrewing the lid, she said, "Now this stuff isn't hydrocortisone. I made it myself from local plants. It was part of a research project I did for a class last year. It's great for rashes, burns, poison ivy, bug bites, you name it."

Michael caught himself scratching and put his hands firmly to his sides. "Whatever, so long as it works."

Maggie leaned Michael up against the sink. She dabbed her finger into the jar and scooped out a blob of the brownish paste. "You're not allergic to anything, are you? Marigold? Sunflower? Walnut?"

"No." There was a tremor of doubt as Michael stared at the glob on the end of Maggie's finger. "So how did you learn how to make this stuff?" He tried to keep his voice deep and not let it crack. It sort of worked.

Maggie laughed. "Relax. I told you. I researched Lenape medicine mostly, plus some other homeopathic medicines."

"Who?"

"The Lenape were the natives that lived in the Eastern Woodlands. Here."

"So this is witch doctor stuff?"

Maggie looked at him harshly. "You know, just because it didn't come out of the white European patriarchy doesn't mean it's bad." Her face softened. "I use this cream all the time." Maggie tilted her head, crossed her eyes and stuck out her tongue.

Michael laughed and stopped caring whether the cream was safe to use as soon as Maggie leaned against him and took his arm in her hand. Her grip was firm, stronger than he expected, and the cream was surprisingly cold. The tiny poke of her finger sent a wonderful electric shiver through his body.

"Sorry I snapped at you before." Like a nurse, Maggie matter-of-factly held his arm and dabbed ointment onto each little red welt. It felt like she might have been squeezing his muscles, but it could have been Michael's imagination.

"I get it," he said. His breath came a little quicker when Maggie turned to face him fully as he leaned against the sink. He thought about leaning in and kissing her right there, but decided that was a bad idea. He could feel nothing but the warmth and the weight of her as she leaned against him, gently dabbing the ointment at each tiny bite. He could feel the gentle rise and fall of the breath in her body as he fell into her deep, brown eyes.

"You should know that I'm complicated. I've got a lot of baggage." Barely above a whisper, her voice came husky. Michael hated talking about stuff like this. He never knew what to say.

Maggie went back to dabbing his arms. Michael let her work for a while, focusing on the silk caress of her hair brushing his arm as she bent over him, her forehead creased with concentration. Her fingers gripped his arm firmly. The supple press of her body against him was like a blanket. She was the coolest girl he had ever met, but there was something else there. Something secret. Mr. Rajai's words came back to him. "A journalist has to be objective." But Mr. Rajai probably never did an interview with a girl like Maggie leaning on him.

Maggie stopped and stepped away from him. She looked afraid. Up until that moment, Maggie had been confidently in charge of everything.

"Are you okay?"

"My parents died when I was nine," she said quietly. Michael had not been expecting to go back to that.

"We were downstairs in the sitting room. Me and my parents were watching TV. We didn't watch television much, especially not in the summer, but there were no guests. It was late in the season. And my mom wanted to watch the news because of Hurricane Katrina. They had just called for the evacuation of New Orleans. I remember that part. It was a long time ago, and my memories from that night are messed up. I don't remember things right. Teams of doctors have spent years telling me that my memories of that night are mostly delusions brought on by trauma. That I probably dreamed a lot of it and then believed the memories of my dreams were actual memories." Maggie laughed. "After awhile, how would you know, right? Especially when you're nine and your parents just got killed."

Michael shrugged. "Dreams usually don't make sense."

Maggie laughed. "And reality makes sense?"

Michael thought about the dead thing with tentacles he could have sworn he saw on the side of the road.

Maggie shook her head. "I don't even know why I'm telling you all this. I don't even know you."

"Maybe that's why."

She looked up at him. Her eyes were wet. "It's like I have this thing inside me, these memories that are trying to come out, like they want to be born, except I don't know if they are really my memories. All the doctors say they're not. The medication was supposed to make it stop, but it doesn't work so I stopped taking it. But that just made the weird memories even stronger. But if they aren't memories, just delusions, that makes sense, right?" Maggie laughed nervously. "I mean, the medication is supposed to stop the delusions, but I stopped taking the medication so the delusions keep coming, right? Except what if they're not delusions?"

Michael tried to imagine what Maggie felt. Sitting on the lid of the toilet, she looked smaller. Fragile. Even when he had woken her up from her nightmare, she looked so strong. So confident. It's what made him like her in the first place. That was gone now, like it had been sucked out of her, leaving a trembling husk. Alone with her, Michael felt responsible for her, but he was helpless to protect her. And she seemed pretty capable of protecting herself. But he was afraid for her. Or maybe he was afraid of her. "You don't have to talk about this."

She looked up with wet eyes, but then she smiled. "Sorry. But it helps me to talk about it. Can't you tell?" Her laugh was wet and honking. Behind him, she must have found her own face in the mirror. She shut her eyes with a dramatic shiver. "Yikes! I can't believe I'm letting you see me like this."

Michael was glad the storm was blowing over. "I've seen worse."

Standing to her full height, the Greek goddess was back. "When a lady says she doesn't feel good about herself, a gentleman could say something sweet and positive to build her back up."

His swagger flexed inside him. "Okay. I'm positive I've seen worse."

Laughing, she punched his shoulder. It hurt. She was strong. "We had a deal. You did the dishes, so now I'm going to take you snorkeling."

The sudden turn made Michael feel a little lost, but he was letting Maggie call the shots. "I just figured you punked out or something."

He put up his arms defensively when she cocked her fist again. She punched him twice in the shoulder, more gently this time. "Two for ducking." Laughing, she grabbed his shoulders firmly and steered him toward the door, then playfully shoved him out. "Get changed. And don't touch the bites." She closed the door. Michael stood in the stairwell alone.

26 CRUISING

Alison hated the helmet Olivia was forcing her to wear. She had cleaned it obsessively, but it still felt dusty and her head itched. She was convinced an army of spiders was laying eggs in her hair by the minute, and forget about what her hair was going to look like when she took the stupid thing off. But Olivia started in with her horror stories about brain-damaged cyclists her father knew who had to spend the rest of their lives taking their meals through a straw, and that was that. If Alison wanted to ride with Olivia, then she had to wear a helmet. Olivia could be so stubborn about stuff like that.

Alison was amazed at the number of bikes and all the different types. There were sleek racing bikes, tough-looking mountain bikes with huge, knobby wheels. Classic beach cruisers, BMX stunt bikes. One stall had enough unicycles to supply a small circus. Some had tiny wheels and seats that were barely a foot off the ground while others towered eight feet. They lasted a few seconds each on one of the smaller ones and decided not to risk broken bones on one of the big ones.

Just for fun they took a few turns on one of the old-fashioned bikes with the giant wheel in front. Alison got it going pretty well—until she wiped out in some bushes. Olivia did better and made two whole laps, but then she could not figure out how to get off, so she just fell over in a laughing heap.

There was one gigantic tricycle that had a huge padded seat that looked like a couch. It was covered in streamers and sequins and plush padding. Riders sat side by side like a pedal boat. After a few laps around the lawn, they decided it was too slow and heavy, and they would probably not get very far on it.

Alison found a stall with the kind of practical, ordinary bikes sold in most bike shops. After all of the other bikes they tested though, these ordinary bicycles seemed a little dull. They explored a few more stalls until Olivia found a low-slung, purple and white chopper with a massive back wheel and a skinny tire on an extended, raked, chrome fork up front.

In minutes, Olivia had it fixed up. She walked the chopper out front, swung her leg over the white-flamed, purple banana saddle and took hold of the high-rise handlebars that streamed with purple and white silk ribbons. The purple and chrome pedals were set forward, so that she had to lean back slightly to ride, with her lower back supported by the raised part of the saddle. Olivia grinned and adjusted the cross-shaped rearview mirrors. "Oh yeah. Check it."

"That's awesome," Alison grinned. "But I still can't decide."

"Well, hurry up!" Olivia clucked her teeth with fake, exaggerated impatience. "I need to ride this thing."

"Don't rush me; I want to get one I'll like." As she spoke, Alison found exactly what she'd been looking for. It was a classic beach cruiser in light blue. The full-vented chrome fenders in front and back came halfway down the dark-blue, spoked wheels. It looked like it was in decent shape, except that its fat, white-wall tires needed air.

"Ooh," Olivia said as she examined the tire. "The tube is cracked."

Alison felt a lead weight of disappointment, but Olivia cheerfully rummaged through some of the drawers in the worktable until she found a supply of new inner tubes, still in their boxes. Olivia found the right size and changed it out in a couple of minutes while Alison watched in amazement.

Olivia stood up grinning. "Done!" She wiped the grease off her hands on a shop towel. "Thanks for your help, by the way. I couldn't have done it without you."

Alison felt a twinge of guilt. "Sorry. I guess I spaced out a little."

"Aliens?" Olivia tossed the rag at her.

Alison caught it and tossed it back. "Bite me!" she laughed.

Olivia made Alison help her clean and lubricate the chain before Alison could mount the plush, leather apple-shaped seat that floated on a pair of chrome springs. The chrome handlebars curved up gracefully and allowed Alison to sit in a comfortable riding position.

"Let's roll," Alison called. The sun was warm on her, and she felt happier and more free than she had all day.

Leaving The Mansion, she had taken the lead down the driveway through the woods. Even in daylight it was full of shadows. Thorny tangles of underbrush seemed to want to pull the huge trees down to lie with the logs that lay in rot, covered in white and red platters of fungus. The only sound came from the crunch of their tires over the gravel as they navigated around large puddles.

In the daylight, the streets were easier to navigate. When they arrived at the boardwalk, Alison felt relaxed. The ride had helped to clear her head, to give her time to think and to sort through her tangle of feelings. Alison stopped her bike and looked out at the sun sparkling on the blue ocean. The surf rolled in a strong, gentle rhythm. The sky was so blue it hurt her eyes.

Great! The awesome sunglasses I bought for this trip are still in my bag. After riding hard through the cool of the woods, Alison felt the heat drying the perspiration on her bare shoulders and arms.

"You're not tired already, are you?" Olivia asked, giving her a playful poke on the shoulder.

"No," Alison felt a little self-conscious about not being in shape like Olivia, no matter how much Olivia tried to downplay it. "It's just really pretty here."

"Would you rather go to the beach?" Olivia asked.

Alison considered going back, getting into some bathing suits and lying on a beach. She could take a nap.

"Earth to Alison," Olivia laughed. "Do you want to head back and go for a swim or keep riding?"

"We did all this work to get the bikes. Let's keep riding," she said simply. "We can swim after lunch." She looked at Olivia out of the tops of her eyes, "You're not going to make me wait an hour after I eat, are you?"

"Shut up," Olivia laughed. "Besides, that's a myth. No, the only other naggy thing I'm going to say is that there's no shade here and we don't have any sunscreen. We're going to fry." She leaned back in the purple banana saddle of her bicycle and pedaled down the boardwalk.

In between rounds of anagrams, they laughed and talked about school—the past, not the future. Neither of them brought up Ashton Academy, Alison's parents, creepy men, aliens, snow globes, giant sapphires, weird bugs or weird birds. If any thought like that threatened to break into the conversation, Alison would pick a nearby landmark and challenge Olivia to race to it, but only halfheartedly. Alison knew she was no match for Olivia. She just felt happy to be riding with her, feeling the warm air blowing past her face and ruffling her hair under the stupid helmet and talking about nothing at all.

They didn't pass many houses along the boardwalk. The ones they did pass mostly looked abandoned and boarded up. Sometimes Alison saw shadows through windows in houses that had people still in them, but there weren't many of those. Once Alison saw an old woman sitting on her steps. She looked poor and dirty, and she looked up at Alison without smiling. It could have just been the wrinkles on her face, but Alison would have sworn the old woman had given her a cold sneer. She reminded Alison of the old woman in the gift shop.

Further along the boardwalk, the motels were mostly collapsed. The few that weren't were dark and needed a lot of fixing up if anybody was ever going to stay there again. Alison didn't think that was likely. A few buildings were just charred skeletons. The air near these still smelled of smoke.

The shops, arcades and stalls were closed, and most of them were boarded up, too. A flash of movement caught Alison's eye. It was in the remains of a miniature golf course, smashed mostly to rubble. A few gorillas looked like they were trying to claw their way out of the sand that buried them. Alison noticed some movement around the splintered boards. Three, maybe four, children, small and dirty, played among the debris. My mother would have a heart attack.

"Whoa!" Olivia startled Alison. She had to stomp on her foot brake to keep her beach cruiser from smacking into Olivia's rear tire. "Check this out." Olivia stood straddling her chopper and pointed.

"Whoa," Alison agreed. In front of them a huge section of the boardwalk had been torn away, and there was a long drop down to the sand below. "If we'd have fallen in there…"

"This boardwalk is pretty messed up." Olivia shook her head. "It sure doesn't look like it did in the picture book."

Alison squinted and shaded her eyes with her hand to see the ruins on the other side of the gap. They didn't look any different from the ruins on their own side of the gap. More scorched hotels and wrecked shops. Houses shattered, half-eaten by time and getting slowly buried by sand. Probably more scowling old ladies and raggedy little kids. "We've been riding for more than an hour. Want to just head back?"

27 INVESTIGATIVE JOURNALIST

In his room, Michael threw on black trunks, a bright yellow tank top and sunglasses. From his bag, he pulled out his new camera. It was still fully charged, so he swapped out the regular lens for the fisheye since everything he had read about underwater photography said to shoot wide. On the second try, the underwater housing sealed correctly. At least Michael hoped it did. Dad had told him he would regret spending all his savings from mowing lawns on the underwater camera housing, since now he had no money to take to college. Dad also pointed out that Michael knew nothing about underwater photography, and was probably going to destroy his camera.

Dad will rip my head off and plant tomatoes down my neck if anything happens to this camera. But it won't. Maybe I never did this before, but there's a little thing called the Internet, Dad, maybe you've heard of it. When I post pictures of me and Maggie underwater, Vito and Zaprisky and all my other friends can suck it. They've probably been blowing my phone up, just to give me crap about this lame trip Mom dragged me on. But wait until I post pictures of Maggie. They're gonna pop their bubble wrap. If the sucky phone service ever comes back.

Sliding into his flip-flops, he swung by his parents' room and knocked to tell his mother that he was going, but she wasn't there. He thought about leaving a note, but decided that by the time she got it, he'd be back. Next year in college he wouldn't be checking in with her every five seconds, so she might as well get used to it. He was about to run back up to Maggie's room, but then decided that would make him look like a desperate stalker. Playing it cool, he headed down to wait in the lobby.

He sat down, first in one chair and then another. He felt jittery and nervous and thought about running his camera back upstairs. *I don't know anything about snorkeling or underwater photography, and I don't want to blow this date. Calm down. It's not a date. It's just something fun to do with a cool chick. Who happens to be amazingly hot.*

Looking around the lobby for a distraction, he decided to check for a soda behind the bar. Finding nothing, he decided he was better off. Caffeine and sugar would only amp him up more. He sat on a barstool. That didn't feel right so he crossed over a sofa. His butt was barely on the seat when he thought that Maggie might think he was trying to get her to sit with him on the sofa and that would make him look like a total creeper. Finally, he settled himself into one of the leather easy chairs—only room for one unless she wanted to sit in his lap. *Really? It's like that? Just chill.*

He clicked on the tall, antique floor lamp beside the chair, but nothing happened. The power was still out. He spotted a copy of the *Cape November News* on the table next to the chair. It was a few days old, but it would still be news to Michael.

Absently he leafed through the sections, but he couldn't focus. Maggie had said something about when a lady does this, a gentleman should do that. He wondered whether she was expecting him to pick her up at her room. She just said to get changed. And then she basically slammed the door in my face. *Stop being so emo.*

Reasoning that the whole mansion was technically her house, he decided to stay where he was. If it were a normal house he would be waiting in the living room, not going up to her bedroom. *Just keep waiting. She's coming. Eventually.*

She was taking her sweet time. Weren't they just going snorkeling? It's not like she needed to do her make-up or whatever it was that women did that took forever getting ready for stuff. He and Dad had to wait in their tuxedos for hours before Mom and Alison finished getting dressed for cousin Rebecca's wedding. But Maggie didn't seem like she was into all that girly stuff. That was one of the things Michael liked about her. Anxiety suddenly clawed at him. *She's upset in the bathroom. I should see if she's okay. Maybe that's what she wants. This might be some kind of test. Forget it. I don't need to get with some head case who's into games.*

Chill! What did Doc O'Brien say all the time in physics? Appreciate the now. It's all we got.

A headline caught Michael's eye: "Cape November News Closing Its Doors After More Than a Century."

Propping his sunglasses up on his head, Michael read the article. *Cape November News* was only a small local paper. There wasn't enough staff. Readership was way down. There it was. All the reasons Mr. Rajai said that cause local papers to close. Then he noticed something else. Another reason for the closure was the disappearance of staff reporter Elizabeth Bromley Denton.

Way to bury your lead, guys. That's no way to sell papers. Michael reread the article and saw that it referenced the other front page story: Cape November News Reporter and Husband Missing along with Editor in Chief."

> *Elizabeth Bromley Denton, staff reporter for the* Cape November News *for the past fifteen years, has been reported missing along with her husband, Stephen Denton, a local graphics designer. Also missing, the paper's editor in chief Jose Pereira. Leading the investigation is Sheriff Charles McGill.*

Michael held the paper up to get a better look at the photo. It was the same cop who pulled Mom over on the highway. The coincidence made Michael's skin crawl. *Take it easy. Probably not that many cops down here.*

Curious, he kept reading.

Denton is best known for her syndicated exposé: Lost in Cape November. Denton explores the strange disappearances occurring in or around Cape November during the last decade and possibly stretching into the last century. Denton's exposé was considered controversial by some for implying a connection between these disappearances and The Church of New Enlightenment in Cape November. (See Lost, Cape November News Archive Vol. 8 May Issue 16).

That's why Maggie freaked out when Dad asked about mass murders. There were no murders, but there have been these strange disappearances.

Michael read on.

When asked whether there was a connection between these three latest disappearances and the CNE, McGill said, "Right now, the worst thing I can do is speculate. Look, last month there were a number of murders in New York City. The president was also visiting the United Nations. Are all those events connected? Did the president kill those New Yorkers? Maybe you reporters should go check it out."

Except they wouldn't check it out. The paper was out of business and a reporter, her husband and the editor in chief were all missing.

The sudden slap of Maggie's flip-flops behind him startled him. He gave a little cry, and she laughed. In spite of his very conscious effort to be mature and not to act like a total creep, Michael's eyes kept getting pulled like paperclips to Maggie's magnetic curves and smooth, tanned thighs peeking out from the opening of the white wrap that covered her from her chest to her knees. Under her arms, she carried two large towels and a small beach bag.

Her long, chestnut hair was in a braided ponytail like silk rope. Grinning, she popped down the sunglasses that had been propped up on her head. "Ready?"

Nearly jumping out of his seat, Michael knocked into the antique floor lamp that probably cost more than his parents' minivan. Catching it before it hit the floor, Michael laughed nervously. "Good thing I have cat-like reflexes."

Struggling to straighten the lampshade, he glanced over at Maggie. She looked like she was holding back a laugh. She let it go when Michael yelped and jumped back as the light bulb flashed. There was a sizzling spark, and the lamp went dark, sending up a tendril of gray smoke. Michael smiled sheepishly at Maggie. "I guess the power's back on."

Maggie laughed. "Now I have to add a light bulb to that bill you're working off."

When she led him past the stable, Michael noticed the open door and the bikes lying on the grass like sleeping cows.

Maggie must have noticed him staring at the bikes. "Would you rather go biking?"

The promise of Maggie in a swimsuit was too close. "We already got changed for snorkeling," he said. "Plus, I can go biking anytime."

Maggie smiled warmly. "You're the guest."

Out on the jetty, the blue-gray stones of the lighthouse towered like a giant's sandcastle rising majestically over the yellow sand of the beach and the stately procession of blue-gray blocks that shaped the jetty.

Michael would have been the first to admit that he knew nothing about architecture, but there was something unusual about the lighthouse. Like somebody plucked it out of some Aztec rainforest. "So how old is this lighthouse?"

"The top part that used to be a lighthouse was built by the Navy during World War I. That's the part that blew up." Maggie looked down at the sand. "That was the accident. The night my parents died."

Maggie was so matter-of-fact about it. Michael stopped walking.

Noticing, Maggie stopped, too. "What?"

"Your parents."

"Yeah?" Maggie nodded. "What about them?"

"It's just...before you sounded more..."

"Upset?" Maggie almost sounded like she was going to laugh. "I know. You know, grief is weird. I mean, my parents died ten years ago. Sometimes it feels like it was a hundred years ago, like it happened to somebody else and not to me. And if you think about it, I'm so different from that nine-year-old girl, it might as well have been somebody else. Other times it feels like it's happening now. Sorry if my grief doesn't meet your expectations."

Michael felt stung. "I didn't mean—you can feel however you need to feel."

"Gee, thanks. I didn't realize I needed permission."

"That's not what I meant." He thought about jumping on a bike and catching up to Alison. "Maybe we should forget snorkeling."

Maggie's angry expression broke into a grin. "Why are you so uptight?" The grin warmed into a genuine smile. "I don't talk about it that often."

"Are you ever going to tell me what's really going on?" Michael said it firmly.

Maggie looked a little startled. "What do you mean?"

"About your parents. About this place."

She looked out at the ocean. "That's a lot to tell."

Michael watched a wave roll and splash against the rocks. "We're going to have a lot of time."

"You're right." Maggie started walking again. Michael was happy to stay and watch her walk for a moment before he followed.

"I come out here all the time." Maggie spoke over her shoulder. "I feel closer to my parents when I come here. Like I'm visiting them."

Talking with Maggie was like walking through a funhouse. Michael never knew what would pop out next. It was a little scary, but he liked it. And he really wanted it to be okay to like her.

"Why does your painting show this tower exploding? Is that part of it? Part of the story about your parents?"

Maggie nodded and kept walking. Michael wished he could have seen her face to get an idea of her expression. "Painting is all part of the healing process." She made air quotes with her fingers. "Hey, thanks for listening to me. I know I'm a pain. A lot of guys don't have your patience."

That might have been the coolest thing a girl had ever said to him. He felt like he could fly. "I like hanging out with you. Everybody's got baggage, right? You heard my family drama earlier and didn't judge me."

Maggie led Michael toward the three huge stones at the shoreline near the end of the jetty opposite the tower. One huge block lay flat across two massive uprights. The blocks reminded him of pictures of Stonehenge. There was an ordinary-looking brick hut that had been built within the three stones. The wall facing Michael had a wooden door.

"How come the hut looks like regular brick?" he asked.

Maggie seemed happy with Michael's observation. "The dolmen is as old as everything else, but somebody, possibly Colonel Coombs, built the hut under the dolmen. I don't know what Coombs used it for—slave quarters maybe? We use it as a boathouse."

Michael's head was swimming. "What's a dolmen?"

"If you were a folklore major you'd know." Maggie laughed. "It's that. The three megaliths, the big stones, in that square arch shape. They're found all over the world." She dropped her voice, sounding mysterious. "Some people call them portal tombs."

Michael considered that. If you took away the brick hut, the three stones would look like a big doorway. "Portal to where?"

Maggie laughed. "The afterlife? The spirit world? An alternate universe of unicorns and llamas? Who knows?" Approaching the more ordinary-looking wall and door that had been built into the stone entranceway, Maggie rifled through the beach bag looking for her keys.

Michael looked at the dolmen and then turned to look at the blue-gray blocks of the jetty and the foundation of The Mansion. "So nobody knows who built any of this?" He absently removed his shirt.

"My grandfather was looking into it."

"Was that his hobby or something?"

Maggie shook her head. "Not exactly. For now, The Mansion is just one of history's mysteries." Maggie's voice faded a bit. Was she staring at Michael's chest? She seemed to notice Michael looking at her and suddenly found something in her bag that must have been super important because she started digging like crazy. Her cheeks looked a little red. "Uh... I hope you brought sunscreen."

Michael smiled. *So she is into me.* "I figured since we were going to be under water I didn't need any."

Maggie smiled thinly back at him, "You still need sunscreen. You want a sunburn on top of your fly bites? I don't have enough cream for all that." She gestured up and down his body with her finger.

"I'll be okay. You fixed the fly bites." It was true. Already the itch was gone, and the sores were not nearly so red. Whatever that cream was, it had worked.

"I have plenty of sunscreen. You can borrow some."

"So when I'm done, what? I scrape it off and give it back?" She didn't look up. Maybe lame jokes were the wrong approach.

"If you're going to be a smart-ass about it I should l just let you fry." Maggie turned up her mouth wryly and unlocked the metal door to the boathouse. Inside it smelled like damp sea breezes, tar and old wood. It was as dark as a cave until Maggie switched on the overhead lights.

"I guess the Lenape didn't install the lights either?"

"Sure they did. They just ran down to Lodge Depot and popped them right in." Maggie stepped toward the back of a weathered rowboat. "Can you give me a hand pulling out the dory?"

"Is that what people are calling it now?" *On a roll!*

Maggie blushed a little and wrinkled her mouth like she was annoyed. "Don't be gross. Just help me with the boat."

"You named your boat Dory?"

Maggie chuckled. "A dory is this type of boat. See the high sides? That was so fishermen could fill it up with fish. The flat bottom makes it easy to pull up onto the beach, even when it's full of fish."

"So the Pilgrims used it for waterskiing or something?"

Maggie laughed as she climbed around to the back of the boat. "I should warn you, it's pretty heavy." She grabbed the sides of the boat and indicated that Michael should also.

She was right. The boat was heavier than he thought, but Michael knew he could manage it. He was impressed by how strong Maggie was. She seemed to hold up her end effortlessly. Michael figured she must have had a lot of practice carrying this thing in and out of here. Michael grunted a little as they maneuvered the boat through the narrow door. "And you're sure this thing isn't going to sink, right?"

"Why? Can't you swim?" Maggie grinned. Michael noticed that she wasn't grunting at all. "Relax. The boat works fine. It's just old like everything else down here."

"You're not old," Michael offered.

"Aunt Penny says I was born old. That I have an old soul."

They set down the boat in front of the boathouse. Michael pushed his sunglasses a little down his nose and looked at her over the top of them. "Your soul looks pretty good to me," he offered with a grin.

Maggie blushed slightly as she smiled. That made Michael a little weak in the knees. He was glad he wasn't still carrying the boat. "C'mon," she said. "Let's get the rest of the gear."

Maggie ducked back into the boathouse and had Michael wait outside while she tossed out a cooler full of bottles of water, snorkels, masks, flippers, floating seat cushions and a small plastic box labeled emergency kit. As Michael caught each item he tossed it into the bottom of the dory.

"It's nice to have a mate," Maggie said, coming out of the boathouse with a huge orange flashlight in her hand.

"Mates like wild animals? Or like pirates?"

"Definitely not like wild animals, and if you keep up the gross jokes I'll make you walk the plank." Maggie laughed and threw the flashlight sharply at Michael's chest. He fumbled, but caught it before it hit the ground.

"I knew what you meant. Sorry." Michael looked at the flashlight in his hands. It was long and orange with a large, round lens. "Did you pull this out of a truck?"

"Anytime you go out on the ocean, you should be prepared for anything Mother Nature might throw at you."

"Like what? An eclipse? I thought we were only going out by the lighthouse," Michael wondered if Maggie was just showing off for him. If so, he did not mind.

"We are." Maggie smiled. "Semper Paratus."

Michael lit up inside. "You like Sharknado?"

Maggie's mouth hung open. "It's the motto of the US Coast Guard."

Michael deflated a little.

Maggie nodded at Michael's camera. "Anyway, sometimes there are cool fish down deep in the shadows. You'll get better pictures with a light. If you get a shot of Cappy, you'll be famous."

Michael laughed. "Your Cape November sea monster?"

Maggie looked surprised. "You know about that? A lot of Bennies don't."

Michael felt like it was an insult, but he wasn't sure. "Bennies?"

Maggie laughed. "Tourists from up north. We call them Bennies. Or Shoobies because they wear shoes on the beach." She looked over the stuff in the bottom of the dory. "Now. Is there anything else you can think of?"

Michael shrugged. "I'm no expert since I've never done this before, so this is only a guess, but I think we might need a couple of oars."

Maggie laughed, "Oh yeah that might help." She turned back inside and came out a moment later with two long oars. After placing them into the boat she said, "You should probably leave your shirt and your flip-flops here. If the boat tips over, you'll just end up losing them."

Michael smiled nervously, "Wow. That's a great line. I'm going to start using that one."

Maggie scowled playfully at him. "Don't get any ideas about this. I'm just your tour guide."

Michael raised his hands like he was warding off any more of her anger about his wisecracks. "Don't worry. I don't have any ideas other than not drowning. Does the boat usually tip over?"

"I wouldn't say usually." Maggie laughed. "It's pretty hard to tip a dory. That's why we use it out here." She untied her sarong and let it drop, "but better safe than sorry."

Michael tried hard not to stare at Maggie's sporty, light blue bikini. A small, black skull and crossbones was embroidered over the left hip. Kicking off her flip-flops she asked, "Ready?"

"Absolutely." Michael wanted to draw attention away from the attention her bikini was drawing from him, so he added, "I'm super stoked to snorkel."

Maggie laughed. "You're such a dork."

28 STRANGER DANGER

"I can't believe I forgot to take water," Olivia groaned as they walked their bikes back along the boardwalk. Her throat was dry. As an athlete, she knew how important it was to stay hydrated. *Sorry, Dad. At least we have helmets.*

"It's not your fault," Alison said. "It's not like we had a plan."

"Yeah, well, I have one now," Olivia said. "Let's take the next side street anyway. We can take the first road that runs next to the boardwalk. There are trees there so at least there will be some shade. When we get closer, we can cut across to Ocean Boulevard. If Olga's is open, maybe we can stop in and get some water. We can even call your parents to come get us."

"No way. They'll freak out. It doesn't matter anyway. My father's probably still golfing."

Olivia noticed that Alison's face was red. Heat and sun. No sunscreen. Alison was so fair-skinned. "How about Maggie? We could call The Mansion. Maybe Maggie has a van or something."

"No. I'm still embarrassed about freaking out this morning. We'll be fine. Let's just keep riding." Alison swung her leg over her saddle.

"You look pretty red." Olivia pedaled up next to Alison.

"You sound like my mother." Alison sounded irritated.

Olivia decided not to say anything for a while.

After miles of silence, they passed an old man in his front yard. Olivia heard Alison call out to him, but he scurried inside. Olivia pedaled faster to get alongside of Alison. "All I did was ask him for water." She sounded surprised and confused.

"Does the phrase "stranger danger" mean anything to you?" The three big men from the night before had been creeping through her thoughts during most of the ride, but Olivia knew better than to say anything else that might set off Alison.

"I'm sorry this vacation sucks," Alison said.

Olivia laughed. "I'm having fun," she said brightly. She did not want Alison to think she was sorry to be there with her. "You know I love biking."

"It's hot and I'm thirsty," Alison said miserably. "And I keep whining. And my butt hurts."

Olivia laughed, "You get used to it if you ride enough."

"That's what I'm afraid of."

Olivia pedaled a little faster, just ahead of Alison. "The sooner we get back, the sooner you can get off that bike." Olivia knew what dehydration did to the body, but she estimated that they were only a mile or two from Olga's.

They were making pretty good time and whenever they passed a cross street, Olivia glanced to her right to make sure the boardwalk was still in sight and they were heading the right way.

Along the road, the buildings didn't look as damaged as everything on the boardwalk, although Olivia noticed that most of the houses still looked empty and forgotten. Other than the old man, Olivia only saw a few other houses that looked like they had any people living in them.

On the next corner, they pedaled past a group of little kids, barefoot and dirty, standing under a dense clump of trees between neglected yards. The kids held sticks and they poked at something on the ground. Oh, god is that an animal?

Most of the kids ignored them, but one little boy looked up at Olivia as she rode by. His stare was stone cold. Soulless. It chilled Olivia to her core, but she wasn't going to say anything about it to Alison.

"Hey!" Alison yelled. Olivia stopped and turned around. Alison stood straddling her bike. "Get away from that," Alison scolded, waving her arms at the kids. "You'll get sick."

The six other kids all looked up at once like wild animals. The way they moved all at the same time freaked Olivia out. And she had never seen children's faces look so hard. So full of hate. They sneered at Alison and Olivia like the girls were something disgusting. All seven children held up their sticks. Olivia noticed the pointy ends dripped red and trailed bits of what looked like bloody meat.

"Alison?" Olivia wanted to get out of there. Fast.

"It's disgusting. These kids are playing with a dead animal. I think it's a cat. Poor kitty." Alison turned back to face the kids. They were closer to her. Moving slowly and all together, like one creature. They held up their drippy, meaty sticks in front of their cold, sneering faces.

Alison didn't seem to notice or to care. "Don't even tell me you kids killed that cat. I will go off on you. That's sick! Where are your parents?"

Their eyes were stony. Their mouths were tight, gray slits like they had never smiled in their lives. Olivia felt the hairs stand up on the back of her neck and her heart thumped faster. "Allie, we need to go."

"But the cat."

"It's dead." Olivia felt panic rising as the kids moved toward them holding their sticks like a Roman legion. Olivia got the feeling that these kids would do to her and Alison exactly what they were doing to that dead cat. She didn't even try to hide her panic. "Allie, NOW!"

It finally seemed to dawn on Alison that these little kids wanted to hurt her and that they could. Alison pedaled away, and the kids stopped walking and stood, still holding their sticks like spears. From a safe distance, Alison called over her shoulder, "Leave innocent animals alone, you sick freaks."

"Allie, we have to get back to The Mansion. We need to get your family and get out of Cape November." Olivia pedaled faster. She could not stop checking her mirrors. "These people out here aren't right in the head."

A few blocks later, Olivia checked the cross-shaped mirror on the handlebar. Her breath caught in her throat when she spotted an old, dilapidated white van. They had passed other cars, but since seeing those kids, Olivia was on edge. Something about the van scared her. She slowed down to let Alison ride alongside her. The van slowed down, too. "Did you notice the van behind us?"

"No."

"Don't turn around!" Olivia warned as Alison began to look. "It's better if they think we don't know."

"Why?" Olivia knew that Alison was giving one-word answers because she was getting winded. She did that on the treadmills at the gym, too.

"I think that van is following us. Can you pedal faster?"

"No. We should…" Alison panted, "get back… to the boardwalk." Her voice became more breathless as they pedaled harder. "Can't …follow us."

Olivia checked the mirror again. The shadowy trees reflecting off the windshield made it impossible to see inside the van. She thought she could make out a pair of long, white chins, just like the big guys she saw at the traffic light and in the parking lot, but she forced herself not to go there in her head.

The girls steered their bikes sharply right and pedaled faster. Olivia let Alison go in front, otherwise she was worried she might lose her. In the mirror, Olivia could see that the van hadn't turned yet. There were only a few houses on the street, and the first one they passed was boarded up and abandoned. The front yard was overgrown with out-of-control bushes and unmowed grass.

"No way!" Alison said.

At the end of the street, Olivia saw them. Two large men in ratty, black, hooded ponchos stepped into the road, blocking the way to the boardwalk.

Olivia felt her gut turn to jelly.

"Quick! In here." Alison slammed her footbrake and skidded into the dirt grooves through the grass. It was a driveway that curved through the trees. Olivia could vaguely make out a large, blue building. Olivia felt choking fear grip her. Through the trees, Olivia saw the white van come around the corner.

"Hurry up, Liv!" Alison rasped.

Olivia stood panting next to Alison. "Where are you going?"

"We should cut through and get back to the boardwalk. Just stay low."

They pushed their bikes to the side of the driveway, trying to stay hidden in the overgrown shrubs. Olivia heard the rattling motor get close and then stop at the end of the driveway.

Alison panted like a dog. "Are those the guys you saw?"

Olivia's mouth stopped working when the doors on the van creaked and rattled open. Trying to stay low and hidden, the girls watched through the tall weeds as a giant in a long, ragged black poncho hobbled slowly up the driveway. When she saw the distinctive, jerky, limping walk, Olivia felt a tear sting her eye.

"Come on," Alison whispered.

Olivia followed, too numb to ask questions. They pulled the bikes to the untrimmed brush at the edge of the driveway that Olivia prayed was thick enough to hide them. She glanced back to see where the guys from the van were. One of them hunched in the driveway. With one boot in each of the two tire paths, the huge man made his wobbling way toward them. The hooded head with the protruding white chin moved rhythmically back and forth, nodding slightly.

Olivia fumbled to get her cell phone out of the pocket of her shorts. The screen, indifferent, said NO SERVICE. She almost screamed when Alison grabbed her wrist. Alison flapped her palm rapidly and Olivia understood that Alison wanted her to lie down. On their bellies, they abandoned the bikes to crawl like soldiers under the low branches toward the blue building.

Every leaf and twig sounded like an avalanche. Her own heartbeat thundered in her head. Olivia could not stop shaking as they crawled around the side of the building. It looked new and modern, not like any other building they'd seen in Cape November. When she saw the pointy roof and steeple, she recognized it as a church. Twisting to see the top, she tried to make sense of the symbol at the point of the steeple.

The curved, half-moon shape reminded Olivia of the symbol for Islam. Her dad was Muslim, and she'd seen that symbol many times. But instead of a star, the points of the moon were connected by a series of parallel lines. That wasn't any symbol she'd ever seen in any mosque. She fumbled around in her mind trying to place the symbol, but nothing clicked.

Olivia looked back down the driveway, and her throat filled with hot sand. The man from the van had found their bikes. Her heart squeezed tight when Alison tapped her on the head. She was up in a low crouch and waving for Olivia to follow her around the side of the church to the back. The yard was a large, unpaved parking lot. Olivia could see the opening of the next street on the far side. Her gut jumped. Another goon stood in the yard, cutting them off again.

Alison dropped and pulled Olivia down beside her. Her hands were sweaty around Olivia's wrist. There were two of them at the end of the street. One in the yard. Back in the driveway, the sliding and shuffling of the dirt told her the first one was coming around the building after them. Olivia's heart dissolved as the reality overwhelmed her. If there was another one in the van, that meant that at least five huge, creepy-looking guys in ponchos were after them and they were trapped.

Suddenly gripping Olivia's wrist hard enough to burn her, Alison tried to pull Olivia out of the bushes. Olivia jerked her wrist free. She stared in disbelief, sure that Alison had lost her mind. *Why is she pulling us back out there? We need to hide!*

Pointing jerkily to a basement window, Alison dove across the driveway and skulked beside the window's screen, trying to tear it open. The dragging footsteps scraped closer up the driveway.

Scurrying next to Alison, Olivia helped her push out the screen. Alison practically shoved Olivia into the dark. Sliding feet first as quickly as she could, Olivia felt something solid under her sneakers. A shelf? Her head was still level with the window. She helped pull Alison through and quickly slid the window closed behind her.

They leaned against the cool cinderblock walls, steadying their balance on the narrow shelf as they ducked below the window. Olivia found Alison's hand and squeezed, but neither of them could stop shaking. She could hear Alison struggle to hold back her gulping gasps for air. Olivia felt hot, grateful tears, and her whole body deflated when the two enormous shadows passed the window without pausing and apparently without noticing.

29 OUT TO SEA

After they dragged the dory out past the breaking waves, Maggie flipped gracefully over the side and sat on a bench seat.

Michael eyed the rocking boat; the sides seemed impossibly high. He looked at Maggie, already comfortably inside. "So, uh, which bench should I aim for?"

She laughed. "If you want to sit on a bench, go to the park."

Michael felt like she was pranking him, and it made him angry and nervous as he dangled helpless in the water. "Excuse me?"

Maggie laughed again. She seemed to enjoy his discomfort. "On a dory we sit on thwarts, and you can park your butt in the middle one, you lubber."

"What's a lubber?" Michael tried to pull himself up with his arms, but he couldn't get it. "Is that like a lover with a speech impediment or something?"

Screaming and laughing as Michael nearly capsized them on his first attempt to get in, Maggie barked like a wrestling coach. "Time it with a wave. Then just pull yourself over the gunwale."

"The what?"

"The sides of the boat." She ran her finger along the wooden rail. "This part on top is called the gunwale."

"Are we snorkeling or studying for the SATs? Enough vocabulary, and help me get in!" Michael tried twice more to get over the gunwale. Both times were epic fails. Each wave pulled them a little farther from the beach. Michael felt a little flutter of panic. "It's too deep now. I can't even touch."

"Wow! You really do suck at this." Maggie seemed to be laughing too hard to offer any new suggestions.

Scenes rushed into his mind from all those movies he'd stayed up late to watch, where someone's in the water with their legs dangling like shark bait. He remembered suddenly how much he liked pools better than the ocean. "Seriously, are there sharks out here?"

"Trust me. A shark's not interested in you."

"How do you know?" Michael looked around uncomfortably. "A shark might think I'm fascinating."

Maggie raised one eyebrow. "Somehow I doubt that."

"Hey, you think I'm interesting," Michael said, but he realized it was too hard to sound charming while spitting out salt water and clinging for life to the side of a boat.

"I'm not a shark." Grinning down at him, she stood and curled the toes on one foot over the gunwale, reaching out with her hands. Michael grabbed on, and she hauled him up the side until he could flop awkwardly onto the flat, narrow bottom of the dory.

"Thanks," Michael said, running his fingers over the scrapes on his six-pack. Awkwardly, he found his seat and felt like Maggie had just pinned him in front of a packed gym.

Effortlessly standing in the wobbling boat, Maggie set her hands imperially on the curves of her hips and looked him up and down. "I can sell you as catch of the day." Her laugh was musical and comfortable. "Okay, sailor, you can make it all up to me by rowing us out past the lighthouse."

Michael turned and looked at the lighthouse, towering at the end of the jetty. "All the way out there?"

"Hey, you wanted to snorkel."

"Snorkel, not enter a triathlon."

Maggie chuckled. "What are your events? Eating, drowning and making lame jokes?"

Michael put on his best hurt voice. "My jokes are not lame."

Maggie rolled her eyes. "Whatever. Anyway, a big, strong guy like you? This should be a piece of cake. I row out here all the time." Maggie put a cushion behind her. Like a big cat, she stretched out, putting her hands behind her head and positioning her feet on either side of Michael's knees. Her electric blue toenail polish glistened with seawater.

Catching himself admiring her bikini body, Michael felt himself go red. Were her eyes closed behind her sunglasses? Could she see him checking her out? The last thing he wanted was for her to think he was some kind of pervy creeper.

"A little faster, sailor," she said. Her voice was liquid. "It's getting hot, and I'd like a breeze."

Michael tipped up the end of the oar and doused her with ocean water. Maggie screamed and sat up laughing. She threw a cushion at him and then leaned over the side and splashed him. They were both laughing and screaming their way through a full-on splash war until the waves started moving them too close to the jetty. Michael got back to business, rowing in steady pulls. Passing along the jetty, he got a closer view of the strange, blue-gray stones. They were laid in some kind of interlocking pattern, but every time he thought he could follow the pattern he noticed something new and had to start over, looking for a different pattern.

"I'm not an expert on lighthouse architecture or anything, but your lighthouse looks weird." He added hastily, "No offense."

"None taken," she said wryly without moving.

Michael looked back at the lighthouse. It was cone-shaped, narrowing at the top where it bulged out in a large bowl shape. He guessed the top was flat and solid, because that's where the lighthouse stuff used to be. The weird blue stones made a confusing pattern. The tower seemed more like something from a science fiction movie than a lighthouse.

Rowing steadily and enjoying the sun, the waves and the breeze, Michael was just wondering whether Maggie had fallen asleep when her voice startled him.

"You're pretty good at this." She propped herself up on her elbows to look at Michael. "It's hard to keep this old boat going where you want it, especially with two people aboard."

"I'm just generally awesome," Michael's swagger grinned and he flexed his chest and back muscles as he rowed.

"It's always rough out here." Maggie sat up. "Usually it's even worse than this. I figured that with you rowing this was going to be a disaster, but you surprised me."

"Thanks a lot," Michael said sarcastically. His swagger was curled up in the fetal position.

"No, you don't understand." Her voice was softer. Gentler. She sat up and leaned forward. Their knees touched. Michael could not tell where her eyes were behind her dark lenses. Automatically, his swagger tightened his core, just in case. Nothing was supposed to jiggle. Her voice was incredible. Part kitten, part tigress. "I was kind of hoping you'd get us into trouble so I would have to save us."

His swagger jumped overboard. Michael teetered between lust and fear. "Why?"

If she noticed the crack in his voice, she must have let it slide. Smiling and looking away like she was suddenly shy, she whispered, "So you would be impressed with me."

Michael wasn't sure if he heard her right over the sound of the boat in the waves. Because what he thought he heard had him convinced that she was messing with him again. "I'm already impressed with you," he said cautiously.

"Shut up," she groaned, pushing his shoulder gently. Facing the waves she said, "So...you couldn't have rowed crew. You don't know your ass from starboard." She poked his chest gently with her electric blue fingernail. "Do you row your girlfriend around when you're trying to impress her?" Maggie leaned back again on the cushion and rested her feet on his knees. The warm press of her skin thrilled him up to his thighs.

He forced himself to play it cool and to just keep rowing at the same steady pace. "I don't have a girlfriend. And what makes you think I'm trying to impress you?"

Maggie giggled impishly. "I would be if I were you." She draped her hands carelessly over the sides.

Michael realized that she could easily be setting him up. He wasn't going to take her bait. "You're already impressed."

"I'm not a shark, remember?" She laughed loudly. It wasn't unpleasant. "So if it wasn't rowing around your girlfriend, singing love songs and eating a picnic lunch, where did you learn to row?"

He looked back at The Mansion and for a moment, wondered whether his dad was golfing with Nelson. "When I was younger, me and my dad would go fishing sometimes. Turns out that neither of us really liked fishing. Kinda boring just sitting there holding a stick, you know?"

"Are you kidding?" Maggie leaned up to look at him like he'd just requested grape jelly on his tuna melt. "Fishing's awesome."

Michael shrugged. "Whatever. He always made me row the boat."

Maggie stretched flat out, her heels slid farther up his thighs. It was becoming hard for Michael to focus on much else. "When you fish, you get to eat what you catch," she practically purred in her tiger-kitten voice.

Sliding back slightly in his bench—thwart—so that her feet were closer to his knees, Michael cleared his throat. "You said I was catch of the day," Michael tried to sound suave, but he knew that he didn't.

Sitting up abruptly, Maggie looked at him with a crooked grin. "Just what are you insinuating?"

"Are you implying that I smell like a fish?"

Laughing, Maggie reached into the bottom of the boat and tossed a small anchor overboard.

Michael watched the coil of rope unwind, pulled by the anchor sinking out of sight. They were out past the tip of the jetty, and the waves were gentler. The lighthouse towered over them.

The boat rocked, but Maggie climbed effortlessly over Michael, moving bags and equipment. "This is really the best spot, but it's too far out to swim to and we'd kill ourselves trying to climb down from the jetty. Plus, who wants to carry all the gear. It's easier just to row."

"It's cool," Michael said. "It was fun rowing out here."

"Are you ready?" Maggie asked.

Michael shrugged. "What do I have to do? I need a mask, right?"

Maggie didn't answer right away. She sat forward on the thwart. "I mean for my story, reporter boy."

It caught Michael off guard. "If you're ready to tell it."

As the dory rocked in the swells, Maggie sat back down, facing Michael. She took a long, deep breath. "This morning, when you came to my room, you wanted to help me because you thought I was in trouble."

Sheepishly, Michael looked out at the horizon to avoid looking at her. "Yeah. Sorry. That was stupid."

"No, Michael. You were right." She looked down into the space between their feet. "I do need your help. Not about that—not directly about that anyway." She sighed heavily. "Or maybe it is. I don't know." She snatched up his hands. "I sound crazy, right?"

"Right now you kinda do." Michael felt little bug legs of uncertainty crawling all over his scalp.

Dropping his hand heavily, Maggie looked into his face as if she were studying him. "I have to start with my parents, the night they died, or none of this will make sense." She scowled and shook her head gently. "It probably won't anyway."

Michael suddenly didn't feel so good about being all the way out here in a boat with a girl he met because she was screaming in her sleep, no matter how hot she was.

If Maggie noticed his discomfort, it didn't seem to bother her. "The official story is that my parents were killed in an accidental explosion when they were trying to fix the motor for the lighthouse. The Navy decommissioned it, but the old gas line that used to supply the lamp was still there. Gas lighthouses are pretty rare, and my parents thought that if they got it back on it could be good for business."

Michael turned in his seat to look at the stone tower. "So what happened?"

Maggie laughed quietly. "Again, this is the official story. My dad was pretty handy, but he wasn't a licensed plumber or anything. He screwed up and blew up the gas line. He and my mother, up there helping him, both got killed." Her voice was low, barely audible over the sloshing boat. Not a purr now. More like a chant she'd recited too often.

Michael stared at Maggie. Her head was turned; he assumed she was looking at the lighthouse, but her eyes were behind dark lenses. He watched the tiny droplets of water sparkling on her shoulders. She didn't say anything else, but there was more that Michel needed to know.

Waiting, Michael listened to the slap of the waves. He wondered if she had changed her mind and didn't want to tell him any more. "So, what's the unofficial story?"

Maggie turned to face him. "This story is a lot harder for me to tell."

"Why?"

She smiled sadly. "It's the story that got me locked up in a mental hospital." Her mouth was tight. Her hands clenched into fists and unclenched again. Resting his hands over hers, Michael nodded, trying to encourage her.

"You're not going to believe me." Her voice was thick and crusted.

"Try me."

Maggie gave a bitter chuckle. "I'm not supposed to believe it myself. They've been keeping me doped up on aripiaprazole and clozapine and about a dozen other pills for half my life to make sure I didn't start believing it."

"Believing what? What happened?"

A change came over her. The confident, sexy powerhouse Michael rowed out with suddenly looked like a frail and frightened child who just watched her parents die. She took another deep breath, and when she sighed it out, her story dragged behind like the tattered tail of a broken kite. "My parents died trying to stop The Church of New Enlightenment."

It caught him off guard. "What is that? I read about that in the newspaper."

"The Church?" Maggie still looked frightened, but she seemed to come back to herself. "What did it say?"

"Not much. It mentioned them in an article about the newspaper closing down. Three people are missing. The editor and a reporter and her husband."

Maggie's face drained. "Elizabeth Denton?"

It stunned him. "You know her?"

Maggie tossed her sunglasses down, covered her face with her palms and flopped her head to her knees. Her braid lay damp down her back like a piece of driftwood.

Feeling awkward and uncertain, Michael tried to comfort her by resting his hand gently on her shoulder. Her skin felt warm in the sun, her muscles tensed with her sobs. Michael looked at the shore and up to the windows of her room. He remembered her painting of the lighthouse blowing up. He looked back at her. Hunched over, her spine made little bumps beneath her freckled skin. "So what happened? What is the Church of whatever-you-said?"

She sat up and straightened her back, looking regal again. The corners of Maggie's lips turned down in a sneer. "It's a cult that calls itself a church. There have always been a handful of them down the Cape. The CNE was just one of the many colorful attractions, another part of the Cape November freak show that helped bring in the tourists. Like the way people go to Amish Country to gawk at people driving buggies and milking cows. But as things went bad down here, more and more of the Enlightened—that's what they call themselves—showed up to buy the cheap property. They have money. A lot of money. They basically took over Cape November. Killed the town. The Enlightened have always had a meetinghouse down near Ocean Boulevard. Just last year they totally renovated it. Put in a few classrooms and who knows what else." Maggie laughed dryly. "When everyone else is closing down, they're getting bigger and better."

Michael felt a little revulsion. He suddenly realized how much he sucked at reading people. She had seemed so cool, but she was just another paranoid bigot. "Isn't that how a lot of prejudiced people talk when any minority group moves in? A few years ago, a community at the Jersey Shore tried to stop Hassidic Jews from moving in and taking over the town." Michael dropped the air quotes. He sighed sadly and looked at the dilapidated outlines of the buildings that used to make the boardwalk awesome. "Everybody's heard that speech, uh-oh, the blacks or the Puerto Ricans or the Jews or the Mexicans or the Italians or Pakistanis or whatever are moving in. There goes the neighborhood."

Maggie shook her head. "It's not that they moved in. The Enlightened have always been here. But about ten years ago, right around the time my parents died, the CNE started driving out everybody else."

"Meaning what?" Michael made an adjustment on the oars to keep them away from the jetty.

"The official story is that they want to build a religious community."

"But?"

Maggie shook her head. "Groups of ten or twenty of them would bang on people's doors at all hours of the day and night demanding that they sell their property. They would congregate in front of restaurants and stores and stuff just to hassle the customers until the customers stopped coming and the place shut down."

"We didn't see anybody like that when we went to Olga's."

Maggie laughed. "They don't mess with Olga."

"Why not? Is she one of them or something?"

Maggie looked at Michael like he'd just sprouted antlers. "You met Olga. Would you mess with her?"

Michael wanted to understand, to believe her. To find a way back to that place where he thought she was the coolest girl on the planet and not a potentially dangerous bigot psycho. "So what do these church people have to do with your parents?"

Maggie leaned down and sorted the equipment in the bottom of the boat. "It was during Hurricane Katrina. I remember that much clearly. The date on the police record matches up, too, so at least this part of the memory is irrefutable. We were in the front room, by the bar. There used to be a television in there, and my parents were watching the news. I was on the floor drawing. I was scared because they were showing pictures of New Orleans and satellite images of the storm. I thought a giant monster was eating New Orleans. That's how the storm looked to me. That famous satellite picture? To me, the eye of the storm looked like a mouth and all the clouds around the outside were like tentacles or something. Anyway, there were noises outside The Mansion. Chanting."

"Chanting?" Michael scooped some water onto his shoulders and chest. The sun was baking, and rowing the dory left him feeling overheated. He helped himself to a water out of the cooler. There was no ice, but at least it was wet on his throat.

Maggie nodded. "Yeah. I know. It sounds nuts to me, too, and they're my memories. I think."

"What were they chanting?"

Maggie shrugged. "I don't remember words. It probably wasn't even English. I just remember the sound, like the melody. It made me feel, I don't know, sad or hopeless or something. I don't even really remember the sound, just the feeling."

"Are you sure the feelings didn't come after? You know, because of your parents?"

Maggie shrugged. "I'm not sure of any of this. But I remember the lights.

Lots of lights, like flashlights or lanterns or something, shining through the windows. That's when my parents told me to hide up in the tower."

"In your room?"

"It wasn't my room back then. It was just another guest room." Maggie ran her fingers through her hair. "I remember thinking that it was weird they wanted me to go all the way up there. I thought they were hiding me because the hurricane monster was coming to eat us, too."

"That doesn't make sense. The hurricane was in New Orleans."

"I was nine, Michael. And my memories of that night are all jumbled up. But I know they told me to hide up in the tower. The official police report says the cops found me up there in a closet with the room key still in my pocket. My parents had to have given me that key; I didn't know where the keys to all the rooms were."

"So was it the church people? What were they doing?"

Shaking her head uncertainly, Maggie shrugged, "I ran up to the tower and looked out the window. All these people in white robes were down here on the jetty."

"They were from The Church of New Enlightenment?"

Maggie nodded. "I don't know that, but that's what my grandfather thought."

"Hang on," Michael was getting that funhouse feeling again. "He was there?"

Maggie shook her head. "No. He told me later."

"How did he know?"

"It was just his theory. He thinks The Church of New Enlightenment is a cult and that they have been practicing *human sacrifice* here at The Mansion for a long, long time."

Michael swallowed. This was a lot to take in. "You think The Church of New Enlightenment sacrificed your parents?"

Again, Maggie shook her head. "Not exactly. I think my parents knew more about the CNE than they ever told me—I was a little kid. But I think that my parents were expecting something bad to happen down at the lighthouse. I mean, they might not have known what exactly or when, but they knew something was coming, and so they prepared."

Michael looked at her, trying to see if she were messing with him or testing him. But she looked one hundred percent serious "You think your parents rigged the tower to blow up on purpose?"

"Exactly."

"Why?"

Maggie shrugged and shook her head. "There were at least twenty people in robes that I saw from the window that night. I could hear them chanting, even from the tower. The lighthouse and the jetty—the stones I mean—made this huge, blue light. Everything was glowing, and The Mansion felt like it was, I don't know, vibrating or something. I saw my father and my mother at the top of the lighthouse. The Enlightened, in their robes, were climbing up the steps after them, chasing them. And then everything exploded. The windows shook. I thought it was the hurricane coming to eat us. It scared me so much. I knew my parents were up there. I ran into a closet to hide. I guess I passed out or fell asleep in there, waiting for my parents to come back, but...when the police finally found me the next morning, they told me my parents had been killed in the explosion. I told them about the blue light and the people in robes chanting. They said there was nobody else at the lighthouse. They never even found my parents' bodies, but the police were sure that it was an accident. That my father blew up the gas line."

Michael tried to keep all the facts straight like a good reporter should. "So this cult or whatever came down here and took over the Cape just to use the lighthouse, your lighthouse, to sacrifice people?"

"The Mansion is so old. There have always been mysteries surrounding it."

"But how come nobody else knows about this cult?"

"Everybody knows about The Church of New Enlightenment, but most people think it's just another oddball religion."

Michael was going to point out that he'd never heard of it, but until that morning, he'd never heard of blintzes or crepes either.

Maggie squeezed Michael's hands and shook her head. "I know it sounds crazy. I grew up thinking I was crazy. They told me I was crazy, and they told me my grandfather was crazy. I wasn't even allowed to see him for a long time."

"Why?"

"Because they said he fed my delusions."

"What's that supposed to mean?"

"It means he believed me. He started to investigate The Mansion and The Church of New Enlightenment, and you know what he found?"

"Aliens?"

Anger flashed across Maggie's face. "Michael you don't understand how serious I am right now. Colonel Coombs was one of the Enlightened."

"The Civil War dude who built The Mansion?"

Her eyes pleaded with Michael. Maggie believed what she was saying; Michael was positive about that, which only left two possibilities. She was crazy. Or she was right.

"Can't you just ask your grandfather?" Michael watched Maggie adjust the rubber strap on a dive mask. He'd almost forgotten they'd come to snorkel.

"My grandfather and Uncle Max disappeared two years ago."

"Your Aunt Penny's boyfriend? I thought they just broke up or something."

Maggie shook her head. "No. He and Grandpa didn't show up for dinner one night. We haven't seen them since."

"And now the reporter and her husband." Michael felt like his brain was shooting off in five directions at once.

Maggie eyed the shoreline suspiciously. "Elizabeth Denton was investigating the CNE. Its ties to The Mansion. The disappearances. All that."

"Did she find anything?"

"The CNE sued the News a few times. The paper stood by her, though, and Elizabeth Denton never retracted anything."

"But did she prove that The Church of New Enlightenment had anything to do with the people who went missing?" He gulped some more water.

"Nothing that would hold up in court. Everything was circumstantial and speculative."

"Meaning what?"

"For starters, they never found any bodies."

Thoughts of Alison and Olivia hit him like a lightning bolt. He fumbled for the rope and started hauling up the anchor.

"What are you doing?" Maggie sounded startled.

"My sister and Olivia are out there!" Michael felt his anger course through his body. "How could you send them out if you knew this was going on?"

"I don't know!" Maggie sounded horrified. "Michael, you have to believe me. I spent my whole life believing I was crazy, remember?"

"Are you?" Michael dropped the anchor to the floor and grabbed the oars. "If this place is so messed up, why did you even let us come here? You shouldn't have even let my mom book a trip here."

"Aunt Penny has no idea about any of this. She's just trying to keep her business so we don't end up homeless. Is that such a crime?"

"So where does she think your grandfather and her boyfriend are? Does she think they eloped or something?"

Maggie sounded angry and tearful. "She really thinks Uncle Max left her. It devastated her. She won't even consider the possibility that the Enlightened might have taken them."

"Didn't he leave a note or anything?" Panic was clawing at his gut. "Did he leave her or didn't he?" Michael was tired of the sun and tired of Maggie.

"I don't know!"

"Did he leave with your grandfather or not?"

"I DON'T KNOW!" Maggie's tiger roar startled Michael. She closed her eyes and took a breath. "My grandfather has always come and gone. Aunt Penny thinks it's because he's sick like me. Schizophrenia is hereditary."

"Is he sick?"

Maggie shrugged. "Grampa's never been to a doctor."

"Why not? If he's schizophrenic—"

Maggie groaned in frustration. "He doesn't think he's sick."

"Crazy people never think they're crazy." Michael knew he said it coldly.

He didn't care.

Maggie's mouth was tight. "Suppose you believed that the principal of your school was actually an evil alien disguised as a human, but you had no way to prove it. What would you do?"

Michael groaned in frustration. "Listen, if I wanted to play stupid mind games, I'd have stayed with Alison." The thought of Alison burst through him like lightning. Again, he pulled hard on the oars.

She grabbed his wrists to stop his rowing. "Wait! Think about it. What would you do, Michael?"

He knew that either he had to play along with Maggie or fight her for the oars. He sighed, exasperated. "I would probably tell somebody."

"Who?" Maggie's voice was flat.

"I don't know. My parents I guess."

"And what do you think they would say? Would they believe that your principal was an alien because you said so? You'd probably never get enough proof to convince them of something so totally crazy, right?"

Michael just wanted her to let go so he could row back.

"You might even start to doubt yourself. It's so crazy and stupid to think that your school principal is an evil alien. Where would you even get an idea like that? Unless you saw him transform once—just for a second—in his office, when nobody else was around. You saw him look like an alien, but only for a split second, and then he looked human again. You'd have this clear, but fragmentary, memory. After a while, you're not even sure; maybe you dreamed it, but it's so sharp in your mind. If you try to tell anybody, your parents, the police, they're all going to say you're crazy. You might even start to think you're crazy."

"I would be crazy!" Michael felt guilty as soon as he said it. "Look, I don't mean to hurt your feelings. It's got to be hard for you, living with all these memories about your parents and everything."

"Don't judge me! Who are you to judge me? You grew up in your little suburban bubble with both your parents in a perfect little world."

"You don't know anything about me, okay?" Michael felt the anger radiate out of him. "It doesn't matter. I'm rowing back."

"Wait, Michael, please." Her eyes softened. "I'm sorry. You're right. I don't know you. But just think about it from my perspective for a second. As crazy as it sounds, you wouldn't be crazy if you were right. You would just be the only one who knew the truth."

Michael stopped rowing. "Let me see if I have all this. Either you and your grandpa are totally nuts or there really is a cult at Cape November that kidnaps people to kill them." Everything in his chest felt hot. His head throbbed. "I have to get Alison and Olivia right now." Michael jerked his hands free and rowed as hard as he could for the shore.

"Wait!" Maggie said. "I spent my whole life thinking I was sick, delusional.

But suppose it turns out The Church of New Enlightenment really does kill people? And my parents died because of it? How can I get people to believe me? Michael, the CNE has been around a long time. They have a lot of money. Probably a lot of connections. They might even have Enlightened in the police, the FBI, who knows?"

Michael ignored her. All he could think about was finding Alison and Olivia and then his parents, and getting as far away from Cape November as he could.

"Michael, please. I need your help."

"Alison and Olivia need my help more."

"It won't take long and then I'll help you find them and I'll refund your parents' money and you can all just go home. But first help me. When you came to my room you said you wanted to help me."

Michael stopped rowing. "Why should I?"

"Because," Maggie slumped, "nobody else will."

Staring at her, at the water and back at the shore that seemed more distant than ever, Michael struggled to put all the pieces together. He swallowed clumps of hateful resentment. "Say that I do." Michael set the oars in the oarlocks and let the boat rock and drift. "Say I believe you and everything you said is true. Then what?"

Maggie sighed. "Then it might not be safe anywhere."

"What does that mean?"

"The CNE is apocalyptic. The Enlightened believe that God, their version of God anyway, is going to wipe out all the non-believers and create a paradise just for them."

Michael laughed. "That's what half the whack-job religions that have ever existed believe. So what?"

"My grandfather thinks that The Church of New Enlightenment has a way to really make it happen."

On disturbing little feet, that idea clawed around Michael's head for a moment. It was either the most paranoid, crazy thing he ever heard anybody say out loud... or it wasn't. He tried to laugh it off. "How could they do that?"

Maggie shrugged. "The stones at The Mansion are ancient. Nobody knows what they really are or what they do."

"Rocks don't do anything. They're rocks." This was getting ridiculous, and Michael was losing his patience. "What are you saying, the whole mansion is some kind of weapon?" Laughing, Michael started rowing again.

"I don't know, but I know where to look." Michael noticed the tiny streaks of gold in Maggie's teary, hazel eyes. She pointed down into the water. "If I'm not crazy, then there's a door down there that leads inside the jetty. My grandfather thought that whatever the CNE was doing, they would do it inside the jetty. My grandfather thought there should be a door and that if that door opens, something big is happening."

"Why?"

"I DON'T KNOW!" Maggie panted a few times. "I don't know if he knew. He disappeared before I could get all the information. He didn't like talking about it. He said the less I knew, the better."

"Because that doesn't sound crazy at all." Michael paused and studied her face. Something in the back of his mind was still waiting for the punch line. None came.

"It does sound crazy. That's my point. If there's no door, then I'm probably just crazy. You and your lovely little family can just go home, and you can forget all about me. But if there is a door, Michael..."

Michael took another look at the shore. He thought about his sister out there with Olivia. Scenes from the morning replayed in his mind, everything they had done before Maggie started all the crazy talk. She had seemed so cool. He had liked her. If she'd kept the whole thing to herself, he would have never known and they would have gone snorkeling and everything would have been...whatever. But then he thought of the day before. Strange birds. Strange dead bodies. In the back of his neck, the hairs prickled.

He sighed. "It's not fair of me to get mad at you for just being honest, even if it came a little late."

"Michael, I—"

"Forget it." Michael took her hand. "You're right. I said I would help you, but then you have to help me find Alison and Olivia, okay?"

"You're helping me, Michael. You can't know how much that means to me." Maggie leaned in and kissed his cheek. "I'm in this all the way with you."

The kiss rippled from his cheek to the rest of him. Michael grinned, "When you say all the way..."

She punched him in the arm, but it didn't feel like she meant it.

Alison slipped her phone from her pocket and peeked through her fingers at the terrifyingly bright screen, but nobody outside seemed to notice the light.

NO SERVICE. She resisted the urge to spike her phone. Olivia's phone was dead, too, and Alison felt fear ooze around her, but she had snuck around in places she shouldn't have before. She couldn't panic.

Once her eyes had adjusted to the pale light from the window, she saw an ordinary tool room, like any school janitor's closet. Mops and brooms leaned in buckets in the corner. There were a few dirty toolboxes; a small worktable was scattered with wrenches, screwdrivers and hammers. Careful not to knock over anything noisy, she and Olivia climbed off the storage shelves to the tile floor. Everything looked clean and well cared for, but the fishy, ocean smell was strong. And rotten.

Another glance up at the window, still empty, satisfied Alison that they were safe. But they couldn't hide in the tool room forever. She stepped gingerly to the door. Olivia shook her head and raised her eyebrows with silent urgency, her eyes wide with terror.

Alison leaned her mouth close to Olivia's ear. The clean smell of shampoo, mingled with the comfortable smell of fresh sweat, was a relief from the reek of low tide. They reminded Alison of her ordinary life before Cape November.

Alison forced herself to whisper and to stay calm. "We can't stay here. They're going to figure out where we went, and then we'll be trapped."

Glancing at the hammers on the worktable, Alison picked one up and held it out. Olivia stared blankly, "Are we building a table?"

Alison didn't want to have to say it. "If one of them tries to get us…"

"I can't hit somebody with a hammer!" Olivia rasped desperately.

"Just take it." Every horror story and urban legend scuttled through her mind. Alison pressed her ear to the workroom door, but she heard nothing. She jumped and swatted at the thing tickling her neck. She and Olivia both chuckled weakly. It had been Olivia's hair.

Nodding at the door, Olivia leaned in whispering, "What's out there?"

Shrugging, Alison reached for the knob. "We can't stay here."

With panic in her eyes, Olivia grabbed Alison's wrist. Alison tried to project her most confident smile. "We might be freaking out for nothing." Alison didn't even believe it herself, but she needed to say it.

Shaking her head, Olivia insisted, "Those creeps are after us."

"Why?" Alison tried to think of a reason, but nothing came.

Olivia shook her head and shrugged limply.

When Alison twisted the doorknob, she knew the click of the door had been tiny, but in the silence of the basement, it sounded like a fireworks show.

The door swung silently outward. She could feel Olivia cringe reflexively beside her. Alison checked the window. No shadows. No faces.

Squeezing Olivia's smooth, strong hand gave Alison enough courage to leave the tool room. At least it stopped her own hand from shaking.

The light from the window didn't stretch beyond the doorway, but Alison could see that they were at the end of a hallway. With the door shut behind them, Alison decided it was safe enough to use the flashlights on their phones. The hall was empty. Except for the fishy smell they could have been in a school or office building.

Alison shined her phone flashlight light as far down the left wall as it reached. Blank. On the opposite side, Olivia's light found a second door a little farther down the wall on the same side as the tool room. The light wasn't strong enough to reach the end of the hallway.

Alison looked back at Olivia. "Ready?"

Olivia managed a weak smile. "Baby steps."

Leaning in, Alison pressed her forehead gently against Olivia's. It was damp with sweat. "We're going to be okay. I promise." Alison wanted desperately for that to be true.

When Alison paused at the second door, Olivia pulled her back. "What are you doing?" She hissed. "Don't just open random doors."

Alison took a deep breath to steady her jingling nervousness. Olivia had scared her with her sudden pull. "We need to find a way out of here." Scanning the door with her phone, Alison found a blue plastic sign. STORAGE. It didn't sound like a way out, but it was worth a shot.

Olivia's lips tightened. She listened at the door a moment, and then shook her head. Alison tried the knob. It clicked like thunder. Pulling the door open a crack showed only a dark sliver. She opened the door a little wider and shined her light in. It was an ordinary storage room. Cardboard boxes. Paper. Office supplies. Cases of water bottles.

Pushing past her, Olivia tore into a case and pulled out two bottles for each of them. Their swallows sounded like Niagara Falls in the dark silence.

After their third bottle, Alison shut the door behind them and led Olivia farther down the hallway until it turned left. The middle of that hall had one door on each side. The sign on the left read CHAPEL. The right read NURSERY.

Opening the chapel, Alison saw rows of folding chairs facing a low altar. Alison's light glinted off a blue, metallic decoration hanging behind the altar. A half-moon with the points joined by parallel lines. "What is that?" she whispered.

"The same thing is up on the steeple," Olivia replied. "I guess it's a religious symbol, but I never saw it before." Stepping past Alison, she whispered, "What's that on the altar?"

Alison recognized it as a musical instrument. "It's a small harp." And then it came together in her head. "That's what the symbol is. It's a harp."

Olivia picked the harp up and gently plucked the strings. The instrument made small, gentle tones. "I guess they use it in the ceremony."

"Let's go." Alison couldn't bring herself to care what the thing was.

Back in the hallway, Alison shut the chapel door behind them. Olivia nudged her and pointed out the dull light shining from under the door to the nursery. They listened, but heard nothing. The knob was cold under Alison's fingers. It moved smoothly. When she pulled the door open, the fish odor was thick and rotten in her nose and mouth.

Olivia held the front of her shirt over her face so that only her watering eyes showed. She motioned for Alison to shut the door.

Alison shook her head. She was glad to stick her nose under Olivia's hair to whisper, "We need a way out."

"It could be dangerous."

"A nursery?" Alison pictured a preschool classroom with beanbags and rainbows and cubbies full of cartoon lunchboxes and blankets for naptime.

Olivia scowled at her. "Does that smell like kindergarten to you? And did you forget about those little psychos who chased us with bloody spears? There might be a whole class of them in there."

Forgetting would have been a relief. Alison had been trying to shake the image of the child with ice cube eyes and a bloody stick in his hand. She looked down the stairs, hoping for a clue. They were made of metal grating. Yellow light came from long fixtures in regular rows down each wall. Alison noticed the familiar rhythmic sound.

"Hear the waves?" Olivia whispered. "We're near the beach."

A way out, Alison mouthed. Anyway, she hoped it was. Olivia shook her head again. Breaking away from Olivia's frightened eyes, Alison looked back down the stairs. All she heard was the gentle lapping of water. The rotten fish smell was unbearable, but she knew there had to be a way out down there. The lights were on. Somebody could be there. A shudder made her tingle all over when she thought of the hard, old faces she'd seen, and the angry kids with their dripping, pointed sticks.

Olivia's whisper rasped in Alison's ear. "Let's check the other hallway first. Please? Maybe there's a better way."

Shutting the door behind them, they continued around the next corner of the hallway. The door labeled Classroom 1 opened to a room with low tables and small chairs. A shelf of books.

"There's that symbol again." Olivia's light showed the harp hanging on the wall above the dry-erase board. "And check out the poster." Olivia was already walking toward it.

Closer, Alison saw that it was a large canvas that looked like it had been painted by kids. A class project? Alison wondered.

Cartoon children, all blue, danced in a circle around a strange, white creature. It stood on dozens of long, wriggling tentacles. Its head was a blobby jellyfish with more tentacles coming out of its neck. It had two huge, blue, cartoon eyes and a wide, blue, cartoon smile. It waved with two puffy-looking lobster claws. One claw held something red and brown. The picture was so strange it made Alison chuckle until she noticed the sides of the poster. Children had drawn cartoon animals but every puppy, kitty, bunny, squirrel or tiger was impaled on its own pointy, cartoon stick. The cartoon blood was vibrant red.

"Just like the kids we saw," Olivia whispered.

That's when Alison realized the thing in the creature's claw was a mangled elephant. The gray paint must not have been dry when the child smeared on the red for blood. The colors had mixed, and the thing looked brown. A queasy gurgling sloshed in Alison's stomach. She took Olivia's hand and backed quickly out of the classroom.

"Olivia, you were right," she whispered. "This place is bad. All bad." Alison felt the panic rise in trembling waves.

"We're going to be okay." Olivia took Alison's hands. "Baby steps." Olivia laughed quietly. "You probably thought I would be the one to lose it."

The sloshing inside her calmed to a manageable flutter, and Alison smiled, looking at her friend's face. It was her only reminder of the world as it used to be, when everything still made sense.

They crossed to Classroom 2; it was basically the same as Classroom 1, but the furniture was larger. There was a poster in the same spot, but it was not a cartoon. It was an intricately drawn diagram with the different parts labeled. Alison thought it looked like some kid's science fair project, but it wasn't showing anything Alison recognized. The title painted at the top read Naiads, Benefactors, Beadles and Stewards.

Alison studied the picture, but she had a hard time making sense of it. Under the title a white blob labeled Naiad was next to a line diagram of a naked woman, labeled Benefactor. A wavy white line labeled with an addition sign went from the blob to the woman's stomach. Little blue arrows showed that something flowed between the woman, the benefactor, the blob and the naiad, along the white line.

"So the white line is some kind of connector tube?" Alison asked.

Olivia shrugged and pointed to a fat block arrow that led down to a second diagram. The naiad was still a blob, but tentacles and a head started to sprout. The benefactor's hair was thinner. Her body looked shrunken, shriveled. The flow of arrows around the white connector tube was fatter and there were more of them.

Another block arrow led to a third diagram. The white connector was gone. The blob had been replaced with a white creature standing upright on six tentacles with two more tentacles for arms. Its head was a large, curved half-moon shape without eyes or facial features. It was labeled Beadle. The woman, shriveled and hairless, was labeled Steward, under which someone had written in Sharpie, "Working Stiff LOL!" The diagram was so strange, but the graffiti looked so ordinary, like kids did to posters at school.

"I know what this is," Olivia startled Alison. "It's a life-cycle diagram. A naiad…"

"It's from Greek mythology, right? A water spirit or something?" Realizing that the only way out was going to be down the steps into the nursery, and terrified of what they might find in there, Alison just wanted to get it all over with.

She listened for footsteps and looked into the hallway expecting to see lights coming.

"Yeah," Olivia said, whispering excitedly. "But it's also the young stage of an aquatic insect like a dragonfly or a mayfly. That white blob is probably a larva. It turns into that other thing with the tentacles. Probably through metamorphosis like insects and frogs, newts, certain kinds of fish…"

"Okay," Alison had no patience for one of Olivia's science lectures. "So it's a blob first, and then it turns into that other thing." That other thing was terrifying, even as a picture. "What about the woman?" As soon as she said it, Alison realized what she was looking at. "Are you saying that the blob uses the woman to change itself?"

"I think so. Look at the white line. It connects to the woman's belly button."

"Like an umbilical cord." Understanding crashed into Alison's head. The naiad attached itself to a woman just like a baby. It sucked nutrients from the woman's body through the tube until it could grow into that other thing. "What's happening to the woman? Her hair's all gone, and she's dried out looking. Does it kill her?"

Olivia tapped the word steward. "A steward is a servant. Why would they call her that if she's dead? There must be some kind of exchange. Look at the arrows, they go both ways."

"Liv," Alison said it sharply, but she was frustrated and afraid. More than anything she just wanted to go home. "We don't need to figure out how it works. We're not in school."

Ignoring Alison, Olivia tapped on the graffiti. "A working stiff is a person stuck in a dull job, right? Someone who just goes to work."

Alison swayed with a helpless feeling of falling. She held her head. "It's a pun, Liv. A stiff is also a dead body, right? So, a working stiff is a dead body that works. Hilarious," she said with bitter sarcasm.

"Right," Olivia said brightly. "So maybe this is some kind of voodoo church, and they believe in zombies."

"'Cause that's not terrifying at all." Icy fingers of horror squeezed Alison's stomach, and she felt sick again. "What backwater, inbred idiots would believe in this crap?"

Olivia looked away from the poster to catch Alison's eye. "Christians say that God created the world in seven days and sent his son to get killed and come back from the dead to save people from going to hell. Is that any less weird?"

"Zombie Jesus?" Alison asked.

"I'm so serious right now," Olivia said calmly. "Think about it. The whole point of a Catholic mass is so that the Catholics can eat the body of Christ."

"Cannibal Christians? This keeps getting better." Alison suddenly hated every religion on the planet.

Olivia laughed, "Every religion sounds crazy to somebody who doesn't believe in it." She tapped the poster. "Apparently, these people believe they can make squid people out of humans while making the humans into…zombie slaves or something."

"It's just like I told Michael about Berkeley. The only things that are real are ideas. If these psychos believe in this stuff, then it's real to them." Alison looked at the images and thought about those horrible kids torturing that cat with their pointed sticks. It made her shiver. "We need to go. Not just out of this psycho church, but out of Cape November."

Olivia chuckled halfheartedly. "Wanna tell your parents now?"

Guilty anger burned at Alison's chest and eyes, but she had nothing to say.

31 DIVER DOWN

Seeing her in her bikini, Michael could watch the magical dance of Maggie's muscles as she bopped effortlessly around the heaving boat. He could have watched all day.

"So now what?" he asked, craning his neck over the gunwale to watch the anchor fall through the clear water. His extra weight combined with the choppy swells, making the boat lean suddenly. With a small squeal, Maggie grabbed the gunwale and kept herself from falling out.

"Just sit still! Please."

She sounded impatient, which Michael found irritating, but he didn't feel like calling her out on it. "What's the plan?"

Michael watched Maggie peel back a tarp and realized that something he'd thought was a pile of equipment was actually a machine bolted onto a small platform in the bow. Since he had been facing backward to row, it had been behind him. "This boat has a motor?"

Laughing, Maggie attached hoses to valves. "It's not for the boat." Two pulls on the starter cord and the motor growled like a lawnmower. Rushing air hissed from the hoses. "It's for hookah diving."

"So…we're not snorkeling?" A nervous knot tightened his guts.

"Not exactly. This is more like scuba diving, only we use a hookah."

Examining the mouthpiece on the end of the hose Maggie handed him, Michael called over the drone of the motor, "Like that stoner cat smoked in Alice in Wonderland?"

"The Caterpillar smoked the hookah. Anyway, this is basically a SCUBA tank, only it's a lot easier to use and it stays up here. We just take the hoses down with us."

"Can't you just breathe through the hose without the machine?"

Maggie laughed and shook her head. "After you go down a foot or two you wouldn't be able to pull any air through a hose because of the water pressure. Your chest can't expand. The hookah makes enough air pressure that we can go down ten meters with no problem."

"How deep is that?"

Maggie smiled. "It's like going from the roof to the basement of a three-story building."

Michael felt things inside him turning to jelly, but he'd never show it. "That's it?"

"We can go deeper, but since this is your first time, I don't want to push it."

"No, ten meters sounds great."

"Anyway, what we're looking for shouldn't be deeper than twenty-five, maybe thirty, feet."

Michael let that word we roll around in his mind while he watched Maggie attach a small flag to a float on the hose. It was red with a white diagonal bar.

"What's that for?"

"Guess you're not a Van Halen fan."

Michael felt that uncomfortable left-behind sensation again. "Weren't they a band?"

"Yeah. And they have a great album called Diver Down with this flag on the cover. Forget it. The flag warns boats there're divers in the water."

Looking around at the empty ocean, Michael said, "I don't think that'll be a problem. Just tell me what to do so my lungs don't explode."

As much as he didn't want it to, her laugh still sounded great. "You're not going to explode. Hookah is a lot easier than SCUBA. Plus, we're going to practice here in the boat first. When we go in the water, we'll practice some more near the surface. When you think you've got the hang of it, we dive. If you don't think you can do it, you can just wait. I won't be long."

Michael would drown before he'd admit he couldn't keep up with her. "No. I said I would help you."

Maggie smiled warmly. "Thanks."

In a few minutes, Michael was comfortable enough with the respirator to try it in the water. Maggie explained how to adjust his flippers, and then she spit inside her mask and rubbed it around with her fingers.

"That's disgusting!" Michael said.

"You want to see down there?" Maggie said. "Spit in the mask, rub it around and rinse it with seawater. Otherwise your mask will fog up."

Michael was still feeling a little dry, but he worked up enough spit in his mouth to coat the lens and the seals.

"You still might get some water in there. It's probably just condensation. Even if it's a small leak, don't panic. As long as your mask is adjusted right, you'll be fine."

"How do I know if it's right?" Little bubbles of fear gurgled in Michael's stomach.

"For starters, make sure none of your hair gets caught. Here. Let me help you."

Maggie adjusted his straps until she was satisfied, and helped him into the water. They stayed near the boat at first, and then she took him down a few feet, and after awhile, a few more. After a long stretch, she brought him back to the surface. "You catch on fast."

"You're a good teacher." Michael had been too focused on learning not to drown to think about Maggie's psycho treasure hunt for an imaginary door. He felt a warmth for her coming back. He was convinced that she was a nutjob, but she was a hot nutjob and fun to hang with.

"You ready to go all the way?"

Michael grinned, "I don't usually have a girl say that to me on the first date."

"First rule of diving is don't piss off the person controlling your air supply." But she smiled. Good sign. "There's still enough fuel in the hookah for about an hour and a half. That's plenty for finding the door."

There went the crazy again. "If the door is there."

Maggie didn't respond. She adjusted her mask and respirator and supervised Michael taking care of his. When he felt as ready as he was going to feel, Michael gave her thumbs-up. Maggie dipped her head and swam down toward the base of the jetty.

All Michael could hear was his own breathing and the blurp of bubbles when he exhaled. He checked the camera strap again, making sure it was still on him. He hoped to at least get some cool underwater pictures out of all this. And if Maggie did find whatever door she was she was looking for, he was going to take pictures of that, too. That would definitely make her happy.

Tracking the flashlight beam, Michael followed Maggie down the underwater mountain. Just like Maggie instructed him, Michael kept his breaths slow and steady. He forced himself to exhale all the way after each breath. Holding his breath while using the hookah would get him into trouble, even if they weren't going very deep. But clearly he and Maggie had different ideas about deep. The water around him was getting colder and more shadowy. It squeezed him and hurt his ears.

Maggie had seemed confident that he could do this, and that made him feel pretty confident, too. And so far he felt okay. More scared than he liked to admit. *She confided in me. Do I trust her more for that? Or is getting me to trust her the only reason she told me her crazy story? Or is she really just straight-up crazy?* Another thought muscled its way to the front of the line of fears and doubts crowding his brain like a sub shop at lunchtime. *Maybe she really is in trouble, and she really needs my help.*

The responsibility of that pressed down in him with more weight than the water. And he wondered whether Alison and Olivia were safe. If they weren't, there wasn't a thing he could do to help them.

As soon as he did whatever she wanted him to do, he was going to find the girls with or without Maggie. He would figure out how he was going to explain it all to Mom and Dad, but things had gotten too weird. It was time to get his family out of Cape November.

Estimating that a two-story house would fit between himself and the surface, and that Maggie was still diving, Michael tried to concentrate on not freaking out. That just made him freak out more. It didn't help at all that Maggie had warned him that freaking out would be very bad. He tried to focus on the scenery to keep the bad thoughts from gaining traction.

They were far enough down that the sunlight was dim, even though the water was surprisingly clear. There wasn't a whole lot to look at. Michael had expected something more colorful and dramatic. Everything was dull brown and sandy. Most of the rocks were shaggy with mossy-looking seaweed. The beam of Maggie's flashlight caught shells and some orange anemones that looked like mushrooms. A couple of scrawny fish and small crabs scattered as they passed. The starfish just lay there. Tall, brown grasses swayed in the breeze of the currents. Michael looked away from the jetty, out into the deep water connecting him to the entire rest of the planet. He tried not to think about the things that lived out there.

Ahead, Maggie stopped swimming and floated vertically. Her flashlight penetrated a dark, rectangular opening that led up into the jetty. Michael knew there was no way a natural cave could be that regular. The opening was about as tall as he was and just a little too wide for him to stretch his arms across it from edge to edge. Floating next to the opening, something below them caught his eye. Maggie started to swim head first up into the cave, but he tapped her on the ankle and got her to point the flashlight down.

A metallic, rectangular object lay at an odd angle on the rocks below the cave. They swam down to it, and Michael lifted a corner. It was heavy, but moveable. Seaweed and barnacles covered the bottom, but the side facing up was smooth and clean. Michael understood that, until a short time ago, this door had covered the passage.

Who opened it? And why?

Back at the entrance, Maggie shined the light up, but the tunnel was longer than her beam could reach. The walls were smooth and lined with smaller versions of the familiar blue-gray bricks. The tunnel was perfectly clean.

It must have been sealed until the door fell off, Michael thought. *That's why nothing is growing in here.*

Maggie pulled down more slack for their hoses. The flashlight showed that the tunnel cut up into the jetty at a steep angle. Maggie grabbed the sides of the tunnel to pull herself in, but Michael stopped her. He shook his head as he drew her gently back. He said he would help. He was going first. He pointed to himself and then up into the tunnel.

Her hair swirled around her like the sea grass as she shook her head firmly. She pointed to her own chest.

Michael didn't see the point in arguing when they couldn't even hear each other, so he swam up into the darkness ahead of Maggie. His calf erupted in pain when she pinched him. She tugged him back by the ankle, but he shook himself free and kept swimming, letting his natural buoyancy lift him, guiding himself along with his hands. Maggie was just below him, as close as she could swim without getting slapped by Michael's flippers.

She shined the light ahead for Michael to follow. The tunnel spiraled up to the left and got steeper until Michael felt like he was swimming up from the bottom of a well. Soon he found the bottom of a ladder. He only had to follow it a few feet before his head popped out into dark, still air. There was just enough room for Maggie next to him. Even in the strange surroundings, Michael noticed as their thighs and hips brushed together.

He also noticed the way that the sloshing water echoed off the stones. Every sound seemed to carry up and out of the tunnel forever.

Maggie pulled out her mouthpiece and spit some water. "We must be above the waterline. This is amazing. I can't believe we're in here." She was barely above a whisper, but it sounded as loud as a hurricane. The mouthpiece bubbled and hissed.

"In where? Are we inside the jetty?" Michael whispered back after spitting his own air hose out. He followed her lead and wound the hose around the rungs of the ladder.

"We only have about forty-five minutes of fuel left at most. A half hour is safer."

"You want to go back?"

Maggie took back the flashlight and aimed it along the metal ladder, but the light just seemed to get sucked up by the darkness. "We're *so* climbing this ladder."

It was a terrible idea, but Michael knew he wasn't going to talk her out of it.

She was already pulling off her flippers, which is how she kneed him squarely in the groin. Sinking pain gushed through his core.

"Oh sorry!" she giggled, apparently trying hard not to.

It still throbbed. "Is that for going first?"

"It was an accident. I swear."

She looked sheepish and guilty, but there was definitely a mischievous light in her eyes. Beautiful or not, he didn't know if he could trust her, and that chewed at him.

Threading her arm through her mask and flippers, Maggie took the lead up the ladder. Right below her, Michael could crane his neck to watch Maggie climb. He felt like a total creep every time he looked, but he had to admit, she looked really good climbing a ladder. Besides, he told himself, it was the only view he had.

32 THE CAVE

Olivia had hoped there would be stairs at the end of the hallway. They could go just up those stairs, find an empty church building with no scary dudes in ponchos. No white van parked outside. Then, easy, breezy, melted cheesy, they'd hop on their bikes and ride away.

But they had found no stairs. And if they had, Olivia was sure the creeps in ponchos and the white van would still be there. They were a long way from home. They headed down the stairs behind the door marked NURSERY.

The yellow lights lining the stairs at least allowed them to put their phones away. Olivia concentrated on keeping her breathing regular. Alison seemed so calm. *She's a lot more used to being in places she shouldn't.*

They moved slowly, setting squeaky sneakers down with cautious, deliberate steps on the stairway's metal grating. Finally, they stood on a metal mesh deck that covered the tumbled stone floor of a large cave. Through the grating under Olivia's sneakers, the stones looked slimy, and many were covered in seaweed and barnacles. She tracked the rows of yellow lighting across the roof of the cave until they stopped. But out slightly to the right, the cave continued past the artificial lights. Daylight filtered in at the far end where the cave opened into the ocean.

"We can go up there." Alison pointed to steps across the deck, past two rows of tables. Alison gasped. And then Olivia saw it, too. Six metal tables. Three of the tables each had a person lying on it, two men and a woman. They seemed to be naked, but most of their bodies were covered with pale goo.

"Are they glued there?" Olivia asked, feeling the horror crawling out of her throat. She tried to make sense of the thick, ropy snot coating the arms, legs, chests and groins of the people on the table. A white, rubbery-looking tube stuck out of each person's belly button and disappeared under the black water. The scene in the cave was just like in the poster. "This isn't possible."

Her skin crawled. Her mind whirled. Olivia was overwhelmed by the sensation that she was in a dream. She had to be. She slapped her own face, pinched her arms, bit her lip until she tasted coppery blood. Olivia's eyes opened when Alison shook her sharply by the shoulders. For half a second Olivia felt relief, but it crumbled away when she saw that they were not in bed. Alison had not been waking her from a nightmare.

"Hey!" Olivia felt the heat of Alison's breath, as she rasped in Olivia's face, and she could smell the shampoo in her thick, curly hair, just over the stench of low tide. "We can't lose it in here. Stay with me or we'll never make it out."

"This is a nightmare, though, right? I just can't wake up."

The quiet determination in Alison's voice was reassuring, even if her words weren't. She took Olivia's hands. The soft touch of Alison's fingers brought Olivia back to a flickering hope for something normal. "This is real. It's happening. Everything we knew before? Where the world was ordinary and this stuff didn't happen? That was the dream."

"What do we do?" Olivia refused to accept that, but she resigned herself to letting the nightmare continue.

Alison's eyes were force and fire. "First we get out of here."

Crouching past the tables, Alison led Olivia toward the other staircase. They slunk along the left wall of the cave, past two empty tables. At the third table, Olivia poked her head up to risk a look at the person lying on it. She felt like one of the prairie dogs she used to love watching at the zoo.

The man on the table was probably middle-aged; he was pale, shriveled like he was shrinking inside and his skin didn't fit anymore.

Who is that? she wondered. What's happening? Does it hurt?

Her face impacted something soft. Alison, who turned to glare at her with an angry finger on her lips. Nodding toward the stairs, Olivia saw the shadow coming down the wall. Then she heard the metallic plunk of footsteps on the grating. Loud and confident, the walker must have felt at home among the surgery tables, the stink of fish and the tubes leading underwater. That thought terrified Olivia. She clenched her stomach to keep from throwing up.

Alison dragged Olivia back toward the stairs they had used earlier, but when they were hidden behind the last table, Alison pushed her so that they both lay face down. The grating bit uncomfortably into Olivia's thighs, elbows and knees.

The bottom hem of a blue robe came into sight down the front stairs. Olivia could not stop shaking. It was not the men who had originally chased them. Their ponchos were black, not blue, and they were larger. The hood was pushed back enough for Olivia to see an old man with a scruffy white beard. He looked like a medieval monk.

He moved around the room like he'd done it a million times, taking a plastic bucket from a small table under the stairs and dipping it in the ocean water. At the first table, he pulled a cloth out of the bucket and wiped down the hairless, dried-up man on it. The old man wrung out the water over the man's mummified face and body and over the white umbilical cord that went into the water below.

The monk chanted in a singsong as he worked. "Another day, two at most, and you will be ready, my sweet. Ready to serve He That Is Magnificent. Ready to leave this world of shadow and illusions. Let He That Is Magnificent enlighten you to reality. Take your place among His army."

He moved to the woman. She looked thin and sickly, but she still had recognizable features and quite a bit of her black hair. "Coming along," he said, wiping and wetting her and the cord. "Patience, my dear. Patience."

"Kill me." The croaking voice echoed off the stones and seemed to startle the man in the blue robe. He looked over at the third table, where Alison and Olivia had been a moment before. "Kill me, please," the man on the table begged. He was fleshy, and his skin still looked normal.

The man in the blue robe clucked his tongue. "That's no way for a benefactor to talk, Mr. Pereira. You have been chosen. It's a great honor." The monk smiled pleasantly. "You've only been here a few days. Soon you will be enlightened."

"No!" the man's voice rattled. His body convulsed as if he wanted to move, but couldn't. Olivia craned her head, but did not see any ropes or restraints. Maybe he's paralyzed, she thought with sudden, overwhelming horror. Whatever gets exchanged through the tube must paralyze people.

When the man on the table begged again to be killed, the old monk's face became a network of malicious, scowling creases. He yelled something inarticulate and wrung out the cloth over his victim's face, filling his mouth with seawater until he gurgled, coughing and spitting, as the monk slapped him viciously again and again with the wet cloth.

The man on the table sobbed. "I can't. Please don't..." The monk cut him off by dumping the bucket over his face. The monk's eyes narrowed to slits. "If you don't stop all this," he hissed, half giggling, "I will soak this cloth in seawater and stuff it back in your mouth like I did on our first day together. Remember how you cried and blubbered like a little boy?" The monk imitated the sound of crying until he trailed off in a coughing fit of crazed laughter. "I know how much you hated that." Cackling, the monk held the cloth up, threatening the helpless man on the table. Satisfied that the man on the table would not say anything else, the old man continued to wash and wet his body and the white cord.

Olivia hyperventilated. She needed to scream, but she knew she couldn't. She reached out for Alison's hand, but it was gone. Panic filled her. Alison was gone. *They got her!* She crawled around desperate to find Alison, but she could not call for her. When she hit her head on the metal table, it clanged like a gong. Olivia froze. Her heart sounded like an avalanche in her own ears.

"Who's that now?" The old man demanded icily, moving cautiously around the table. "Nobody's supposed to be here but me today." He set down his bucket and walked toward Olivia.

She scurried back, her hands and feet making tiny squeaks on the deck, no matter how quietly she tried to move.

"There you are, little mouse," he said. Closer, Olivia could see that under his hood, his face was bony, his eyes hollow and so blue they were almost white. "I didn't know He That Is Magnificent was going to send me another benefactor so soon." He reached his bony hands out toward Olivia. There was a wet, sickening crunch, and the old man's head lolled drunkenly to one side. He staggered, wobbling when the second crunch knocked his head the other way. He crumpled softly to the deck.

Alison stood behind him, panting. The hammer clattered loudly to the deck.

Olivia stood and stared at the limp form in the piles of robes. "Allie? I think you killed him."

"Good," she hissed angrily. She wiped viciously at her nose and eyes. "Look what he's doing to them." She gestured toward the people on the tables. She sniffled hard. "I thought we could make it to the stairs while he was working. I thought you saw me, but then you weren't behind me. I heard that guy begging on the table. It made me sick. And then I saw that old psycho coming after you. I guess I snapped."

Olivia shivered at the wreck of the old man at their feet. Her stomach lurched. She threw up. "Sorry."

Alison shook her head like it didn't even matter. "We're leaving. Now!" She turned and trotted toward the stairs. Her foot was on the first step when she stopped so suddenly, Olivia ran into her back.

"What?" Olivia felt the panic of knowing that something else was coming to kill them.

"I can't." Alison turned around and edged past Olivia. "I can't just leave these people."

"We can't do anything," Olivia hissed. "We need to call the cops. They need an ambulance." Olivia wasn't so sure doctors could help, but she felt pretty sure that they couldn't do anything for them.

Alison ran to the man on the table and shook him. "Hey? Mister? Mister, can you get up?"

"Kill me," the man rasped. "It's in me."

"What is?"

"A mind…in my head. Someone else. Something else." His wheezy voice wilted.

Olivia caught up to Alison and looked at his face, creased with lines of agony. His eyes were watery and pale. "Can you see?" Olivia asked.

"Kill me. Taking me. Evil." The man let out a choked sob.

Alison elbowed past Olivia and grabbed the cord. She made a disgusted sound. "Help me pull it out."

It was fatter than Olivia could get her hand around. Slimy and cold, like raw meat. Just touching it made Olivia think she might throw up again. They pulled and tugged. The man screamed. There was thrashing in the water behind them. Olivia saw the pale suggestion of something beneath the surface.

"This isn't working," Olivia said. "We have to cut it."

"How?" Alison asked.

Olivia ran over to the worktable where the old man got the bucket. She spotted a set of long, shiny knives. They reminded her of a video she once saw in social studies about Civil War hospitals. That had been back in the dream she used to call reality.

Setting down her hammer, Olivia picked up a large, straight knife with a long, shiny blade.

Alison held out her hand, but Olivia shook her head and forced out a weak smile. "I got it. Just help me hold it still."

With one hand, Olivia gripped the cold, slimy musculature of the umbilical cord. Its veiny tubes throbbed. She raised the knife and glanced over at Alison. Gripping the cord with both hands, her face red, she nodded.

The man on the table groaned pathetically. Olivia took a deep breath. Her father made her watch medical shows all the time. Her mother once brought home a whole suckling pig for a New Year's Eve party and guided Olivia on removing its eyes and cutting out the organs. Divorced or not, Olivia's parents agreed that Olivia would grow up to be a surgeon. Neither of them missed an opportunity to make her lose her squeamishness, but none of that had prepared her for what she had to do in the cave.

Her stomach did little flips as she brought the blade near the pulsing tendril in her hand. She took a deep breath. In her head, she counted *One. Two.* As she thought three, she exhaled and sliced through the white flesh. The man shrieked, and behind them in the water, the white blob pulsed and thrashed, splashing them. Blood and purplish liquid bubbled out of the gash Olivia had made in the thick, hose-like appendage, along with a thick, lumpy, white substance like fat on a piece of marbled beef.

Olivia felt her stomach heave. From up the stairs, there was a terrible, agitated rumbling and shuffling over the floor. Olivia shivered when she recognized the unnatural shuffle of the men in the ponchos.

"Hurry, Liv, finish it," Alison's voice quavered.

Olivia forced her mind into a state of complete focus like when she raced. She took one more breath. Two more slices and the cord was writhing on the ground, spewing bloody, white jelly. Her heart sprang in her chest as the man on the table shrieked and strained against the crusted mucus gluing him down. His whole body thrashed like he was having a seizure, and then his head flopped to one side and he let out a long, gurgling hiss before blood and white clumps came spasmodically out of his mouth.

"Is he dead?" Olivia could barely breathe.

Alison stepped away. "I don't know. We have to go." Her voice was flat, frayed.

Olivia saw the bottom of a long poncho come haltingly down the stairs. "It's them," she whispered. "From the picture." The knife clattered to the floor. "That's what they are. What this is!"

Alison acted like she hadn't heard. Snatching up the knife and tucking it into the waistband of her shorts, she whispered, "We have to swim."

Olivia looked at the dark water and thought about the pulsating, white blob she had seen. It made her feel weak and hollow. "We don't know what's out there."

"We know what's in here." Alison had already moved to the edge of the deck. She glanced at the steps and motioned for Olivia to duck down right before she slipped quietly into the water. Face down on the deck, Olivia forced herself to breathe slowly and tried to stop shaking. Alison was already swimming. Olivia knew Alison expected her to follow, but she was afraid to swim. *That's ironic.*

Moving on palms and toes, she followed Alison silently into the water and caught up easily. It was almost painful to watch Alison struggle to do something between a crawl and a dog paddle. As they moved closer to the mouth of the cave, the waves got stronger. If she weren't trying to pace Alison, Olivia would have been out already, but she wasn't going to leave Alison alone.

Flipping into a backstroke, Olivia craned her neck to look back toward the nursery. Fear knotted her insides. Two things in ponchos stood bobbing their heads at the edge of the deck.

One dropped its poncho, revealing a large, white body. From that distance, Olivia could not make out much detail, but there was no question that it was one of those things from the diagram. A beadle.

A sick roller-coaster feeling swelled in her stomach, like she was plummeting down a slope. The beadle dove into the water.

"Allie?" Olivia whispered. "We have to hurry."

"They found us?" Alison sounded more angry than afraid.

"Just swim faster."

"Damn it, just tell me! Did they find us?"

"Yes!" Olivia flipped back over and tucked her head into a competitive freestyle stroke, but after a few yards she stopped to tread water. Alison couldn't keep up with her. She remembered the knife and pulled it from Alison's waistband. "I'm taking the knife."

"Why?"

"One of those things is coming. Swim as fast as you can. Get out of the water."

"What about you?"

"Just go!"

Forcing herself to control her breathing, Olivia leaned back and kicked hard for the cave mouth. Her sneakers popped off, but she kept kicking, holding the knife in front of her chest, bracing herself, ready to slash anything that grabbed her legs to drag her down. She tried to spot the pale form under the dark water, to see where it would come from, but as she swam closer to open ocean beyond the cave mouth, the waves were higher. She couldn't see over them.

Fatigue settled on her like a blanket. The long bike ride, the crawling, hiding, climbing, swimming and mostly the fear, had burned out her adrenaline. How exhausted Alison must be. She couldn't see her. Olivia kicked hard to get upright and see above the waves. When she saw Alison clear the tunnel and head for the rocks, she breathed again.

She had no idea where the thing was that had followed them into the water.

Holding the knife in her teeth like a pirate, she never took her eyes off Alison as she quickly closed the distance to the rocks.

If it had been any rougher they would have been smashed against the boulders. Olivia watched Alison try to time a large, lazy swell rolling in from deep water. She rode the wave onto a large outcropping of rocks, but landed so hard Olivia winced just watching her.

At least she was out of the water. She was safe. Olivia thought about the pale, white form gliding under the surface and swam hard for the rocks. She took the knife in her hand again to yell out for Alison over the pounding surf. Scrambling on her bloody hands and knees, Alison reached back for Olivia.

Riding a swell, Olivia grabbed Alison's wrist, slick with blood and seawater. As Alison hauled her onto the rocks, pain like hot needles bit Olivia's ankle. The fire spread up her leg.

She screamed. The white tentacle wrapped around her ankle. It would have pulled her into the water, except Alison squatted behind her, holding her under the arms and around the chest, screaming painfully in her ear. Their bare feet slid over the slick, wet rock as the thing pulled them toward the water's edge.

Ignoring the fiery needles in her ankle, Olivia tried to understand what she was seeing. The thing wriggled farther out of the water, chasing them. Its long, snaky fingers at the end of the tentacle pierced her with toothed suckers. It had white, gelatinous skin and a long, moon-shaped head with no eyes or nose or any features except a completely round mouth. As it opened to chomp Olivia's thigh, she saw many rows of jagged teeth.

Roaring savagely, Olivia slashed at the head, slicing a gash and driving it back. Then she hacked blindly at the tentacle. The first swipe missed completely, sparking off the rock, but the second swing chopped into the monster's white, flabby skin just behind the tentacle fingers. The sharp tentacles unwound from Olivia's ankle and slid limply into the water as the monster threw itself back and disappeared under the waves.

Without the extra weight, Olivia tumbled backwards onto Alison on the hot, hard rocks. Screaming, they scrambled like crabs away from the water. They were almost up to the boardwalk when they paused, panting and still tangled together. Olivia held her breath, waiting for the thing to leap out of the water after them, but there was only the rhythmic crashing of the waves. When she felt Alison's arms around her neck and shoulders, Olivia melted, sobbing softly.

"It's just like the picture. They really make these things!" The thought whirled in Olivia's head, driving out everything else.

Alison sobbed. "That old guy was going to do it to you. You understand that, right? That's why I had to. I snapped. I'm sorry. I didn't even think. I just…Liv, I killed him. He was alive, and now he's not."

It scared her how little she cared that Alison killed the old man. The thing Olivia could not escape was that poor man on the table, begging to die. The begging was an earworm from a nightmare. She could not stop seeing the old man reaching for her. Or feeling the barbed-wire tentacle grabbing her ankle. The fire in her throbbing wound ignited her whole body with rage.

"No!" Olivia said it savagely.

Alison gasped, recoiling.

Olivia pushed herself back from Alison and looked into her dark eyes. "These sick freaks are the real killers. You had no choice. Look what they were doing to those people on the tables. You think they cared about them?"

Shaking her head, Alison said, "I've done lots of bad things, but not like this. Nothing like this."

"You saved my life!" Olivia grabbed Alison's shoulders. "We have to get back. We have to get your family and Maggie and Olga and everybody normal out of this town. We have to tell them what happened. EXACTLY what happened. Whatever's going on here, it's serious. And it's dangerous."

Alison looked like she was caught between laughing and crying. "Nobody's going to believe us. What are we supposed to say, that we got attacked by squid monsters?"

"Look at my ankle! Are we making that up?" Olivia could not stop hearing the man on the table begging to die. The welts on her ankle from the tentacle still burned. And the memory of the old man's head flopped to the side like a rag doll when Alison bashed him with the hammer replayed over and over again in her mind.

Alison shut her eyes and let out a long sigh. "We don't even know what we saw, and we're the ones who saw it."

Olivia felt so tired. She looked at Alison. Her eyes were sharp and intense. She had that look. "What? What is it?"

"Maggie," Alison said flatly.

"What about her?"

"She must know something. She lives here. The nightmares?" Alison's face turned a shade paler, and her mouth dropped open. "Michael. He's with her back at The Mansion. And who even knows where my parents are? They have no clue."

The gashes around her ankle hurt, but Olivia could put weight on it. Kneeling, Alison pressed around the cuts with her fingers. "It's not that deep. More like bad scrapes. I don't think you'll need stitches, just a bandage probably."

Panic ballooned in Olivia's stomach as she felt the fire spread around her ankle and crawl like fingers up her leg. "Allie, I might be poisoned."

Full of fear, Alison looked up at her. "It's a little red, but it doesn't look that bad. Should I pee on it?"

That made Olivia laugh. "Only a real friend would offer to pee on me. But that's a myth. Seawater might help, but we're not going anywhere near the water.

Maybe if we get back we can find some vinegar. But pee might make it worse."

"When we get back." Alison's eyes were fiery.

"We don't know what that thing is." Studying Alison's beautiful freckles made Olivia sad. She fought back tears. "A blue-ringed octopus bite doesn't show any symptoms for ten to twenty minutes."

"Then what?" Alison looked worried.

"You die." Olivia felt sick and panicky.

"Go rinse it!" Alison popped up to her feet and started to pull up Olivia.

Olivia shook her head, but it hurt, like it was full of heavy marbles rolling around and crashing into the inside of her skull. "I'm not going near the water. That thing could be waiting."

"You're not going to die." Alison sounded confident. But Olivia knew she was a gifted liar. She examined the cuts on Olivia's ankle again. "If you were poisoned, you'd feel a lot worse than you do, right?"

"Sure," Olivia said. She didn't feel like it was the best time to share how sick she was starting to feel.

"Did it bite you?" Alison knelt, inspecting the cuts carefully.

"No. It just grabbed me." Olivia shuddered remembering the long, white tentacle attached to her ankle. "But jellyfish venom is in their stingers. Octopus venom is in their beaks."

Alison looked up at her. "You can walk on it, right?"

Gingerly, Olivia moved around, experimenting with her weight. It hurt. The hot rocks and barnacles under her feet didn't help any. "I had a coach once on a travel team. She said an athlete had to know the difference between getting hurt and getting injured. Hurt meant you could keep going. Injured meant you had to stop."

Looking up at Olivia, Alison tilted her head. "She sounds like a jerk." Alison ran her hands lightly up and down Olivia's leg. "It might be a little hot, I can't really tell. You're all wet still. When we get back to The Mansion we'll get some peroxide and a bandage." Alison stood up. "Maybe you should take a Benadryl or something just in case there was any poison."

Olivia knew that an antihistamine was useless against serious venom. A trip to the hospital might not even help. And how could she tell a doctor what poisoned her? Olivia sighed deeply. The lighthouse at The Mansion was just a splinter against the sky. "Maybe I should just find someplace to hide here. You can run back and get help. Call the cops and an ambulance for me and for the people down in the cave."

Alison ran her hand on Olivia's forehead. "Are you sure you're okay? You sound delirious." She rested her hand gently on her forehead. "Do you have a fever?"

That made Olivia smile. "I'm serious. You can go faster without me." Olivia laughed and winced. "Ironic, huh?"

33 CATHEDRAL OF NEW ENLIGHTENMENT

"I'm at the top." The climb left Maggie sounding breathless.

Michael cleared the top rung and stood dripping beside her at the end of a stone hallway that sloped gently up from the vertical shaft. The air was hot, damp and heavy. They both glistened with sweat. Michael didn't need to duck, but he could touch the ceiling and both walls without stretching. He had never felt claustrophobic before, but he had never been in a weird underground passage before either. He stared at Maggie, not quite sure what to believe or even what to think of her.

"Okay. Seriously. How did you know this was here?" His own voice startled him in the strangling silence.

Maggie's voice was just a night breeze. "I didn't."

"But you were looking for it."

She turned to face him. "It was just a hunch based on crap my grandfather said. I didn't really think I would find anything."

"That's some pretty amazing guesswork, Maggie. You play the lottery?"

Her eyes narrowed. "It wasn't a guess. It was a hunch." Her eyes softened, and she lowered her face toward the ground. "I didn't know this would be here." She sighed. "Now that I found it, I don't know if I should feel relieved or terrified. That's why I brought you. I was afraid to come alone. Either way, this was going to be life-changing for me." She looked up at him with damp eyes. "I had no one else to ask."

"What do you mean?" Michael debated in his head for a moment before putting his hand on her upper arm.

She looked at his hand and smiled. "If this wasn't here, then I am just delusional and my parents died in an accident. Everything is normal except me, just like the police report said."

He squeezed the muscles of her shoulder gently. She didn't pull away.

"But it is here." Maggie's eyes were damp. "Everything I know about my life is wrong, Michael. And what I thought was a delusion is reality. My parents were killed fighting a dangerous cult, and they're doing something bad right in my backyard."

"We don't know that yet."

She arched her eyebrow, and Michael knew she was right. The weight of it all felt as crushing and claustrophobic as the tunnel. He tried to imagine what it must be like to learn that everything you thought you knew about your life was wrong. "All this time you thought you were just sick?"

"All the doctors and counselors, even Aunt Penny, they just made me think I was delusional, but don't you see?" She squeezed both his hands. "My parents weren't crazy. My grandfather wasn't crazy. This proves it." Her eyes looked vibrant. "I'm not crazy."

"A tunnel proves all that?"

"This tunnel shouldn't exist!"

"I don't want to piss in your Cheerios here, but this place could have been made by pirates or smugglers … the Underground Railroad. It doesn't really prove anything about the Church of the Christmas Lights or whatever you call it."

"Church of New Enlightenment." Smiling, Maggie turned back around and walked up the hallway. She called over her shoulder. "You're right. That's why we need to keep going."

"What about the air? If the fuel runs out we'll be trapped down here."

"Maybe. There could be another way out." Maggie said. "But you're right. You should probably go back." She kept walking.

Michael turned to face the ladder, but without her flashlight, he couldn't see it. He couldn't see anything. He thought about leaving Maggie down there. He could grope his way back to the ladder, get back to the dory, get his family and get out. He didn't need to get mixed up in Maggie's psycho drama. And then he felt horribly guilty for thinking it. Even if he wanted to, he could never live with himself if he left her. Especially knowing what he knew about her. And he really didn't want to. He said he would help her, and one thing Michael knew was that a man should say what he means and mean what he says.

But even if he didn't abandon her, Michael wondered whether going back to The Mansion would be the best way to help her. He ran a few scenarios through his mind where, without a flashlight, he managed to get all the way back up to the boat, miraculously get it back to the beach, figure out where to get gas for the hookah, figure out where to row back to and how to hook the gear back up again correctly, and swim the hose back down the tunnel for Maggie to get back up. In no version of that did he make it to an ending where nobody drowned, so he turned and trotted after the flashlight beam.

They padded along for a while, neither of them talking until Maggie said, "End of the line."

Looking past her, Michael saw the end of the hallway. In the right wall there was a pointed door. The wood looked old, the planks thick and heavy. It was big enough that they could have easily walked through it side by side. But it was closed.

He took the large metal ring in his hand and looked expectantly at Maggie. Glowing lines of reflected light played across her face and body.

She hesitated, looking back and forth between Michael and the door. Then she nodded faintly.

Michael twisted the ring, and it moved slightly. He used both hands and twisted as hard as he could. The ring turned a little more. His body dripped in the close, stifling air.

"Let me help you." Setting the light on the floor, Maggie pressed next to him, their bodies slippery with sweat. She shook her hands as dry as she could get them and grabbed the ring. Their shadows were huge against the wood. She gave a one-two-three count, and they both twisted the ring. It turned slowly until, with a metallic shriek, it twisted loose. A metallic clang came from within the door.

"We got it," Michael said, untangling himself from Maggie. He leaned gently against the door with his shoulder, and it swung silently inward on massive metal hinges.

The door was almost a foot thick. Leaning through, Maggie shined the flashlight down to the left. By the time the beam found another wall, it was only a dull, thin glow on the huge blocks, but they saw something different in the pattern.

Maggie steadied the light. She whispered, "Another door. See it? Way in the back? Could be our way out."

Michael wondered why she was whispering, and then he leaned through the opening. Far across the darkness, the other door shimmered faintly. The enormous emptiness of the place made him feel like a single krill in the mouth of a whale. He whispered, "What is this place?"

"It feels ancient." Maggie moved the light beam around. There was another wall across from them, not as far away as the first one they saw that had the door in it. Eventually the beam found the corner where the two walls met far to the left. "And it's so big."

"That's what she said." Michael had to break the tension.

Maggie snorted out a stifled laugh. "There's a Lenape legend, well, most anthropologists say that the legend isn't technically Lenape, but they seem to have been aware of it. Some of their lore mentions a longhouse built by the *manetuwak*."

"The what?" His mouth felt dry.

"Evil spirits. The Lenape feared it. Shunned it."

"Sounds like that was probably a good idea. I wish the white man thought of that, but instead, here we are."

Maggie didn't reply. She shined the light over the opposite wall until it found something other than huge blue-gray blocks.

"Is that a painting?" Walking toward it, blinding pain erupted in Michael's toes and knee. Cursing, he staggered in the dark, and his hip ground into something hard that stuck straight up from the ground. He caught himself on it before he fell.

"MICHAEL!" Maggie sounded terrified. Her voice echoed around in the dark.

"Aww. You really do care," he groaned, trying to get a rise out of her. "It's okay. I just ran into something. A rock, I think."

With the flashlight, Maggie revealed a low, stone pedestal standing straight up out of the ground, as tall as her hip. The top had a small groove, about two fingers wide, carved into it. "What's this for?" she wondered.

"Circumcisions?" It wasn't until after he checked his camera, still strapped around his neck, that Michael realized his toes throbbed. Wiggling and flexing didn't make them feel any better, but it helped him convince himself that nothing was broken. "Come on. Let's find that painting so we can get out of here." He was still worried about Alison and Olivia, but the mystery he was working on with Maggie was becoming impossible to resist.

As Maggie crossed the room, the flashlight beam wobbled between the colorful image and the floor. Michael didn't want to trip over any new surprises, but other than that weird pedestal, the floor was empty. The stones felt warm and smooth under his bare feet. His right foot hurt if he put too much weight on it, but he didn't want to mention it to Maggie. She might think he was a wimp.

When they were close enough, Michael saw that the painting was framed in rounded, rectangular stones that came to a point at the top like both of the doors they'd seen. The painting itself was of an enormous, erupting volcano. The mountainside was toppling into the ocean, creating a massive tsunami that was swamping a Greek-looking city.

Maggie gasped. "A flooded Greek city. Do you think that's supposed to be Atlantis?"

Michael had no idea. "I don't know. It's a really nice, family picture though," Michael said sarcastically, "Let's get it to a museum. Kids'll be lining up around the block."

"If you think they'd like that one, take a look at this one." A few feet to their left, Maggie lit up another painting. "That's Rome. See the Coliseum and the Pantheon? I know that because I used to play a lot of Assassin's Creed. And Mom said video games weren't educational. What's with the *kaiju*?"

"The what?"

Feeling a little smug that she didn't know everything, he nodded at the strange creature in the painting. Rome was engulfed in flames, and an enormous jellyfish-looking thing towered over the city like in a Japanese monster movie. At the sight of the monster, Michael felt a little heave in his stomach, like the time he was out on his bike and saw a dead possum covered in maggots. Or the day before when he'd seen that carcass on the side of the road.

The monster was pale white. It stood on huge tentacles and had a fat, blobby body, with dozens of smaller tentacles coming out of it, along with two huge claws, like a crab or a lobster. The claws smashed through the Coliseum. "That's not how the history books say Rome fell."

"Maybe the history books are wrong." Maggie stood on her toes to examine the painting. "Or maybe this is just wishful thinking."

"What kind of mutant ass-head would wish for this?" Michael felt his stomach turning as he looked at the smaller tentacles snatching up dozens of shrieking men, women and children in togas and dropping them into the thing's mouth. At least that's what Michael figured the round hole at the top of the *kaiju's* body was. It bristled with jagged teeth.

Turning to look at him, Maggie said, "Human sacrifice?"

"This is what the Church of what's-its-face is into?"

"The Church of New Enlightenment." She moved down the wall to the left, stopping whenever the light landed on a new picture. At the end of the wall nearest to the corner the painting showed the manger scene Michael recognized from Christmastime. Mary, Joseph, an ox, a donkey and the three wise men stood around a little cradle. But white tentacles slithered out of the straw, crushing baby Jesus like boa constrictors. Next to the Nativity, Michael recognized Buddha meditating under a tree. Michael had seen this scene before, but in this version, white tentacles came out of the ground and penetrated his eyes and mouth, killing the Buddha.

"I think that's Krishna in the next painting." Michael heard Maggie swallow. She pointed to the blue young man getting ripped apart by white tentacles.

"These are sick! Who would ever paint this?" Michael demanded.

"Don't you get it, Michael?" Maggie's voice was shaking and full of tears. "It is real. What I saw, what my grandfather believed? The Church of New Enlightenment really is some kind of death cult, but it's even worse than he thought."

Michael fought down the fear and anger rising inside him. "Alison and Olivia are out there with this death cult."

"It doesn't matter," Maggie sounded sad. Defeated.

Michael felt his blood catch fire. "The hell it doesn't!"

Maggie's eyes got big. "That's not what I mean. Look at these pictures. Look at what these people want to do. Nowhere is safe."

Michael looked at the nightmare images. "This is just some meth-head's coloring book. These paintings don't mean anything."

"We have to take some pictures of these paintings."

"No. We have to get out of here."

Maggie clenched her fists. "Michael, everything I thought I knew is a lie! And look at this place! Look at what these people are about. We have to do something." She slumped against the wall and slid down until her butt was on the floor and her head rested on her knees. Her body shook with her quiet sobs.

Michael sat beside her. He rested his hand gently on her shoulder. "This is tough for you. I get that."

She pierced him with her red, teary eyes. "No! You don't get it."

Michael studied the worried lines creasing her forehead. He tried to brush some damp hair off her face, but she swatted his hand away. Then she snatched his hand in both of hers and pressed it to her face. She took a deep breath and kept her eyes closed. "Michael, what if the Church of New Enlightenment really is responsible for all the disappearances and everything else going on down here, and this place tells us why?"

"I don't understand," Michael did not pull his hand free.

"I can't explain it all to you now, but we need to take pictures of these paintings. They're our only clue, the only proof. We might not be able to get back here."

"We?" Michael jerked his hand back and stood up. "Look, I said I'd help you and I am, but this is it. I'm never coming back to this place or to The Mansion or to Cape November."

She stood slowly until she was eye to eye with Michael. "Right. Just get everybody important and run. This isn't your problem. Until it becomes your problem."

Michael felt a twinge of guilt. "It's not like that. It's just...my family's out there."

Maggie looked at him coldly. "My family's dead." She shined the light on the scene of baby Jesus and the tentacles. "Just take the pictures. Then we can go. Okay? It might be my only chance."

"To do what?"

"TO PROVE I'M NOT CRAZY!" Her voice echoed off the ancient stone. "To figure out what these people are really doing so we—so I— can figure out how to stop them."

"How are these pictures going to help?"

"If nothing else I can expose The Church of New Enlightenment for what it is."

"Isn't that what the reporter was trying to do?" Michael said. "That didn't work out too good for her. Do you really want that?" He looked at her face. Her eyes flashed with intensity.

"So what? I shouldn't do anything?" Maggie looked away from him and brushed the hair away that had fallen across her face.

"Why don't you leave, too? Come with me."

She gave a long sigh. "It's not that simple. This is my home. And besides, do you really think The Church of New Enlightenment is going to stop at Cape November?"

A million thoughts swirled in Michael's mind. "I don't know what they're going to do."

"Don't you see? Look at what's happening here at Cape November. The way they've taken over. They're getting stronger. They're growing."

Michael lifted the camera that hung around his neck and took a few shots of the paintings. "So what are you going to do with these pictures?"

"I have to show them to Olga first."

Michael laughed at the ridiculous idea. "What's she going to do, cook them?"

She stared coolly, and it made him feel small and self-conscious. "People can be more than one thing. You can be a hotshot wrestler and an aspiring journalist, why can't Olga be a brilliant cook and a brilliant local historian?"

"She's a historian?"

"Where do you think I got interested in folklore? I used to ride my bike to her place all the time when I was a kid. She was like a grandmother to me. My real grandmother died before I was born."

"Did you tell Olga about what you saw? About your parents? Your dreams and your memories?"

"Of course."

"What did she say?" Michael felt his heart racing a little faster.

Maggie chuckled quietly, shaking her head. "I never understood what she meant until now. She said, 'If you are not ashamed to think it, don't be ashamed to say it.'"

"I don't understand." Michael wanted to find his family. And even though the stone room was huge, he was starting to feel claustrophobic again.

Maggie laughed bitterly. "My whole life they made me think I was nuts. They poisoned my mind with lies, and they poisoned my body with drugs. They drove a wedge between me and everyone and everything I ever loved." She choked back a sob. "They made me feel ashamed."

"But you were right."

Maggie looked up at him, her eyes glistened with the tears she was holding back. "Olga knew that. That's what she meant."

"How? Did she know about all this?"

Maggie breathed out heavily. "I don't know. That's why I have to show her these paintings."

Once they had taken pictures of the paintings they had already seen, they moved farther to the right where there was a set of smaller paintings, arranged like comic book panels. The first panel showed the monster swimming in the ocean, surrounded by white sperm whales. The whales gave Michael a swirling sense of *deja vu*. He'd just been thinking about Moby Dick, but he couldn't remember when or even why.

The whales looked small next to the monster, but it was clear in the second panel that they were fighting. The monster crushed whales in its tentacles and cut others in half with its claws. Rivers of red blood poured everywhere. In a different panel, the whales charged the monster, driving it down into an eerie blue glow at the bottom of the ocean.

Michael suddenly understood. "So we're dealing with a church, right? And they worship this jellyfish thing? It's like their God or whatever?"

Maggie shrugged. "I guess."

"So this place is some kind of cathedral, right? It's a big room. High ceiling. The paintings on the walls are like stained glass windows. Maybe this church comes to worship here."

"But it's right behind my house. We would have seen it."

"How? We're under the jetty. If they all come in the way we did, you'd never know."

"I would see the boats."

"So maybe they only use it on, like, holidays or whatever. Special occasions. Or maybe they used to use it, but don't anymore. They might not know it's here either."

Maggie's lips curled into a wry smile. "Then why was the door open?"

"It wasn't. It was stuck, remember?"

She shook her head. "The first door. The trap door down on the jetty. Somebody had to open that."

Michael shrugged helplessly. "Maybe it fell off on its own."

"It's as good a theory as anything right now." Maggie smiled at Michael. "Come on. There's one more wall to check." Maggie led Michael up to the wall near the door where Michael had tripped over the pedestal. His toes still hurt, but it was down to a dull, distant ache.

Michael decided that if they were going to think of this place as a cathedral, then the wall near the pedestal had to be the front since it was where an altar would be in a regular church or cathedral. When they got closer to it, Michael saw that the painting took up the entire front wall. Maggie had to move the light around to reveal the entire image.

The monster stood on its tentacles on top of a flaming globe strewn with mangled corpses of men, women and children representing every creed and color. Michael felt the hair stand on the back of his neck.

The images were crudely painted, but very clear. Michael recognized The Eiffel Tower. Big Ben. The Sidney Opera House. The Great Wall. The Forbidden City. The Golden Gate Bridge. The Statue of Liberty. The Taj Mahal. The Great Pyramid. The Parthenon. The ones he didn't know, Maggie named. Hagia Sofia. Kaaba. The Dome of the Rock. Everything was burning.

Michael stared at the image of the monster. It might have been a trick of his eyes, but it seemed to pulse slightly with its own light. "Mags, turn off the flashlight a sec. I think I see something."

After the click, the darkness was overwhelming. Michael heard Maggie moving to turn the light back on. "Wait. Look at the painting." He could just start to see the image of the monster. Like a glow-in-the-dark toy it glimmered slightly with a faint, blue light. "Was it doing this the whole time?"

"We would have seen it," Maggie whispered. "We're right next to the pedestal where you tripped before."

"So why is it glowing now?" Michael wanted to touch the glow, but it was too high.

"I have no idea, but I think it's getting brighter," Maggie said.

Michael stared. It was hard to say for sure. "It could just be that our eyes are adjusting, so it only looks brighter."

Maggie stared with her mouth open slightly. "Think you can get a picture of the glow?"

The light of Michael's viewfinder was almost enough to drown out the glow of the painting. He made sure the flash was off. It took five tries and many aperture adjustments to get one faint, blurry shot of the ghostly, glowing image.

"I'm turning the light back on, okay? Take a couple more and then we have to figure out how we're getting out of here. And Michael?"

He turned to face her.

She wrapped her hand around his back and kissed him gently on the cheek. "Thank you."

34 FIGHTING BACK

A dizzy detachment made Alison feel like she was watching everything from somewhere else. Like it was happening to someone else. But her throat burned as if it was full of sand and seawater. Her head throbbed. Her feet, hands and knees were bruised and bleeding. It was all happening to her. The worst part was that, over and over, she kept feeling the dull thud in her hands when the hammer bashed the old man's head.

Glancing toward the water, she waited for the nightmare thing to wriggle up like in a horror movie. But all she saw were the little smears of blood from their injuries like a trail of breadcrumbs on the rocks.

"Do you need to lean on me, Liv?" Olivia was toughing it out, but Alison could see she was in pain.

"I'm fine." Olivia smiled, but even that looked painful.

Alison tried to ignore the thud travelling up her arms and the vision of the old man's head snapping like a broken doll. She forced it away. "We need to get our bikes."

Olivia's eyes went wide. "You're not serious."

"We have to get to the bikes," Alison said firmly. They would never make it on foot. Olivia had to see that.

"We're not going back to the church. Are you crazy? We barely got out the first time. We have to run to The Mansion and get your parents."

"Run?" Catching up to Olivia and grabbing her arm, Alison felt hopeless fear rising in her. She forced it down. "Look how far that is. You can barely walk. If they're chasing us, we'll never make it. But our bikes are right down that street." The street rested in the shade of old trees. Alison would have liked walking down it if the stuffing hadn't just come out of the world. A vision of the old man's snapping head haunted her again.

Waving at it like a fly, Alison looked toward the ruined boardwalk just ahead of them. "It will be easier for you to ride than to walk, right? And a lot faster."

"We can't go back there." Olivia's voice cracked. "I won't."

Alison hoped Olivia wasn't on the edge of a breakdown. She felt such a calm otherness about the situation and wondered whether she had already had a breakdown herself. *Don't murderers go crazy sometimes?* Alison thought about the nasty kids with their sharp sticks poking the poor dead cat. She wondered whether she could have bashed their brains in ,too, if she'd needed to. She looked at the knife in Olivia's hand. *Cut their throats? Stab them in the chest? I've turned into a serial killer. Cut it out. That monster in the water is still alive.*

Protect Olivia. Get home.

Checking up and down the boardwalk, she looked into the shadows of the crumbling buildings. Those monsters could be anywhere. "How many of those things were there?"

Olivia shook her head. Her eyes were closed, and she looked like she was in pain. "Two at the end of the street and probably three in the van if they were the same three I saw."

A pang of remorse shot through Alison. If I had just believed Olivia in the first place, none of this would have happened. The thud travelled up her arms again. The old man's head flopped in her memory. And then a flash of white tentacles grabbing Olivia. Alison forced it all down. "Who was driving the van? Those things can't drive."

Olivia twisted up her face. "How do you know?"

"They don't have eyes."

Olivia shrugged and wiggled her toes on the injured side. "Neither do jellyfish."

"Jellyfish can't drive either."

"Funny." Olivia's mouth turned down in an irritated scowl. "Do you know how many animals thrive without any eyesight? Take any troglobite, like the Kaua'i cave wolf spider. Totally blind, right? But they sense vibrations and…"

"Okay, this isn't science class." Alison held up her hand. Talking about the science stuff seemed to perk up Olivia. Maybe it was distracting her. Alison thought about the old man trying to grab Olivia. To hurt her. The crunchy thud shook her forearms again. She waited a bit this time, allowing herself to explore the memory before forcing it away.

Satisfied that there was nothing on the boardwalk, Alison scampered across and ducked around the corner of a crumbling building that looked like it used to sell waffles and ice cream. She motioned for Olivia to follow.

Olivia knelt, wincing. Alison asked, "You still okay?"

Olivia nodded. She looked a little pale.

The white van still sat in front of the church, about half-a-block from the beach. Alison couldn't see them, but unless somebody had moved them, their bikes would be right there in the bushes.

"The monsters are there," Olivia whispered. "And one of them is going to be pretty ticked off."

"I don't see them." Alison strained to see through the shadows. She looked carefully for movement in the van.

"They're there." Olivia spoke slowly, like she had to think about every word. "Only one of them chased us out of the cave. The other ones have to be there."

Alison felt herself slipping back into calm detachment. "They think we're just a couple of scared girls."

"We *are* a couple of scared girls." Tears bubbled in the corners of Olivia's eyes.

Alison took Olivia's hand. "They are going to get back into their child-molester van and start looking for us."

"They're going to find us if we just stay here."

"But we're not staying here. We're gonna get the bikes." Alison didn't know if she was going to be able to talk Olivia into this one. And watching Olivia's face get paler by the minute, she knew they were running out of time.

"Liv, it's the only way. Please. We might be a couple of scared girls, but we're not *just* a couple of scared girls." Alison needed Olivia to feel it. She grabbed Olivia's hand and brought the knife to eye level. "I killed somebody today. For you. We freed one of those people, the prisoners."

"He died!" Olivia hissed.

Alison felt something growing inside her. She was still afraid, but this new thing was sick of it. "Maybe. But at least he's not still getting his insides sucked out by that thing in the water. And it probably died, too. And the thing that grabbed you? You slashed it."

"So?"

"We're not helpless."

Olivia's eyes looked sad, sick and tired. But a fire burned in Alison's chest. "How do you know they're not scared of us?"

Taking Olivia by the hand, Alison led her as quickly as she could toward the white van.

"I thought we were waiting." Olivia winced on every step. She dripped sweat.

"You look terrible."

Olivia laughed weakly. "Wow. You've never said that to me before."

"No time to wait." Alison pulled Olivia into the shadows under the trees. "You need help. Plan B."

"I thought this was Plan B."

Stooping, Alison led Olivia along the grassy shoulder of the road toward the front of the church where the van hunched like a gargoyle. Alison directed them inside the tree line, behind the screen of underbrush, angling toward the spot where she hoped the bikes still were.

Crouching at the edge of the driveway, Alison saw the sun glint off the chrome handlebars, and she could breathe again. Even the phantom thudding in her forearms seemed a little fainter. She almost missed it.

In the front door of the church, in the grassy lane to the yard and in the van, nothing moved. Alison didn't see or hear anything. "Ready?"

"No," Olivia hissed back.

Alison crawled slowly away from the cover of the underbrush. Her heart snapped when Olivia suddenly grabbed her wrist. Alison turned, feeling small and afraid. Olivia pointed wide-eyed to the thing in the driver's seat. Only the tip of its long, white chin stuck out from under the hood of its poncho, but Alison knew what it was.

Forget the bikes. Olivia mouthed.

Alison thought for a moment, considering whether they could just keep hiding and sneak all the way back to The Mansion. Even if they made it, and Alison did not think that was likely, it would have taken them hours. Olivia didn't have hours. She leaned into Olivia's ear. Her hair was still damp. The comfortable scent of shampoo mixed with briny seawater and sweat smelled like an ordinary day at the beach, but a glance down at the blue, veiny tendrils snaking up Olivia's leg from her wounded ankle was enough to snap Alison right back to Cape November. "I'll get the bikes. You slash the back tire."

"Are you nuts?" Olivia whispered back.

"Don't worry. You'll be fine. It'll just hiss."

Olivia looked annoyed. "Obviously. There's not enough air pressure to make it explode. That's not what I mean. I just can't do it. I don't know how."

Alison had to chuckle. "There's nothing to know. Just stab the tire with the point of the knife. It's sharp so it should go right in." Before Olivia could refuse, Alison slipped through the grass toward the bikes. She should have been the one to slash the tires, but Olivia's ankle was bad and she looked like she was getting weaker by the second. Olivia wouldn't be able to move both bikes. *So now I'm the athlete, and she's the delinquent. Perfect.*

Dragging the bikes through the grass toward the road, Alison did not take her eyes off Olivia, crouching by the side of the van. The engine was running, and Alison heard the hum of its air conditioner. *Those stupid fish things probably hate the heat more than I do.* With all that noise, the thing behind the wheel wasn't going to notice Olivia. *Hopefully.*

Alison had to get the bikes into the road, facing the boardwalk, but she didn't want to get spotted in the rearview mirror of the van. *Those things don't have eyes. Do they even use the mirrors? How can they possibly drive if they can't see?* She blocked it out. She would have plenty of time to debate monster physiology when Olivia was in a safe, air-conditioned hospital room.

It had not been part of the original plan in her head, but now that she thought it over, the boardwalk really was the best route back to The Mansion. Even with four good tires, the van couldn't follow them on the boardwalk. Plan C. Just sneak the bikes onto the boardwalk and get away. Olivia didn't even need to slash the tires. Alison felt so stupid. Why hadn't she thought it through before. She panicked and now. Olivia was taking a risk she didn't need to take.

Alison made hissing sounds and waved, but Olivia was too focused on the job, and the noise from the van insulated Olivia along with the driver.

Helplessly, Alison watched Olivia grip the handle of the knife in both hands and lean the point against the tire. She looked back at Alison. Alison shook her head furiously. Her head throbbed when she did it. Stress. Dehydration.

Looking scared and pale, Olivia set her jaw and looked back at the blade and the tire. Alison could not make her understand.

Olivia's whole body heaved when she took a deep breath. Closing her eyes,

Olivia pushed the point into the sidewall of the tire. Without any drama, the blade slid in. From where she was squatting, Alison couldn't hear anything as the tire deflated down to its metal rim. Alison allowed herself to exhale.

When Olivia looked back, grinning at Alison, Alison gave her an enthusiastic thumbs-up and waved frantically, calling her back.

But Olivia crawled along the side of the van to the front tire on the passenger side and stabbed the blade into that tire, too. With no air in either of its right tires, the van leaned to its right side. The driver didn't seem to notice. Wincing, Olivia crawled away, but Alison's heart hammered. Her nails drew blood from her palms.

The church door banged open. Two fish things shambled down the stairs. The one still wearing its poncho pointed at Olivia. The naked one with the slashed face held one of its tentacles, dripping pale ooze, close to its body. Two other creatures hobbled around the side of the church from the back lot.

"Run!" Alison yelled. She could hardly breathe as she watched Olivia get to her feet. With a metallic pop, the driver's door opened. Alison saw the fifth fish thing step out and circle to the back to the van. It stopped short and rose up menacingly when it found Olivia.

Screaming, Olivia slashed at it with her knife. The monster ducked back and its hood fell away revealing its white, half-moon head. Alison glanced up at the monsters bobbing down the driveway. She only had seconds.

Olivia lunged again, but the driver swatted the knife away with a tentacle. It clattered in the street. Screaming, Alison snatched up a large rock and smashed it into the back of the thing's head, crumpling it to the ground with a wet thud. Pale liquid pooled around the crushed jelly that used to be its head.

Pushing nauseous thoughts of the dead old man away, Alison watched the four other monsters reach for Olivia with their tentacles. Olivia dodged them and leaped over the fallen driver. She screamed when she landed and had to grab Alison to keep from falling.

"Olivia!" Alison slung her arm across her shoulders and half dragged Olivia to the bikes.

"I'm okay, I'm okay!" Olivia yelled. "Let's go!"

Alison gave Olivia a push to get her started and slipped under a white tentacle that swiped at her head as she ran with her own bike. The creature waddled after her, but Alison outran it and jumped onto her bike. Looking back, she saw that the fish things were at their van, pushing into each other as they crowded into the doors. As she rounded the corner onto the boardwalk, Alison saw the van trying to drive on its two flapping tires.

When she wasn't checking over her shoulder, Alison checked the side streets, but she never saw a white van or anyone else. Olivia seemed to be pedaling slower and slower

35 DOOMSDAY PAINTING

"Hang on." Michael felt a sickening lump of fear in his gut. "Look."

He directed Maggie's hands so that the beam showed the lower corners of the painting. Figures in white robes stood around the monster's tentacles, their arms up in the air like they were celebrating. Huge, hideous black birds circled above them.

"Those are the birds that attacked me and my dad."

Wide-eyed, Maggie brought her hand to her mouth. She looked terrified. "We need to get out of here. We have to find your family."

Michael felt like he'd been kicked in the chest. "Are you kidding? That's what I said before you dragged me down here!" When Maggie dropped her eyes, looking sad and sorry, Michael felt hot shame. He knew he shouldn't have yelled at her. "I'm sorry. This isn't your fault." He laughed, but not because it felt good. "Who could have known about any of this?"

Her eyes snapped back up, catching his. "I DID know. I just didn't believe it. I let them make me think I was crazy." She laughed nervously. "I've been having dreams of birds like this for weeks."

"When we came to your room this morning?"

She nodded slowly, keeping her eyes on the painting like she was afraid the birds would fly off the stones and attack them.

Michael felt betrayed. "When I told you I hit one of these birds with my car, you didn't think you should tell me that you dreamed about them? I mean…it's got to mean something, right?"

Maggie's lip curled. "You said you hit a big bird. Lots of people hit birds, Michael. Did I think it was a weird coincidence? Obviously. But so what? Life's full of weird coincidences."

"There were more of them."

"More birds? Like this?"

"After the first bird, a whole bunch of other birds—all the same kind—started attacking us."

Maggie's eyebrows curved down like the cone of a smoldering volcano. "Who's keeping secrets now?"

Sour guilt curdled in him for having been so judgmental before. "You're right. I should have told you everything, but at the time, I thought that if I said anything, you would think I was…" Michael couldn't drag the word out.

Maggie's hands went to her hips and she laughed. "Crazy? One weird thing happens to you and you're worried about labels? About getting judged?" She sighed and shook her head. "This is the problem with mental health in our culture. Did you know that most insurance companies won't cover mental healthcare unless you attempt suicide? How messed up is that? If you get the flu or cancer nobody judges you, but if you have any kind of mental health problem..."

Michael held up one finger, indicating Maggie should pause. "As soon as we get out of here we can fight the man together."

Scowling, she said. "Mental health is a serious issue, Michael."

"So is not dying."

Chuckling, Maggie checked her watch. "The hookah is definitely out of fuel by now."

Little bubbles of panic erupted in Michael's stomach. "Let's hope that other door goes someplace."

Aiming the flashlight at the back wall, Maggie padded toward it, but after a few steps, she stopped short.

"Here's one we didn't see before." She shined the flashlight to their left, onto the painting that was on the wall next to the door they had used when they first entered the cathedral. It had been behind them, which is why they hadn't noticed it. Maggie tilted her head like a puzzled dog. "It's a painting of this room. Of the cathedral itself."

Michael oriented himself within the perspective of the painting. "There's that pedestal I tripped over." Michael pointed to it. "What are they doing with it?"

Stepping closer, Michael could see a man in a green robe playing a strange-looking harp. The bottom of the harp rested in the groove at the top of the pedestal.

"I guess it's not for circumcisions," Maggie said.

Michael tried to put together the details of the painting. The cathedral was full of people in robes, but the perspective was from behind them, so other than the harp player, Michael could only see backs and hoods. And even the harp player's face was hidden under his hood. The congregation faced the front wall, but the doomsday painting wasn't there. Instead of the front wall, the cathedral opened onto a gray beach. Really, it looked more like a desert, but it was next to a body of water that looked like an ocean.

It could have been a landscape painting, bleak and inhospitable, but ordinary, except for the things in the foreground. White, blubbery creatures that looked like a cross between a man and a jellyfish. Each creature carried a large, lumpy cocoon out of the cathedral and onto the beach. "You didn't dream about those things, too, did you?" Michael asked.

Despite the soggy heat, Maggie seemed to shiver slightly. "Not yet. Hopefully not ever. What are they carrying?" Maggie asked.

Michael leaned in for a closer look. "Oh my God, Maggie." Michael felt faintly nauseous as he made out the shadowy outline of a person inside each pod.

"What are we dealing with here?"

Maggie shook her head and shrugged. "When Michelangelo painted *The Last Judgment,* he was representing a Christian belief about the Second Coming of Christ."

"Those things are pretty disgusting-looking for a painting about God."

Maggie laughed. "It's not a picture of God the way we're used to, but have you seen Michelangelo's *The Last Judgment?* Saint Bartholomew is holding his own flayed skin that was torn from his body when he was martyred."

Michael really needed some fresh air.

"And then Michelangelo replaced Bartholomew's face on the skin in the painting with his own. In the same painting, he has a naked cardinal getting bit by a snake right on his junk."

Cringing at that description, Michael thought that Maggie was enjoying his discomfort a little too much. He felt the same way he did when Alison showed off how smart she was, just to make him feel stupid. He didn't need that from Maggie, too. "What's your point?"

"Michelangelo painted a gruesome vision of the end of the world in the Sistine Chapel."

"So this is The Church of New Enlightenment's Last Judgment?"

Cocking her head toward the larger doomsday painting, Maggie said, "That one probably is. This one looks more like a picture of a ceremony. Maybe it's the ceremony that's supposed to happen when the other one happens. A ritual celebration welcoming the end of the world. What the Norse called *Ragnarok.*"

"What's that?" Michael felt lost. His mind kept wandering to Alison and Olivia and his parents. He hoped they were all okay.

"*Ragnarok* is when humanity loses all the old traditions and loyalties and the gods fight the giants in a final battle."

"And the Gods win and everybody goes to *Asgard* or whatever?"

Maggie laughed and shook her head. "Not exactly. The universe gets destroyed."

"I guess I can stop saving for a car now."

Taking his hand, Maggie said, "*Ragnarok* marks the end of one cycle of time so that a new cycle can start."

"The Vikings believed in rags 'n rocks or whatever you call it, but it never happened. We're still here. In 1982, Prince wrote 1999 about the world ending. But 2000 came and went, and nothing changed. Even the computer bug that had everybody freaked out, Y2K? That never did anything. It was all hype. My buddy Jablonski and me did a presentation on the hysteria in the media around the change of the millennium."

"September Eleventh happened in 2001." Maggie spoke quietly, like she was saying a prayer. "You don't think that marked the end of one cycle and the beginning of something new? The world has never been quite the same since."

Michael studied the doomsday painting again. "We know it's a ceremony, right? Because of the robes? And look at the guy down in front with the harp. Probably leading them, right? But what about those other things?" Michael gestured with his chin toward the creatures with tentacles who walked like men.

Maggie looked closer and shrugged. "The Church of New Enlightenment's version of angels or something?"

Michael laughed. "Angels don't look like that."

It surprised Michael when Maggie laughed, too. "Have you ever seen an angel?"

Again, Michael felt the jaws of a trap closing around him. "Don't start in with me like my sister does. I'm sure you're some kind of genius, too, just like she is, but that doesn't mean I'm stupid."

Maggie's features softened. She looked at him tenderly. "I'm not trying to make you feel stupid. I'm just trying to talk this thing through for myself. No one credible has ever seen an angel, but everybody thinks they know what an angel is supposed to look like."

"Good-looking dude with wings. So?"

"Human beings probably came up with a description to match their understanding."

"Huh?" Michael felt the close, sweltering heat of the place at the back of his neck. He really wanted to leave.

"Angels are supposed to be these perfect beings, somewhere between human and God. God lives in Heaven, which is up in the sky, so we give a human the wings of a bird—the only feature of a bird a human has ever envied—and we make an angel."

"I still don't see your point."

"This church worships a god who doesn't live in the sky, but the ocean. So, their angels are halfway between a human and that thing," Maggie made a sweeping gesture that took in the gigantic monstrosity in each of the paintings. "Their angels have tentacles, not wings."

A window opened in Michael's mind, letting in a shaft of bright, terrible light. "So those angels are carrying people off. The people in the pods. Is that to Heaven or to Hell?"

Maggie sighed heavily, Michael could not tell if she was becoming impatient with him or just overwhelmed by what they were learning. "The CNE probably has a whole different understanding of Heaven and Hell."

"What difference does it make? This is all a bunch of BS anyway. These people are just nuts. None of this is real."

"What about the birds?"

The heavy air caught in his throat but his chest opened up when he felt the warmth of Maggie's hand on his shoulder. "Think about the pictures in a church. Don't they show things that are important to that religion? Some of it is one hundred percent real, like the execution of martyrs. There's a historical record to back up a lot of those gruesome deaths."

"Yeah, but monsters?"

Maggie looked nervously around, "Forget the monsters. Look at the people." Her face suddenly went a little white, and she paced. "When the Aztecs sacrificed people to Quetzalcoatl, it didn't matter whether or not Quetzalcoatl really showed up to collect his offering. What mattered was that the people believed that he did, and that made them willing to kill for the sake of their god."

"Human sacrifice?" The beads of sweat suddenly felt like ice trickling down Michael's back.

"We need to get out of here," Maggie said urgently.

Michael laughed, but he didn't find anything funny. "Welcome to team Let's Get the Hell Out of Here! I've been pitching for that team since we got here."

Maggie shined the light toward the back wall, opposite the doomsday painting. "We have to try that other door."

Michael grabbed her upper arm, stopping her.

"Ow! Hey! Let go!"

Dropping Maggie's arm, Michael shushed her so he could concentrate on the faint, sizzling hiss in the air. "What is that?" Michael noticed that the glow from the doomsday painting had gotten brighter. "Kill the light."

When Maggie switched the flashlight off, the blue glow coming from the painting was bright enough for Michael to see her clearly. Noticing that Maggie wasn't following as he stepped cautiously toward the glow. Michael turned around. Maggie's skin seemed to glow in the pale, blue light. Michael's shadow stretched along the stones and over her feet, and it looked like she was wearing gray socks.

"I think we should go, Michael." Her eyes looked scared, but her lips showed tight determination.

"You're the one who wanted to come here and know everything." He gestured over his shoulder with his thumb. "Something is seriously up with this painting." Michael realized that he had raised his voice to be heard over the electric sizzle in the air. Its loud vibration tickled his ear. And then he figured out that it wasn't the sound. Something was on his ear. Something else stung his ankle, and another hot needle poked his back.

He cried out and shook his head, swatting at his ear. Sharp pain made him wince and yell. His stomach knotted in terror as he realized the flies were on him.

He looked up and saw Maggie's face, wide with her horror. In a sudden flash, she was lit up brightly, shading her eyes with her arms. Huddled into herself, she held her hand out to him. "Run, Michael! Something's coming out of the wall!"

Michael only took one step before the air erupted in a single blue lightning flash. The hissing, static thunder shook the stones. It didn't sound like any thunder Michael had ever heard. The sheer weight of the sound dropped him painfully to the floor.

He heard a high whistle. With horror, he realized that he'd lost his hearing from the thunder. He shook his head and worked his jaw, trying to get his hearing back, but his head was washed in a constant ring.

The blue light faded almost to nothing, and in that blind moment, one sound cut through the fuzz in his ears. The black birds shrieked.

36 NOBODY'S HOME

Alison's legs felt like led by the time they pedaled up to The Mansion. A knot of fear tied itself into her stomach when she didn't see her parents' minivan. At the steps Olivia sagged, collapsing off her bike into Alison's arms. Alison dragged her inside and helped her onto one of the leather sofas.

"Hey! Help us!" Alison called. "We need help here!"

The large empty mansion sucked up her voice, but no reply came.

"Mom? Dad?" Alison called up the stairs. "Michael? Where are you?" Alison thought about the terrifying people and other things she'd seen. Her stomach knot got tighter. She was afraid to yell anymore. She didn't know who or what might answer.

"Allie?" Olivia always had to be so tough. She managed to stand, but drooped on the back of a chair, pale and dripping sweat.

Alison guided her back to the couch. "You need a hospital. MOM! DAD! Where are they?"

Olivia's voice cracked. "We need water."

Alison found a glass, filled it, and helped Olivia take a few swallows. She was too weak to hold the glass herself. Alison panicked.

When Olivia finished her water—it took way too long—Alison ran to the phone at the bar. Dead. When her phone showed a blank screen, she spiked it to shatter on the floor. "Liv, I have to run upstairs to find my family. We need help, and I don't know where anybody is."

"Take me with you." Olivia struggled again to her feet.

"Whoa! You stay right here." There was no way Olivia could make the stairs.

Sitting back down, Olivia shook her head and winced like it hurt. "Don't leave me here alone. Please."

The cuts around Olivia's ankle still oozed blood, and the blue, toxic tendrils made a network from the wound halfway up her thigh. Alison shivered, wondering what was creeping toward Olivia's heart. "I need to get you help, Olivia. That thing poisoned you." Alison felt a helpless churning inside her. She looked at the front door, wishing for her parents to walk through it, but terrified those creatures would show up instead.

Olivia swayed on the couch like she could pass out at any moment. "Okay. Just hang on." Alison squatted down and leaned Olivia across her shoulders. Olivia's body burned with fever. Alison wrapped her arm around one of Olivia's thighs and grabbed her wrist in the fireman's carry, the one wrestling move Michael ever taught her.

With Olivia draped across her shoulders, Alison's thighs burned as she carried her up the stairs to their room. Her heart skipped when she realized it wasn't locked. Someone's here! No. Calm down. We never locked it when we left with Michael. We didn't even take our keys. She felt her breath come back to her. Alison couldn't believe it had only been that morning. It seemed a lifetime ago. In a different world.

Gently, she lay Olivia in the bed. Alison allowed herself one moment to remember how they had lay there together earlier, two ordinary girls talking through life's ordinary problems. She looked at Olivia's face. She was only half awake, and her skin was on fire. Hot tears blinded Alison. *Olivia can't die!*

Alison sobbed so hard it hurt as she ran into the hall and pounded on her parents' door. No one came. Michael's room was empty, too.

She ran to the bathroom and told herself she was not allowed to panic. *Olivia needs me.* She soaked towels in cold water and ran to the bed. She put one towel over Olivia's face and chest to cool the fever. As she did it, Alison thought of the thing in the water and the thing she crushed with a rock, and the old man. The dead old man. She longed to feel the thud in her arms again, but that memory had faded on the bike ride back. She looked at Olivia's fluttering eyelids, and an atomic rage mushroomed in Alison's guts. She knew that if that old man had shown up at that moment, she would have happily buried the hammer in his teeth.

Alison wrapped the second towel around Olivia's thigh, twisting the ends tight to make a crude a tourniquet between the poison tendrils and Olivia's heart. She'd seen that in a movie once when someone had been bitten by a snake. She didn't remember much else. She couldn't even remember if the guy lived.

"Liv? Can you hear me?" Olivia's eyelids fluttered slightly. Alison felt everything squash inside her. "I love you, Olivia. You have to fight. Stay strong for me. I can't lose you. Not now." She leaned down and pressed her lips to Olivia's burning forehead. "Olivia, please!"

A faint tapping sound startled Alison. Her breath caught in her chest. When it came again, she placed it outside the window. She ran to the curtain. Michael! Stupid Michael with his stupid, wonderful pranks!

Sliding the curtains back, Alison saw the five enormous, white creatures, stuck to the windows like nightmare starfish. Without their ponchos, their tentacles writhed against the glass, smearing it with clear ooze as they slapped the panes, trying to break in.

Alison screamed and jumped away. Her foot caught on her bag and she fell onto her back. The impact forced all the air from her lungs in a choking gasp. Struggling to breathe, she flailed to get up. Her hand struck something cool and smooth in her bag.

Her whole bag glowed with dazzling pink light. It hurt her eyes to look at it. She scrambled to her knees and pulled out the snow globe. The pink light was blinding. Alison had to squint like she was staring at the sun. The snow globe felt heavier and seemed to move with its own momentum. Alison felt as if she was holding a strong magnet that pulled her hand up and toward the window. Outside, the jellyfish creatures dropped off the window and huddled on the balcony. They held their tentacles in front of them as if they were trying to protect themselves from the overwhelming pink light.

Alison felt weightless and powerful. She followed the energetic pull of the snow globe toward the window. Like a psychedelic lightning lamp, tendrils of pink light shot out of the snow globe, striking the creatures. Glowing with pink light, they recoiled and jumped off the balcony.

The snow globe dimmed, but the pink light still glowed. Alison felt as if she'd just sprinted a mile. Her heart hammered in her ears. Sweat dripped. Her lungs ached. Her muscles hurt.

When the magnetic pull tugged again it startled her. It drew her toward the bed. Alison fought to keep her hand down, but she could not fight the pull of whatever energy was coming through the snow globe. She tried to drop it, but her hand felt paralyzed. Alison grunted and tried to stop her legs, but step by step she shuffled toward Olivia, her bare feet sliding across the smooth wood. Alison felt the hot tears in her eyes. She could not breathe. *It's going to kill her!*

The snow globe pulled Alison's arm straight out so hard that she stumbled forward. The pink light swelled and condensed and curled out toward Olivia's ankle. Alison suddenly felt calm and relaxed, as if she was sitting in cool shade, feeling a gentle breeze. The pink light, soft and gauzy, enveloped Olivia's leg. Alison watched amazed, as the blue poison retreated back down Olivia's calf, sucked up into the pink light. A moment later and the snow globe was just a snow globe again. The little miniature creatures floated gently in the sparkling water. Olivia's ankle didn't even have a scar.

Olivia yawned and stretched. "I'm so thirsty."

Sobbing like an earthquake, Alison threw her arms around her friend.

37 ANABASIS

He stepped on the bug he'd swatted off his ear and then rolled across his shoulders to kill the one on his back. Michael felt the gooey crunch of the bug under his weight. The one that had been on his ankle was gone, but Michael knew it would be back.

Spinning across his shoulders to his feet, sharp pain from his toes lit him up, but that wasn't why he screamed. The scream was because he had to dodge away from the huge bird snapping at his face. He caught the thing's long throat in his hands, its skin like sandpaper covered in icy jelly.

He realized he was still screaming even as he squeezed and held the bird out at arm's length. The thing thrashed and clawed at his belly, trying to gut him with its claws even as it snapped its beak at his arm. Michael tried to crush its neck, but the bird's muscles and tendons were like steel cables.

It thrashed wildly, trying to twist free of Michael's grip, slashing at his forearms with its claws. Michael knew that if one claw dug in it would cut to his bone, so he held it firmly, matching its movements so it couldn't get any leverage while shaking the bird hard the way a dog would, trying to snap its neck.

"I caught one!" He risked a glance up for Maggie.

The blue glow from the painting had almost faded completely, but there was enough light to see Maggie, mouth twisted in disgust, slapping flies from her arms and legs and stomping them into the ground. A ruddy slime stained her feet, her wild swatting and stomping dance a psychedelic strobe as the flashlight swept the room with blinding light and shadows.

Maggie screamed, and the strobe made one crazy arc across the ceiling. Michael saw the second bird waddle and lunge at her leg. She smashed the heel of the flashlight down on its head. Even from ten feet away and with his ears still ringing, Michael heard the crunch of its skull and the squawk the thing made as it died on the floor at Maggie's feet.

Michael adjusted his grip to make sure the creature in his hands didn't wriggle out. Something burned his forearm. A thin red line of blood appeared on his skin where the bird had clawed him.

Careless, he thought, when he realized that the bird had grazed him. He knew that if he made another mistake he would lose his arm. Or die.

Maggie screamed something, but Michael couldn't make it out. His ears still rang, although sounds were getting clearer. She ran to him, brandishing the flashlight like a club and shouting. With the whistling in his ears, he couldn't understand her words, but he understood her frightened, desperate face and the wild circles she made with her hands.

Spinning so the bird was between himself and Maggie, she batted its head with the heavy end of the flashlight, partially caving it in as black goo spattered them both. It thrashed and clawed. She smashed it again with the flashlight. Michael dropped it twitching on the floor. Maggie clubbed it until it stopped moving, then clubbed it again.

"Okay! It's dead!" Even to himself Michael's voice sounded like he was shouting through a pillow. He doubted she could hear him, so he grabbed her arm.

She snarled at him like a cornered cat. Michael thought she was going to attack him with the gory light. Raising his hands, he stepped back. A droplet of blood dripped from his arm to the stones.

Panting heavily, her face softened until she looked like herself again. She dripped with sweat and was spattered with black gore. Bug guts stained her feet. The flashlight clattered to the floor as she sank to her knees.

"I've heard of assault and battery, but that was ridiculous," Michael said uselessly from under the swimming pool of mud that still filled his ears. He pressed on the cut on his forearm. It felt slightly bruised, but after a minute or so, it stopped bleeding and a sticky scab started to form.

He could tell from the puzzled tilt of her head and the kink in her eyebrows that Maggie had no idea what he'd said. She made a twirling gesture near her ear. Michael figured she was trying to tell him that her hearing was shot. Or that she was crazy.

He held out his hand, and she allowed him to help her to her feet. Michael pointed to the back door. She kept holding his hand, and they walked toward the back of the cathedral.

"Can you hear yet?" Her voice sounded like a bad phone connection.

Michael nodded, yelling back, "You?"

Closing her eyes, she shook her head. "Getting better, but shouting hurts."

"Sorry," he mouthed.

Michael pulled her up short as she reached for the ring in the door.

She turned to glare at him, angry and confused.

He mouthed the words carefully, pointing to his lips. Are…you… sure? He exaggerated raising his eyebrows to emphasize his question.

She looked impatient. Annoyed. "You can talk. Just don't scream."

"Are you sure?"

He heard her laughter, faintly. She shrugged and shook her head. Michael laughed, too, when he understood her gesture. There was nothing sure anymore. Not about this place and not about anything else. He nodded, and the door ring turned silently in her hand. Michael wondered why this one was so much easier to turn. Maybe it had been used more regularly. That concerned him, but it also gave him hope that it would lead somewhere.

Maggie looked back at him, her face anxious and uncertain. He had no idea whether opening this door would be a way out or another disaster, so he did what he always did when he didn't know what to do. He shrugged and nodded.

She pulled the huge door open. Leaning in next to Maggie, Michael looked through the opening and followed the beam of the flashlight up a long, straight corridor, which sloped gently upward like a ramp. The floor was paved with flat stones like the cathedral, but the walls were made of jagged, irregular boulders of various sizes, almost like a cave.

Slowly they made their way up the slope. Under his feet, Michael noticed the stone floor was getting cooler. The air felt cool and damp.

After a few more minutes of walking, he noticed the whisper of their feet on the stones. From time to time he heard the faint plunk of a falling water droplet. He realized that the humming in his ears had almost gone away. "How's your hearing?" His voice sounded muddled and distant, yet painfully close and loud at the same time.

"Getting better I think. You?"

"You sound more clear. That's definitely a step up."

She smiled at him. "Is it a step up because you can hear or because you can hear me?"

He felt something warm in his chest. "A little of both I think."

She smiled and looked away, back up the ramp. "Those were the birds, right? The same kind that attacked you on the highway?"

"Yeah." Michael nodded. It hurt his head.

"I dreamed them, too. It's weird. In my dream, almost the same thing happened. I think. I can't remember the details. Just the birds."

A creeping feeling overwhelmed him, and he had to stop walking. "Was I in your dream?"

Maggie closed her eyes and looked like she was concentrating. Remembering. "I really don't remember. Maybe."

"So what's it mean?"

"I don't know."

"How do they get out?"

"Of the painting?"

Michael had to laugh. "What are you talking about? No. I meant how do they get out of the cathedral."

Maggie shook her head. "There must be some opening or something in the ceiling that lets them get out of the cathedral."

"Yeah." Michael envisioned the monsters crawling through slits in the stone. "We're under the lighthouse, right? Those things can fly up to the ceiling and probably have a way to crawl out to look for food."

"But what are they?" Maggie sounded more than frustrated. She sounded angry. "The painting lit up, and there was that—lightning or whatever—and then they were all over us. The flies and the birds."

Michael stopped walking again. He felt the world was slipping away from him. Like he was on a merry-go-round that kept speeding up. "What are you talking about?"

"Are you kidding?" Maggie laughed, and Michael got the uncomfortable feeling she was laughing at him. He didn't like it.

"What?" he asked.

"That room was empty. We checked all around, remember? There were no bugs or birds. Then the painting starts to glow, there's a big thunderbolt and wham-bam-thank-you-ma'am. What else could it be?"

Michael laughed then. "There has to be—like—a crack in the wall or another door we didn't see. There's probably another room or something where those things have a nest."

Maggie stopped and looked at him with her arching eyebrow.

Michael was torn between wanting to kiss her and punch her. "So what, then? You're saying the painting is some kind of magic door or something? Should I start looking for a lion and a witch?"

"I never said it was magic," she said flatly. She walked more quickly up the ramp.

"What then?" Michael demanded. "What else makes something appear out of thin air."

"Not out of thin air, Michael. Out of that painting. Are you saying you didn't feel the thunderbolt or whatever the hell that was?"

"I felt it. I'm still half deaf from it."

"What do you think that was exactly?"

"I don't know. Lightning?"

"Underground?"

Before Michael could say anything, he saw that they had reached the end of the ramp and the flashlight beam found a rough ceiling made of boards. They looked old, but not that sturdy, Michael decided.

He crouched in the highest point in the ramp, where the floor almost met the ceiling, squared his back against the boards, positioning himself over his feet.

"What are you doing?" Maggie looked amused and confused.

"Basically a squat." Michael tried to sound confident.

"Why?" Maggie shook her head.

Michael tightened his thighs and pressed his back into the old boards.

"Are you an idiot?" Maggie asked.

Michael ignored her and pushed harder. Wood splinters bit his shoulder blades, and his quads burned. He concentrated on pressing his heels down into the stones, and the boards creaked in protest. He looked up at Maggie. Her eyes were wide, but whether she was impressed or just surprised, he couldn't tell.

He gave himself a short break and borrowed the light to examine the boards. At the edge, one board had separated slightly from its neighbor. "See? Loose nail. We can get out of here."

He repositioned himself as high as he could, squatting like a coiled spring. He pressed up, roaring with the effort. Two boards popped loose.

Maggie helped him wiggle them free. The space was too small for him, but Maggie put her foot in Michael's hand so that he could boost her up and squeeze through. She gave a surprised, yelping laugh.

"What?"

"I don't believe it. You just broke through the floor of the boathouse. Hang on I'll get you out."

Michael waited and a moment later, white light streamed through the cracks between the boards. "I got the lights on. Let me find something to rip up the boards."

Michael listened to her rummaging around above him.

"Step back," she ordered. A moment later, there was a loud thwack as she hit the board with a hammer. Through the gap, Michael saw her squat beside the board and pry the nails loose with the claw end. A moment later, she pulled him up by his wrists and he stood with her, looking around the boathouse.

"I can still sell you as catch of the day." She grinned at him.

"Are you implying that I smell like a fish?"

Laughing, Maggie wrinkled her nose. "I know I've smelled better. Sweat and seawater isn't the new summer fragrance."

Michael leaned in and sniffed her hair and neck. Laughing, she pulled back, but only slightly. "You smell fine to me. Anyway, you can take as many showers as you want."

"A shower wouldn't hurt you any," she said.

"Is that an invitation?" Michael exaggerated raising his eyebrows.

"Hey, this has been a great first date; let's not push it."

Michael laughed. "Before I do anything I need to find my family and make sure everybody's okay."

She kept the flashlight and tossed him the hammer. Then she picked up a small shovel.

"Are we burying something?" he asked.

She shrugged. "What if another one of those birds finds us?"

Michael thought about the horrors in the cathedral and felt a small shudder. "I think we've killed enough weird animals for one day. We wouldn't want to get into trouble with the weird animal protection agency or anything."

Maggie laughed. "You think those things are endangered?"

Michael nodded at Maggie's shovel and grinned confidently. "They will be if they mess with us again." At least, he hoped it was confident.

"We should go back and get one of the dead ones to show somebody. Maybe figure out what it is and where it came from."

Michael looked down into shadows under the missing floorboards. "First let's make sure everybody's safe."

As they walked out of the boathouse and back up the path to The Mansion, Michael looked out across the water and saw the dory bobbing in the waves. It felt like a month ago when he and Maggie rowed out there to dive. He allowed himself a moment to remember how amazing Maggie looked lying in the boat, glistening in the sun.

Michael didn't turn around to talk. "Maggie?"

"Yeah?" Her voice came quietly behind him.

"Out on the boat…I felt like…"

"What?" She sounded slightly breathless. Michael figured it was probably from walking up the hill to The Mansion.

"Were you…are we…"

She startled him by taking his hand and pulling him to a stop next to a large wooden cabinet built against the side of The Mansion. She stepped in front of him to face him. "I did need your help, but I swear I wasn't just using you." She leaned up on her toes and pecked his lips. "When this is all over, I'd love to go to the movies or something."

She opened the door, and Michael saw a shower. "Are there any movie theaters down the Cape?"

Laughing, she turned on the water and rinsed herself with the liquid soap. "Sorry, but if I don't clean the guts off I might puke. You should, too. You'll feel better."

She dried herself with a towel from a plastic storage trunk while Michael hastily rinsed away the brine and grime. He soaped the cut on his arm; a hard, thin scab had formed. He decided it was superficial, like the pain in his toes.

He kept looking out of the shower stall anxiously. Hoping nothing was going to fly out of the boathouse through the…"What did you call the three rocks that make the archway?"

From under the towel, Maggie said, "It's a dolmen. Why?"

"You said that people believe they're portals, right? To the spirit world or whatever?"

Maggie stopped toweling and looked at Michael, her face slack. "You're right. The dolmen isn't a portal, but what if the painting is?"

Michael opened his mouth and drank a few big mouthfuls before he turned off the water and took the towel Maggie held out for him. "So the dolmen is a portal to a portal?" He laughed, but he couldn't shake the feeling that he was getting caught up in Maggie's delusions. There couldn't be a real portal to somewhere else. That was crazy. It had to be. He hoped it was. But the birds and the bugs had been there.

"Let's get a move on," Maggie called.

His thoughts scattered. He watched her turn and trot up the path. For a moment he let himself forget about monster birds and bugs, mysterious portals and the aches and bruises blossoming around his body.

He caught up to her as they passed through the high grass between The Mansion and the stable; Michael noticed that the stable was still open and the bikes that his sister and Olivia had left standing around were still there. He wondered if they were still out.

"The girls must be back," Maggie said, rounding the corner of The Mansion.

Michael saw the two bikes abandoned at the bottom of the steps. Alison would leave a mess like that, but Olivia was a neat freak. Back home she was always cleaning up after Alison. He didn't see the minivan either, and he wondered where his parents were. He grabbed Maggie's arm, holding her back on the stairs. "Wait. Something's wrong."

She looked back at him and then up at The Mansion, sitting silently in front of them. "We'll take it slow." She hefted the shovel and led him up the groaning stairs and through the creaking front door. The Mansion felt still and empty, but the foyer and the sitting lounge looked pretty much as Michael remembered it, except for the glass on the counter.

"Somebody was here."

Maggie ducked behind the bar and filled two more large glasses of water. Michael ignored Maggie's warning to drink slowly. The slight ache he felt after his fifth glass was worth it, but it made the empty rumble in his stomach sharper.

Thumping his glass down on the bar, he picked up his hammer. "Let's check upstairs."

Maggie nodded and picked up the shovel and the flashlight. Slowly, she led them step by creaking step upstairs.

"Alison?" Michael knocked on his sister's door. "It's me."

The door sprung open and Alison jumped at Michael, making his chest convulse with startled fear as she wrapped her arms around him and hugged him tight. He felt his heart hammering between them.

"Thank God!" Alison's tears felt hot on his neck.

38 MIND AND BODY

It was as if the toothed suckers of the cold tentacle still grabbed her. Alison's snow globe had worked like a miracle. The wound was healed on Olivia's ankle, but it was still raw in her mind. She forced herself to listen to Maggie and Michael talk over each other even as the walls closed in claustrophobically around her.

When Michael described the ladder and the tunnel, her own swim through the cave and that thing in the water made her shaky and sick. She couldn't stop seeing the children with their dripping, red sticks, mutilating the dead cat. On the table, under webs of mucus, the man's eyes were still pleading and desperate. Olivia's skin crawled as Maggie described the paintings in the cathedral. And her heart clamped at every jump Michael made, as he bounced around the room recreating their fight with the birds and the bugs.

To get out of her own head, Olivia concentrated on Maggie and Michael. She watched them move. Still in their swimsuits, they were both so beautiful, two perfect people. Michael was lean and powerful, Maggie curvy and graceful. Everyone always went on and on about how beautiful Olivia was, but she didn't buy it. Whenever she looked in the mirror, all she saw was flaws. Maggie seemed flawless, and it filled her with a sad longing for something that could never be.

Olivia watched the flashing of their eyes as Maggie and Michael touched each other's hands and arms, and finished each other's sentences. They liked each other, Olivia decided; they just might not know it yet. It was sweet.

Something bitter rankled inside her. It took her a moment to recognize that it wasn't envy exactly. She didn't begrudge Michael and Maggie their hetero-happiness. She just wished she could have something like it with someone, and that finding it didn't have to be so hard.

Sitting up in bed, Olivia allowed herself to soak in the amazing contours of Maggie's toned body. For too long, Olivia hadn't felt she was allowed to explore that part of herself. It was hard to do, especially in high school where everybody was still figuring out who liked what. One good thing about transferring to an all-girls school, Olivia realized, was that the chances of finding a girlfriend were a lot better. She promised herself then and there that if she were still alive when all of this was over, she would find a girlfriend. After facing down death, she owed that to herself. She deserved to be happy, too.

Maggie's story about her parents made Olivia feel a heavy sadness. If she'd told it the day before, Olivia would have dismissed Maggie as totally delusional and suffering from PTSD. But not after what they'd seen.

It was almost impossible for Olivia to put herself in Maggie's shoes. Maggie had spent all those years thinking she was sick, but it was the world that was sick.

Then again, was it really so different to find out that when you're a girl who likes girls, a lot of people think you're bad just for feeling how you feel? Or to find out that you have relatives in Senegal who won't talk to your father because he married a white woman? Not even after the divorce.

When it was their turn, Olivia let Alison do the talking for both of them. She was better at it anyway, and Olivia, although she was feeling better, wasn't up for retelling that story.

The toothed suckers wrapped her leg and pulled her again toward the crashing waves. Olivia forced the memory down, but still felt slightly nauseous. Sipping water, she listened to Alison tell the total insanity that had just happened to them. The only part she left out, Olivia noticed, was when Alison had killed the old monk in the cave.

Olivia was used to keeping Alison's secrets, and even if this was the biggest ever, Olivia felt absolutely no remorse for the death of the monk. She would happily lie under oath to protect Alison in court if it ever came to that. But it made sense that Alison would not want to tell her brother about it. Not yet anyway, and not with Maggie there.

Olivia didn't spend too much time worrying about Alison's choices. She was too focused on her own health. It was impossible really, from everything Olivia knew about medicine anyway, but that pink light from the snow globe had healed her. Alison didn't seem to care how it worked, only that it had. She must have asked Olivia a hundred times how she was feeling.

As long as Olivia said she felt good or better or fine, that was good enough for Alison. It was just as well that Alison wasn't interested in the technical details, because it would have been hard for Olivia to describe exactly how she was feeling.

The best Olivia could do was to say that she felt lined up, like things were fitting back where they belonged. The poisonous stuff that wasn't supposed to be part of her body was gone, and she, her own mind, was pouring back into herself. But that was almost like her mind and her body were separate things.

Olivia chuckled to herself. She and Mr. W. once had an argument that lasted for two weeks about the philosopher René Descartes and his idea called dualism. Descartes said that the body and the mind were two different things that weren't even connected, since the body was physical while the mind was something totally non-physical. That was why it was dualism. Dual. Two. Mind and body. Always separate.

Descartes had to explain why, even though they were separate and different, the mind and the body were able to connect. The mind could make the body hit its thumb with a hammer, and the smashed thumb could then make the mind feel pain. But Descartes never could explain how the body and the mind talked to each other. That bothered Olivia.

How could some famous philosopher offer no explanation for his big idea and get away with it? But Mr. W. had said that there was another philosopher named Malebranche who had an explanation. The mind and the body are not connected at all. God makes the movements of body match the thoughts of the mind. People have free will and make free choices, but God knows what these choices are going to be, so he can move the body appropriately to match a person's free choices. So, when a mind decides to hit its thumb with a hammer, God is the one who moves the body, and then God puts the pain into the mind. The body and the mind have no effect on each other. God does it all. It was almost like people were just characters in the story God tells.

So, God killed the monk in the cave, Olivia concluded. Alison chose to swing the hammer and bash in his skull. It was consistent with her character. But if God didn't collaborate, if God didn't move Alison's hand, it wouldn't have happened. Did God want the monk dead, too?

Olivia shifted in bed and tuned back into Alison's story. She was describing how she used the snow globe to drive away the beadles on the window and then to heal Olivia. Before Alison had used the snow globe—which was obviously not just a snow globe—Olivia's whole body had felt as if it was turning to a cold, dense sludge that sucked her mind down into it. She could feel herself, or the part of her mind she thought of as herself, getting pulled helplessly into a cold darkness with a terrifying, tumbling feeling of falling in slow motion. At that moment, it sure felt like her mind and her body were two different things.

Maybe Descartes had a point, Olivia thought. When the poison had been in her, just talking had been a struggle, especially in those last few minutes when they had arrived back at The Mansion. Olivia could think the words, but she could not get herself to say them. Her body had become a prison, and her mind was trying to break out. If Alison hadn't used the snow globe, Olivia was certain that her mind would have been trapped in the cold, dark sludge that had taken over her body.

Was that death or something else? Olivia shuddered. Cold claws of fear gripped her throat and shoulders. Does your mind, or your soul, just get stuck in cold sludge? Or maybe the poison wasn't really killing her; it was just paralyzing her. Trapping her mind like a fly between two panes of glass.

Alison had saved her from that. With a snow globe? The weight of it settled into her mind. Olivia knew magic wasn't real. More precisely, Olivia knew that what people have called magic was just misunderstood science. And she was desperate to understand the science of the snow globe.

That wasn't the only question the snow globe raised for Olivia, though. She liked to think that she had a strong sense of right and wrong, but if Alison had not stolen the snow globe, Olivia would be dead. If Alison had not killed the old monk, Olivia would be glued to a table with a tube in her belly. Another wave of nausea twisted through her gut. She forced her thoughts back to her question.

Alison committed two crimes—if killing the monk was a crime. I would lie to protect her for it, which is also a crime. Is all of that good or bad? Stealing is wrong, but without the snow globe, I would be dead. The old man was evil, but does that make killing him right? Even in self-defense? But it wasn't even self-defense. Alison was protecting me, not herself.

This was too much for Olivia's brain to handle at the moment. It was easier to think about the science of the snow globe.

The pink light has to use some kind of technology, but what? Lasers? Nanobots? Ultrasound? Microorganisms? Nothing like that exists. We're years, maybe even centuries, away from that kind of technology.

Olivia needed a lot more information. The important thing was that the amazing pink light coming out of that snow globe had saved her life. When the pink light was in her, and that was the only way to describe the way the light had felt, it had been like floating in a tub of perfectly refreshing water.

There had been something else, too. When the poison was in her, she felt so utterly hopeless, worthless even, like nothing at all mattered. Not her. Not Alison. Not the world. It was all pointless and useless. And then the light had flowed into her, and she felt just the opposite.

While the light was flowing, she was important. Not just her, everything was important. She had understood the place and purpose of every single thing in the universe, and it all had made perfect sense. It was all connected. She wondered whether that was what God feels.

But there was one more thing. Something terrible had been just out of her reach, but coming. As soon as the light went out of her, though, all these ideas crumbled like a dream that just slips away, leaving only feelings that were frustratingly strong and vague at the same time.

Had it all been just a hallucination, some side effect of the poison or of the pink light? *Did I really experience that understanding or was it just a dream? How could I ever know the difference?*

"Okay, so what is a beadle?" Maggie asked, interrupting Olivia's reflections. Alison had brought the story back to their room, right before Maggie and Michael had found them.

"It's one of those creatures they make out of the people they kidnap. I already told you. That's what attacked us and poisoned Olivia. She would have died if the snow globe didn't have, like, magic powers or whatever."

Olivia caught the irritation in Alison's voice. She didn't think it was a good time to point out that the snow globe was powered by science, not magic.

"I wonder if that was Elizabeth Denton you found on the table." Maggie stared off into a corner.

"Who?" Alison asked.

Michael told them about a newspaper story he'd read. Missing people. Olivia could only half-listen.

"Could be," Alison concluded. "There were three of them."

"What did they look like?" Maggie asked.

"They didn't look good." The corners of Alison's mouth turned down in disgust. "They were all shriveled-looking."

Olivia winced and watched Maggie pace to the window, presumably to look out at the ocean. "So…all the other words you saw on the poster mean something else. A benefactor is someone who does something good for somebody else. A steward is a caretaker. A naiad is either a mythical water spirit or the larval stage of a dragonfly or something, right? Based on what you saw on the diagram, Elizabeth Denton and the others were benefactors for the naiads. The good they did," Maggie put air quotes around the word good, "was they fed the naiads. But when that was done they became stewards for the beadles. What does that mean?"

Alison shrugged, "They help the beadles I guess, like servants or something."

"Okay, but what's a beadle?" Maggie repeated.

When they all turned to face her, Olivia felt her face get red. She took another sip of water. "I thought you guys knew."

"Only you would know something like that." Olivia thought Michael meant that as a compliment, even if it sounded like he was throwing shade.

"Olivia assumes everyone is as smart as she is. It's the only stupid thing she does. You don't have to answer, Liv. You're not a dictionary. You just rest." Alison continued to stroke Olivia's hair, but Alison's snark made Olivia cringe. The last thing they needed was a fight.

Olivia smiled and squeezed Alison's hand. "I'm fine." Her voice felt a little raw, but she was happy that her brain was coming back online. "A beadle is someone who works for a church. They basically handle operations."

"So like a janitor?" Michael asked.

Olivia shook her head. It didn't hurt as much. Her headache was mild, and she thought it was probably more due to hunger and dehydration than to any lasting effects of the poison. At least she hoped that was it.

After a few more sips of water her stomach growled, but she stuck to Michael's question. "A beadle makes sure that all the members of the church are following the rules, especially during services. Sometimes they check on members who don't show up. They can be ushers, pass around the collection baskets, help organize festivals and fundraising, that kind of thing." She swung her legs over the bed and sat up.

"Whoa! Where do you think you're going?" Alison's eyes were full of fire and fear.

Olivia smiled at her, trying to be reassuring. "I'm okay, Allie. Really."

"As soon as Mom and Dad get back, you're going to the hospital."

Visions of white rooms, bright lights and needles crowded Olivia's head. She thought of lying on a hospital bed and the images of the people on the tables in the cave made her feel weak and cold. "I don't need a hospital." She tried to sound light and effortless to reassure Alison that she was okay. "What would I even say happened?" She held up her ankle. "The snow globe took care of the poison. There's not even a scar."

"Do you know how crazy you sound right now?" Alison scolded.

"Not as crazy as I would sound explaining this all to a doctor," Olivia said. She tried to sound breezy for Alison.

"You need a doctor, Olivia. You're supposed to be the sensible one here."

Olivia laughed. "I was attacked by a sea monster that a cult made by sacrificing people in a cave. Does any of that sound sensible?" She let her gaze drift out the window. The sun, setting on the opposite side of The Mansion, cast long, wriggling shadows over the waves and painted the horizon pink and orange. The ocean met the sky along a blade of deep blue. "It's really a shame that such a beautiful place has so many bad things happening."

Maggie laughed dryly, "Welcome to Planet Earth."

"Beadles are church officials." Michael ticked a list off on his fingers. It was like he hadn't even been listening to their conversation. Olivia knew this wasn't unusual for him. "The Church of New Enlightenment calls those monsters beadles. Beadles organize the church, right, Olivia? They prepare for festivals and stuff?"

"So?" Alison huffed.

Michael raised his eyebrows and lowered his voice. "So what do you think they're getting ready for?"

Maggie's eyes went wide, and she suddenly looked like she was in pain.

Michael put his arm around her. "Hey," he said softly. "You okay?"

Her eyes looked terrified. "The door, Michael. The door we found. The beadles opened that to get in and out of the cathedral."

"Why?"

Maggie laughed like she didn't believe he was serious. "You saw the pictures, Michael. They're getting ready for their big ceremony."

Michael looked like he had no idea what she was saying. "What ceremony?"

"They're calling that thing." Maggie gasped. "It's Cappy!"

Michael tilted his head. "The sea monster?" He laughed loudly. "You're tripping. They might be a bunch of dangerous psychos, but there's not going to be any Second Coming of some sea monster."

Maggie's eyes narrowed, and her lips pursed into a scowl. "Keep telling yourself that if it makes you feel better, Michael, but I've been hiding from the uncomfortable truth for way too long. And by the way, as a person with mental health issues, I find the term psycho offensive."

Michael's mouth dropped open. Maggie had caught him off guard, but it surprised Olivia, too. In other circumstances, she would have found it amusing, especially the flustered look on Michael's face. She wondered whether she had a shot with Maggie after all.

"I'm sorry, Maggie." He turned to face her, looking so awkward it was kind of sweet.

Maggie's face softened. "Forget it."

Michael shrugged and started pacing again. "But there is a big difference between a mentally ill person and a group of dangerous murderers who—"

"Quit while you're ahead, genius," Alison said.

He turned on her, pointing his finger. "I don't need any help from you."

Alison laughed at him. "That's not how it looks from here."

Michael held up both hands. "Just forget it, okay. The important thing is that these freaks…" Michael paused and raised his eyebrows at Maggie like he was waiting for her permission or approval. Her face didn't change. "Suppose they really do want to bring a monster through that magic painting to destroy the world. What are we supposed to do exactly?"

"As a person who believes in science and reason, I find the term *magic* offensive," Olivia said quietly.

"Look, Olivia," Michael said, "I know you were poisoned and you almost died and all, but now really isn't the time for one of your nerd bombs to go off."

Before the cave, she would have wanted to crawl into the nearest hole. That made Olivia smile. "It's not a nerd bomb, Michael. There's no magic stronger than information."

"Listen to her, stupid!" Alison snapped. "She knows what she's talking about." Alison's eyes were wide and waiting.

Olivia wasn't so confident, but the description of the glowing painting and the sudden appearance of the birds and the flies in the cathedral had gotten her thinking. The pink light wasn't magic. It was technology more advanced than anything on Earth. With that kind of power, the improbable became possible. "That painting is a wormhole."

Michael threw up his hands and stomped in a tight circle. "Please! Even I know that wormholes aren't real."

"They're real, we've just never seen one." The more angry Michael got, the calmer Olivia felt.

"If we've never seen one, how could somebody make one in Maggie's backyard?" Michael dismissed Olivia with a swatting gesture.

"*We* can't, but that doesn't mean someone else didn't figure it out." Olivia couldn't believe she was saying it herself, but nothing else made sense. "It's like what Sherlock Holmes says. When you rule out the impossible, whatever is left, no matter how improbable, has to be true. What you saw in the cathedral is a wormhole, and aliens built it."

"Aliens?" Alison sounded stunned. "You said there were no aliens."

"I'm rethinking that."

"What do you mean?" Olivia watched Maggie's core muscles tensing. She felt a flutter, but drove it away. "I don't think aliens from our universe could get here. The window is too small." Olivia fished for a way to explain a complicated idea in a few sentences. "The distances are too great between stars that might have planets with intelligent life. Life is too fragile, and civilizations don't last long enough for deep space exploration to ever find life on other planets."

"So aliens or no aliens?" Michael asked. "What are we saying here?"

"I hadn't really considered aliens from a parallel universe, because we have no hard evidence that multiverse theory is right, plus the only way to get to another universe would be through a wormhole, and we've never observed one of those either."

"This is all just sci-fi crap!" Michael slapped the back of his hand into his opposite palm.

Olivia took another sip of water and a deep breath. "Einstein didn't think so. People used to think black holes were only theoretical, too, but now we find them all the time."

"Who cares?" Michael sounded irritated. "Instead of worrying about the little green men, we should be worried about the people from the church."

Olivia knew Michael was being narrow-minded because he was scared. Who could blame him? But after her experience with the poison and the pink light, Olivia saw things differently. "Some scientists think wormholes might blink in and out of existence all the time by themselves, but just for a few nanoseconds. They would be super small too—we're talking Planck scale with insanely high levels of energy in an insanely tiny amount of space. At that size and with those energy levels, quantum uncertainty increases until Newtonian physics breaks down. Time, location, cause and effect...all of it goes out the window."

"Or out the wormhole," Alison muttered.

"That's not what's in the cathedral," Maggie said. "The painting is about thirty feet tall. If that's a wormhole, it's not small."

Olivia felt energized. Almost like the pink light was still in her. "Right. But if you have exotic matter, that's matter with a negative energy density and possibly positive pressure—or vise versa, anyway, with exotic energy it is theoretically possible to enlarge one of those spontaneous wormholes and stabilize it. Exotic matter is only theoretical, at least in our universe, but suppose exotic matter is common in the universe that's on the other side of the wormhole? Exotic matter to us would be ordinary matter to them."

"How do you even know there is another universe?" Michael groaned.

"Just let her finish!" Alison scolded.

"Again, in theory, as soon as anything that wasn't exotic matter entered the field of the wormhole, the whole thing should collapse, but once you can build something out of exotic matter in the first place, stabilizing it shouldn't be that hard. Again, this is just a theory."

"So is gravity," Maggie said, "but that seems to work pretty well."

Olivia laughed. "Right. But the hard part would be combining the exotic matter with ordinary matter. The two kinds of matter should annihilate each other. But this is already far beyond our current understanding of the Standard Model anyway. The point is, an advanced civilization from a parallel universe might have tunneled here though a wormhole."

"And our universe's entrance to it is the painting in the cathedral?" Maggie asked.

"It's possible," Olivia said. Ideas danced in her head like colorful, squawking birds. She tried to get each one into the right cage, just long enough to make sense of it, before it flew away. "That might explain the mysterious stone blocks around The Mansion. I thought they might be some kind of synthetic sapphire, but I couldn't figure out why. But now I get it. Sapphire has high dielectric strength so it insulates against high voltages, and it can store energy right in the crystal structure. Sapphire works great in a capacitor. Also, it's the second hardest gem after diamonds. Synthetic sapphire keeps your phone from getting scratched. It conducts forty times more electricity than copper."

Michael's mouth hung open. "So you have, like, zero life?"

Alison pushed him away, but gently. "So the blue blocks all around here, they're what? Batteries for the wormhole or something? Is that what you mean?"

Olivia laughed, "If someone made synthetic sapphire—or another form of aluminum oxide—and synthesized it with exotic matter, it could act like a kind of a battery for the exotic energy you'd need to create and stabilize the wormhole."

"Is that even possible?" Alison asked.

"No," Olivia laughed. She felt a thrilling tickle in her stomach as cutting-edge science bubbled through her head. "Not for us, but maybe for somebody more advanced."

"Aliens." Michael scowled, sounding pretty doubtful.

Maggie put her hands to her temples and closed her eyes. "So The Church of New Enlightenment is trying to open a wormhole to bring in a creature from a parallel universe?"

"Why?" Michael asked.

Maggie's eyes popped open. "Because they think it's God. That's why there's a church!"

"So all we have to do is blow it up or something," Alison said.

"Oh is that it? Just blow up a wormhole? Sure! Last week I blew up three wormholes before breakfast!" Michael laughed, but he didn't sound happy. "Are you guys nuts? If Olivia is even close to right, we need to get NASA and maybe the Pope on this. We don't know how to blow up a wormhole. We're just kids on vacation, remember?"

"I'm not, Michael." Maggie's eyes were fierce and cold. "I'm responsible for this place. Like it or not, I'm already in this."

"Okay," Michael sighed. He raised his palms toward Maggie, but he sounded impatient. "You're this responsible adult who drinks coffee and knows how to snorkel and make crepes and all that. We're not. And we're not Seal Team Six either. There's nothing we could possibly do to stop this cult or these aliens or whatever they are. We seriously need the cops or the FBI or the Army or something."

Maggie's eyes widened like Michael had surprised her, but it surprised Olivia when Maggie stepped to him and took both his hands. "There's a lot you could do, Michael. You're strong. You're smart. Brave. And you care about people. You care about me. At least," Maggie dropped his hand and looked toward the ground between them, "I think you do."

Turning suddenly toward Olivia and Alison, Maggie sounded almost manic. "You two already beat these things once. That's our big advantage. They underestimate us. People have been getting lost down here for a long time. Does it look like the FBI is running to the rescue? Or NASA or the Pope? The CNE gets away with it because nobody is trying to stop them. The Enlightened are working right out in the open under everybody's nose because nobody has ever taken the time to figure out what they're up to."

"Because if you run around talking about wormholes and aliens, they're going to lock you up and throw away the key!" Michael looked sheepishly at Maggie. "No offense."

Maggie laughed long and loud. "I've wasted ten years thinking I was crazy and doing nothing while this cult killed my family and destroyed my home."

"Now what?" Alison asked quietly.

"We have to get to Olga's. We need to show Olga those pictures. She might be able to help us."

"What do you mean we?" Michael said. "Could everybody just hang on a minute?"

Maggie scowled. "What? You want to just run back to your privileged little suburban life and ignore this until it bites you on the ass?" Maggie turned her back to him and faced the window.

"That's not what I meant." Michael scowled, and Olivia saw the knotty muscles in his shoulders contract. Olivia had seen him get angry. It wasn't pretty. She felt her own body tensing, bracing for the shouting and the violence she knew was coming.

But Michael took a long deep breath. When he spoke again, his voice was softer. "I do care about you. All of you. We all need to stay safe."

Maggie looked at the floor. "Michael…"

He held her gently by the shoulders. "It's dangerous out there."

"We can do it together and keep each other safe." Maggie sounded hopeful. Olivia understood that hope. It wasn't just about The Mansion. Maggie was a lonely outsider, too, just like her. Without Alison, Olivia would have been utterly alone. Who else did Maggie have?

"I can't just leave them here." He nodded toward Olivia and Alison. "Let's just wait for…"

"We're going." Alison's eyes were defiant.

"Olivia's sick." Michael folded his arms and shook his head firmly.

Maggie looked out the window. "I don't know. Those beadle things found the girls here once. They can do it again."

Maggie's words were like an icy hook around Olivia's throat while the memory of the tentacle burned her ankle.

"We still have the snow globe." Alison stood and held it up. Olivia didn't realize that Alison had been holding it the whole time. It probably made her feel safer.

Maggie's face softened. "You don't know what that thing is or how it really works. It might not work again. Or those things might get stronger. Or there might be other things. We just don't know enough. That's why we need to get to Olga's. If we tell her everything we found out, she might have an idea of what to do. She's lived here a long time, and she and my grandfather were friends."

"We still should wait for my parents to come back," Michael pointed out.

A sad, fearful cloud passed Maggie's face. "Mine never did. Neither did Uncle Max or my grandfather."

Her words hung in the air until they punched like a fist in Olivia's stomach. Alison stood abruptly and, for the first time since they got back, she left the bed to pace around the room.

Alison sounded like she was having trouble breathing. Her face was so red it almost hid her freckles. "Maggie, are you serious right now? You think that Mom and Dad..." Alison covered her face with her hands. "My parents had a fight this morning. They just needed time to calm down."

"I'm sorry, Alison," Maggie said calmly.

"What's that supposed to mean?" Alison demanded. "Do you want my parents to be dead so I can be like you?"

"ALISON!" Michael rushed to Maggie's side, but she looked calm.

"No, Alison. I wouldn't wish that on anyone." Maggie's voice was small and quiet. "But your parents have been gone all day."

"You don't know that," Alison stalked up to Maggie. Olivia cringed, afraid that Alison might hit her, but Maggie didn't flinch. She didn't show any emotion at all.

Alison stood face to face with Maggie, but she was shorter, so she had to look up at Maggie to stare her down. "We haven't been here all day. They might have come home and gone back out again."

"You know Mom. They would have left us a note or something." Michael sighed heavily.

Alison turned on Michael, sounding furious and on the edge of tears. "Why are you taking her side, Michael? Is it just because she's hot and you want her?"

Michael's face turned red, and his fists clenched. Maggie stared awkwardly out the window. She folded her arms, covering herself.

"Alison!" Olivia stood up. She felt dizzy, but only for a moment. Low blood sugar.

Alison rushed to Olivia's side. "You need to stay in bed."

Olivia shook her off. "No, Allie, I'm fine. But you need to listen. You're way out of line."

Alison's face was red and tight.

Olivia spoke quietly and gently. "Maggie is trying to help. Allie, after everything we saw today...What if something did happen to your parents?"

"No!" Alison snarled like an animal and ran out of the room. Olivia heard her stomp up the hall. Michael looked confused and helpless. Maggie's face was blank.

"HAH!" Alison sounded triumphant. "This is why you can't panic. You end up doing stupid things." Her voice echoed outside the room, and then her feet pounded back down the hall. She swept into the room waving a yellow piece of paper like a flag.

"See? They did leave a note. They went out for dinner!" Alison beamed. Olivia knew Alison was happy that her parents were okay, but suspected that the fact that Alison had been right didn't hurt any either. That was Alison.

Maggie smiled sadly. "Good. I'm glad they're safe at least."

"And they're together." Olivia was not surprised that Alison was still thinking about her parents' marriage after all this. She was so stubborn.

"We should just wait here for them to come back then, right?" Michael suggested. "It's not safe on the roads. They probably went back to Olga's. Do you know the number?" Michael picked up the phone on the nightstand. "There's no dial tone. What do I dial to get out?"

"Nine, but if the phone was working, you'd have a dial tone already."

Michael mashed the buttons and then slammed the phone down. "Nothing."

"Smashing it won't help." Maggie sighed. "Do I really need to add a new phone to your bill?"

Dark anger swept across Michael's face, but then it softened, and he laughed at some private joke between them. "Depends. Am I going to have to do more dishes or row another boat?"

Smiling, Maggie closed her eyes and took a big breath. "Listen, we should just get to Olga's fast. Hopefully your parents are there. You can tell them what's happening or not. You can just get out of Cape November."

"What about you?" Alison asked. Olivia could not tell whether Alison was being compassionate or suspicious. Both, she concluded.

Maggie stood silent for a moment. "I'm not leaving," she said finally. "This is my home."

"What can you do if you stay?" Michael sounded worried.

"What can you do if you go?" Maggie replied, still with her sad smile.

"Maggie, I can't let anything else happen to my sister and Olivia."

"That's our choice, Michael," Alison said. "You don't get to tell us what to do."

"I have to protect you."

"No, you don't!" Alison's eyes flashed.

Michael slammed his fist on the nightstand. "You think you need to protect Mom and Dad's marriage, but I can't stop you from getting yourself killed?"

Olivia closed her eyes and covered her ears. She couldn't listen to the fighting anymore. The Church of New Enlightenment and its monsters had almost killed her the way they had killed Maggie's family. She couldn't let that happen to anybody else. Ever.

Out the window, the gorgeous sunset sparkled over the ocean. In it, Olivia found what she needed.

"It's like all that stuff they teach us about bullying." She turned to face the others. Each one looked sad and afraid. Her stomach growled and felt hollow. "Bullies win when bystanders don't stand up for the victims. If good people don't do anything, bad people win."

Maggie spoke quietly. "The best lack all conviction, while the worst are full of passionate intensity."

"What?" Michael asked.

Maggie shook her head. "It's a line from a poem by Yeats. I had to memorize it once. Know what it's called?"

"Obviously not," Michael spat.

Maggie looked back out the window. "Second Coming."

Michael chuckled. "Perfect." He paced furiously for a moment. "That's all great for school assemblies and political speeches and poems, but this is serious. These monsters, these people, they're really dangerous."

"No kidding," Olivia said. "Everything's dangerous. Terrorism, pollution, war, poverty, crime, ignorance, hatred, racism, homophobia, injustice, each one is a monster. We all have choices. We deal with a problem or we ignore it. But ignoring it is still a choice. It's choosing to do nothing while the monster kills somebody else and you hope it's not you next time."

Michael sat heavily on the edge of the bed. His big shoulders moved up and down with his breath. "So what's the play?"

Maggie put her hand on his shoulder. Olivia thought it looked tender, loving even. She spoke softly. "I'm going to put on some real clothes, then I'm going to Olga's. You can wait here or come with me. It's your choice."

"Wait!" Michael popped up and looked them each in the face. "Nobody goes anywhere alone tonight. Can we at least all agree to that?"

"Still Batman?" Alison grinned.

Michael laughed, sounding bashful and nervous. "Yeah. Right."

"To me you are," Maggie said. She tousled his hair like he was ten years old, but Michael didn't seem to mind.

Alison turned to stare into Olivia's eyes. She'd never looked more intense. "You almost died today. I can't lose you again."

Olivia felt warmth spread from her chest to her face. "That's exactly why we need to go and stop these people."

"But are you up for it?" Alison put her hand tenderly on Olivia's face. Olivia pressed Alison's palm against her cheek and nodded, happy that nothing hurt in her head anymore. The foggy feeling had cleared, and her ankle felt strong. Everything seemed back to normal. At least in her mind and body. She walked to the wardrobe and started to look for some clothes. "What do people wear to save the world?"

40 OVERPROTECTIVE

Alison and Olivia quickly pulled on tee shirts and shorts and their last pairs of sneakers. "We can't lose these or we'll be running away from monsters barefoot." A small shiver ran through her.

Michael demanded to stay in the room and just turn his back while they changed, but eventually he agreed to wait in the bathroom to give them privacy. Alison caught him with his ear against the door, and he got angry when she accused him of being a sick perv. Alison noticed that Olivia was laughing. Maggie wasn't.

The argument didn't last long. Alison realized that Michael really was worried about them. He was being annoying because in his own Michael way, he was trying to keep them safe. But now Alison needed the bathroom. That had created a new problem.

"You're not staying with me in the bathroom, Michael," Alison warned, "and I really gotta go, so get out."

"I'll turn around and cover my ears." Michael did that, so Alison poked him in his ribs to get his attention. Michael yelped. "Hey!"

"Get out!" Alison pointed to Michael's room. "You get changed and then we can all go upstairs to Maggie's."

"Fine," he said grumpily, "but let me check the bathroom."

"We're standing in it!"

With both fists clenched, Michael craned his neck to check the shower and then he did a sweep of his own room. "Okay, we're clear. I'll go get changed. You take your dump or whatever…"

"MICHAEL!"

He waved Alison off and stretched to look past her to the other room. "Olivia, you and Maggie watch that door. If anything happens, just yell really loud and I'll come."

"Michael, I really think you've lost your mind," Olivia said.

"Just yell," Michael insisted.

"What are you going to do if we start yelling?" Alison asked. She had never seen Michael so jittery.

"I'll kick some ass." Michael laughed like it was obvious and then he looked annoyed. "Man! I left my poker up in Maggie's room this morning."

"Take ours," Olivia offered.

"No. You might need it." Alison knew that he was totally serious, which only made the whole thing funnier.

"What's so funny?" Michael sounded defensive.

"It's just the stress," Alison said, because the truth was too hard to talk about: If more of those beadle things came to get them, it wouldn't matter who had the poker. "But I know that if anything happens to me in the bathroom, I can just yell, and you'll come in and kick ass. I got it."

Michael nodded, but looked a little less confident.

"What if something happens to you in your room while you're getting changed?" Maggie asked from the other room. Alison noticed that she was doing a pretty bad job of hiding a smirk. Alison felt a pang of guilt for the way she had acted earlier. She had said some pretty disgusting things.

Michael looked at Maggie like that was the dumbest thing anybody had ever asked him.

"You'll kick ass?" Olivia sounded uncertain.

Michael winked and pointed at her with his fingers shaped like a gun.

Maggie rolled her eyes as she shut the bathroom door on her side.

"I don't know why you think you're in charge anyway," Alison said as she closed the other door on him.

From his own room, Michael's voice came though muffled. "I'm just being careful."

It surprised Alison how much Michael was worrying about them. Okay, so this was an extreme situation, but still, he'd never been protective of her. Daniela Acevedo's big brother Ramon would follow her boyfriends home in his car and threaten to cut their junk off if they did anything to Daniela. It was probably good that Ramon had no idea what Daniela was doing to her boyfriends.

Alison had never had a serious boyfriend, and anyway, she made a point of keeping her family out of her personal life. If Michael had ever heard about someone giving Alison a hard time at school or whatever, he never said anything about it. Alison had always assumed that this was because he was clueless or that he didn't care that much.

But the way Michael had been pacing the room, checking doors and windows over and over again, Alison began to think that he had let her fight her own battles because he thought she needed to; it was his way of showing he cared. He wanted her to be tough. But now the danger was so big that he couldn't hang back.

In a few minutes, Alison knocked on Michael's door. He had been asking her if she was okay about every thirty seconds since she'd been in there. Opening the door, he appeared in black cargo shorts, sneakers and a plain black tee shirt. He also had his backpack on.

"What's the backpack for?" Olivia asked.

Michael shrugged. "Right now I got my camera in there."

"And why are you dressed like it's the first day of ninja school?" Alison couldn't pass it up.

"Didn't you ever play manhunt?" Michael scowled at her. "If we end up needing to hide, you're better off in black."

She hadn't thought of that, but Michael had a good point. Alison and Olivia headed back to their room to change again. Michael agreed to wait in his own room as long as they promised not to shut the bathroom doors.

Changing again into dark gray chinos and a black tank top, she went back into her brother's room and sat in a chair to put her sneakers back on. "See, Michael, you always say I overpack."

"That's only because I'm always the one carrying your suitcase."

"Such a gentleman," Olivia teased, coming through the bathroom door into Michael's room.

"What are you wearing?" Michael asked with obvious disapproval.

"I don't have any black with me. This is the best I can do." Olivia modeled her purple, long-sleeved tee shirt and blue sports leggings.

"She owns a lot of pastels and bright colors," Alison explained.

He shrugged. "Did you bring the poker?"

"Reporting for duty," Maggie said, coming in behind Olivia. She held the tool out in front of her.

Michael nodded, "Come on. We have to hit the road."

Alison looked up at Michael. Anxiety gnawed at her gut. "What if they're not at Olga's?"

He shook his head firmly. "You know Dad. Where else are they going to go? Besides, have you looked around this town? There's nothing here. You have the snow globe, right?"

Alison held up her backpack, having already dumped it, and put the snow globe in, wrapped in a sweatshirt. She noticed that it wasn't glowing or acting like anything other than a snow globe, except for the erratic way the sea monster and the whale floated inside it.

Maggie handed Olivia the flashlight. "You can put this in yours."

Olivia slid the flashlight into her backpack as they pressed together behind Michael and the poker. If it came to it, Michael was the strongest and probably the best equipped to beat a monster with a fireplace poker. It struck Alison as strange, almost funny, that they were starting the night the same way that they had started the morning. And how had that turned out?

41 SWAGGER

Michael was relieved that they had gotten to Maggie's room with no trouble at all. He was ready to kick ass, but he was happy that he didn't have to. While they had been waiting for her to change, Olivia had flipped through a book from Maggie's shelf.

"You gonna throw books at the monsters?" Michael said it gently.

"It's got a section on wormholes," Olivia said calmly. "If there is a wormhole in the cathedral, we should know what we're dealing with." She sighed and tossed the book onto the bed. "I don't know how much this book will help anyway. If the painting really is a wormhole, it's the only one in existence as far as I know."

"Maybe you'll become famous for discovering it," Michael offered, figuring it would make Olivia happy. "If we live that long."

Maggie had changed quickly into a black tank top, black cargo pants and black hiking boots. Her backpack was soft, brown leather.

"Let's pick up some supplies," she said.

"Supplies for what?" Michael asked. They were wasting too much time.

"You know what they say," Maggie said cheerfully, "luck favors the prepared."

Alison huffed, "No. Louis Pasteur said, 'Fortune favors the prepared mind.' Sorry, but I hate it when people get quotes wrong. It's a pet peeve."

Maggie's lip curled slightly, but she didn't say anything.

Alison's whole smarty-pants thing really irritated Michael. "You don't have to correct people all the time. It's annoying."

Alison shrugged. "Mr. W. had that quote on a poster hanging in his room. He would always point to it whenever somebody said they didn't understand why they had to learn something. He'd always tell us to learn as much as we could about everything because you never know what you're going to end up needing."

"Sometimes knowledge is the best weapon," Olivia said.

Typical nerd. "I'm sticking with the poker."

Maggie opened her door. "Let's get to the kitchen."

"Why are we going to the kitchen? You want to bake cookies for the monsters while we read to them?" Michael wondered whether he should have just left the three of them and pedaled to Olga's on his own. He would have been there already.

Maggie ignored him and took the fireplace poker Michael had left there earlier and handed it to Alison. Then she took the poker from her own fireplace. "Michael's right. We do need to get going."

"Thank you!" Michael couldn't believe somebody agreed with him for once, instead of making him feel like an idiot.

With the power back on it was easier and a lot less scary to move through The Mansion and they reached the kitchen in no time. It was a stop Michael didn't want to make, but he kept his mouth shut about it because he knew they would all just yell at him.

He was hungry, but he didn't want to waste time eating. Anyway, he figured they could get food once they were safe at Olga's, after they found Mom and Dad. But Alison whined that she needed something or she wouldn't have enough energy to pedal. Typical Alison. That's exactly why she had to see a fat doctor.

Michael was surprised when Maggie agreed with Alison, adding, "If we hit any trouble on the road, we might not get to Olga's for a long time. If we get there at all."

That was exactly the kind of thing he didn't need to hear, but when he saw the shelves in the back of the kitchen stocked with cans and jars, he realized that his sister was right. He was starving. He took a huge jar of peanut butter off a shelf and began shoveling it into his mouth with his fingers as he pulled open the refrigerator door, and found the cold cuts.

When they ate all of the ham and cheese, Maggie handed them a box of granola bars. They ate a few and then stuffed the rest into their backpacks along with the cheese sticks Michael found with the cold cuts.

They drank water and sports drinks and put extra bottles in their bags. Maggie went to the shelf full of tools and found another flashlight and some extra batteries. She slipped that into her own bag. She held out a hammer for Olivia. "You're the only one without a weapon. Take this."

"I...I don't think I could use that on anybody," Olivia sounded breathless and looked at Alison out of the tops of her eyelids.

Maggie raised one eyebrow. "If you need to save yourself or one of us, I think you will."

Olivia looked at Alison like she wanted to ask her something, but she didn't say anything. Neither did Alison, but Michael noticed that Alison shook her head slightly. There was something she didn't want Olivia to say out loud. Olivia shivered with her eyes closed and let Maggie drop the hammer into her backpack.

Maggie stuffed her own bag with screwdrivers, a couple of adjustable wrenches, some rope, some elastic bungee cords, duct tape. She looked up, noticed their staring and stood to her full height.

"You really think you're going to need all that?" Michael asked.

Putting her hands on her hips, Maggie said, "The point of being prepared is that you don't always know what you're preparing for."

"You look like you're preparing for a carpenter's convention," Michael grinned. The food had improved his mood considerably. "Whoa, I was just messing with you."

Maggie had pulled a dangerous-looking hunting knife out of its sheath. "I know." She grinned as she flicked her thumb across the blade, testing its sharpness, Michael assumed. Nodding like she was satisfied, she slammed the knife back into the sheath and attached it to her belt. "Ready?"

Maggie led them to the front door, but Michael stepped up to the knob. "I'll take the lead, okay?"

"Why?"

"Just wait here a second." Michael turned the knob and opened the door. He motioned for them to wait while he crept down the porch steps, cringing every time a board creaked, and they seemed to creak every time he took a step.

The porch light was on, but that only made the darkness beyond the pale yellow glow seem that much darker. At the bottom of the porch stairs, Michael waited, trying to allow his eyes to adjust to the visual maze of light and shadow on the edge of the trees around the yard. Under the trees was only darkness.

Sweat trickled down his temple. His heart slammed in his ribs as footsteps clattered behind him. Maggie, Olivia and Alison had come down to stand beside him. Maggie and Olivia used their flashlights to probe the shadows.

"I told you to wait," Michael hissed.

"You're not the boss, Michael," Alison whispered. Michael saw that she didn't take her eyes off the ring of darkness that lurked just beyond the porch light.

"Those things could be out here."

"Exactly," Maggie whispered. "That's why we need to stick together."

"Shouldn't we take these?" Alison nodded at the two bikes they had left lying on their sides at the foot of the porch stairs.

Michael appraised them and thought about the ride ahead. "They have gears?"

Olivia shook her head. "Beach cruisers."

He looked up at Maggie, "You have twenty-niners out there?"

"What's that?" It was almost a relief that Maggie didn't know what he meant.

"Mountain bikes with twenty-nine-inch rims," Olivia said. "Last year my dad got me an awesome twenty-niner, full suspension, disk brakes, carbon frame, the works. It flies over roots and rocks on the downhills." Olivia beamed.

It surprised Michael. He didn't realize what a gearhead she was.

"I don't really know what kinds of bikes are out there," Maggie admitted. "Uncle Max took care of the bikes. He built custom motorcycles and stuff. I'm more into diving. Anyway, what difference does it make?"

Michael was happy to explain it to her. "Twenty-niners are fast because of the bigger rims, but they still give a lot of control."

Olivia whispered, "There are twenty-niners, couple of full suspension gravity bikes—not that there's a lot of downhill around here—oh, and there are a couple of fat bikes."

"Fat bikes?" Alison asked.

"Those bikes with the huge, fat tires we saw out there," Olivia explained.

Michael rubbed his chin, calculating whether he would be better off underinflating the oversize tires on a few fat bike tires. He looked at Maggie, "You're not taking us over a lot of sand, right?"

"I am not riding along the beach," Alison said. "Those things live in the water, I think."

"She's right," Olivia agreed. "Twenty-niners take curbs like they're not even there, and they're smooth and fast over pavement. They would be perfect for us right now."

Michael offered Olivia a fist bump. That girl was all right.

As he looked across the ocean of darkness outside of the reach of the porch light, he could feel his heart racing, and all the food he'd just inhaled was starting to feel like a lump in his stomach. Little beads of sweat bubbled out all over his body, but the night breeze coming off the ocean was chilly. He took a deep breath. Somehow he had to keep the girls safe, but he knew how stubborn Alison was, and Maggie was proving just as bad.

"Will you please wait here while I check the stables?"

"Hell no," Alison said.

His heart hammered in his chest. "I need to make sure it's safe."

"You did say that no one should go anywhere alone, right?" Olivia reminded him.

Michael felt like the air on his body weighed a ton, like everything was pressing down on him. "Look, maybe this whole thing is a bad idea."

Maggie's infuriating eyebrow popped up at him. "If you and the girls want to wait here…"

Michael's chest tightened. He needed to punch something. Or someone. Where were those beadle things? "Fine. But stay behind me." Before any of them could argue, he turned and stalked toward the stables.

The woods around The Mansion screeched and chirped and cracked and moaned in the breeze. Every sound made Michael jump in his skin. He had to keep reminding himself that the woods were just making all the ordinary sounds that woods make. He gripped the poker like a baseball bat. Sweat made his palms slippery. He kept waiting for a shadow to lunge at them.

He jumped and gave a startled yelp when Maggie grabbed his shoulder, "Slow down. It's dark. We're getting ahead of Alison and Olivia. We don't need anybody tripping out here."

Michael felt his forehead boil. His ears hissed and his head hurt. Why won't they just listen? "That's why I asked you to wait at The Mansion."

"You can sprain your ankle, too, fearless leader. Just slow down and be careful." She rubbed his shoulder and smiled weakly at him, but her face was tight and creased with worry.

His blood pounded in his temples. His chest felt tight, and his shoulders tingled. For a second he thought he was having a heart attack. And then he wished one of those fish things would show up so he could bury the poker in its face. All his muscles tightened, and he raised the poker over his head, threatening the shadows, "These fish heads better be careful! They're messing with the wrong people this time!"

His voice echoed in the trees, and invisible wings flapped off screeching in the darkness. Michael's stomach jerked shut like he'd been punched. He tasted peanut butter in the back of his throat as he waited for the birds to swoop out of the darkness to attack them, but the woods were still and silent.

"Shut up, you idiot!" Alison hissed, smacking his arm. "What the hell is your problem?"

Maggie's eyes were cold, angry slits. She whispered sternly, "Your Macho-the-Barbarian thing could get us all killed! Maybe you should wait at The Mansion." She pushed past him and took the lead toward the stable. Alison stayed back, apparently just to glare at him some more.

He jumped when he felt the hand on his back. But it was only Olivia, gently rubbing between his shoulder blades. "You okay?"

His breath came in short, panting gasps. He felt furious and humiliated. His swagger shriveled up inside him, but he realized women were just as brave and strong as men, but they were always so practical and realistic. If they were scared they would just accept that they were scared and deal with it. Men weren't supposed to be scared, so they invented swagger. They talked tough until they fooled themselves into feeling fearless.

It was like something his driving teacher had taught him. Michael was nervous to drive sixty-five miles an hour the first time he got on the highway. So Mr. Berkowitz made him do seventy-five for a full two minutes. Then when Michael slowed back down to sixty-five it felt relatively slow and comfortable. All the tough talk and trash talk Michael had grown up with in school yards and ball fields and gyms and locker rooms full of boys struggling to become men, was really just seventy-five miles an hour of swagger so that when they needed sixty-five miles an hour worth of courage, they would be comfortable with it.

The weight on him felt less heavy. He smiled at Olivia, and for the first time, he knew that they really were friends. "Thanks. I'm good. Sorry I sort of lost it there."

"You should be, Michael," Alison sneered.

Olivia put up her hand. "Allie, he was just scared, okay? We all are. And he's worried because he cares about us." She looked up at him, "Let's get on some kick-ass twenty-niners."

When she fist-bumped him, Michael laughed. He couldn't believe that all these years they had bikes in common, and he never knew it. But then he'd never taken the time to ask. Maybe they could be friends, too. That gave him all the courage he needed for the moment.

Alison punched him lightly in the arm. "Just don't be a moron."

42 LIGHTS IN THE DARK

The beam of Maggie's flashlight bounced ahead of them on the grassy path. As they got closer to the stable, Olivia saw the yellow valley of lamp light stretched flat between looming mountains of shadow cast by the partially open doors. Beyond that little path of light, Olivia could only imagine what waited for them, hunched in the dark stable.

Maggie heaved the doors open, sounding only slightly louder than a garbage truck. Olivia's stomach flipped as she stared into the slouching shadows, but nothing moved in the stable or under the trees around them.

Michael stood next to the doors in a batter's stance with his poker. Wincing, Olivia added the shine of her flashlight to Maggie's. The beams shook with their hands, but everything else was still.

"Looks clear." Olivia wondered whether Maggie felt as confident as she sounded.

"The bikes we need are in the back on the left," Olivia whispered. She didn't think she sounded confident at all, but it was hard to sound confident with spasms of fear wriggling through her body. She concentrated on slowing her breath, just as she did before races. "They're with the other mountain bikes. I only saw three twenty-niners. All hard tails, but with front shocks. There might be another one hiding."

"This might help." Maggie spoke in an ordinary tone, but to Olivia, she might as well have been using a megaphone. The click of the light switch sounded like the whack of a baseball, and the little bulbs hanging down the center of the stable could have lit up center field.

"Let's get to work," Maggie said.

Michael insisted he stand guard. Olivia tensed as she braced for another fight, but Maggie calmly explained that she and Alison couldn't work on the bikes. Michael could get them all on the road faster. After a tense silence, he agreed. As the tension thawed in the back of her neck, Olivia appreciated how stressed Alison must have felt around her parents.

Olivia's shaking fingers wouldn't cooperate. It frustrated her that she kept dropping the valve caps and the small screwdriver she used to adjust the derailleurs. Every few seconds she found herself checking the door where Alison and Maggie stood guard, but no huge pale shape of a beadle came wriggling in.

In her own ears her breath sounded loud and labored. She took a break and shook out her hands while she watched Michael change a cracked inner tube on the full-suspension fat bike he found, two stalls down from the twenty-niners. He worked fast. He knew what he was doing. It would have even impressed her father, and that wasn't easy. That thought calmed the anxious crackle making her hands shake. Her face finally relaxed into almost a smile.

From the far side of his repair stand, Michael must have noticed Olivia's staring. He stood up from his work to look past the bar ends that stuck up like a pair of antlers off the handlebars of the fat bike. He must have thought she was admiring the bike and not him. "Sweet ride, right? The fat tires and huge ass rims are going to cost me some giddy-up, but whatever."

"You're strong," Olivia said. "It won't matter." She wiped some sweat out of her eyes with the part of her forearm that was least greasy. "Anyway, with those huge, moon-buggy wheels, you're going to ride straight over everything."

"Chromoly frame, though," Michael said.

"Still lighter than steel," Olivia replied. She was enjoying their little game. Talking shop in the shop. "We all need to stick together anyway, and we're riding in the dark. Speed isn't going to be a factor." And then everything came back to her in a queasy rush. She checked the door. Alison was strapping the pokers to the backpacks. Everything felt quiet.

"How are you guys making out?" Maggie called.

"Almost there. And hey, if anything shows up, give a holler." Michael bobbed his eyebrows impishly at Olivia.

"And you'll come kick its ass," Maggie droned. "Just get the bikes done."

Michael grinned at Olivia, whispering, "She's into me, right?"

Olivia was amazed at how Michael's brain worked. She laughed and went back to adjusting the derailleur. "Maybe, I guess."

He stepped around his bike stand and lowered his voice even more. "Hey, make sure my sister gets carbon fiber frame. It's the lightest and will be the easiest to ride so she won't get tired."

"I will." *That's sweet. He's worried about her keeping up, but he's still worried about her feelings, too.* That's why he had whispered. Olivia had to stand up for her, though. "Alison's a lot tougher than you think."

The way Michael looked at Olivia, with his face all scrunched up like he was trying to solve a puzzle, made Olivia feel self-conscious and exposed. "What?" she demanded.

Michael's eyes darted around nervously. "You're like a...you're...you like girls, right?"

Olivia felt relieved, but also irritated. "Not that it's any of your business, but yes."

Michael smiled and put up his hands like he was surrendering. He retreated behind the stand and went back to working on the tire. "I'm not judging you or anything. It's just...I don't know...we're, like friends, aren't we? I just wanted to know. Sorry. I wasn't trying to start anything."

Olivia felt the bristles on her back smoothing out. The breath she'd held eased out. "You're right; we are friends. I am gay. I thought you knew."

Thinking that was the end of it, Olivia went back to the adjustment screw on her derailleur. But Michael kept staring. Olivia set down the screwdriver. "What now?"

"So you and my sister…"

"Yeah?" Olivia had a pretty good idea where this was going, but she didn't want it to get there.

"Are you—like—a thing?" Michael leaned his head forward and dropped his voice. "It's cool if you are."

Olivia wanted to be angry, but she had to laugh. "It's absolutely none of your business, but we're not a thing. She's straight. We're best friends."

Michael looked doubtful. "You sound like maybe you're disappointed."

Did she? Olivia wasn't sure if she sounded disappointed or if Michael just heard it that way. She felt her face get hot. "Okay, now you've crossed the line. Seriously, this conversation is making me uncomfortable, Michael."

Michael used a set of tire-levers to tuck the tire back into the rim. "We're just talking here. Friends do that. You don't have to get mad."

Olivia felt guilty. She had nothing to be ashamed of, and after everything that happened, Olivia knew she should have felt grateful. Michael was reaching out as a friend. "It's okay. You're right. It was a fair question. I don't mean to be defensive."

"So do you have a girlfriend?"

Why wasn't he letting this go? Why were boys so obsessed with lesbians? "Michael, I don't know where you're going with this, but now isn't the best time."

"It's a simple yes or no question."

Olivia sighed, frustrated by his question and by her answer. "No, okay? I do not have a girlfriend."

"That wasn't so hard, was it?" He grinned at her with his charming blue eyes while he spun the completed tire.

Olivia chuckled in spite of her best efforts not to. "Yeah. So, if you know any single lesbians…"

Michael winked and took his bike off the stand. "I'll keep my eye out for a hot chick for you."

"You don't get to watch, so don't even ask." For good measure, Olivia tossed a shop towel at him.

Michael and Olivia rolled the four bikes out in front of the stable so they could all strap on their helmets and saddle up. Maggie looked the bikes over and told them to pull off all the reflectors. She duct taped the flashlights to her handlebars and to Olivia's.

"Keep them off unless it's an emergency. If anyone or anything is looking for us, we don't want to make it easy for them," she said. "The moon is coming up. Once our eyes adjust to the dark, we'll see enough to ride as long as we take it easy."

"Follow me," Michael said.

Maggie shook her head and touched her own chest. "It'll be me, then Alison, Olivia and then you." She cut Michael off with her hand before he could say anything. "I know these old horse trails from back when the stable was really a stable. I can keep us off the main roads and get us to The Boulevard in under an hour." She smiled at Michael. "Plus we need somebody good to watch our backs."

"Fine. My pythons trust you." He gave that goofy smile of his while he raised his arms and flexed his biceps. It made them all laugh.

The first quarter mile or so was rough. Olivia jumped at every shadow and felt a little jolt of fear at even the slightest hint of movement from the trees. But as her eyes adjusted and she could see more, she settled in. The constant crunch and occasional clatter of Michael's wheels and gears behind her were reassuring, and her own bike felt solid under her. It was the first time she'd felt in control of anything for a while.

Olivia wished she'd taken this mountain bike earlier instead of that chopper thing. It had looked cool, but rode like a kid's tricycle. The beadles would have had zero chance of catching her on this. Creepy white van or not, she could have outrun them by just jumping sidewalks, cutting through yards and finding trails. But it didn't matter; Alison couldn't have done all that no matter what bike she'd been on.

And anyway, she realized, if they hadn't hidden in the church, they wouldn't have known about the beadles. They would have even less of a clue what The Church of New Enlightenment was up to.

And now I might find a real wormhole. That thought fluttered in Olivia's stomach. *On the other hand, Alison wouldn't have killed the monk, the creature wouldn't have poisoned me and Alison wouldn't have used the snow globe.*

The same question continued to haunt her: *Is it good or bad that we ended up here? All Mrs. Nunios wanted was a family vacation. How did she pick Cape November of all places? If Mrs. Nunios had picked Friendly Point we would have just hung out on the beach like regular people on a regular vacation.*

That reminded Olivia of Sanjay. In ninth grade, right before the end of the year, a senior named Sanjay died in a car accident on the way home from prom. Everybody assumed it had been a drunk driving thing, but it turned out that the truck driver who hit them had been texting. It wasn't Sanjay's fault at all.

At the funeral, Sanjay's mother said something that struck Olivia. If Sanjay or that truck driver just left five minutes later or five minutes earlier, they would not have crashed at the intersection when the truck ran the stop sign. Five minutes either way, by either driver, and her son would still be alive.

Was it fate, free will or chance that brought us to Cape November? Einstein said that God doesn't play dice, but Heisenberg showed that uncertainty was a basic feature of nature. Was it really part of God's plan for Sanjay to get killed by a texting truck driver? Did God want Sanjay's family to suffer as some kind of punishment or test? Was God even there? Hello God; it's me, Olivia.

Focusing on her bike, Olivia noticed a skip in her rear derailleur causing the chain to skip between fourth and fifth gear. The way she'd been rushing with her shaky fingers and Michael getting her all flustered, it was a small miracle that the whole gear cassette didn't fall off.

She felt the anxiety squeeze her chest, and she focused on slowing her breath to calm down. The skip was not a big deal. The bike would get her to Olga's. If everything went according to plan, they would be riding in the minivan soon with Mr. and Mrs. Nunios, anyway.

Olivia flicked the shifter with her thumb to drop down a gear. The clicking and clattering of the chain over the gears sounded only a little like a chainsaw on the dark trail. She cringed and hoped she would not have to change gears again.

Maggie had been right about the light. With the moon shining, Olivia had no trouble seeing the trail. It was a little overgrown, but it was a horse trail, wider than a typical single-track. Now and then, something thorny growing into the trail would claw her face, hands or legs, but it was easy terrain. The path had gentle curves, low, gradual hills, and the gravelly dirt was packed hard and smooth.

Now and then a root or a rock would catch her off guard and thunderbolt the whole bike, sending a sharp reminder up the saddle that Olivia needed to stay more alert. But the twenty-nine inch wheels did their thing, and she more or less rolled over obstacles with little drama.

Ahead of her, Alison was going slow and steady. Every so often, she would make little yelping noises if her bike took a bad bump. Sometimes, when she climbed a small rise, she would grunt.

Where a corrugated metal drainpipe crossed the trail at a stream, Alison got stuck and lost her balance. She had to step off the pedals to keep from falling, and Olivia skidded to a stop just before crashing into her. Michael rolled to a smooth stop behind them. Nobody said anything. Alison pushed the bike over the pipe, got back on the saddle and kept riding until they caught up to Maggie, who waited a little farther down the trail. She must have stopped when she heard them.

It was quicker going than Olivia had expected. They kept a fast pace through the woods, even though it was dark under the trees—or maybe because it was dark under the trees. After about half an hour, the trail dumped them onto a road without lights. They glided like shadows with knobby tires purring on the pavement.

What difference does it even make? The beadles have no eyes. However they found us the first time, it wasn't by sight. Could they use some kind of sonar?

However a beadle navigated, they weren't the only things to be afraid of. Olivia's mind kept getting pulled like a magnet to the memories of the children with bloody sticks and the monk in the cave.

Who else is in The Church of New Enlightenment? It can't just be old men and little kids and monsters. And really, the little kids would have probably ignored them like the other old people they saw in town if Alison hadn't stopped to yell at them about the cat. And the old man in the cave was only after us because we were in his cave, basically delivering him two free benefactors. So, the only ones who were really after us were the monsters, but why? We aren't anybody special. We've never even been here before. What did they want? If it hadn't been for the snow globe...

It all came together in Olivia's mind. She pedaled hard to get up next to Alison, who gave a startled yelp.

"You scared me," Alison sounded breathless, but whether because she'd been startled or because she'd been riding hard, Olivia couldn't tell.

"I think the fish monsters are after you because of the snow globe."

"Duh," Alison said.

Olivia wasn't expecting that. "You knew?"

Alison shrugged. "Why else would they be after us?"

Michael pedaled up to the other side of Alison. "We should stay in single file," he said. "And we're trying to keep it quiet. You can talk about my awesomeness later."

Up ahead, Olivia saw Maggie turn around in her saddle. She coasted until they all caught up. "Is something wrong?"

"We know why the beadles are after us. It's because of the snow globe." Olivia still felt like it was news.

Maggie scanned the dark houses and the overgrown yards on the sides of the road. "We shouldn't stay out in the open. The next part of the trail is ahead on the right," she spoke just loudly enough to be heard over the wheels and the wind. "Let's get off this street fast, okay? We can talk about this at Olga's."

"But the snow globe blasted them," Michael protested. "Why would they be after something that can kill them?"

"I don't know if it kills them or just hurts them," Alison looked around nervously. "But that's exactly why they want it. Then nobody can use it on them." She sounded so certain. So Alison.

Michael shook his head, "But you didn't even have it with you when they came after you at the church."

"Maybe they didn't know she didn't have it," Olivia pointed out.

"No," Alison corrected her, "they did know I didn't have it. That's why they came after us. I was unarmed. If they got rid of me, then there was nobody to use the snow globe on them."

"But you didn't even know you could use it as a weapon yet," Olivia said.

"They didn't know that," Alison said. "You're the one who said it scared them away in the parking lot. Maybe they thought I was coming after them.

That's why they ran away from us."

"Guys, seriously," Maggie said. "Not now."

The sudden blast of light in their faces stung Olivia's eyes. She heard the roar of an engine and the screech of tires on the road.

"Look out!" Maggie screamed.

Olivia swerved her bike to the left side of the road as the white van passed so close that she could feel the heat of the motor wash up her legs from the pavement. She jumped off the bike and turned around.

"ALISON!" Olivia turned on her flashlight and wrenched the handlebars around. Alison was on her side on the curb across the road. Her hands shook as Olivia tore the flashlight out of the tape and ran across to her. Alison was already scrambling to her feet, hauling up the bike, but her elbow was bleeding, and there was a long scrape on the side of her helmet. "Did they hit you?"

Alison shook her head and winced. "I got out of the way, but I fell over the curb."

"Are you hurt? Can you run?"

Olivia heard the dragon roar of the van's engine as it turned around at the end of the street and lined up for a second run at them.

Maggie skidded to a stop beside them. She dropped the bike and snatched the fireplace poker free from the backpack. Up the street, the engine revved, and the van lurched toward them.

"The trail is right there!" Maggie nodded toward the woods just behind them. "The van can't follow us." Her voice was high and thin with fear. "Can you ride?"

Olivia grabbed Alison's wrist and pulled her toward the trail. "JUST RUN!"

Alison jerked her arm free. "Where's Michael?"

Olivia shined her light up and down the road, but couldn't see him. The headlights bounced wildly as the van closed on them.

"Move!" Maggie commanded. She pulled Alison's other arm.

"We can't leave Michael," Alison sounded panicky. "Did they run him over?" With frantic, jerky writhing, she pulled off her backpack. "I have to get the snow globe!"

Olivia heard a terrifying, roaring scream that ran in chills up her back. And then she recognized the voice that roared. Michael charged out from the trees and jumped the curb, carrying enough speed to coast alongside of the rushing van.

It swerved toward him to run him down, but he avoided it. Keeping one hand on his handlebars, he waved his fireplace poker over his head like a knight's battle-axe, slamming it into the driver's half-open window.

Glass shattered, and the van swerved away, but he leaned in to track with it. Standing up on his pedals, Michael stabbed his poker like a spear through the van's shattered window. It wobbled out of control for a second before it jumped the curb and slammed into a tree. Something white and wet spattered into the windshield, shattering it and flopping out flabbily over the hood. Smoke and fluids poured out of the front of the van. The side door creaked open, and three huge beadles in hooded ponchos shambled out to hobble after Michael.

Laughing and whooping, Michael rode away from the smoking wreck, silhouetted in the one headlight that wasn't shattered.

"I got one of those things!" he called. "Right in its ugly face!"

"Come on!" Maggie shouted. She and Alison were back on their bikes and had ridden about half a block up. Maggie waved her light in the air like a beacon to the horse trail.

Olivia dropped her own flashlight in her backpack and hopped on her own bike to follow them. She had to laugh when she caught up to Michael. He had stopped in the middle of the road, apparently just to give the three shambling beadles the finger. "That's for my parents' windshield!"

43 LA FAMIGLIA

Alison's thighs burned. Her arms ached. Her butt hurt. Her bangs hung sweaty on her face. The helmet squeezed her head.

Bikes sucked.

When the trees broke and she bounced, painfully, down the curb into the street, Alison heard Maggie's voice ahead. "No more trail now. Only a few more blocks." Alison felt like laughing and crying.

"Just keep your eyes out," Maggie cautioned.

"Trust me; their van is dead," Michael called from behind.

"They might have other vans," Maggie reminded them.

"And who knows what else," Olivia added.

At the front door of Olga's, Alison dropped her bike on the sidewalk and followed Maggie inside. The lights were low, so they didn't hurt her eyes, but everything seemed bright after being in the dark for so long. All the tables were empty. Alison's stomach dropped.

"Youz guys are back?" Alison recognized Sal. He was smiling and had his arms out like he wanted to give them a hug. "Wait! Maggie? Oh my God, look at this! Zi-Zi! *Vieni qui!* It's Maggie!"

"Where are my parents?" Alison demanded.

Sal looked at her from across the tops of his eyeglasses. "Huh? How should I know?"

Alison felt the fear choking her. "My parents said they were coming here for dinner."

Sal shrugged like the collapse of Alison's world meant nothing to him. "We ain't had nobody in here all night. I tell ya, business is down the tubes."

Alison felt something crack inside her. She heard a blood-chilling shriek, but it wasn't until she charged Sal, clawing and punching at his chest and face, that she realized the sound had come out of her.

His glasses flew across the floor. She beat against his shoulders and back until her arms stopped moving. Someone had grabbed her. Maggie! Alison thrashed and shrieked until she tore free. Words hemorrhaged out of her. "Get off me! What did you people do to my parents? I killed one of you already. If you hurt my parents, I swear I'll kill you all."

Powerful arms wrapped around her, nearly crushing her. Panic filled her like ice. The monsters had caught her. She was going to a metal table. She was going to die. She thrashed and struggled, but realized she couldn't move.

"Calm down, Alison," Michael's voice was gentle, but strong. It brought Alison back from wherever she'd gone. Racking sobs squeezed her chest. Her clothes were soaked with sweat. She went limp, and Michael's bear hug became an ordinary, comforting, loving hug. She sobbed into his chest while he stroked her hair.

"Can we get her some water, please?" Maggie asked quietly.

Alison calmed down enough to notice people appearing through the kitchen door. She recognized Vinny and Tony, but not the big men in tracksuits. One was completely bald; the other had a thin moustache and jet-black hair slicked straight over his scalp. Alison felt shaky and weak when she noticed the guns slung over their shoulders.

"Why do they have rifles?" Alison almost didn't recognize her own croaking voice.

"They're shotguns, kid," Slick explained cheerfully.

"For personal defense of home and property," the bald guy added.

"Second Amendment, badabeep-badaboop, we don't want no trouble." Slick grinned and smoothed his moustache.

The bald one asked, "Maggooch, who are these kids? Why're they beating up Sal?"

"Get her out of here now!" Sal held a napkin on his bleeding lip. "I never want to see her or any of them again, Mag, got me? If you feel like coming back in here ever, I better not see you with these *duefacci... disgrazi—*"

Sal jerked to his left, startled. Olivia held Sal's glasses out to him. He snatched them from her and held them up to the light. "You're lucky they ain't cracked. You know how much these cost?"

"Sal, please," Maggie said. "Let me explain."

"You got nothin' to explain. This little girl comes in here all wild and attacks me in my own place? *DISGRAZIA!* Talking about her parents? He loomed over Alison. *"ADUZIPAZZ'!"* He waved his hand up next to his face in a half-twirling motion that Alison figured meant something in Italian.

"Is not you place, Sal. This my place." Alison recognized Olga's heavy accent. She stood in the doorway of the kitchen between the two huge men with the guns. She carried a large glass of water over to Alison. "You drink. You feel better."

Olga looked up at Michael, and his iron arms relaxed their grip. But Alison still couldn't move. She felt pinned in place by Olga's eyes, dark and shining. Alison saw hardness in them, but kindness, too. Olga's eyes looked strong and wise. They radiated lines and creases that stopped at the tops of her high, bony cheeks.

Alison took the water and gulped it, quickly draining the glass.

"Vin," Olga called, "bring lotta water. And tell Tony to throw on some macaroni."

"We're not hungry, Zi-Zi," Maggie said. "We need help."

"You eat and we help, eh?" Olga looked them all over. When she got to

Alison, she clucked her tongue. *"Poverina."*

Gently, Olga took Alison's arm and looked at the scrape. "We fix everything." Olga gestured with her bony arm toward the large round table where Alison remembered sitting with her parents. The sobs exploded out of her, and her face felt like a hot pan all the way under her hair. She grabbed Michael and Olivia. "No! We have to go get Mom and Dad!"

"We don't know where they are," Michael said.

Why is he always so stupid? "They're at the church! They got them. We have to get there before they get glued to the tables!"

"What is she talking about?" Sal asked.

Alison stalked toward the door.

"Alison, wait," Olivia pleaded, trotting behind her. "We can't just run back out there."

She turned around to look at Olivia. "Liv, we have to go get my parents before it's too late."

"But Michael's right, we don't know where they are."

Alison felt the fire in her turn to ice. "Seriously? You're not going to help me? They're at the church!" She clenched her fists to keep from screaming.

"You don't know that. And even if they are, we don't know where the church is."

"It's by the beach, Olivia! We're running out of time."

"The beach is miles long! I don't remember where it is, do you?"

Alison felt her stomach lurch tight. "No. But I know it's out there somewhere."

"Hang on. You talking about The Church of New Enlightenment?" Sal asked. "It's over on Shore Drive. Should I drive them over, Zi? See what's going on?"

Alison felt hope lift inside her, only to get dragged down by guilt. She'd just attacked Sal for no reason and now he wanted to help? Guilt was replaced by doubt and suspicion. "Why would you help me?"

Sal dabbed at his bloody lip and laughed. "With your temper, I figure you must be part Sicilian or something." He laughed. "Look, you're scared. You need to find your Mom and Dad. I can help. No hard feelings?"

Alison shook Sal's extended hand. "I'm really sorry."

Sal made a swatting gesture with his hand. "Fuggettaboutit." He turned to Olga, "Whaddaya think Zi? I got my Caddy out back. Should I run by the church?"

"The church is no good." Olga's face looked hard. She shook her head. "Is no safe to go. No now."

"Zi-Zi, did something happen here, too?" Maggie asked. "Why are Carmine and Frankie here?"

"The reporter," Olga said. "She gone. Phones all dead. That's it. Now the

Church gonna move. You see."

"But what are they going to do?" Maggie asked.

The edges of Olga's mouth turned down. "Go find her parents first, eh? When you come back we see what we can do."

Alison turned to Sal. At the moment he seemed to be her only hope of finding her parents. "Take me to the church. Please, I have to find my parents before it's too late."

Sal looked up at Carmine and Frankie. "You boys feel like taking a ride?"

"Carmine, you go with Sal. Take the kids. Find they parents. But Frankie, you stay here in case I need you."

"Zi-Zi, what's going on?" Maggie asked.

"It's time. Just like the night when you parents…" Olga shook her head. "Go. We talk later, but now you go."

44 QUIET AS A CHURCH

Michael allowed himself to melt a little deeper into the soft leather seats of Sal's old Cadillac. It felt like he was gliding over the ground. Even the bumps in the road felt soft. Michael swore that when it was time for him to buy a car, he was going to find a big old Cadillac.

Sal pulled smoothly into the grassy driveway of the church.

"No good," Carmine shook his big, bald head. "Too easy for somebody to block us in. Park across the street and up a little ways. And turn around in case we gotta get out fast."

Sal parked like Carmine wanted, and they got out. Michael scanned the road as they crossed. There were no streetlights anywhere, and none of them had turned on their flashlights.

"We go in dark," Carmine had said. "Stay outta sight."

Past the end of the street to his right, Michael felt a tingle of wonder at the stars shining over the ocean, like a million eyes looking down on them, not giving a crap. Out to his left was just empty street, empty houses and trees waving in the night wind. They didn't give a crap either.

Michael's hands started hurting, and he realized that he'd been practically strangling the chrome fire axe he'd borrowed from Olga's. Carmine had told him to take it.

You can't run in there with just your swagger in your hands. Only Carmine hadn't said swagger.

The church didn't look anything like Michel had expected. He thought it was going to look more like the cathedral he'd found with Maggie. Old stones, weird paintings, creepy. But the church was a neat, clean, modern-looking building. It looked a lot like the church his parents dragged him to on Christmas and Easter, except this church was dark and it looked like there was no one in it. The only thing even a little weird about it was the curved, bow-shaped symbol on top of the steeple.

He asked Maggie about it. She was guarding the back of their line with him, holding the fireplace poker.

"It's the main symbol of The Church of New Enlightenment," she whispered. "It's a harp."

"Why a harp?"

"It's like the cross or the crescent and star, or the Star of David. It's just a symbol."

"But why a harp?" Michael had to admit the harp cast a beautiful silhouette against the stars. "What's it mean?"

"It means they're boombots," Sal whispered gruffly. He still sounded angry that Maggie had made him leave his air-conditioned Caddy. She had convinced him that it was too dangerous for anybody to be alone. Sal said a few things in Italian. The only thing Michael understood was that they didn't sound friendly and they made Carmine laugh. But there Sal was, right behind Carmine and his shotgun. Michael knew firsthand how persuasive Maggie was. It made him feel a tingle in his gut that wasn't unpleasant. He wondered what would happen with the two of them, when this was all over. But he could only let himself wonder for a moment.

"So are Carmine and Frankie..." Michael wasn't sure how to ask it. "Will I get whacked for asking?"

"What?"

"Are they...you know...connected?"

Maggie arched her eyebrow, and then stifled a laugh. "The mafia?"

Michael was glad it was dark, so Maggie couldn't see his face get red. "The way they're dressed, the guns..."

"So you just went all Italian stereotype? Olga wouldn't let criminals in the family."

"Okay, but you have to admit, they look like mobsters." Michael couldn't believe she didn't see it. "Tracksuits?"

"Comfortable," Maggie shot back.

"Shotguns?"

"Hunters. They're big time NRA guys. They take guns everywhere. Don't worry, Eliot Ness, they're licensed."

If Maggie was throwing shade, Michael didn't get it. "Who?"

Maggie shook her head, still chuckling. "Maybe you shouldn't watch so much TV. Try reading."

Michael dropped it. Alison had led them up the dirt tire grooves in the grassy driveway to the side of the church. Back in the car, she had mentioned something about a basement window. She was kind of rambling. Michael hoped that, as usual, Alison was just overreacting. Mom and Dad probably had just changed their minds about dinner. They were going to get back to The Mansion at the same time that their kids were at a strange church, committing several crimes with two sketchy guys they just met. And one had a shotgun.

Michael tried to count the laws they were breaking. There was Carmine's gun. Michael doubted he had a license to carry that thing around. And they were already trespassing, getting ready for some breaking and entering. Depending on what they found inside there might be an assault or maybe even murder. *Why aren't we getting the police again? But if we called them now, they'd lock us up, NRA or not.*

The thought of the police and jail sent a nauseous chill through his gut. He'd seen too many shows about prison. Michael wondered what Alison had meant earlier when she said she had already killed somebody.

Did she mean the thing I killed in the van? That was no person, unless somebody was wearing a mask, but why would anybody go to all that trouble? Why would anybody try to kill us with a van in the first place? No. That creature was real, and I buried a fireplace poker in its face.

Michael felt a small quiver of fear and a sour lump of revulsion, but mostly he felt an almost unbelievable rush of power that surged through him and made the fine hairs on his arm stand up. He'd killed a creature that had been trying to kill them. He protected them all. He was a man.

He could still clearly recall the soft, jelly head. There was a skin on it, like a plastic bag, on the outside. The skin was firm, almost hard, and rubbery like a fake leather jacket. Under the leather was just white goo.

Michael felt it in his hands again, the way the point of the poker pierced the rubbery skin. He could not stop feeling it tear and pop. And then there was a faint, sweet, rotten-meat smell that, for a second, overpowered the gassy smoke of the old engine. And then the thing's jelly head just sucked in the poker until it tore out the opposite side of the thing's head. That's when Michael had almost lost his balance and fallen under the van. That would have killed him. Probably should have, but he kept it together. Swagger.

The thing must have been dead. Michael stabbed it through the brain. If that even was its brain. But if it wasn't, when the van hit the tree, its face splattered into the windshield.

So, Michael knew he had killed something. But Alison had said that she had killed one of you already. Was that just one of Alison's dramatic rants? All the stress catching up to her? Michael hadn't had a chance to ask her about what she had said, but he was pretty sure that even if he did, she wouldn't tell him anything.

"Here's the window," Alison whispered.

"Zoot' u' basciament?" Sal grumbled.

She knelt down, running her fingers around the edges. "I got it open before."

"Scusi, please." Carmine gently moved Alison aside. With sudden, startling savagery, he kicked the window in with his white loafers, smashing the frame and raining glass onto the floor inside. "It's open."

"Could you please keep it down?" Maggie hissed. "We don't need the whole world to know what we're doing." She shined her light into a small tool room. Slivers of glass sparkled on the floor and the shelf under the window. "There's glass everywhere. Try not to sever an artery when you climb in."

Like some kind of *parkour* ninja, Maggie slipped through the window in one smooth motion. She helped the rest of them climb down one by one. Sal had trouble, but he was pushing seventy, Michael guessed. Carmine had such a hard time fitting it was almost funny, except they were breaking into a weird church to look for Mom and Dad who might be dead or glued to a table. Michael forced that thought away.

"This way," Alison said. She pointed the flashlight she'd taken down the hall. Their shoes squeaked and scraped the floor, but other than that, they were nearly silent as they followed Alison around the corner to the door marked Nursery. The fishy, ocean smell was overpowering. Michael had to force down a gag reflex.

When she opened the door, Carmine pulled Alison back and shook his head. He pointed at all them and made a stop gesture with his hand, telling them all to wait. His pinky ring glinted in the beam when he took the flashlight from Alison.

Michael heard the quiet scruff of Carmine's white loafers on the metal grating as he crept down the stairs. Soon the glow of his flashlight was hidden behind the angle of the ceiling. For a few seconds, there was no sound at all except Michael's own breath and the quick thump of his heart. Then the stair lights came on, and Carmine whistled for them.

Michael's heart pounded as he ran down the stairs behind Alison. He was torn between wanting to find his parents there and not wanting to find his parents there. The cave room was just as Alison had described it. The two neat rows of metal tables were all empty.

"Whatever they were doing, they ain't doing it now," Sal said.

"These tables are spotless." Maggie squeaked her finger along a metal surface. "Alison, your parents were probably never here."

Olivia shined her light into the water next to the tables, but whatever she was looking for, she didn't find it. "No naiads now."

"*Cazzo! Ma che quest'?*" Carmine asked.

Sal ran his hand over one of the tables. "It looks like some kind of schifozza hospital."

"It is," Maggie said. "The girls said they use this place..." Maggie closed her eyes and sighed. "I'll explain later. At least, I'll try. We need to get out of here, though."

"Where are my parents?" Alison demanded.

"We should check back at The Mansion," Olivia suggested. She stood close to Alison, rubbing her back. Alison leaned her head on Olivia's shoulder.

Alison said they had to check the whole church first, so she took them on a tour of the other rooms she had already seen. The chapel looked like a chapel, and the diagrams in the classrooms were creepy, but there was no sign of Mom and Dad. Michael felt his heart beating nervously as they went up the other set of metal steps. At the top of the stairs, the wooden door was locked.

"Now what?" Sal asked.

Carmine looked at Michael. "Ey, cagoozzalunga, you got an axe."

Michael's face felt hot. His breath was coming in shallow gasps. "You want me to break down the door?"

Carmine shrugged, "I mean, you can try knocking first."

They gave him some space and Michael swung. The axe thudded into the door and got stuck.

Carmine and Sal laughed.

"Come on, kid," Sal said. "I know you got more than that. You gotta get mad."

Michael was furious. Humiliated. He gritted his teeth and swung savagely. In three more chops, he was sweating and out of breath, but the wood around the locked doorknob was in splinters.

Carmine's white loafer popped it open. "We're gonna make a man out of you yet, kid."

The door led to a small office. Michael almost didn't bother to try the phone and when he found it dead he was sorry he did. Carmine laughed at him when he tried to wipe off his fingerprints with the end of his shirt. "Yeah, kid, that'll really mix 'em up down at the crime lab."

The office opened out into a sort of locker room. Robes of various colors hung in several cubbies along one wall, and there was a big counter in the middle with cabinets under it. A door on the far side of the room led out into the actual church where the altar and the seats were. Everything was decorated with that harp symbol. Behind the altar was a big, modern-art, outline-looking version of the creature from the paintings in the cathedral. When he noticed it, Michael nudged Maggie to show her. She nodded, and her eyebrow arched, but whatever she thought about it, she kept it to herself.

The rest of the church was all pews. Shining a light on a few of the windows showed that they were decorated with blue, green or white panes of stained glass. There were no images or pictures like there had been in the cathedral.

Back in the car, Michael felt his heart beating as they approached The Mansion. It was hammering when they went inside, and it felt like it stopped completely when they got to Mom and Dad's room. It was dark, and nobody answered when Michael pounded on it.

"It doesn't look like they've been here," Olivia whispered.

"I don't understand." Alison sounded like she was just on the edge of crying. "What happened to them?"

"Maybe they went somewhere else," Olivia said quietly.

Without saying anything else, Alison headed back toward the stairs.

"Let's get back to Olga's and figure out our next move," Maggie suggested.

"Va bene," Carmine said. *"Ho fame."*

"Yer always hungry, ya mamaluke," Sal grumbled.

Squeezed in with Olivia on her lap, Alison cried quietly into her back the whole way from The Mansion. By the time Sal parked in Olga's yard, she had nothing left inside her.

Maggie got out of the car and turned, extending her hand to help Alison. Guilt poured like hot cement in Alison's gut. The terrible feelings, the worry, the grief, the guilt she felt about her own missing parents, she realized, had been Maggie's whole life. And back in The Mansion, Alison had been a real bitch to her.

"Maggie..." The words caught in Alison's throat. Maggie's eyes were narrow and hard, but they softened. "I'm really sorry about your parents. And about the horrible things I said to you." Alison noticed the tears in Maggie's eyes when she hugged her.

When Olga led them to the table, the same table where Alison had sat with her family, the final few dry, lonely sobs escaped her, and then she felt empty, numb, and so cold.

The last time she'd sat there, she'd been on vacation. Her family had eaten and laughed; the world was normal. She had only worried that her parents might get divorced. Now she worried they were dead.

Olga clucked softly. *"Poverina,* you tell me everything and we see, eh?"

Vinny had set out large pitchers of water and wine and then ducked back into the kitchen, reappearing with baskets of warm bread. His fast, sure steps made Alison feel, for a moment anyway, like maybe the world could go back to normal. She sat at the table and gulped down a glass of cold water. It made her feel that much colder, but her throat was dry and sore from sobbing.

Olga poured Alison a half a glass of wine in the same kind of short, fat glass she'd used for the water, and then she poured a half a glass for herself. *"Pane e vino sono la vita.* Bread and wine are life. Drink a little sip. Calm you nerves."

Alison thought about what Doctor Kale Smoothie would have said about bread and wine are life. Too many carbs, she figured. Maybe Alison had been born into the wrong family. Like a guilty knife, that thought stabbed her right through the heart. Another tear stung her eye; apparently there had been one more hiding inside her.

Alison swallowed her grief as she sipped the wine. She didn't want to feel anything. The fruity tang warmed her mouth, throat and stomach. Her head felt a little lighter, and she took a full breath. Olga's dark eyes looked calm and strong as she sipped her wine. Her hard face softened when she smiled, showing Alison a gold tooth in among the others.

Olivia sat on Alison's other side with Michael next to her. Across the table, Maggie took her place next to Olga. After they set out a huge platter of spaghetti, meatballs and sausages, Vinny and Tony joined the table. It almost felt like a family dinner, except Mom and Dad were missing and Carmine and Frankie ate by the door with their shotguns leaning on their table.

Her hand shook violently as Alison tore a hunk of bread, and Olivia had to guide her into the green olive oil. Nothing tasted like anything. The bread and wine couldn't drive all the fluttery things out of her stomach.

"Now," Olga said in her thick, broken English, "you tell me what happen, eh?"

Maggie sighed and shook her head. "Zi-Zi, I don't even know where to start."

Alison did. She knew exactly where to start. She took out the snow globe and placed it on the table in front of Olga while Olga and her relatives gasped and said things in Italian. "It starts here," Alison said.

That was all Alison could say. She let Olivia talk about the snow globe—she left out how Alison had stolen it. Michael took over when they talked about the bird on the highway. And the dead beadle. Michael sounded certain that that's what he'd seen on the side of the road. Alison knew he was probably right, too, but she still didn't know why it had been there, except that it had something to do with the snow globe.

At that point, Olivia had to jump in and explain what a beadle was, but that took the whole story out of sequence, so Maggie brought it back to their snorkeling trip under the lighthouse. When Maggie mentioned the door under the jetty, Olga's dark eyes got wide and she leaned forward, but she didn't say anything while Maggie talked about the cathedral and the paintings. On the viewfinder of his camera, Michael showed them all the pictures he'd taken.

Alison could not say a word when Olivia talked about the cave in the church basement. The benefactors, naiads, stewards and beadles. The poison and the pink light. Alison just watched the strange figures floating slowly around the snow globe, following their own laws of motion. She zoned in and out of the story as she picked at her food. That was almost funny to her. There was a huge platter of amazing food and she had every reason to eat it, but she could barely look at it. All she wanted was to do was put her head down and sleep for a month and then wake up and find that it had all been a nightmare.

She glanced at Carmine and Frankie, eating by the door with their big guns. They made Alison feel afraid and safe at the same time. It felt like she had been running forever and this day had lasted her whole life.

"Hang on. Go back a minute and lemme get this straight," Sal leaned forward, rubbing his long hands together. "The creeps with the hoods, they're not people? Not human?"

"Definitely not," Olivia said.

"But we see 'em around sometimes," Vinny said. "They work for the church."

"That's why they call them beadles," Olivia said.

Alison let Olivia explain more about beadles and the rest of what they saw in the church basement. Alison felt relieved when Olivia didn't mention the monk in the cave, but so what if she had? So what if Alison did kill him? She'd kill a hundred monks if it meant saving her parents. She felt the monk's head smash again under the hammer. She had lost count of how many times she had felt the wet impact travel up her hands and forearms. It made her feel guilty and sick inside.

Anyway, what can these people possibly think of me now? Especially Sal. She had attacked him for no reason at all, and he was still being nice to her. Alison felt a jolt of fear. Suddenly she was afraid of herself. Like maybe she attacked Sal because she'd already killed the monk. Now that she was a murderer, could she kill anybody? *Did I become a monster? Have I always been one?*

A shiver rocked her. She looked around at all the others jabbering about monsters and cults. She grabbed Olivia's hand, just to feel something familiar. Something normal. Just to know that she was there.

Olivia squeezed her fingers. "You doing all right?" Olivia had that little line in the middle of her forehead she always got when she worried.

Alison lied and nodded. The squeeze of Olivia's hand made her heart stop vibrating. She took a deep breath and looked at Olga. "The Enlightened kidnap people and use them to make those monsters they call beadles. Olivia and I saw them doing it, but this time it was empty."

"When youz was there last time, you really saw them people on the table? And the monsters?"

Alison nodded.

"Any Enlightened? Did anybody see youz?"

Alison felt the old man's head going soft under the hammer again. The thud crunched up her forearms. She could not look any of them in the face. She drowned her eyes in the bowl of green oil on the table in front of her. "An old man came down. He was dressed in a robe, like a monk. It was his job to make the beadles, I think." Alison's tongue felt thick and clumsy. She heard herself stuttering out the words. "We were hiding, but he…he found Olivia. I was so scared."

Alison felt her guilty heart, clawing against her ribs, like it wanted to escape and betray her. She could hardly breathe. She drank a glass of water and poured another. "He was going to kill her, make her into one of those things like the other people we saw on the table. Under that web of goo. Glued down." Alison couldn't speak. She glanced up and saw everyone else looking at her. Waiting for her. She felt the squeeze of Olivia's hand and let it out. "I killed him."

Michael's mouth hung open. The worried line in Olivia's forehead was deeper. She looked so sad and afraid. Vinny and Tony looked nervously into their half-empty plates. Maggie's mouth was tight and her eyebrow arched up. Alison felt ashamed and alone.

"I didn't mean to. I was scared, okay? I found a hammer, that was all I had. I just…hit him. I didn't have time to think." Alison tightened her hands. With one she squeezed Olivia's. With the other, she tried to dig her nails into the wood at the edge of the table. The silence that followed weighed a ton. Alison looked down again, watching the little crumbs of bread and pepper suspended in the green oil.

"Fuggaddaboutit," Frankie said breezily, startling her. "Sometimes ya gotta whack somebody." But Carmine was the only one who laughed.

Olga nodded when Alison faced her again. The edges of Olga's mouth turned down thoughtfully; she closed her eyes a moment, nodding.

Michael's mouth moved like he was trying to say something. Olivia squeezed her hand hard, and tears streamed silently down her face. The others looked at Olga as if they were waiting.

Finally, Olga spoke quietly. "To kill a man…This is a hard thing you do, but you do it for Olivia." Olga smiled at Olivia. *"Che bellisima."*

Alison felt sick. She could not look at Olga's face.

"You no a murderer, eh? You…You like a soldier. You gotta live with what you do, but you do it to protect somebody you love. This no make you bad. You kill him because you good and because you love you friend."

Alison risked a peek at Olivia. Her beautiful face was red, and she shook with silent sobs.

"Dio Mio," Olga sighed. "We knew this day was coming. Nobody is innocent anymore. Look at the world. Everything look like it fall apart. *I politici sono tutti sfacchimi.* They make people hate one another just to make votes, eh? Nobody love nobody no more. Everybody angry. Everybody scared. No good. We all gotta live in this world together, but people kill each other in the news every day. But you, *poverina,* you no like that."

Alison felt Olga's hand cover her own. Her hand was so much bigger than Alison expected, and she felt Olga's strength in the grip of her fingers. Her skin was smooth like old leather. Risking a look into Olga's bottomless eyes, Alison was surprised to see tears clinging to the corners.

"You are good and you love," Olga whispered. "That's why you had to kill that man. God's gonna forgive you."

The words hit Alison in her chest and took her breath away. She had not considered God in all of this. She never thought about forgiveness.

Olga touched the gold crucifix that hung on her neck. "For me, there's only the Catholic Church. The Pope, eh? And Jesus say you gotta love you enemy. Turn you cheek and forgive. But you can't let that man kill Olivia, eh?"

Olga nodded thoughtfully, and then continued in her heavy accent, "I know other church is good for other people, too. There's church for everybody. Christian. Jewish. Muslim. Buddha. Hindu. God talk to people in lotta ways. You know, some people got no church, but they still can be good people. Maybe they talk to God in their own way. Maybe they don't talk to God at all. That's okay. God love them anyway because that's what God is. Love, eh? And God say we gotta take care each other. Love everybody. *Compassione."* Olga flashed her gold-toothed smile. For the first time in a long time, Alison felt safe.

But then Olga's wrinkles hardened like she was turning to stone. "If somebody tell you to hate somebody else, that can no be from God. God no want us to hate nobody. Church of New Enlightenment is no a church of love. Is church of hate. So is no a church of God. Something else."

"*Il diavolo?*" Sal asked. "*Satana?*"

Olga shook her head. "Maybe something worse."

"What do you mean, Olga?" Vinny asked. "They're just a bunch of *coogootz*, no?"

The way Vinny said it almost made Alison laugh, but before she could, Olga turned her stony face toward her nephew. Her word was hard. "No."

"But that's what you always said." Vinny sounded nervous, and Alison could feel his doubt, his fear, his world, crumbling like hers did. "You said the Enlightened were just these crazy, misguided people and we should pray for them."

Olga closed her eyes and shook her head slowly from side to side. "I been Cape November many, many years. The Enlightened always been around. But I know the stories, too. *Racconti,* eh, how you say folktales. The Lenni Lenape had stories of people who disappear, too. For thousand years, Lenape children no go too far or the *yakwahe* gonna get 'em. I think what you see, how you say, beadles? This is what the Lenape call *yakwahe.*" Olga smiled sadly, showing her gold tooth. "Maggie, you know what the Lenape say about Mahtantu."

"Sure," Maggie said. "It's basically the Lenni Lenape name for the Devil. Once Christian missionaries came to this area, they used the words interchangeably."

"But is no the same." Olga seemed to warn them by wagging her sturdy forefinger.

Alison's eyes felt so heavy. Her whole body felt heavy. But her mind could not stop racing. She had heard enough stories about monsters. She just wanted to find her parents and go home, but she had this awful feeling she never would.

When Olga picked up the snow globe, Alison snapped awake. Olga turned it in her hands. After studying it for a few moments, she looked at Alison. "This shoot the beadles?"

Alison nodded. "And it healed Olivia. Do you know what it is?"

"Put it away. You should no leave out." Shaking her head, Olga handed the snow globe back to Alison. She felt nervous as she rewrapped it in the sweatshirt and stuffed it into her backpack.

Olga sighed heavily. "I never hear any story about this. I don't know what's the whale, but look at the monster. Cape November got its own stories, too." Olga turned to Maggie. "Maggie, we no call him Mahtantu, but we gotta monster, too, eh?"

"Cappy." Maggie nodded, her eyes intense. "Every culture has stories of sea monsters. The Bible talks about Leviathan. The Norse talk about the kraken. Here at Cape November, we have Cappy."

Alison jumped when Michael laughed. "I'm supposed to pee my pants at something called Cappy?"

Maggie looked annoyed. "When those big superstorms first started coming and then the fires, old people said Cappy was pissed off because the people down the Cape had gotten too big. Built too much. Cappy was a story I grew up with. It was in the air we breathed. I never thought about it. In the hospital, they told me to forget about Cappy because it was part of what was creating my delusions. That's what my therapists all said. And at Cartesian, my professors dismissed the Cappy stories. They said local legends and cryptid stories were only good for learning about the culture that came up with them. Cappy stories were just a xenophobic projection of our collective mistrust of the Enlightened." Maggie laughed bitterly. "Some nerdbomb, right, Michael?"

Michael chuckled. Alison wished she could.

Olga nodded solemnly. "*I raconnti,* how you say the folktales, they always say something true. They no just come from no place. The Mansion, the lighthouse, people say it's for Cappy. He make it. The Lenape say manetuwak, evil spirits, build The Mansion and Mahtantu live there. We say is for Cappy. Maybe it is for the Enlightened." Olga took a sip of wine "Anyway, these are the stories people used to tell here. But people no talk about Cappy for many years. Not since The Church of New Enlightenment become so big."

"Because they didn't want anyone to think it was real," Maggie whispered. "They didn't want people thinking about Cappy at all."

"Because it's not just a story," Olivia said. "The things the Lenape called *yakwahe* almost killed us."

"I killed one of them, too," Michael said. He sat up a little taller. It almost made Alison smile, but Michael added, "And Alison killed one of the freaks that…"

Rage and guilt exploded in her. Alison turned on her brother, "Stop it, Michael! I'm sorry I killed that old man. He was bad, and I'm glad he's dead, but I'm still sorry I killed him. It's not a joke."

"No! It's not a joke!" Michael snapped. "It's war!" Michael slapped the table with both his palms.

"Take it easy, kid," Sal said. "You'll give yourself a heart attack."

Michael stood up abruptly, his chair clattered to the floor. "What if these people really do have Mom and Dad? What if they do hurt them or kill them, Alison? Who would you kill then?"

"I don't know, Michael." Alison felt so cold and drained and empty.

Michael picked up his chair and sat heavily into it. In the quiet that followed, Maggie fidgeted with her napkin, crumpling it and stretching it in her hands. "Zi-Zi, you used to talk about Cappy when I was little. Why did you stop?"

Olga sighed sadly. "I no talk about it to you because you grandfather say no. After you parents die, you grandfather, he say if everybody, even you, think you…*pazz'?*" Olga grasped with her fingers, as if the word she wanted was stuck in the air.

"Mentally ill?" Maggie said wryly.

"Ah, si, mental ill. If you mental ill, then you safe. Safe from them. The Enlightened no worry about you. Leave you and Zia Penny and Zio Max alone. For many years, I do this, but no more."

"Why?" Maggie asked. "Why is all this happening now? The girls got attacked. The door was open under the jetty. Are the beadles setting up the cathedral for their ceremony?"

Olga nodded solemnly. Her hand still covered Alison's. Her gold tooth winked in the low light. When Olga sighed, Alison could feel the weight she carried. "Everybody who's no Enlightened leave. Just a few of us left now. An' we all scared. Good people run or hide. Nobody trust nobody. Not even me. I tell Carmine and Frankie come down because even I am afraid now. Afraid of what The Church of New Enlightenment gonna do." She shook her head sadly, and Alison could feel Olga's grief in the grip of her fingers. "Cape November now like a…*casa haunte*, eh?" Olga nodded. "The stories say Cappy get strong when people suffer. When people afraid. When there is no more love, no more hope. That make Cappy strong. When he strong enough, he come back. Then? Goodbye, Jack."

"Who's Jack?" Michael asked.

"It's just an expression, kid." Sal said quietly. "It means everything's going down the tubes."

Maggie's face went slightly slack. Her eyes seemed like they were looking at something far away. "I remember something else from when I was really little. Something my Mom would sing. Like a little nursery rhyme. "When people are crying, Cappy gets strong. When people start dying, start singing his song."

"Your mother sang that to you?" Michael asked.

"Explains a lot, right?" Maggie chuckled quietly. "The doctors thought so, too," Maggie said. "They did everything they could to make me forget, and I guess it worked. Until the stories came to life and started killing people."

"But what's it mean?" Vinny asked.

"I know a lot of songs," Tony said, "but none about making Cappy stronger."

"It's just a saying, though, right?" Vinny asked. "Just part of the folktale?"

Olga chuckled and shook her head sadly. "Maggie, you grandfather, he no think is just a story. He think Mahtantu and Cappy are what The Church of New Enlightenment call God. And he think that the Enlightened can call it here."

"They're going to sing to it?" Michael asked.

"Prayer has always been connected with songs," Maggie said. But then her eyes went wide with fear. "That's why the symbol is a harp."

"Maggie," Vinny said. "Come on. It's just a story. How are they going to use a song to call a sea monster? It's crazy."

Startling Alison, Olivia blurted, "Because Mahtantu or Cappy, or whatever you want to call it, is an alien." All the faces turned to look at her as if she had announced that ocean turned to guacamole.

Olivia took a long, deep breath and a sip of water. "Let's just say I'm right and The Mansion has a wormhole built into it—"

"A what?" Carmine asked from across the room.

"Oh. Sorry," Olivia smiled at him. "A wormhole is like a door. This one goes to another universe."

Carmine held up his hand. "You lost me."

Olivia smiled. "Think of it like this. Cappy's in another room. The Enlightened think they can open the door and bring it into our room. It's probably the whole reason the CNE even exists." Olivia's mouth turned into a surprised circle. "That explains the beadles!"

"How?" Maggie asked.

Alison tried not to roll her eyes, but she wondered why Olivia even bothered explaining herself to people. Before Olivia could say anything else, Alison explained it herself. "The alien must have adapted to reproduce using humans. The things we saw in the water, the naiads, those are like larvae or something. The church figured out how to use humans to make the larvae into the beadles."

"Exactly!" Olivia added. "Those beadles have to be some kind of alien-human hybrid."

"Can they do that?" Sal asked.

Olivia shrugged. "They did it. We've seen them."

"But if it's over there and we're over here, how are the larvae getting through the door?" Vinny finished his glass of wine and poured another. "This is nuts."

"The wormhole isn't totally shut," Olivia said. "Because of quantum fluctuation the wormhole opens on its own sometimes, just a sliver. The Enlightened, or maybe the beadles, themselves bring the Naiads over to our side. But that's how the birds and the flies are getting through."

"But what are they?" Michael asked.

Olivia was beaming. "I'm sure they're just other organisms native to the alien biome."

Michael shook his head, wearing that same dumb look he always wore when he talked to Alison or Olivia. At least it gave Alison something to laugh about. It felt so normal to translate Olivia to English.

"She means the bugs and the birds are other animals that live in the same place as Cappy. When the doorway pops open for the naiads, some get through. It's like when you open a door in the summer and moths fly in."

"Those must be some moths." Tony took another forkful of pasta.

"They get here, and they look for food and reproduce, just like any other invasive species." Olivia sounded like it should have been obvious, like everyone else was as smart as she was.

"Hang on!" Sal said. "I only went to school up to eighth grade, but if I understand what you're saying, the beadles are babies. So don't that mean they can grow up to be like the giant monster youz seen in the pictures down in the cathedral?"

"Not necessarily," Olivia said. "Since they've been crossbred with humans, they might not get much larger than the ones we've already seen."

Alison thought about the huge creatures they already saw and shuddered.

"So if we figure out how to stop The Church of New Enlightenment from bringing over Cappy, will we find our parents?" Michael asked.

His question stung. Alison had gone several whole seconds not worrying about them, and now that she remembered, she felt the guilty knife stab her gut again.

"Maybe," Maggie said. "But how? What are we supposed to do?"

"It has to do with the song," Olivia suggested. "The song, the sounds, maybe it's the vibrations or something. That harp you mentioned might have something to do with controlling the wormhole."

Maggie snapped her fingers. "The pedestal, Michael. The pedestal you tripped over. The harp goes in the pedestal. That's part of the stonework of the whole place! Where's that picture?" Michael found the picture and showed them in the camera's viewfinder. After he passed around the picture of the painting with a guy playing the harp, Maggie clapped her hand to her forehead. "Of course! I can't believe I'm so stupid! They use the harp to call Cappy."

"Okay," Michael said, "So, we need to find the harp, right? If they need the harp to open the wormhole, then all we have to do is grab the harp. No harp, no wormhole. No problem."

Part of Alison's mind knew she would have laughed if she weren't so worried about her parents.

"I don't know from this harp." Olga turned to face Maggie. "You grandfather go because he was looking for how to stop The Church of New Enlightenment."

Maggie's face went slack. "He didn't go. They killed him. Or they turned him and Uncle Max into those beadles."

Olga shook her head. "No, Maggie. He go with you Uncle Max to learn how to stop this. He tell me if he no come back, I should tell you and Aunt Penny to go. We all should go. Leave Cape November and don't come back no more."

"But it's been two years, Zi-Zi," Maggie wiped a tear. "When were you going to tell us he wasn't coming back?"

Olga's mouth became hard and rigid. "Tomorrow I was gonna tell you. Carmine and Frankie, they here to help us leave in case the Enlightened give us trouble." She leaned over and took Maggie's hand. "But you grandfather will come back. He will stop this." She nodded like she was done discussing it.

Maggie's fingers curled around a napkin. "But where is he? Where did he go?"

Olga shrugged and shook her head. "This, I don't know. He don't tell me."

"They've been gone for two years! Why didn't you tell Aunt Penny about Uncle Max? She thought he left us. Do you know what she's been through? Aunt Penny said…"

"You Aunt Penny didn't know nothing about this. You grandfather never tell her anything about The Church of New Enlightenment. After you mama and you papa die," Olga shook her head sadly and crossed herself with her hand, "you grandpa want to keep you and Aunt Penny safe."

Tears streamed from Maggie's eyes.

The creases deepened on Olga's face. *"Cara mia,* You grandfather say the less you know, the safer you gonna be."

Maggie's laugh was hard. "Does it look like anybody's safe?"

45 FIRE AND ICE

Olivia jumped, and her heart felt like a wild drum when Frankie's chair scraped the floor. He popped up and went to the door with his shotgun.

"Who are these jadrools?"

"Who?" Carmine asked, joining Frankie.

Olivia's blood hissed through her ears.

Michael's voice rasped, "Take Olivia. Hide in the kitchen. Now!"

"Huh?" She saw Alison blink, as if she didn't quite hear him, but then her eyes blazed. "No! We stick together, remember?"

Olivia saw Michael's neck muscles tighten. He picked up his axe and snarled, "Alison, those things are after you. You need to stay safe."

"So do you," she growled back.

"What the hell is this?" Frankie's voice was shaky. Olivia was terrified of whatever was scaring a man with a shotgun.

Frankie and Carmine backed away from the door, raising their shotguns to their shoulders. "Everybody in the kitchen!"

Olivia could barely breathe. The curtains were closed, but she knew something bad was outside. The memory of tentacles and poison forced its way into her head.

Unwrapping the snow globe, Alison muttered, "Not this time. Not again."

"Kitchen!" Carmine yelled. "Everybody out the back door! Time to get out!" Keeping his shotgun leveled at the front door, Carmine moved to the large window and parted the curtain slightly. *"Cazzo!"*

The plate-glass collapsed in shrieking pieces, raining shards of Olga's name across the tiled floor. Pale arms wrapped around Carmine. Gray hands clawed at his face and wrists. His shotgun blasted the ceiling causing plaster and dust to crumble around him before the arms dragged him out into the night, pulling the curtain out with him.

Fear and disgust churned her gut, and she had to gag down everything her stomach was trying to puke all over the table. She couldn't see Carmine under the savage pile of people squirming on top of him, but she heard him scream and the wet, popping sounds as they ripped him apart.

A hot tear stung her eye. She couldn't speak. She could barely force herself to breathe. She was sure her heart was about to explode inside her.

Outside the window about two dozen people shuffled toward Olga's front door, although Olivia wasn't sure they even were people. They were naked and totally hairless, but had no breasts or genitals, only belly buttons the size of a fist. Their cracked, crusty skin was pale gray, purple-blue or sickly yellow. A few looked raw and red. Olivia thought of scabs that had come to life. Walking infections. Her guts flipped.

Looking mindless and diseased, the scab-people crawled over the glass and over one another to tumble inside, scrambling over the ones who had already flopped in.

Olivia's guts cramped and heaved. She vomited on the floor.

"Come! Come!" Olga screamed from the kitchen. "We go now!"

Olivia couldn't breathe. She could not stop hearing Carmine getting ripped apart, and it made her gag again. Frankie fired again and again into the stewards who had smashed through the front door. With her ears still ringing, Olivia saw the holes the buckshot punched into their crusted skin. There was no blood. A few of the stewards looked up, but they kept trampling through the shattered window and the splintered door.

Olivia might have screamed when the stewards lurched toward Alison, who was still shaking the useless snow globe at them. Wrapping her arms around Alison's chest, she half-tackled her away from the grabbing hands that wanted to tear Alison's muscles off her bones.

"It's not working!" Alison shrieked.

"They're not beadles!" Olivia screamed.

Lunging, the stewards clawed at Alison with their scabby arms, knocking one another out of the way to grab for her. A crusty gray hand closed around Alison's wrist.

The flash of silver in front of her face made Olivia scream and jump back. She saw Michael holding the axe. He'd chopped off the thing's hand, but the steward still clubbed at Alison with its stump. Its severed hand clawed at the ground by her feet. When Alison stomped it, it squashed like clay under her sneaker.

"Gross!" Alison squealed.

Michael jabbed the flat top of the axe into the thing's face. It staggered, and Olivia saw the perfect indentation of the axe in its forehead.

"Go!" Michael screamed.

"Everybody go to Sal!" Olga screamed, but Olivia could barely hear her over the noise and the whistle in her ears from the shotgun blast. "In the car. In back!"

Frankie backed away and kept his shotgun pointed at the knot of stewards, but didn't shoot. He stood just outside the door while everyone else fled into the kitchen. As soon as Olivia cleared the door, she heard tables and chairs smash as the stewards surged after them. Frankie's shotgun rang out again and again. Olivia gritted her teeth and clenched her fists as she waited. When the screaming and the wet, ripping sounds came, Olivia closed her eyes and let the hot tears run down her face.

Someone, it might have been Maggie, dragged Olivia through the kitchen, past the stoves and the sinks toward the back door. Alison was there, and Olivia grabbed her hand and squeezed it. Alison was the last shred of courage she could cling to before she fell into hopeless panic.

"You gotta be kidding me," Vinny said when he got to the back door. Through the window, lights from the kitchen made the grass glow silver. Olivia's stomach heaved again when she saw five stewards already on the back steps. More came scuttling around the side of the restaurant to the yard. The light cast long, crooked shadows on the grass. She knew they would never make it to Sal's car. She clung tight to Alison. It was all she could do.

"No!" Vinny yelled helplessly as the ragged men grabbed him and pulled him down the stairs. Olga, Tony and Sal screamed and ran after him. The stewards swarmed them, too.

Olivia squeezed her eyes tight and gritted her teeth, waiting for the terrible sounds. Her heart nearly popped when she heard Alison shriek, "NO!" Everything seemed to stop. Her yelp echoed through the treetops. "Just take it!" Alison screamed.

Olivia opened her eyes in time to see the snow globe at the top and of its arc. Alison had thrown it far into the yard. Olivia lost it in the shadows.

Like dogs, the stewards scrambled to where it thudded in the grass.

"The ones inside are leaving, too!" Maggie called, from the door to the dining room.

Olivia stood on her toes to see past Michael. The stewards held tight to Olga, Tony, Sal and Vinnie, but it didn't look like they were hurting them.

Still unable to take a full breath, Olivia watched the stewards surround the snow globe. One picked it up, pressed it to its chest and loped out of the yard toward the road. Like baboons, the others bounded after it. She watched Olga and her family struggle helplessly across the shoulders of the stewards that carried them away.

Suddenly Olivia felt clammy, ice-cold hands grab her shoulders. "Get away!" She thrashed, writhing to break away from the frozen vice that tried to drag her out the kitchen door and into the yard.

Michael roared a wordless, animal sound and buried his axe into the head of the steward that had her. Olivia screamed and broke away. The steward staggered backwards on rubbery legs and fell down the few steps to the grass.

"How's that for a splitting headache, freak!" Michael yelled.

Olivia shivered, and fought not to dry-heave when the steward sat up. There was no blood at all, but a wedge-shaped groove divided the thing's face all the way down to its upper lip. Olivia could clearly see inside the steward's head. In the kitchen lights, it appeared to be made of solid, bruise-colored clay.

"What happens when they change?" Alison whispered. "They're not even human anymore." Olivia heard the panic in Alison's voice and tightly gripped her hand.

If it was hurt, the thing with the split skull wasn't acting like it. It raised its arms and staggered back up the stairs. Its dead yellow eyes, now far apart from one another, spun independently, each in its own socket. The steward tried to get back to the kitchen, but missed the step and stumbled, tumbling forward, closing its arms in the empty space about a foot in front of the door.

Down on one knee on the steps, it tilted its split, purple-black head. Olivia got the clear impression that it was trying to understand what the problem was. Why it couldn't see. Its ruptured mouth smiled and nodded, the two halves of its split head flapping slightly. With its hands, it squeezed its head back together, kneading and pressing the gouge to create a lumpy seam up the center of his face and over the top of his bald, crusty scalp. Its nose was mostly folded into the seam and one eye ended up a lot higher than the other. Olivia was lightheaded, and her stomach heaved the rest of its contents into the sink.

There were still two other stewards at the bottom of the steps. They were both a mottled, greenish gray. Silently, they moved their bodies in a quick, rhythmic, rocking motion.

"What are they doing?" Maggie asked. "What is that?"

The strange, utterly silent way their chests heaved and jiggled up and down looked weirdly familiar, which sent a crawling feeing down Olivia's arms. Horror tingled through her as Olivia figured out what she was seeing. "Whatever used to be human in them is laughing." The dry croak of her own voice startled her.

"How?" Alison asked. She sounded like she was only barely holding down her own stomach.

"Vestigial traces of their autonomic nervous systems?" Olivia heard herself saying. She laughed dizzily, realizing that her own autonomic reflexes had just answered Alison for her. Alison could explain it all to the others if she needed to; Olivia didn't care. Her grip on the world had just floated away from her. Or she floated away from the world. Whatever. It made no difference. Relativity! That one random word popped into her mind and made her laugh uncontrollably. There were voices. It might have been Alison or Maggie. It didn't matter anymore. Olivia realized that she had been stuck in the worst nightmare she'd ever had, but all she needed to do was wake herself up.

Still laughing, she slapped her own face again and again. Each slap was a little harder than the one before. It stung her cheeks. She tasted blood. From far away, someone screamed her name. It was Alison. Olivia noticed her hands had stopped moving. The world took on the solid, hard edges of reality again, and she realized that Michael held her wrists. She felt a flutter of panic, and she pulled and struggled, but could not break his grip.

"Olivia, chill!" he said.

"STAR DEW!" Alison yelled.

That sounded so funny, the laughter ripped out of Olivia uncontrollably.

Either her nightmare was starting to collapse or Alison had lost her mind, too. Olivia didn't know, and she laughed again when she realized that she didn't care."

"SWAT RED!" Alison had her hands on both of Olivia's cheeks. They still burned from slapping herself. "Come on, Liv! Straw Ed."

Olivia felt a deep pang of grief as the world came back into focus. Alison's eyes were wide with fear; freckles dotted her red face. Olivia knew she was in Olga's ordinary-looking kitchen. A stainless steel counter stood in the center. There were large stoves and ovens. Pots and pans hung on racks along the walls. A few soaked in the sink. Utensils stood ready in shining metal containers. She felt her brain stirring like old soup. She could only come up with one anagram for steward. "T'was Red?"

She jumped when she felt the arms wrap around her, but they were warm and soft. Alison held her and whispered in her ear. "Close enough."

Olivia never wanted that moment to end. Olivia was a balloon in the wind, and Alison was the only tether. *But she's a strong tether!*

Out the door, the nightmare still skulked stubbornly in the dark at the bottom of the steps. The two others faced the one who had shoved its own split skull back together. They awkwardly slapped one scabby hand against the other while twisting up their cracked, crusted faces into repulsive, silent mockeries of a smile.

Olivia knew she had to survive in whatever reality this was. She couldn't afford to fall apart again. She forced herself to look at the stewards. It was the only way she could make herself not feel helplessly terrified of them. She felt a swirl of revulsion as she understood what they were doing. "They're clapping because their buddy figured out how to shove his face back together."

Alison's voice sounded so sad. Hopeless. "I really hope they don't remember being human."

"How is this even possible? They don't even have any insides. They're just...clay...scabby...things."

Michael poured sweat. "Get out of here!" He screamed and waved his axe at them as if they were raccoons on a garbage can.

Maggie pulled him back and shut the door. "Maybe they'll leave. The others calmed down and cleared out already. Maybe these will, too."

"They wanted the snow globe." Alison's face tightened into a scowl. Olivia knew that look. Alison was furious at herself.

"But they took Olga and her family!" Michael sounded exhausted and on the edge of crying. Olivia suddenly realized how much stronger he had made her feel, because hearing him sound so broken rekindled the fear in her own gut like wind across the embers of a cold fire.

Maggie put her hand on his shoulder. "They took them, but they didn't hurt them. Not like Carmine and Frankie." Maggie shivered. Olivia felt sad to see her pretty face was streaked with dirt and someone's spattered blood. "As long as they're alive we can still get them back."

"You think those things..." Michael put his hand over his face. "Mom and Dad."

"I don't know." Maggie kept her voice steady, but Olivia noticed the tears carving wet trails through the grime on her face.

"Why did they go?" Alison's anger made her voice shrill and sharp.

"You gave them the snow globe," Maggie said.

Alison slammed her face into her hands. "I know! I messed up! I just helped them do whatever bad thing they're doing! I'm sorry. I didn't know what to do. They were going to kill them!"

"Alison," Maggie's voice was a quiet coo. She patted the air with her hands. "You saved their lives."

"But the snow globe!" Alison's voice cracked. "It was all we had!"

"We'll figure it out," Maggie said.

The part of Olivia's mind that wasn't constantly replaying the soggy, grinding deaths of Carmine and Frankie admired Maggie's calm strength. Olivia had to be strong too. For Alison.

She counted her breaths and forced herself to focus. She felt the solid floor under her sneakers. The cold metal of the sink pressed the back of her thighs as she leaned against it. The sweat that ran in tiny streams down her arms and neck. The thump of her heart finally slowed down.

Olivia washed her face and cupped her hands to drink from the faucet. The cold water soothed her throat and cooled her stomach. She bent down to let the water run over her head and neck. When she stood up she felt maybe she could keep it together, at least for a little while longer.

Out the kitchen window, she watched Scarface smile a big, hideous smile. He seemed to be looking at his companions, nodding to them. He smiled too far, and his upper lip split open again. He and the other stewards looked suddenly round-mouthed and troubled, but Scarface kneaded his crusted upper lip back together. They clapped like toddlers and headed for the stairs.

"They're coming back," Michael growled.

The door thumped once. A long, dead silence followed. Olivia kept swallowing, but she couldn't lose the disgusting taste in her mouth. Her throat still burned, and she noticed a chunk from her stomach that was still lodged in her nose. It shot out when she screamed.

Scarface smashed its misshapen head through the door, and it buckled away from the frame. Olivia couldn't look away. She couldn't move. While her mind had been floating off into madness, her body had grown roots that fixed her to the floor.

Scarface lunged past Michael and grabbed Alison's arm. She shrieked and buried her knee in its groin, leaving a perfect indentation in the scabby clay. The steward didn't seem to notice.

Olivia snatched a heavy frying pan from a rack. There was a muffled clang as she clocked Scarface in the head as hard as she could. Her wrists hurt from the impact, and the pan gonged to the floor.

The side of Scarface's already mangled head was completely flattened, and the thing staggered from the impact, but it didn't seem hurt.

Michael grabbed his sister away from the steward.

A thunderous eruption made Olivia jump. Past the puff of smoke, Maggie still held Frankie's shotgun up to her shoulder. It was covered with blood. Probably Frankie's.

Scarface had several small, round holes in the middle of its face. Its crooked, yellow eyes were gone. It staggered in the doorway, teetered on the top of the steps for a moment, and Olivia could see that the back of its head, where the buckshot pellets had come out, was prickling with points like lemon meringue pie. Scarface stumbled down the steps onto the two yellow stewards below. They picked up Scarface and turned him back up the steps. Their bare feet made dull, heavy thuds on the wooden stairs toward the kitchen.

Michael raised his axe and stood by the door.

"Wait!" It surprised Olivia to see Alison yelling from the door of the huge, walk-in freezer. And then she understood Alison's plan. "Lead them here!"

Olivia held her breath and stood with Maggie near the door to the dining room. Maggie had lowered the shotgun. She couldn't shoot a steward without hitting Michael or Alison. Scarface staggered through the kitchen, swinging his arms wildly, knocking over stacks of pots and dishes. Metal containers of cooking utensils clattered to the floor as he bumbled around the kitchen in no particular direction. Olivia realized that the steward was blind because Maggie had shot its eyes out.

The stewards silently lunged after Michael. Each jerky step brought them a little closer to Alison. One of the other stewards lunged forward. Unlike the blind Scarface, this one's coordination made Olivia hold her breath. Her nails bit into her palms. With its yellow fingers, it clawed the air where Michael's face had been just a heartbeat before.

Michael retreated around the counters in the middle of the kitchen where they formed an aisle. Only one steward could fit at a time. The thing charged again with both hands out. Michael swept his forearms out in a circular motion that deflected the steward's grasp while he sidestepped and pushed the steward further into its off-balance lunge. It stumbled and fell face down into the back of the freezer.

"Move!" Alison had circled around the counter, behind the second steward. She dropped her shoulder and rammed it forward until it tripped over the one on the floor. Michael slammed the freezer door shut and slid the metal pin through the latch. The stewards thudded against the door, but the heavy freezer held. The door was so thick, Olivia barely heard them pounding. She felt a tiny spark of hope. Those two, at least, were trapped.

"What about this one?" Maggie called. She kept the shotgun pointed at Scarface since it had moved away from Alison and Michael.

Alison grabbed a broom and poked Scarface in the ribs—or where the ribs should have been—with the handle. As soon as it turned and pawed for the handle, she pulled it back and jabbed it from the opposite side. It turned back again.

"Hah! You like that?" Alison's eyes were manic. Gleeful.

Something way down inside Olivia felt a twinge of guilt because watching Alison torment the thing was fun. But she doubted Scarface actually felt tormented. It didn't seem to feel anything. The smiles and clapping were just autonomic reflexes. They had to be.

Whatever Scarface had once been, a mother or a father, a doctor or a supermarket cashier, all Olivia let herself see was a revolting, murderous monstrosity. That was all that was left of the person Scarface had been. Watching Alison make it dance like a puppet, Olivia realized that she enjoyed hating it, because it was everything that terrified her.

"I can do this all day if I have to!" Alison jeered.

The steward kept swiping at the broom, trying to grab it, but Alison pulled the handle out of reach and poked it from a different direction, making it spin. "These things are even stupider than the beadles."

"And uglier," Michael said.

Olivia gasped when he hacked off one of Scarface's legs. It fell to the side, clawing the ground and the edge of the counter. With quick chops, Michael totally dismembered and decapitated it.

Olivia felt another nauseous wave roll through her, but she kept everything inside her in place. Even when the torso wriggled on the ground, flipping itself over and over. The dented, mangled head lay like a rock, its mouth opening and closing, like it wanted to talk. The four limbs twitched and flexed. One arm crawled away on its fingers.

Alison stomped the hand, crushing it like dough under the heel of her sneaker. "Open the oven, Michael."

Michael set his axe on the counter and slammed the doors of the pizza oven open. Each crashing sound made Olivia jump.

"You guys aren't serious," Maggie said. But Olivia knew better.

Alison tossed in the arm with the crushed hand and then she tossed in a leg. The leg wriggled out, so Michael chopped it in half at the knee and stuffed both pieces back in. He chopped the other leg in half and threw it in with the first. Alison grabbed the second arm, crushed the hand and tossed it in.

Michael slammed the door. It made Olivia jump.

Alison and Michael cursed and turned their faces away as they each picked up an end of the wriggling torso and tossed it into the lower oven the way they might have tossed a kid into a swimming pool. Alison used the broom to shove it in farther. Michael threw in the head and slammed the second door.

Olivia jumped again.

"That's for Carmine!" Michael screamed at the oven door and gave it the finger. And then he turned the oven dials all the way on.

"No, you idiot!" Alison yelled, slapping Michael's hand away.

The oven hissed as the gas flowed. It clicked as the ignition started the flame and whooshed when it caught. There was a crackle. A louder hiss. A rumbling, rushing sound. Tongues of flame shot out the sides of the oven doors, almost blasting them open. Michael stumbled back. He felt for his eyebrows.

Even across the room, Olivia's face felt hot from the flames. When greasy black smoke poured out, Michael gagged and put his arm over his mouth. Groping for his axe, he staggered toward the dining room door. Through the smoke, Olivia could just make out Alison trying to turn the oven off, but she gave up and, coughing and choking, staggered after him, wiping her eyes as the kitchen filled with rotten, meaty smoke.

Olivia held her breath and put her hands over her mouth and nose.

"Let's go," Maggie said quietly. She turned to go back into the dining room.

Holding her hands over her face to keep out the stench, Olivia heard the oven doors rattling. She was glad the oven had no window because she didn't want to see what was inside, its autonomic nervous system trying to escape the heat. The tears stung her eyes. Olivia was pretty sure it was just from the smoke.

46 NOTHING TO LOSE

Alison's lungs and throat burned, and stinging tears practically blinded her. *Why did Michael broil that thing? What's wrong with him?* Stumbling half-blind, she followed the others out the door to the dining room.

"Michael, you're such a moron! You don't cook alien mystery meat!" She took one breath of clean air, and it caught in her throat. Michael, Maggie and Olivia sat against one wall surrounded by a sea of rubble and shattered furniture.

Alison recognized the bloated-looking man in the khaki uniform with the gold sheriff's star pinned over his flabby breast. He had just removed his ranger-style hat and was perching it on a table, giving Alison a clear view of his bald, mottled head and his pockmarked face. His eyes were still hidden behind metallic mirrored lenses.

"Alison, just run!" Maggie yelled.

Alison's heart jammed inside her. For an instant she imagined herself jumping back into the kitchen, through the choking smoke and escaping into the yard, alone except for every horrible thing on the Cape hunting her down. Her breath came, helpless and shallow, as the weight of that settled over her. She took a few faltering steps toward the others.

Smiling and licking his wet lips, the sheriff rested a fat, clammy-looking hand on his pistol. "You seem to have grasped that running would be an extraordinarily bad idea, Miss Nunios."

The repulsive flash of his nubby teeth and arrogant curl of his lip showed that he knew the bottom had fallen out of her stomach. He was counting on it.

"Let's not kid ourselves, Miss Nunios. We remember each other from our encounter on the highway. I certainly remember you." His laugh was wet and meaty. "This is a small jurisdiction, and as sheriff, I don't pull traffic duty often. Your family left an impression. I find my instincts were correct." He looked at the wreckage of the dining room. "Apparently, I should have detained you for further questioning. But what happens in the dark shall be brought to light. Come take a seat next to your accomplices."

Glaring at the sheriff, hoping that if she hated him enough she could cause him to have a heart attack, Alison took her seat next to Olivia.

"Accomplices? I guess we're not too worried about due process in this town," Olivia declared. Alison was surprised to hear Olivia mouth off to authority. This was a new Olivia. "We can't be an accomplice if we didn't commit a crime."

"HA!" The cop croaked, "We have another smart one!" Olivia stared straight ahead like a prisoner in one of those war movies Michael liked to watch.

It turned Alison's stomach when the sheriff brought his damp, mottled face to within inches of Olivia's. He turned to smile at Alison while he whispered dramatically in Olivia's ear, loudly enough for them all to hear him. "Now suppose you were to suffer an accident while in custody, young lady? Perhaps while you were resisting arrest?"

"I'm not resisting arrest," Olivia stated flatly, still staring.

The sheriff spewed another wet-meat laugh. "So says the criminal."

"You're going to lose your badge. I'll get you locked up for violating our civil rights and abusing your office." Olivia still stared straight ahead, but her voice was as hard as steel and sharp as razors. "It's cops like you that make people hate cops."

The sheriff put up his swollen hands, pretending to protect himself. "Black Lives Matter? All lives matter?" The sheriff laughed and shook his head. "How about no lives matter? Not yours anyway."

It took everything Alison had left not to punch him in his fat face. And then it all became crystal clear. *He's one of them!* "Are you even a real cop or just another beadle?"

"One hundred percent bona fide officer of the peace, Miss Nunios." He leaned down, pressing his face close to Olivia's. She cringed, and Alison cringed with her.

"You want your rights?" he hissed. "You have the right to remain silent."

"You're arresting us?" Alison squeaked and hated it. Tongue-tied and confused, she resented the off-balance, helpless way the sheriff made her feel. "We didn't do this." As soon as she said it, she was mad at herself for not thinking of anything better.

The sheriff laughed. "A suspect who says she didn't do it! How original!"

Alison felt like she'd swallowed an electric fan. It spun in her stomach as the sheriff paced in front of them. His shoes scraped the tiles as he walked slowly, saying nothing for an uncomfortably long time. Finally, he announced, "As a formality, let me identify myself. I'm Sheriff McGill of the Cape November County Sheriff's Office. This interrogation can go easy or hard. You want to tell me what happened?"

Alison hated his smug, arrogant smirk so much it made her head hurt.

"We were attacked." Michael said firmly. "These creatures broke in here. They wrecked the place. They killed Carmine and Frankie. Look in the freezer!" Michael's voice cracked. "There are two of them in the freezer. Go look. They're not even people anymore."

The cop turned his mirrors on Michael, and Alison felt everything inside her go soft. *Why can't he ever just shut up?* "Not people anymore? What did you do to them, you sociopath? Are you confessing to having placed your victims in the freezer of this establishment?"

"Victims?" Michael laughed a hard, mean-sounding laugh. "We're the victims. Come look!" Michael stood up, but the cop shoved him down, hard. Faster than Alison could see it, his pistol was against Michael's temple. Alison stopped breathing. She bit her lip until she tasted blood.

"Get out of that chair again and I will put you down like a sick animal. Got me, boy?" The sheriff took his gun off Michael's temple, but he kept it pointed at him. "You seem like you're on drugs, Mr. Nunios."

Michael gulped hard. "I'm not on drugs," he said quietly.

"Put your gun away. We're unarmed!" Olivia protested.

Alison's heart skipped at the cracking sound when the sheriff backhanded Olivia across the face, snapping her head to the side and leaving an ugly handprint on her cheek. But Olivia straightened herself up and continued to stare straight ahead, her eyes as cold as a frozen flagpole.

Good for you, Liv. Don't give him the satisfaction. Tears stung Alison's eyes.

"Axes, knives, fireplace pokers," the sheriff ticked each item off on his pudgy fingers. "Weapons come in all shapes and sizes. And in case you forgot, Maggie here, of Maggie's Haunted Mansion, was carrying a loaded shotgun. Unarmed indeed."

"She put it down," Michael said sullenly.

"Thus, you are all still alive." The sheriff smiled. With a leathery hiss, he slid his pistol back into its holster. "I told you I could be generous."

"How do you know me?" Maggie asked.

The sheriff chuckled. "Mama Leadfoot and Daddy Duffer told me where they were staying during the traffic stop. I surmised the rest."

Alison refused to feel afraid when he trained his mirrors back on her and croaked, "So where are your parents? You know, an old man was brutally murdered down in the church basement. Real tragedy. I'm having the murder weapon dusted for prints. Obviously an amateur, and none too bright, either. I mean, the whole ocean was right there, but this halfwit left the hammer sitting right next to the victim."

Everything froze inside her. She knew she could have buried a hammer in the sheriff's face and never felt remorse. "Maybe if you did your job better, stuff like that wouldn't happen." Alison forced herself sound as flippant as she could.

Maggie's voice was quiet and trembling. "I can vouch for them. They've been staying with me. They're all guests in The Mansion."

"And look at the hospitality you've shown them." The sheriff laughed as he motioned to the rubble of Olga's dining room. His mirrors turned to Maggie. "Refresh my memory. Your uncle decided to skip out on his obligations…what? Two years ago? Leaving your poor Aunt Penny to pick up the pieces? So, where's Aunt Penny? Shopping with Mama Leadfoot?"

"She's out of town on business—which is none of yours." Maggie sounded flustered. "How do you know me?"

The sheriff's flabby smile broadened. "Like I said, this is a small jurisdiction." He took a big, rumbling breath. "It's my job to know everything that happens here."

"So, then you should know what happened to the old man," Alison said. She had to get him on defense to give herself a second to think.

He laughed a big, flabby laugh and focused his mirrors like a pair of magnifying glasses. Alison felt like a bug. "How do you know I don't, Miss Nunios?"

He cleared something wet-sounding from his throat. Alison felt a heave of revulsion. He turned his mirrors back on Maggie. "I hope that's true about your aunt. I hope it doesn't turn out that she's one of those bodies in the freezer or one of these bloodstains on the floor." Maggie turned pale. Alison felt the fan in her stomach spin faster.

The sheriff trained his metal eyes back on Alison. "Again I ask you: Where is Mama Leadfoot?"

"Again I tell you," Alison imitated the wet rumble of his voice, "we don't know."

"We think our parents were kidnapped," Michael blurted. Alison tightened her gut and tried not to let the sheriff see her cringe. *Michael, just shut up!*

"Aww, now why would you think a crazy thing like that? It's that kind of irrational paranoia that makes me think you're on drugs, son," the sheriff croaked. "Maybe your folks are just out getting that windshield fixed, huh? Or maybe your parents are just enjoying a nice dinner away from you annoying brats." He stood up and turned around, showing them his wide back as he seemed to survey the rest of the room. "Are you familiar with Occam's Razor, kids?"

"Simple theories are better than complicated theories when you're looking for truth," Olivia recited quietly.

He spun back to look at Olivia. Alison could just see the tops of the sheriff's eyebrows rise above his mirrors. "Impressive. Maybe you're smarter than I gave you credit for." The sheriff slowly dragged a wooden chair across the tiles, setting Alison's teeth on edge. "We got a nine-one-one call about the trouble you caused here."

"That's impossible." Maggie's voice was tight. "From who? The phones are dead."

"From w-h-o-m." The sheriff dragged the word out slowly, chuckling "Language is the first thing to go in a dying civilization." He sighed expansively, "After founding the city of Alexandria and its great library, Alexander the Great spread the learning of Greece and Egypt around the ancient world. Conquest isn't always a bad thing, see? When the Romans lost control of Europe to the barbarian hordes, the Muslims, along with a handful of European monks, preserved all that ancient knowledge until Europe remembered to look for it again in the Renaissance. That was long before the once-mighty Catholic Church started holding hands and singing kumbaya with every heathen freak on the planet, you understand." The sheriff laughed. "The Catholic Church was for real then. It could torture and kill non-believers. Or anybody else causing trouble for that matter."

"You mean scientists, gays and women accused of witchcraft?" Alison spat.

"The church kept law and order. We need more of that today, don't you think? A new church that can show people how things really are. Enlighten them? The idea of God is laughable. A God who's all-powerful and all-knowing, but who routinely allows his most faithful believers to suffer? What kind of sick God is that anyway? And where's God been? We haven't heard much from God, have we? There's all this war and suffering, people dying of disease and starvation, and where's God? All those mysterious ways he works in sounds like a cover story for a God who isn't really there." The sheriff chuckled. "Unlike most churches who take it on faith that God is listening, The Church of New Enlightenment have seen the face of He That Is Magnificent. He will save the worthy few and get rid of the rest." He smiled at Alison. "In a way, you're lucky. You get a front row seat at the dawn of a new world. The Church of New Enlightenment is going to raze the so-called civilization we've got now and replace it with something better. Without mercy, every man, woman and child who is not part of our solution…well, let's just say they won't be a problem much longer. I'm here to offer you a chance to get in on the ground floor while you still can." He smiled.

Alison felt herself burn with hatred and rage. "A group of idiots that wants to wipe out everybody who doesn't agree with them?" Alison sneered with as much contempt as she could in her voice. "How original."

The sheriff laughed. "There have always been bleeding hearts who don't understand how many eggs you have to crack to make an omelet." The sheriff released a thick, wet sigh, and the chair creaked under his bulk as he sat heavily. "The strong don't need the weak…well, maybe in the same way that wolves need sheep." His smile erupted into a deep, rumbling laugh that ended in a choking, coughing fit.

He knew how scared she was, no matter how much she told herself she wasn't. That infuriated her. She hated how naked he made her feel.

"Bite me."

The sheriff laughed and set his hat on his soft-looking head. "A storm is coming, Miss Nunios, and you're going to find out soon enough how absolutely insignificant you really are. You and your whole world." He looked at the wreckage of the room and noticed the smoke that poured out of the kitchen and filled the ceiling near the door. "The only reason you're still alive is so He That Is Magnificent can feast on your tears."

"What's that supposed to mean?" Alison sneered. The beads of sweat under her scalp itched. She felt so grimy and dirty, but she would not let the sheriff see her scratch.

Pausing on his way to the door, the sheriff rotated slowly around. "You still think you can win, and you're going to try. He That Is Magnificent is counting on it. But I'll do you one better. Your parents are guests of The Church of New Enlightenment. They're receiving excellent care and I venture to say that they're even happy. They have no idea that they're going to die in agony in our cathedral." The sheriff waddled back and leaned down to stare Alison in the face. She cringed and leaned away, trying not to gag on his rotten fish breath. "You still have a small chance to save them. Understand that I'm not telling you this to help you. You will fail, but it's good if you believe you won't. He That Is Magnificent will enjoy your failure, so I want you to try to save them."

Alison let herself breathe just enough to get the words out. "I want you to use some mouthwash."

Straightening up, the sheriff walked heavily toward the door. "He That Is Magnificent is pleased you still have fight in you. That you still have hope. Because when that hope is snatched out of your hands, your suffering will be that much sweeter. Suffering is best in people who still hope right up to the end. Hopeless people have nothing to lose. Where's the fun in that?" Laughing, the sheriff walked out the door. His boots crunched across the broken glass on the sidewalk. His car door thudded. The sound of the car engine faded. The sheriff finally left, and Alison felt as if everything good had been dragged out of the world behind him.

47 PATHOSYNTHESIS

Rage tore through Michael's chest. If that cop didn't have a gun, he would have smashed his face into the floor with a chair. Helpless fury boiled over, and he snatched his chair and heaved it across the room to splinter against the opposite wall.

"Michael!" Alison screamed.

He had to laugh at that. "What? Afraid I'm going to break something? Afraid somebody's going to call the cops?"

"Just chill," Maggie said gently, almost like she was pleading. It made Michael feel like an ass. She closed her eyes and took a breath. "We need to think. To figure out our next move."

That was even funnier than Alison yelling at him. "There is no next move." He stopped and closed his eyes for a moment. Listening to the air blowing in and out of him like a storm. "The Church of New Enlightenment has been getting away with everything because the sheriff is one of them."

"And if he's in on it, who knows who else is." Olivia rested her forehead on her hands and her elbows on her knees, so she looked like she was talking to the floor."

"This doesn't change anything," Alison said quietly.

"What chance do we have?" Michael's rage boiled over again. He clenched his whole body and roared into the air, as if he could vent his frustration like steam in a kettle.

"Feel better?" Alison sneered.

"No!" Michael screamed. "I don't!"

"Why did he even come here?" Maggie asked quietly. It was like she hadn't even heard his scream.

"To mess with our heads," Alison said.

That's her big genius theory? Michael turned to punch the wall, but stopped himself. The last thing he needed was a broken hand. Not that it would have mattered. "That's stupid."

Alison turned on him with her eyes flashing fire. "Really, Mr. Throw-Chairs-Around-The-Room? I'm stupid?"

His heart hammering, he stalked to tower over his sister. "I never said you were stupid, Alison."

"Guys, come on!" Olivia stood straight with her fists clenched. "You two need to keep it together for once." Her eyes looked so sad and tired. It caught him off guard. He realized with a pang of guilt that they were all in it as much as he was, but they were staying calm. Suddenly he felt like a monster himself for blowing up at everybody. "Sorry. I guess I lost it there for a sec."

"Join the club." Olivia smiled at him weakly.

Alison's eyes narrowed angrily at him, and Michael braced himself, waiting for her to roast him, but then her eyes grew softer. She slid him another chair. Michael sat down.

"Look, the sheriff could have killed us," Alison said. "He could have arrested us. He could have kidnapped us and taken us to the church or turned us into beadles, or who even knows what. But he didn't. Why?"

"It almost sounded like he was trying to recruit us, there at the end," Maggie said. "Like he wanted us to join the church."

"He had to know that wasn't going to happen," Michael said. He wished they already had a plan. Thinking one up was making his head hurt.

"He thinks it's over already," Olivia said quietly. "The Church of New Enlightenment has the snow globe now. They think they won."

His throat had gotten so dry that screaming made it sore. He rummaged through his backpack for an orange sports drink. It was warm, but that didn't matter. He had to get the revolting smoke taste out of his mouth.

"Do you think they need the snow globe to open the wormhole?" Alison asked.

Olivia shook her head and shrugged. "I have no idea. Maybe. It must have high energy."

"It wasn't in the paintings," Maggie pointed out. She sipped at a water bottle. "The only thing we saw in the paintings was a guy playing a harp. No snow globe."

"So what is it?" Olivia asked.

"And why did they want it so bad?" Michael demanded.

"It's a weapon, right?" Maggie asked.

"It did squat against the stewards," Michael pointed out.

"Maybe it was out of energy," Maggie suggested.

"It healed Olivia," Alison added. "Maybe they need to heal their people."

"They just need to control it!" Michael couldn't believe he was the only one to figure it out. All those smart people, but he got it. He knew it. "In a video game, if you're up against a screen boss and you lose your best weapon, a lot of times you can't beat the game."

"This isn't a video game, Michael," Alison groaned.

"No, but he's right," Maggie smiled at him. Michael felt a warm glow in his chest. "They need to make sure that you can't show up with the snow globe and wreck their chance to open the wormhole and bring out Cappy."

The name felt like fingernails getting dragged across a chalkboard in Michael's ears. "We're really sticking with that?"

"What?" Maggie asked.

"That dumb name." Michael felt the laugh coming, and he couldn't stop it.

"I mean, Cappy's coming to destroy the world! Watch out, Cappy's going to get you!"

Maggie laughed, and the tense creases melted into a warm smile. "That's a thing down the Cape. If you grew up here, you'd get it."

Laughing felt good. It was the one normal thing that he'd felt in a long time. "We have to think of something better than Cappy."

"We could call it Mahtantu," Maggie said, still chuckling. It made the warm glow spread in Michael's chest.

But Michael wasn't even going to try to say that name. He knew it would just be another chance for Alison to make him feel stupid when he said it wrong. "Forget it. We'll stick with Cappy."

Olivia sat rigid with her back straight. "So the sheriff just came to deliver the message. Just to make us squirm. But we're still here because the CNE needs us for some reason."

Alison shrugged. "He told us why. He wants us to have hope."

"He was just yanking out chains!" Michael groaned. Nothing made sense. "They hate everyone who's not in the church. Why encourage us?"

Maggie looked up at him. Her eyes looked red and puffy, but he saw an even deeper sadness in them. It made him think of Maggie's parents, gone for so long, and the long, twisting road she'd been on between reality and delusion. He felt another pang of guilt for being the guy who brought the cold slap of reality.

"They want us to have hope so they can take it away," Alison said quietly. "That's what he meant when he said hopeless people have nothing to lose."

"Why?" Michael tried to wrap his mind around the whole thing, but it was like trying to hug a tractor-trailer. "What difference does it make to them if we have hope or not? They already have Mom and Dad. What do we have left to lose?"

Maggie nodded and smiled sadly. She repeated the rhyme she had said before, but added a haunting melody. "When people are crying, Cappy gets strong. When people start dying, start singing his song. What if this alien, whatever it is, gets stronger when people suffer?"

Olivia tilted her head like a puzzled dog. "That would require a level of empathy..." she closed her eyes and pushed her fingertips against her temples. When she popped up out of her chair, Michael flinched.

Olivia turned to face them. "Suppose we really are dealing with an alien mind, see? And that mind can literally feed on the feelings of others. It makes perfect sense that an organism that lives on emotions would look for an environment where there was maximum suffering. Pain creates strong emotional reactions; human suffering could potentially provide the best energy for the alien. Most organisms alter their environments to suit their needs, right? Like beavers? They build dams to make deep ponds because it protects their lodges."

Michael had no idea that was why beavers built dams, and he had even less of an idea what Olivia was talking about. "Beavers?"

Olivia's pretty face scrunched up in bewilderment, like she couldn't understand why Michael was confused. "The point is that this telepathic alien is using The Church of New Enlightenment to spread suffering because it feeds on the suffering."

Michael had practically grown up with Olivia, so he usually forgot how gorgeous she was, but when she smiled up at him, she looked so beautiful and innocent, that for a second, Michael almost missed the fact that what she was saying was completely insane. "You can't eat feelings."

Her forehead creased and Michael knew that he had annoyed her. He saw Alison take a big breath, but before she had a chance to unload on him, Olivia, with her eyes shut, held up her finger impatiently. "We can't eat feelings, but we're not this alien." Olivia paced around the room, wading through the smashed rubble of wrecked furniture. "Think about it. Emotions are just electric signals from the amygdala, right?"

"Are they?" Michael hated all this school talk. He really wanted to hit something.

"What if you had a creature that was perfectly adapted to receive those electrical signals?" Olivia continued to pace. "To feed off them?"

"That's a pretty small amount of energy," Maggie said. "The thing in that painting, if that's what we're dealing with, is huge."

"But suppose it just sits there over time, letting all that energy build up? It didn't happen overnight, but eventually, water carved the Grand Canyon." Olivia snapped her fingers. "Of course! This thing must have been over there collecting energy for years. Maybe even thousands of years. And if the alien does collect mental energy from other organisms, then a religion is a perfect food source. All that mental energy of the faithful, coming to worship at the cathedral, over time, all those thoughts, directed at that creature who must be a perfect receiver, just sitting on the other side getting stronger and stronger."

"Isn't the wormhole closed?" Maggie asked.

Olivia shrugged, "It's permeable, remember? And who knows, maybe a telepathic creature like that can receive thoughts whether the wormhole is open or not."

"The stones might be energy conductors, right?" Maggie offered. "Maybe they conduct thoughts and feelings to the creature."

"How is anything supposed to get energy from thoughts?" Michael said. He almost wished the stewards would come back so that he could bury his axe in their heads.

"Energy is energy, Michael," Alison said. "It's not really that different from plants that get energy from light." Alison sounded annoyed, and that annoyed Michael. "They have chloroplasts that use the electromagnetic energy in light to make sugar. Why can't this alien use the electromagnetic energy of emotions to do the same thing?" Alison stood with her hands on her hips.

Olivia looked up at the ceiling and half-whispered, "Pathosynthesis."

Michael laughed. "Are you people listening to yourselves?"

"So what's your big theory?" Alison sneered.

Olivia tilted her head slightly, and Maggie arched her eyebrow. He felt all the fire go out in him. His stomach was an angry knot. "So we have a telepathic alien that eats emotions. Maybe we can ask it to tell our futures while we're at it."

"That's clairvoyance," Olivia explained. "Telepathy is when one mind can pick up the thoughts of another. You know, mind reading."

It made him want to throw another chair. "Whatever! How do we get Mom and Dad?"

"It wants us to go after them," Maggie said. "The sheriff said he wants us to try so that their god can watch us fail."

"To enjoy the suffering," Olivia added, nodding. "It's feeding."

"You're saying that the only reason that sheriff left us here is so that we could suffer, because that's going to help feed their monster-god?"

Olivia nodded. "I didn't say it, the sheriff did."

"That really pisses me off!" Alison said.

"Hang on." Michael wanted to scream, but he managed to keep his cool. "If they want us alive, why did they send those things after us?"

"Duh! For the snow globe!" Alison said. "As soon as I gave it to them, they left."

"Not all of them." Michael felt the knot in his gut get tighter. He could not understand why he was the only one who saw that they were wasting time. "They kidnapped Olga and her family. Was that just to make them suffer, too?"

Olivia shrugged. "Probably."

"But those last ones stuck around for us." Rage boiled up in him again. He popped out of his chair and stomped toward the kitchen just to scream at them. "We kicked your asses though, didn't we! Stuffed you in a freezer and roasted your ass in an oven! Who's suffering now?" Michael spat on the ground. He looked up and saw that the entire wall behind the oven was in flames. The sour, meaty smoke hit him in the face, and he stumbled back choking with tears stinging his eyes.

"You showed them," Alison said.

Michael was coughing too hard to come back at her.

"But there were only three," Olivia said. She seemed like she was just going to ignore Michael, and he was still coughing too hard to speak. "There were only three of them and four of us," she continued. "It was some kind of test, maybe. Maybe they were testing us or they might have been testing the stewards, to see what they were capable of. Anyway, if they were serious about taking us, they would have left more behind, wouldn't they?"

That ticked him off. Michael managed to cough out, "Carmine and Frankie are dead, Olivia. That's not serious?" He kicked a piece of a chair that suddenly annoyed him just for existing.

"The important thing now is how are we going to stop them?" Alison demanded, stamping her foot.

"What makes you think we can?" He felt like everything was slipping away.

"What makes you think we can't?" For once, Alison did not have any snark or sarcasm in her voice. That got Michael's attention.

She walked slowly up to Michael. He rarely looked her in the eyes and now that he was, he felt so vulnerable. Images of all the terrible things they'd seen and done flashed through his mind, but also memories of their ordinary life before. Stupid little moments came flooding back, like the time on a family vacation when she shot a straw paper at him in a restaurant and hit a man at another table. The time she played video games with him to cheer him up after he lost the state semi-finals. The way she hugged him on graduation and said she was proud of him. He realized that she was connected to just about everything he was connected to. The anger melted, and he felt guilty for all their pointless fighting. He knew that no matter what she said, Alison would always have his back. And he would have hers. He felt a painful longing in his chest and he realized it was love. She was his sister, and he loved her no matter how much she drove him crazy.

"We have to get to the cathedral, Michael." She said it quietly, keeping him fixed with her brown eyes. "Whatever they're doing, they're doing it there."

The idea sounded so insane, Michael worried for a moment that Alison had lost it, just like Olivia had before. "So your big plan is, we roll up on the monsters that have been trying to kill us and be, like, what up, scary dudes? We're here to kick your asses!" Michael had to laugh at that. "It's ballsy, I'll give you that."

Alison didn't say anything. The way she just kept staring at his eyes made him nervous, so he looked at Olivia and Maggie, hoping one of them would bring them all to their senses, but they both nodded. For a second, he thought they were only on her side because of, like, girl power or whatever, but then he realized that Alison was right more often than he liked to admit. He sighed, heavy with the knowledge of that. "Okay, what's the plan?"

"I'm getting my snow globe back." Alison pulled on her backpack and picked up her fireplace poker.

Michael felt a fist of fear and worry as she headed toward the door. "You can't go out there! It's too dangerous."

Alison turned around. She looked so sad it scared him. "Michael, this is the one place in the whole Cape we know Mom and Dad aren't."

"It's also on fire," Olivia added.

"WHAT?"

Maggie's voice was flat and matter-of-fact. "The thing in the oven must have caught fire."

Michael slid into the straps of his own pack and picked up his axe. He looked at Maggie and Olivia. "Ready to say, 'What up? We're here to kick your ass?'"

They both laughed, and it made Michael feel lighter inside. He felt a little heavier when Maggie handed her fireplace poker to Olivia and picked up poor Frankie's shotgun. But, after every crazy, terrifying thing they'd already survived, what was one more? He wasn't so scared of dying, not anymore. It just made him a little sad that he didn't get enough time to do all the things regular people did when they didn't die. "Hey, forget the bikes. Let's take Sal's Caddy. We might as well go out in style."

48 FLYTRAP

The night before, when they had gotten back from driving to the empty church, when Carmine and Frankie were still alive, and Olga's place wasn't burning down, Michael had noticed that Sal never locked his car and kept the keys in the visor. Carmine had scolded him about it, but Sal had said, "Don't let them mamalukes scare you, Carmine. Cape November is still a safe town. You ever hear about a car getting stolen down here? Fuggettaboutit."

At the time, Michael had laughed, but replaying their conversation in his mind filled him with fear. Carmine was dead. Sal had been kidnapped.

Safe town.

In the alley between Olga's and the building next door, the air was sticky and hot, but the breeze coming off the ocean felt cold. Black night was getting pushed away by a hard, gray dawn.

Michael stopped and waved for the others to wait behind him. Something sharp jabbed him in the side. Michael screamed, his heart raced. But he realized that Alison had just run into him with the fireplace poker.

Under his shirt, Michael rubbed this new scrape. "Jeez, Al, don't we have enough problems? That really hurt."

"Don't be such a baby," she scoffed.

"Why'd you stop? Did you see something?" Maggie moved toward the front with her shotgun.

Heavy clouds scudded across the sky. The trees bent in a stiff wind that ruffled the grass. The light coming down made no shadows. "No."

Alison scowled at him. "So why did you stop?"

The new scrape stung, but Michael's hand didn't show any blood. The scrape was nothing. It just hurt. "You want to run right out there? We don't know what's waiting for us."

Alison pushed past him. "The sheriff wants us to go to the cathedral, Michael, he basically told us to."

Michael grabbed her shoulder and pulled her back into the alley. "That's exactly why we need to be careful."

"We could get trapped if we stay here." Olivia looked out toward the street behind them. "Plus, the building's on fire."

"Go make sure Sal's keys are there." Maggie brought her shotgun to her shoulder while gently moving Alison behind her. "I'll cover you."

The shotgun made little bubbles dance in Michael's stomach. "What if you shoot me?"

Maggie chuckled. "I'm a pretty good shot."

"Pretty good?" The bubbles danced faster.

"Just go!" Alison groaned. "We're wasting time."

Michael glanced up at Olivia, hoping she had a better idea, but she just mouthed hurry.

The grass needed mowing. It tickled his legs, and he hated the crawling sensation. When the wind blew, he thought something was crawling toward him. His fingers ached from gripping the axe so tightly. He gave up trying to stop his hands shaking. Keeping close to the side of the restaurant, he paused at the bottom of the stairs. Flames crackled in the doorway and the stench of burnt meat wafted over him, making him gag. He knew the faint thumping he heard was coming from the freezer.

The Cadillac was just ahead in the long, gravel driveway that led straight out to the side street, past the yards of two other houses. Glancing back toward the alley he saw Alison, still scowling, waving him on with her hand. Maggie was sweeping the yard with the shotgun.

The door handle was cool and damp with morning dew. He lifted the latch, and the large door squawked. Michael froze. The squawk hadn't come from the door. Three monster birds, like the ones they had seen on their first day here, perched on the roof, away from the flames.

The first bird dove at Michael. He put up his axe to block it, but before it reached him, Maggie's shotgun thundered and the thing's head ripped apart. It spun in the air and fell on the far side of the car. Michael's chest hammered. The other birds still perched calmly on the roof. They scuttled sideways, away from the spreading fire. One cawed, and Michael held up his axe. "Yeah? You want some of this?"

"How many more?" Maggie leaned out of the alley like she was trying to see the roof.

"Two!" Michael wanted them gone. "Shoot them!"

"Only one shell left."

He felt his stomach drop. "That would've been good to know before!"

"Yeah, well, we know it now. You two, run to the car! Michael, open the back."

It took two tries before he could fumble the back door open with his shaking hands. He guarded it with his axe as Alison and Olivia sprinted across the yard. A second bird flapped into flight, but Maggie blasted it before it cleared the roof. It collapsed and tumbled over the eves, thudding to the grass next to the kitchen steps.

Olivia and Alison dove into the huge back seat. Michael closed the doors and walked halfway toward Maggie, keeping his eye on the bird and his axe ready. "Let's go, Maggie. I got you."

Dropping the empty gun, Maggie sprinted to him. She stopped and spun around, and he felt her hands grip his shoulders. "Back toward the car, but move slow," he whispered, not taking his eye off the last bird. It sat on the roof and tracked them with its eyes, but didn't move.

The bird opened its huge wings and dove off the roof. Michael screamed and Maggie echoed it painfully in his ear, but he never even got to swing. The bird banked and flapped away from the yard, disappearing over the trees. Michael felt like a god. "HA!" He spun to hug Maggie. "We did it! We scared it away."

Maggie was looking up, but not where the bird had flown. Her eyes were wide and her mouth hung open with terror. He turned and held up his axe, waiting for another bird to strike. The clouds were even darker, and they shredded into each other in what must have been high wind. But clouds would not have put that look on Maggie's face.

Scanning the sky, he saw one cloud move apart from the others. He tried to understand what was chasing them, but then his insides went soft as he recognized it as a swarm of flies. The air buzzed and hummed.

The cloud was already atop the trees at the edge of the yard. With his hair standing, Michael half fell into the driver's seat and slammed the door with a solid, reassuring thunk.

Olivia and Alison screamed behind him. He opened the visor, but the keys didn't fall out. Panic swelled; he couldn't breathe. He swept his hands wildly around the visor and then pulled down the other one.

"What are you doing?" Maggie shrieked. "Drive!"

Michael kept looking in the seats. There were no cup holders. No coin holders. Nowhere else to check. "Check the glove compartment!"

"They must have started colonizing the Cape. Uch! The flies just ate the dead bird." Olivia was breathless. "There's nothing left. Just bones and feathers."

"Maybe they're full now," Alison said weakly.

"Probably not if they're reproducing," Maggie said.

"Michael, you said the keys were here!" Maggie screamed.

"I said to wait and let me check!" Michael looked outside his window. He saw the keys glinting in the grass. "Sal must have dropped them when they took him."

"That would've been good to know before!" Maggie yelled.

Michael couldn't respond. He grabbed the door handle, but Maggie leaped across the car and slapped his hand away.

"Do NOT open that door," Alison barked from the back seat.

The gray morning turned into midnight as the car went totally dark.

"They're covering the car!" Olivia screamed.

Maggie popped on the flashlight, and Michael's stomach did a full flip when the light hit the windows. Each covered with a wriggling wall of crawling legs and snapping fangs.

"We have to get out of here," Alison whispered.

"Hold this!" Maggie handed him her light.

It snapped Michael out of his terrified fog. "What are you doing?" He pointed the light into Maggie's bag, since that was where she was looking; the reflected glow lit up the pulsing, black carpet over the windshield. Michael felt sick.

"Move," Maggie commanded, elbowing him back against the seat. "Hold the light on the steering column."

"The what?"

"Here," Maggie pointed. "Where the key goes. Just shine it there."

"Look out, Michael!" Olivia screamed. "They're coming in through the air conditioner."

Michael's stomach churned as the flies began to bubble through the air vents. He slammed them shut, crunching the bugs into a gooey mess. New panic erupted as he scanned the console for the air intake. He breathed a little easier when he saw that that the lever was already set to recirculate the air in the car since Sal had been running the air conditioner last night. "This isn't going to hold them long."

"This won't take long." Maggie had the screwdriver inserted into the key slot. She hammered it in a little farther, then twisted the handle.

The engine roared to life. The flies backed off the car, and for a moment, there was daylight, but the bugs came right back down and the car was dark again.

"Drive!" Maggie commanded.

Michael hesitated, confused by the controls.

"What are you doing? Let's go!"

"I can't see. I need the..." Michael twisted the control for the windshield wipers, smearing the glass with any gooey dead flies not bright enough or quick enough to get out of the way. He sprayed the guts with the window cleaner while shifting into drive. The engine roared, and the tires spun on the dirt and gravel, fishtailing down the driveway and out of the yard. Michael took his foot off the gas with his heart thumping and his knuckles frozen around the steering wheel. His parents' minivan was front-wheel drive. He'd never peeled out before.

"Michael, come on!" Alison screamed, her voice high with terror.

The sudden movement startled the bugs off the car. Daylight flooded in. With squeals of metal, the car careened off the trees on the left side and then on the right, but Michael managed to steer out to the street without plowing head-on into anything. Olivia was thrown against the backrest as he floored the accelerator.

"Sorry, Liv." The car careened over a curb, destroying a mailbox and part of a picket fence before fishtailing onto the street again. Everything he'd ever learned about driving was gone. There was no plan, no thought. He drove on pure instinct and reflexes.

He got to the main road, accelerating smoothly. The red needle leaned across the long rectangle of the speedometer. He was already going seventy. He hit the brakes hard, throwing everyone forward, screaming and cursing at him.

"Sorry, but this isn't the little hatchback I road-tested on!"

"Just don't run over any chocks!" Alison yelled behind him.

He didn't need that. "Not now, Alison, I swear!" In the rearview mirror, he saw that the flies could not keep up with the car, but the disgusting cloud followed at a distance.

"Michael, we have to lose these things!" Olivia pleaded.

"Working on it!" Michael relaxed his grip on the wheel and breathed deliberately to calm himself down. "I think I'm starting to get the hang of this baby."

"Just keep doing what you're doing." Maggie sounded calm and reassuring. "We've got a little space, but crashing now would be bad."

"Do NOT crash, Michael," Alison scolded.

"It's okay, they're dropping pretty far back," Michael announced when he checked the mirror again. "I think we're going to be okay."

The sky opened and rain slammed like rocks over the car. The winds kept shifting, sometimes blowing the rain straight into the windshield, sometimes straight across the hood.

Michael had the wipers turned all the way up and figured out how to get the lights on. Outside it was as dark as dusk. He stayed on the main roads until the headlights lit up the signs for the highway. He turned onto the entrance ramp for the northbound side.

In a few seconds the red needle showed eighty. Every gruesome video he'd ever seen about the dangers of hydroplaning rushed into his head. He checked the rearview mirror. There was not a fly in sight. He took his foot off the gas and slowed to sixty. Michael swelled with pride and let the car's power surge through him. It was the first time he'd driven without one of his parents in the car. Not only was he driving a big old Cadillac, his driving had saved them all.

His swagger wanted to do a victory dance, but he decided just to play it cool. Like it was no big deal, saving them all from a killer bug swarm in a hurricane. All part of a day's work. "We're going to drive up to the next exit, make sure those flies are good and gone, and then turn around and head back to The Mansion to finish this."

"Slow down," Alison said. "You're going to kill us before the monsters can."

"We're fine," Michael said, feeling confident. It wasn't like Alison had a driver's license yet. After going eighty in the rain, sixty felt like a crawl. In a few minutes, he found the exit and turned around, heading back toward Cape November and The Mansion.

"I really didn't think we were going to make it out of there," Maggie said.

"You were awesome." She smiled, making him want to drive even faster, but the traffic safety videos kept playing in his head. The rain pounded the windshield.

"Thanks," was all he could get out. He glanced over at Maggie. She was dirty and sweaty, and banged up. She had never looked hotter. "You're the real hero. You shot two of those birds and we never would have made it if you didn't get the car started."

Back in the dory, her ability to jack a car would have been just another reason for him not to trust her, to be suspicious, to judge her by the privileged, suburban, middle class values that journalists were supposed to watch out for. But now her skill just made her cool and exciting. He didn't care how many cars she might have stolen. She had saved their lives. "So how did you know how to do that?"

"What?" Maggie's eyebrow arched.

"Start the car like that?"

"Oh that," Maggie laughed. "Don't worry. I'm not a car thief. I roomed with a car thief in one of my many stays at Cartesian University Hospital. Jessica was a compulsive car thief." She held up her hands. "For the record, this was the first time I ever tried to start a car with a screwdriver. I wasn't even sure it would work." She sounded nervous when she laughed.

"Thank God it did," Alison said. He'd almost forgotten they were back there.

Maggie turned to talk to them. "Jessica always said older cars were really easy. Just bang in a screwdriver and you're on your way. Newer cars are a lot harder. You have to take apart the steering column and cut wires and stuff. Jessica got busted while she was doing one of those. And the cars they make now with electronic ignitions and the key codes and all that? Almost impossible. Anyway, it's a good thing Sal drove an old car."

Michael exited the highway and followed the signs back to Cape November. Maggie had to point out a few turns to get them heading back toward The Mansion.

As the Cadillac got closer to The Mansion's long driveway, Olivia said what Michael had been thinking as the traffic got heavier. "If nobody comes down the Cape anymore, who are all these people?"

"They must be here for the festivities," Maggie said sourly.

49 A PLAN WITH FREE BATHROBES

They were almost at the driveway. Olivia scrunched down in her seat, afraid to be noticed. The traffic reminded her of a homecoming game.

"Michael, pull over and pretend to be on the phone," Alison ordered.

"I don't have a phone."

"Just fake it!"

"Why?" Michael sounded like he thought Alison was nuts; Olivia wondered what she was thinking.

"If you're on the phone, you won't look as suspicious when you pull over."

"Okay, but why am I pulling over?"

Alison looked at Olivia, and her eyebrows wrinkled with impatience. At this point, Olivia trusted Alison almost automatically and she knew that Alison always found it irritating when other people questioned her, especially at times like this. Alison rolled her eyes. "We need a plan. How are we getting in?"

"She's right," Maggie said.

"I know I'm right," Alison snapped. Olivia rested her hand on Alison's forearm. When Alison looked at her with her eyes on fire, Olivia darted her eyes toward Maggie. Be nice," she mouthed.

Alison's face softened and her lips wrinkled down. "Maggie, I'm sorry. I didn't mean to snap at you."

Maggie kept looking out the windshield. Absently, she said, "I didn't notice."

Michael pulled to the side of the road and held his cupped hand to his face. "Okay…yeah, it's pissing rain, and we're stuck on the side of the road, surrounded by a whole church load of freaks who want to kill us…what's that? You say at least Michael drove like a boss and got everybody away from the killer fly swarm? No, I'm not sure how much longer I'm supposed to keep talking to my hand. My sister didn't tell me that part of the plan."

Even Alison started laughing. That made Olivia relax. She studied the other cars, blurry through the wet window. But then her head snapped back against the seat when Michael suddenly pulled out again. Olivia's heart thumped.

"Whoa! Where are you going?" Alison scowled. Her cheeks flashed red. "I didn't tell you to drive yet."

"Nobody put you in charge," Michael spat. "Waiting by the side of the road is only going to make people notice us more."

"Michael, hang on. We need a plan." Maggie sounded like keeping all the urgency inside was becoming a struggle for her.

Michael shrugged. "We sneak in there, find the snow globe and kick their ass. Done."

Maggie laughed. "That's not a plan." And then her face lost all its humor. "Hang on." She turned around to look at Alison. "Is he serious?"

"Michael, that's not a plan," Alison explained slowly. "It's an insult to plans."

When Michael didn't slow down or even seem like he had heard a word anybody had said, Alison started punching his arms and shoulders and slapping his head. "We can't screw this up, Michael!"

The car swerved drunkenly as Michael swatted away her hand.

"Knock it off, both of you!" Maggie barked. "If you crash it's all over."

"We can't just wait around for them to find us!" Michael roared back, slamming the wheel with his palm.

"So you want to just turn ourselves in to the sheriff?" Alison screamed back. "Why not just put a big bow on my head?"

"Don't tempt me." Michael shook his head angrily.

It was eerie how much Alison and Michael reminded Olivia of Mr. and Mrs. Nunios. It hadn't always been easy to be a fly on the wall during some of their fights, but she had learned to sit quietly and not draw attention to herself as she waited for it to pass. They were usually so focused on fighting with each other, they forgot she was even there.

"That's it!" Olivia couldn't help cheering a little, but it all made perfect sense. "We just walk right in with everybody else."

When Alison turned her angry eyes on Olivia, it made her feel horribly alone. She hated when Alison got mad at her.

"Have you lost your mind?" Alison hissed.

Olivia wondered for a moment whether she had, but as she worked it through, the plan didn't seem that crazy. "Nobody knows us except the sheriff, right? None of these regular Enlightened know us. So, all we have to do is walk in with them. Once we're inside we can just watch everything until we see what we're dealing with."

"The robes!" Maggie said.

Olivia had no idea why robes were making Maggie so happy all of a sudden.

"In the paintings, everybody had robes with hoods, remember, Michael?"

"So?" Michael gripped the steering wheel hard and stared out the front. He really was turning into his father right before Olivia's eyes.

"If we put some hoods on, they'll never even see our faces. We can hide in plain sight." Maggie leaned back triumphantly in her seat.

Alison leaned back and sighed. "That might work."

Olivia looked again at the cars out the window. None of the other drivers seemed to notice the Cadillac as Michael merged into the line rolling slowly up the gravel driveway toward The Mansion. No one was directing traffic, but all the drivers seemed to know where to go. Michael merged smoothly and stayed behind the taillights of the car in front of him.

As they came out of the woods, Olivia noticed that the circular driveway around the fountain was clogged with parked cars, trucks, SUVs and minivans. Some vehicles looked new and expensive. Others looked older and more beat up.

Michael followed the other new arrivals and parked in the line that was forming in front of the stable.

Maggie turned to Michael. "It will look suspicious if we sit here with the engine running."

Michael looked confused as he tried to figure out how to shut the engine off.

Maggie chuckled and reached across the car to twist the screwdriver and pull it out. The car rumbled a couple of moments and then was silent.

Michael raised his eyebrows and looked across at her. "Maybe I should go to reform school. You learn better stuff than I learned in regular school."

Maggie scowled wryly at him, "I beg your pardon. It was a distinguished medical facility."

"Hospital ... JuVee ... Whatever."

Olivia braced herself for Maggie to get mad, but she laughed. She must really like him.

As each car parked around them, men, women and children got out. They looked like regular people going to church. Some wore suits and sundresses. Others were in chinos and button-downs. Most of them pulled on their hooded robes quickly against the rain.

Olivia looked at The Church of New Enlightenment children, chasing their siblings through puddles, holding hands with their parents getting scolded for getting their nice clothes dirty. She tried to imagine their faces hard and angry, poking a dead cat with a bloody stick.

"Nailed it," Michael said. He held his fist up for Maggie to bump it. "See?" Michael sounded confident, like he knew all along that things would play out this way. "All we have to do now is get ourselves a couple of those bathrobes and we're in."

"The sheriff was right," Maggie scowled at him, "you have watched too much TV."

"How do we get the robes?" Alison asked.

"That's easy," Michael said brightly. "We wait for a few of them to go off alone to take a leak, then we jump them, take their robes and stuff them in the trunk of the Caddy."

"Very funny," Maggie chuckled. "Seriously."

Michael smiled at her, like he was talking to a child. "This Caddy has a huge trunk."

Maggie looked at Michael as if she was trying to swallow a jawbreaker whole.

Michael shrugged. "All we have to do is hang out over by the—"

"Slow down, cowboy," Maggie said. "Let's think this one through."

Olivia wished they would all shut up for half a second so she could think. She felt helpless and useless as everyone else talked over each other just to get their opinions heard.

"What if one of us looks around for some robes," Alison suggested. "Maybe somebody left some, like, unattended."

Michael shook his head, "There's way too many people around."

Alison smacked Michael on the shoulder. "But not too many for busting somebody on the head and stuffing them in a trunk? What is wrong with you?"

"It's totally doable." Michael said it like it was the most obvious thing in the world. He made eye contact with Olivia. She didn't know how else to make him understand. "Michael, it's a bad idea."

He leaned back into his seat and smacked the steering wheel. "Okay, I guess we'll do it your way," he grumbled. "Whatever way that is."

Olivia watched the gray clouds sliding over the ocean, soaking everything with rain. If only her head would stop hurting. She needed sleep. She took a water bottle out of her bag and sipped.

"There!" Alison pointed at a row of folding tables piled high with robes. People were grabbing them and holding them over their heads as they squelched to the boathouse. "It's just like Sheila Goldman's bat mitzvah. Remember, Liv, they handed out the little souvenir beanies for the boys who weren't Jewish."

"Yarmulkes," Olivia said.

"Told you," Michael said.

Olivia tilted her head and strained to hear a faint sound that might have been the wind. Or something else. "Do you guys hear that? Is that chanting?"

They all got quiet. The wind howled and whistled, but mixed into that, Olivia heard the hum of human voices.

"It's definitely chanting," Maggie said. Olivia saw her shiver. After hearing Maggie's story about her own parents, Olivia could not imagine how hard this all must have been for her. She put her hand on Maggie's shoulder. "You okay?"

Maggie startled, then nodded and gave Olivia's hand a squeeze. "Not really. But thanks."

"The ceremony." Alison announced. "It must be starting."

Michael started to get out, but hesitated with his hand on the door handle. "Hang on. Maybe there's another secret tunnel from The Mansion to the boathouse."

"Why would there be a second tunnel?" Maggie replied as if Michael suggested that the rain might suddenly turn into butterscotch.

Michael shrugged. "Why is there a secret cathedral under the jetty? Why are there weird monsters running around? Why is there a cult of freaks kidnapping people? Should I keep going?"

Maggie shook her head. "We can't start looking through The Mansion just hoping to find another secret passage."

"We go with Olivia's plan," Alison said.

Michael sighed. "At least her plan comes with free bathrobes." He opened his door and the storm poured in.

50 FRONT ROW SEATS

His hands ached for the reassuring handle of his axe, but they had to ditch their weapons in the car along with their backpacks. It would have been hard to carry a fireplace poker and still pull off the whole respectable church-goer look.

Besides feeling naked without his axe, Michael felt isolated under his hood. It made him nervous to be unable to make eye contact with the others. To avoid drawing attention, they didn't even whisper.

Hoping the real church members would think he was praying, he kept his head down, bobbing in time with the chanting. Alison, Olivia and Maggie better have enough sense to fake it, too. Michael had gone to enough of his friends' bar mitzvahs and confirmations to know there were busybodies in every church, even in crazy, end-of-the-world, monster-cult churches. And those busybodies were always watching out for slackers. Michael did not want to get caught by some crotchety church lady.

They hadn't discussed it first or Michael would have told Alison to find them seats as far back as possible. He couldn't understand how his sister, who was supposed to be some kind of genius, didn't see that they would be much safer in back. The Enlightened were a lot less likely to notice them, and when things went bad they'd be near the exit. But genius Alison led them right up the center aisle toward the front row. Walking last in their line, Michael couldn't even whisper a word to stop her.

Michael kept waiting for Alison to duck into any of the dozens of open seats in the middle section, but she passed row after row. As they got scary close to the doomsday painting, he cringed under his hood, waiting for one of the ushers—human ushers, not beadles—to stop them, to tell them the front section was reserved for somebody important, or at least, for somebody who belonged to the CNE. But nobody said a word.

Crazy Alison led them to the first row next to the ocean door that he and Maggie had used earlier, when they had climbed up from the tunnel. Back when the world only seemed a little bit strange.

Getting in was a lot easier the second time. Nobody had to snorkel or climb a ladder. Outside they had waited in a short line in the pouring rain for a little bit. After they picked up their white robes, following the crowd down into the empty boathouse was no problem.

The Enlightened must have worked all night to clear out all the stuff. Even the floorboards had been ripped up. Passing under the dolmen, he followed the others straight down the stone ramp toward the cathedral like it was the most normal thing in the world. It was unnerving to see the cathedral so full of life.

When he and Maggie first found it, it had seemed ancient and forgotten. But apparently, they'd been late to the party. Now the cathedral was packed with people in folding chairs acting like they owned the place. He supposed they did.

Adults, kids, old people, men, women, it didn't matter; everybody seemed to know every single weird word to every single weird prayer they were chanting, in whatever weird language they were chanting in. Michael couldn't recognize any of the words. Even the sounds were strange. European, African, Asian and Arabic languages all used sounds he knew. Human sounds. The pattern and tone of people speaking a foreign language was at least familiar, even if he didn't understand what was said. But this was like nothing he had ever heard. At times, it sounded like people weren't even making words, just grunts, chirps or coughs, all in perfect unison. The strangeness made his skin crawl.

On the way to their seats, Michael couldn't see too many faces under the hoods. A nose here, a chin there, a cheek once in a while. People's hands revealed the usual mix of skin tones he would have expected anywhere. One thing he could say about The Church of New Enlightenment, they weren't racist. Every color of whacko was welcome. He wondered whether *whacko* was another off-limits word for Maggie.

It hadn't taken Michael long to notice the difference between the people who brought their own robes and those who wore the free ones. The free ones were plain and looked cheap, like a graduation gown. The people who showed up in cheap cars got in line for the free robes. The personal robes looked thick and expensive, embroidered with harps or blue patterns that looked like tentacles. The people who wore those robes had been in the sweet cars. But everybody was sitting wherever in the cathedral. Rich or poor, everybody got the same welcome at The Church of New Enlightenment. Equal opportunity whackos. How refreshing.

The entire space was lit up with oil lamps. Even the ramp down had dozens of small lamps on shelves carved into the stone walls. Michael hadn't noticed the shelves the first time he and Maggie had gone up the ramp. Add that to the long list of things he hadn't known about then.

As they had moved farther into the cathedral, Michael saw a huge chandelier suspended in the middle of the ceiling. That hadn't been there before. The Enlightened must have brought it in and hung it just for the ceremony. If they could clean out the whole boathouse and rip up the floor, hanging a big lamp wasn't such a big deal.

The chandelier was made of dark metal, twisted into dozens of tentacles, each holding several lamps. It hung by a thick rope. Michael traced the rope up to where it looped over a pulley in the ceiling and back down to the large metal cleat anchored to the stone wall right next to the door that led out to the tunnel and the ocean. He hadn't noticed the cleat before either, but it had been dark and there had been a lot to take in the first time. He did notice that the ocean door was now open.

The lamps in the chandelier made eerie, flickering shadows. The terrible paintings glowed with rich colors, the blood reds especially vivid. Michael shivered and risked a look at the doomsday painting. Even in the lamplight he could see that the blue glow was brighter than before. The stones all around the painting seemed to be glowing blue, too, but he couldn't be sure it wasn't just a trick of the lamplight.

In front of the doomsday painting, beside the pedestal where Michael had almost broken his toe, a podium draped with a rich, blue cloth had been set up. The same cloth draped two small tables that stood behind the podium. Michael was no expert, but it looked like silk. One of the tables was empty. The other had a large, white pillow on it. The knife resting on that pillow looked like it was made of some kind of black glass. The blade was wavy on both sides, and it caught the lamplight in its edges. The point on it made his insides tingle.

A woman standing at the podium led the congregation in their chanting. Her arms were raised so that the sleeves of her blue robe sagged down, revealing her dark arms. Except for the white of her teeth, her dark face was barely visible beneath her hood. Michael had just settled in his folding chair when the chanting stopped. He glanced at the open door, and his heart raced. A door was only left open if someone, or something, was supposed to use it. Behind him, he heard the shuffling of shoes on the stone floor and the scrape of chairs as stragglers took their seats. In another moment, the cathedral was completely silent. Not a whisper, fidget or cough. He resisted the urge to turn around and make sure that people were still really sitting behind him.

His own breath and heartbeat were deafening in the overwhelming quiet. The rustle of Maggie's robe sounded like a truck. He jumped a little when her warm hand closed around his. Their fingers interlaced. A memory popped into Michael's mind. His family had gone to a big amusement park when he was nine. There was a famous roller coaster, and Michael had begged his father to take him on it. Dad hated roller coasters, but he agreed. Mom had to hang back with Alison who was throwing a massive temper tantrum because she was too short to ride.

On the coaster, Michael was strapped in and couldn't move. As it rattled and jolted up the steep slope, he went from excited to scared to petrified to panicked. He knew that once the roller coaster got over the top, there would be a terrifying fall, almost straight down. He was headed for it with no way to stop it. Just thinking about it all these years later gave him a bubbling fear deep in his gut. He remembered how he screamed and begged his father to get him off, to stop the ride. His father said that it was too late to stop, but he reached out and took Michael's hand and said that he was scared, too, but that they would do it together and everything would be okay. They rode three more times that day.

Sitting in the silent cathedral, Michael was overwhelmed by that same helpless panic. A tear dripped from his eye, and he was glad for the hood. He wanted the ride to stop, but it was too late. The fall was coming. He squeezed Maggie's hand.

Up at the podium, the lady in the blue hood stood with her fists raised. She swept them down to her sides, and with one voice, the congregation swelled into a song. Michael didn't know much about music, but whatever it was the congregation sang didn't sound like any kind of music Michael had ever heard. The jumpy, mismatched melody made him feel anxious.

People sang in a harmony that almost hurt Michael's ears, but they were all in perfect unison with each other. The woman at the podium was practically shrieking a melody that was a little different from what the crowd was singing, but fit in with it.

Somebody small in a blue cloak came up the center aisle. It looked like a kid. Middle schooler maybe? Under the hood, Michael couldn't tell. The kid held up a black metal statue of the jellyfish monster on a long wooden pole. As he reached the front, he bowed and stuck the end of the pole into a metal holder on the ground next to the podium. All part of the opening ceremony, Michael guessed. Backing away from the statue, the kid walked to the center of the doomsday painting, just in front of the stone pedestal, put up both palms and bowed low to the painting. Then he stood, back to the wall, facing the congregation.

Michael figured the singing would be loud enough to cover him, so he leaned his hood closer to Maggie and whispered. "They're killing people and everything because they think that their bogus jellyfish god wants them to do it?" He tried to whisper. "What a bunch of idiots."

Maggie rasped back, "Ganesh is half-man, half-elephant."

For a second, Michael thought Maggie had lost her mind. "Huh?"

The edges of Maggie's hood shook, giving Michael the impression that she must be shaking her head. "Never mind. Just think about how the crucifixion of Jesus looks to non-Christians. A bloody man with nails in his hands and feet? It's like worshiping a horror movie."

It was official, Michael decided. "Religions are all really weird."

The sharp poke in his back nearly stopped Michael's heart for a second. He turned around to see a short, round old woman. The robe didn't quite close around her large body, and it dragged the floor because she was so short. Her red, cooked-apple face jutted slightly from her cheap, borrowed hood. Michael could see her car wreck of a scowl when she held a thick, stubby finger up to her tight, purple lips.

Michael held up his hand and mouthed, I'm sorry.

Busybody. Michael faced the front again. She made Michael nervous. She could end up blowing the whole thing. Michael started nodding his head and moving his mouth like he was singing along.

A second kid paraded up the aisle. Long, blonde curls stuck out from the hood, so Michael guessed that this one was probably a girl. She carried a huge book with a black cover. The cover looked like it was made of leather that was old and cracked. Taking a distinct, square path, like a soldier on guard duty, the girl set the book on the podium, went through the same bowing routine and joined the first kid by the wall.

Alison and Olivia gasped at the same time. Michael looked up the aisle and saw the four black-hooded robes. His heart skipped a little. These were only human-sized, too short for beadles. He heard the clinking and spotted their ankle and wrist chains. The hoods were more like black sacks thrown over their heads. But what turned his stomach was the neck chain that joined them together, and the small, robed child holding the chain, like a kid out walking a dog.

The old bat behind him could drop dead for all Michael cared. He squeezed Maggie's hand and shook it to her attention.

She pulled her hand free and turned to glare at him. "That hurt," she hissed.

"Sorry." He leaned close and whispered, "Look. There's four of them. That's probably Olga and her family."

Maggie looked the four prisoners over. "I don't know. Maybe. We have to wait."

"Seriously, what kind of sick religion chains people up?"

Maggie took his hand again. "Just about all of them at one time or another."

He felt a sharp poke in his back. When Michael turned around to pretend to apologize to the old woman, he used the opportunity to look over the rest of the procession.

Michael's stomach went all wiggly. Even in the blue hood, Michael recognized the short, bloated nastiness of Sheriff McGill. He walked—waddled—behind the prisoners and carried a large, white pillow. Michael felt his breath catch when he saw the snow globe, sitting like a large jewel in the middle of the pillow. He glanced at Alison. She was biting her lip so hard it was ready to bleed.

The child made the prisoners kneel along the wall right in front of Michael and the others, and then he went back toward the congregation. Probably to join his parents, Michael assumed.

The prisoners faced the congregation, but the sacks still covered their faces. The sheriff gave the singer a brief nod as he passed the podium to place the snow globe on its pillow on top of the empty table. He bowed like the kids had and took his place next to the prisoners.

Fear and rage gnawed Michael's insides. The sheriff was only ten feet away. All any of them needed to do was look up at the wrong time and the sheriff would spot them. At the same time, he felt a powerful urge to jump out of his seat and beat the sheriff to death with his bare hands no matter what the consequences. Clenching his teeth, he bowed his head and pulled his hood a little lower and turned to watch the rest of the procession.

The last person Michael saw in the twisted little parade appeared to be a man. He was tall and thin, and since he was the only one in a green robe, Michael figured he must have been the main priest.

The priest walked slowly and held a harp high over his head, the symbol of The Church of New Enlightenment. The frame looked like it was made out of the same kind of stone as everything else around The Mansion. The strings were shiny silver. There was a ripple going through the song because each time the harp passed a row, the people stopped singing to gasp or to utter words, prayers probably, in their weird language.

By the time the priest brought the harp to the front, the singing reached a loud climax. The leader raised her fists, crossing her wrists. All at once, the voices snapped off. The tiniest echo wobbled in the stone ceiling and then, deep silence.

The priest stood in front of the doomsday painting mumbling. Michael lost count of how many times he bowed, still holding the harp over his head. Then, like he was handling explosives, he gently set the curve of the harp into the groove of the pedestal. There was a quiet scrape when the stone met stone.

Keeping his hood low, Michael looked out from under the tops of his eyelids, hoping to sneak a glimpse of the sheriff. The sheriff's hood was pulled back just enough to show his face. His pale, round cheeks puffed out, his thin lips curved around his nubby teeth. The sheriff's smile was as cruel as a kick to the gut. Michael didn't understand why he was smiling. Who was he looking at? It was someone in their row. Michael leaned forward and turned. Maggie and Olivia's hoods pointed almost straight at the floor. Alison's pointed straight at the sheriff.

51 RIGHT AND WRONG

Alison was done hiding. She glared at the sheriff, hoping he could feel all the fire and ice raging in her. He smiled at her. He would smile just to scare her, like he knew something. Some secret. He was playing with her just to torment her. Like those kids with the dead cat. But Alison was no cat. The sheriff and the rest of The Church of New Enlightenment didn't know her, but they would find out.

The string bean-looking old guy in the green robe took his place behind the podium. The singer stood next to the sheriff behind Olga, Sal, Tony and Vinnie. Alison hadn't seen their faces; they were still wearing bags over their heads, but four prisoners? Who else could they be?

The priest pulled a long, green ribbon that had been marking a page in the big book. Lifting his arms in prayer, his green sleeves slid down revealing his arms. They looked scrawny and white, like a skeleton's.

Looking down at the book, only the priest's bony chin stuck out from the bottom of his hood. Seeing him tied a knot in Alison's stomach. He looked too much like a beadle. Alison looked carefully at the priest's lips and teeth, at the bones of his chin and what she could see of his cheeks. His skin looked so old, thin and brittle as his lips creased into a scowl that Alison thought the old guy might tear if he moved his mouth.

The priest let his stick arms flop to his side, and he let out a big, exasperated-sounding breath as he rotated the book on the podium. Alison snickered, enjoying the fact that for their big ceremony, some dumb kid had put the book upside down on the podium.

The priest's hood turned toward the girl who had carried the book. Alison knew he was glaring at her under his hood. Poor kid. Her blonde curls sagged down her shoulders as she bowed her head to face the floor. It seemed like she was shaking under her robe. Alison felt a hot wave of pity for her. She was just some girl who probably only got mixed up in this church because her parents had basically brainwashed her.

With the book going the right way, the priest lifted his stick-arms again and began chanting in a slow singsong that reverberated from the stone walls and the domed ceiling. Alison had no idea what the priest was saying. Alison wondered if he used a language she had even heard of. She sure didn't recognize it, and it sounded awful. Just hearing the chant gave her a clanging, jarring feeling inside.

It felt as if the chanting went on forever. When the priest wasn't chanting, everyone else was. Sometimes they all chanted together. Finally, the woman came back to the podium to lead another song. Olivia dug her nails into Alison's hand. Alison yelped and turned to look at her.

Olivia still managed to look stunning, even when furious. "Why did you look at the sheriff? You made eye contact on purpose; don't even act like you didn't." Olivia was freaking out so badly, it was almost funny.

"I know."

"He knows we're here now!" she hissed.

"I wanted him to know." Alison didn't expect Olivia to understand. "It looks like his master plan is just to bore us to death, anyway."

"Except for the people kneeling with bags on their heads! We can't screw this up, and now you blew our cover."

Alison studied Olivia. Her eyes were red from crying, her caramel skin was drawn tight over flawless cheekbones. Her full, perfect lips were puckered tight. Olivia always worried. Getting caught or getting judged or what people thought of her. She worried about disappointing her teachers or her coaches or her parents. Even of disappointing Alison.

"I don't want cover," Alison stated. She turned back to the sheriff and faintly, up her wrists and elbows, she again felt the thud of the monk's smashed head. "I want to kill him."

She felt Olivia's tight grip on her hand. Surprised, she turned back. Olivia had tears in her eyes. "No!" She rasped.

Alison's breath caught in her throat. "No what?"

Olivia's scowl was hard. Her eyes were blazing. "You can't just kill him, Alison. I won't let you."

Alison wasn't sure whether to laugh or slap Olivia across the face. "He's got my parents. If not him, one of these douchebags." She nodded to the rest of the congregation.

Olivia shook her head. "There's right and there's wrong, Alison."

"Yeah! We're right and they're wrong." Tears stung her eyes. She couldn't believe Olivia was even saying this. "They kill people. Look at those prisoners up there. You think they're going to give them hot chocolate and crepes?"

Olivia nodded. "I know. You might have to kill him to save them, just like you killed the old monk to save me. But if you plan on killing him, just to punish him or to stop him, or just because you hate him, then how are you any better than they are?" She shook her head. "You always push it, Alison. You need to stop."

"Push what?" Alison struggled to whisper when all she wanted to do was scream.

"The way you get into trouble, break rules, do bad things like stealing the snow globe."

"If I didn't steal it you would have died." Alison tried to breathe away the fire Olivia was lighting inside her.

Olivia's eyes looked wide, wild and desperate. "Alison, you have to promise me that you know the difference. That you know the limits."

"Of what?" She pulled her hand out of Olivia's.

Olivia grabbed her hand back and would not let Alison pull away again. "Of right and wrong. Of good and bad." Olivia grabbed Alison's face and forced their eyes to meet.

Alison looked into the face of an angel. Olivia had so many gifts, but she was weak. "There are no limits," she spat.

Olivia grabbed the back of Alison's neck under her hood, hard enough to hurt. "You're wrong, Alison. There are limits." Her grip relaxed and Olivia tried to pull Alison into a hug, but Alison stiffened up and pulled way. Olivia looked afraid. She bit her perfect lower lip.

"You're too good for me now? Don't worry, I'm sure the rich girls at your new goody two-shoes academy are all better than me." It terrified Alison how much she suddenly hated Olivia. She would not cry. "I killed that old man for you, and you're going to judge me and give me a lecture about morals? You'd be dead if I were as weak as you."

Olivia pulled her hand away. She was devastated. "You're wrong, Alison." Olivia retreated into her hood. Alison could barely hear her. "If you ever tried, you'd see how hard it is to do the right thing."

She suddenly felt so empty. Alison ached to take back everything she'd just said. But it was too late. The words were already out there. She reached for Olivia's hand, expecting her to pull away. Relief and shame washed through her like two streams of hot and cold water.

"You're right, Olivia," Alison whispered. She could not even count the times Olivia had worked so hard and had taken so many risks to keep Alison from doing stupid things. And she always stuck by her when Alison didn't listen to her. "You're always right. I'm sorry. For everything. I'm... I'm lucky I have you."

Olivia turned back to Alison. Her flawless cheeks were red and streaked with tears. "I'm lucky, too, Allie. That's why, if we make it out of this—"

"When we make it out of this."

Olivia smiled and might have even laughed a little. "When we make it out of this, Alison, you still need to be you."

When they hugged, neither pulled away.

52 TANGLED

Michael heard the commotion coming from Alison and Olivia, but he had no way to shut them up. The lump in his throat went down when nobody else around them said or did anything about it. Even the busybody behind him didn't poke anybody. Whatever was going on with them, the sheriff must have liked it. His smile got bigger and bigger, and he started licking his wet lips with his dark tongue, like he was slurping up a slug. Revolted, Michael looked away.

After the last song, there was a long, silent pause. The priest stood with his head bowed. The congregation bowed their heads, too.

The priest looked up and pulled back his hood enough to show his face, framed with stringy, white hair. Gaunt and pale, the man looked like he was in desperate need of a cheeseburger. The priest cleared his throat and surprised Michael by speaking perfect English.

"Friends, we are truly blessed to be alive. The deliverance of He That Is Magnificent is finally realized." His voice seemed way too strong to be coming out of such a scrawny old man.

"How long our people have waited? Since the Earth was young. That was when He That Is Magnificent first called his faithful servant, Kar." The priest opened his hands and gestured around the cathedral. "It was here that Kar first learned his purpose and ours. We walk in his footsteps and finish the task that he set out for us as told to him by He That Is Magnificent."

The priest gripped the sides of the podium and leaned toward the congregation. "For too long has He That Is Magnificent been in bondage. For too long have we had to keep the faith by crouching in shadows, hunted and persecuted by the ignorant and the infidels." The priest choked back a sob. "No more! This is the joyous day when all shall be enlightened. The infidels will suffer and die! He That Is Magnificent shall feast on their misery and grow strong! Thus shall the Earth become his plaything!" The priest's voice echoed from the bare stones.

Something moved to Michael's right. He felt his blood clot in his arteries when a beadle came squirming through the ocean door. And then another. And then there were three. And then four. These were bigger than the ones from the van. Much bigger, maybe twice as tall as Michael. They stood in a line behind the four kneeling prisoners.

"It is time to free He That Is Magnificent!" called the priest. He took his place at the harp, just like in the painting. The melody was haunting and hypnotic; achingly tender and beautiful, but also eerie and evil. The melody grew as the priest played faster and the tune got more complex. He threw his head back and cried out almost continuously, but whether in pleasure or pain, Michael couldn't tell. It sounded both familiar and strange. Michael was drawn to it and repelled at the same time. Maggie squeezed his hand tight.

As the priest played, the glow from the painting became stronger. The stones around it glowed, too. Michael noticed that all the stones, the whole cathedral, pulsed with blue light that kept getting brighter.

The sheriff walked behind each prisoner and, one by one, snatched off each hood. Olga's eyes were closed, and her mouth moved. Michael figured she was praying. Sal and Vinny knelt stone-faced and silent with tears streaming down their cheeks. Tony's hood came off. He blinked and looked around, and then the cathedral filled with his operatic voice. His *Ave Maria* shook the stones.

The blue light dimmed slightly, but Michael noticed. Based on the people he heard shouting and crying out behind him, everybody else noticed, too, and they didn't sound happy about it. The priest scowled like he was annoyed, but he kept playing.

The sheriff laughed, snatched the knife from the table and plunged it into Tony's chest. His beautiful voice gurgled and choked. He collapsed to the stones. Behind him, Michael heard gasps. A few screams. Children cried. The stones glowed brighter again.

"No!" Alison shrieked, leaping out of her seat. There was a blur of movement in the aisle. It was the old busybody who had poked him. Michael couldn't believe she could run so fast. She charged the sheriff, blindsiding him. She snatched the knife from his hands and hacked the rope that held the chandelier.

Michael jumped up and turned in time to watch the Enlightened knock over chairs and one another, but they couldn't get out of the way. The massive, black tentacles crashed down on them. People under the wreckage screamed. The lamps shattered and splashed flaming oil over them. Some people cried and called out names. Michael saw the child who had led the prisoners in on the chain. His white robe was spattered red. His hood was off, and blood streamed over his face from a gash on his head. The child screamed for his mother. Michael felt a lump of pity and horror in his gut. And then the back of Michael's shoulders crawled when the rest of the congregation didn't lift a finger to help the people crushed and burning under the chandelier. Instead they started singing a melody that matched the tune of the harp. Michael clenched his jaw and his fists as he finally recognized the tune. It was the song Maggie had sung about Cappy.

Snapping his head around to look at her, Maggie's hood was off. She screamed and lunged forward, but Olivia held her wrist. Maggie sank to her knees as the sheriff, still laughing, sank the knife into Vinny and then Sal. The old busybody lay crumpled at the sheriff's feet.

Electric thunder sizzled and the wall behind the priest erupted in blue lightning. It spread, radiating until the entire painting seemed to glow from behind. It looked as if a powerful blue fire, as bright as the sun, burned through the painting from the other side. Michael squinted and had to block the light with his sleeve.

Dizzy and disoriented, he struggled to understand what he was seeing; it didn't matter whether or not he believed it. Behind the priest there was no wall anymore. The whole back of the cathedral was gone except the floor. Michael wasn't just looking outside through a window; he *was* outside. A cold, salty wind blew in his face. He could hear the rolling green waves that crashed along the beach in front of him. His breath came in shallow bursts. His heart was a drumroll throbbing in his head. He turned to check the back of the cathedral. Past the broken bodies under the chandelier, people still sang. Everything was still underground and still made of stone blocks. They were glowing, but they were still solidly there.

But the front of the cathedral stuck out like a tongue onto a beach of swirling red dust and pointy rocks that stretched far off to the left and the right where gray mountains loomed in the distance like jagged teeth. All of it under a churning sky, the color of old bruises. Over the rolling thump of the waves, Michael heard a sucking gurgle from far out in the water. Looking down the slope of rust-colored dirt, something huge boiled under the green ocean. If he didn't sit, he was afraid he'd pass out.

The priest kept playing, the congregation kept singing, but the sound seemed to come from the stones of the cathedral. They glowed almost white.

Back on her feet, the old woman screamed. Knocking the singer aside, she grabbed the snow globe off its pillow and held it over her head in both hands. The triumphant glow on her face melted away. The snow globe stayed dark.

"It's not yours anymore," the sheriff called in his wet voice. Michael heard him clearly over the terrifying music. She didn't make a sound as he slid the knife into her belly. She dropped to the floor. The dark bloodstain spread through her white robe, pooling on the stones.

Michael's heart raced. He had no axe. He had nothing. He looked at Maggie, but her face told him that she was as desperate and bewildered as he. He looked over at Olivia. She snatched at Alison's robe, but Alison slipped out of it and ran to the front.

Michael jumped forward as the sheriff turned to stab Olga. Alison caught his wrist. Michael's heart froze. The sheriff laughed and backhanded her to the ground, holding the wicked point of the knife to her throat, drawing a single drop of blood. Michael stopped and raised his hands, surrendering.

One of the beadles snaked its tentacles around her arms, legs and chest. Others wrapped Michael, Maggie and Olivia. Michael waited for the pain of the stingers, but nothing came. He looked at the others. The only one who squirmed and struggled was Alison who was too stubborn to realize that they had lost and that they were going to die.

Throwing back his hood to reveal his smooth, slimy-looking head, the sheriff showed his nubby teeth. It made Michael sick.

"Not to worry," the sheriff croaked. "Their stingers are retractable. I bet you didn't know that." Alison struggled in the tentacles. Maggie and Olivia stood still, their faces creased with fear. At Michael's feet, the old woman was curled up like a baby on the floor, moaning softly. She might have been crying.

Over the thunder of the music, the sheriff laughed. "Honestly, I am glad you were stupid enough to try and stop all this. I really didn't think you'd have the guts, but I suppose you had no choice since you think we have your parents."

"You do!" Alison snarled. A tentacle wrapped her throat, but the sheriff patted it, and it stopped tightening.

"As much as it pains me to say it, Miss Nunios, we don't."

Alison's eyebrows knitted together. Her mouth moved, but she didn't say anything.

The sheriff looked down at the old woman, moaning on the floor, trying uselessly to stop the flow of blood out of her gut with her wet, red hands. He turned his mirrored lenses back to Michael. "The beadles that have you will not move an inch unless I tell them to. They're like living ropes when they need to be. You're welcome to try and wiggle out. Fun is fun, right? Just know that when it's time, these beadles are going to peel your flesh from your bones and rip your heads right off your bodies. It will be slow agony." Chuckling, the sheriff turned to Alison. "Miss Nunios, you get to be the last to die. He That Is Magnificent will savor your suffering when you watch the people you love die a slow, horrible death." The sheriff chuckled and shook his head.

The old woman moaned as the sheriff picked up the snow globe from the pool of blood. It smeared the pillow red when he put it back.

Michael clenched his fists and squirmed in the tentacles. He felt as if he was being strangled by a boa constrictor. He clenched his body as his thoughts hammered his head. They could have left town. They didn't need to be here. Not for any of it. His parents weren't here. They were dying for nothing! He looked at Maggie. Her hood had come off when the beadle had grabbed her. She was crying and looked sadly up at him.

"I'm so sorry, Michael!" she cried, shaking her head. "I'm so sorry I dragged you into this. This is all my fault."

Guilt bit him sharply, right in the heart. Guilt and shame. Her parents were dead. And this church of murderers was opening a wormhole or whatever to bring in a monster. Just like Olivia thought.

Michael knew it didn't matter where he was. He was in this. They all were. He struggled to break free, to go to Maggie. To hold her and tell her it was all right. "I'm not sorry. None of this is your fault, Maggie. We had to help you." Michael slammed his head back into the gummy wall behind him. The beadle didn't move. "We had to try."

She closed her eyes. "I've been trying, Michael. Look where it got me." She hung limp in the creature's grip. "And now look where it got you. All of you."

He looked over at Alison, still screaming and thrashing, trying to get out. Seeing her sparked him. Alison wasn't giving up. Neither would he. "Hey!" Maggie opened her eyes and found him. "This isn't over yet."

53 IMPOSSIBILITIES

Alison's head swam. The back of the cathedral had magically turned into a beach. Not magic, Alison reminded herself. It was just like Olivia had said, The Church of New Enlightenment had opened a wormhole. Apparently nobody bothered to tell them that wormholes shouldn't exist.

Far down the beach, in front of the mountains, things were moving. Alison recognized them as the stewards. Her breath stopped. There must have been a hundred. More, probably. She ached for all those poor people, killed to make beadles. *Beadles. If there are stewards…*

The water seethed and churned as hundreds of beadles crawled out of the water. They stood dripping in the surf for a moment before lumbering up the beach. The army of beadles and stewards closed on the cathedral. In a few more minutes they would be inside. But Alison could not even think about how that was going to play out because out in the dark water, impossibly huge, a new nightmare bubbled up.

Alison startled and yelped when something grabbed her ankle. Not a monster. It was the old woman. Tracing her trail of blood across the stones, Alison felt sick and angry. But when she recognized the old woman from the gift shop, it was as if her brain shorted out. She couldn't think at all. "You!"

"Who is she?" Michael demanded. "You know her?"

The old woman coughed blood. "The Neumenon is yours now."

Alison didn't understand. She looked up at Olivia, who must have recognized the old woman, too, because her mouth was a shocked circle.

Thrashing against the smothering tentacles, Alison screamed at the old woman. "What is it? What are you saying?"

The old woman rolled onto her back. Dark red goo leaked out of her teeth when she tried to smile. "I tried to make you leave, to keep you safe. I had already killed one. More would come. I didn't think it would choose you." The old woman's eyes closed.

"What would? What chose me?"

"The Noumenon," the old woman said. She half smiled, but her forehead was creased with pain. Her head lolled. She coughed up more blood. "I didn't want you to have it. Too dangerous." She smiled through her red teeth. The old woman's eyes drooped closed.

"Who is this woman?" Michael was nearly screaming. "What's happening?"

Alison looked over at the snow globe on the stained pillow and then up at Olivia. Olivia nodded forcefully. She thought the woman was talking about the snow globe, too. The old woman's eyes were still closed. Alison screamed and pushed against the tentacles. The old woman couldn't die. She wasn't allowed to die. Alison had to understand. "What do you mean it chose me? What is it? What do I do?"

Alison pushed and pulled against the tentacles, but they were solid. "The snow globe? It's called the Noumenon? What's that mean? Hey! I'm talking to you!"

Screaming again, Alison battered her head against the beadle's body. It was like hitting a leather sofa. Her wrists burned and bled as she thrashed to pull out of the thing's grip. Out of breath and with her heart pounding, Alison had to rest. Sweat poured down her back.

"Why do you know her?" Michael asked.

Alison looked at him. His face was tense and confused. She looked back at the snow globe, the Noumenon, again. "She's the old woman from the gift shop."

"Where you got the snow globe?" Michael's voice cracked. His black hair was plastered on his head with sweat.

"Yeah," Alison said. "The Noumenon."

"What is it?" Michael looked at Olivia. Olivia shook her head.

Movement out on the beach caught Alison's eye. The sheriff stood with Olga on the top of the beach. He hoisted her by her neck chain so that only her toes scraped the ground.

Still on the harp, the priest yelled over the noise in his huge voice, "We present He That Is Magnificent with a final gift to bind our covenant. The old woman has suffered much, and her suffering gives strength to He That Is Magnificent."

Looking down the beach, Alison knew the army of monsters would be on them in less than a minute. The sheriff raised the knife over Olga. She looked up into the sky and moved her mouth, praying. Alison closed her eyes and turned away as the sheriff brought the knife down. When she looked again, her stomach convulsed and her eyes burned with tears. Olga was just a crumpled heap on the ground.

The priest called out in his other language, but then he spoke in English. "He That Is Magnificent, we beg of you to come and enlighten our world!"

Maggie screamed. "The thing from the painting!"

Past the priest who still played the harp, and past the sheriff who turned to face it, Alison watched the white mass that grew out of the crashing waves. Through the huge curtain of water flowing off its sides, Alison saw the oozy creature rise, like the birth of a white, blubbery mountain.

She held her breath as the horror cleared the waterline. A city block would have fit inside the cavern at the top of its fleshy, white head. That giant mouth was lined with pointy teeth the size of school buses. Alison felt weak and sick when she saw the hundreds of massive feelers squirming all around under the thing's head from where its neck should be. Each feeler was long as a skyscraper.

The creature soared up on dozens of tentacles, each as massive as an office tower. They undulated like the legs on a centipede, carrying the monstrosity onto the dust and toward the cathedral. As it loomed on the edge of the beach, it raised one of its stadium-sized lobster claws.

The horde of beadles paused and rushed off to the left. The stewards turned around to run back in the direction they had come from. For a second, Alison thought they were running away from it. She looked at Olivia, but she was as bewildered at Alison.

Closing her eyes, Maggie tilted her head to the side and arched her eyebrow. "Listen! Do you hear that sound?"

"All I hear is singing," Michael said.

"No. There's something else, too," Maggie said.

"Thunder?" Olivia suggested.

Alison caught the low, steady rumble.

"No," Michael said. "Sounds more like a plane or a helicopter. Maybe it's the army!" Michael's eyes were round and enthusiastic.

"No!" Maggie gasped. She closed her eyes tight and screamed, squirming and thrashing against the beadle. It didn't move. She looked up at Alison, her eyes pleading. She sounded breathless. "It can't be, but I'd know that sound anywhere!" She threw her head back and cried out.

Looking out to the beach, Alison saw a large, red plume, rising like a dust devil behind the army of stewards. They weren't running away; they were charging whatever it was that made the dust and the rumble. The monster turned its massive body slowly, and with a whistling rush, it's claw cut the air and hit the beach like a meteor. Alison felt the shock in her chest. Seconds later, bits of rock rained on the cathedral, but nobody stopped singing. Not even when the cloud of red dust wafted in from the beach like a fog, making Alison choke. The church people coughed and hacked, but everybody still sang.

On the beach, Alison saw a bobbing light cut through the dust cloud. The rumbling roar became louder and clearer. Alison recognized the sound of a motor. The circle of light got bigger, and then she saw a blurry outline. In another few seconds, she gave up on trying to understand why she was seeing a man on a motorcycle.

54 SACRIFICE

It was the motorcycle that gave Olivia a strange giddy feeling that this whole thing might be a dream after all; that reality had slipped away and she was stuck in a delusion. Of course, if she had lost her mind and this whole thing were just a hallucination, she had no way to know it. She would have to wake up to know whether she was dreaming, and she'd already tried to wake herself from this nightmare too many times.

She tugged at the tentacles around her. Firm and thick as fire hoses, they felt real enough, but that didn't prove anything. Things always felt real in dreams, and anyway Olivia felt as awake as she had ever felt in her life. If reality was the thing that didn't change no matter what she thought about it, then this improbable wormhole with its improbable aliens was reality. Whether she experienced things that existed only in her own mind or that existed out in the world beyond her didn't matter. Either way, she was stuck in those tentacles and people were dying.

Michael wore a pained expression as he tried to muscle his way out. Maggie had her eyes closed, hands moving under her robe as she tried to break free. Sweat smeared the dirt that blended with the freckles on Alison's red cheeks. This was no dream, and these monsters were not a nightmare. They were aliens. Just thinking that ran against everything Olivia had ever understood. An alien the size of a mountain, that had no business being here, was lumbering out of the ocean, heading for her world through a wormhole that shouldn't exist.

Olivia could accept all that. The thing that could have only made sense in the sideways logic of a dream was the man riding a motorcycle through that army of aliens.

Even if there were a hole through spacetime that led to another universe, and even if that other universe had a planet in it with dangerous aliens who wanted to get to Earth, why was there also a very human-looking man on a very Earth-looking motorcycle?

Looking again, she realized she'd been wrong. It was two human men on a motorcycle. The bike was enormous, and it smashed stewards out of the way like toys. They spun off the sides of the huge faring or were crushed under its fat wheels. That gave Olivia a little lift of hope, even as it made her feel like she was slipping farther away from sanity.

The biker was one of the biggest men Olivia had ever seen. He would have stood out on a professional football field or wrestling ring. His dirty blonde hair and long goatee blew around under his black helmet and large, spattered goggles. A few beadles had gotten close enough to swipe at him, but their tentacles slid off the biker's leather jacket, apparently without hurting him.

The second man was short and scrawny with a bushy white moustache. Olivia hadn't noticed him at first because he'd been hidden behind the enormous biker. He wore a silver helmet and a white suit. Olivia thought the biker had been protecting the little guy, but she realized she'd had it backwards. The man in the suit was holding off the aliens with a shotgun that he fired from the back of the motorcycle.

"I can't believe it!" Maggie's eyes bugged out and tears streamed down her face.

Olivia's mind put the pieces together, and it clicked like an anagram puzzle. "Is that your grandfather and your uncle?"

Maggie screamed and beat her body against the beadle. "Let me go! I have to get to them!"

"What's happening?" Michael demanded.

"It's them!" Maggie cried. "I don't know how, but it's them!"

"It's her missing uncle and her grandfather!"

Michael looked back out as Max smashed the motorcycle through the mob of stewards and beadles, skidding to a stop on the cathedral's stones next to the priest.

"That is not what I was expecting," Michael said.

The smaller man, Maggie's grandfather Olivia assumed, hopped off the back and aimed the shotgun at the priest, who shrieked and backed away, holding his hands up.

Olivia looked around at the glowing stones, waiting for the wormhole to close since the priest had stopped playing the harp, but nothing changed. Another strand frayed off her tiny thread of hope.

Maggie's grandfather snatched the harp out of its groove on the pedestal and looked around. The wormhole still stood open, and monstrosities continued to close in.

"Dagnabbit! We're too late for Plan B, Max. Back to Plan A!" Maggie's grandfather turned and blasted the face of a beadle that approached him. The thing fell backwards into other beadles. Horror slithered through Olivia's gut when the other beadles fell on the dead one in a feeding frenzy.

Max put the motorcycle on its kickstand and snatched the harp from the small man, spiking it to the ground. A twisting shriek echoed through the stones, piercing Olivia's ears. The others winced, too. Even the beadles twitched. The stones pulsed with the sound and the wormhole flickered, but stayed intact.

The little man snatched the harp back. "That ain't gonna work, ya' chucklehead!"

The priest looked around and made a small, dancing leap. His old, withered face grinned like a skeleton's. "You're too late! The gateway is fully charged. Nothing can stop that which has been foretold!"

The biker punched the priest in the face. The ancient man's head snapped back and he sprawled onto the sand. In less than a second, he was shrieking as three stewards pulled him apart. Beadles devoured the pieces.

Beadles and stewards surrounded the two men at the pedestal, but three more blasts from the shotgun drove them back. Maggie's grandfather reloaded with shells from the pocket of his suit jacket and fired off a few more rounds. The beadles that didn't fall and the stewards that weren't staggering around drunkenly with their faces shot in joined the main horde pouring into the cathedral from the beach. Olivia had to close her eyes when the monsters grabbed the worshipers closest to the front. The stones echoed with panicked screams and shrieks of men, women and children.

"I thought they were all on the same side!" Michael screamed.

Olivia felt nauseous as two screaming people in robes tried to pull a child away from a hungry beadle. She squeezed her eyes shut. Who could possibly suffer more than those parents? Their child was dying a horrible death because their religion had betrayed them and sold them a lie. Olivia hated how right she had been. This religion was a perfect food source for a telepathic creature that thrived on suffering.

Feeling sick and shaky, Olivia understood perfectly. This was no god. It didn't care who worshipped it. It was just an animal looking for a meal. No different from a bear in a garbage dumpster. Except this bear was telepathic and half-a-mile tall.

The Enlightened who escaped the first wave trampled over each other, scrambling for the ramp. Olivia refused to open her eyes, and she screamed to block out the sounds of people getting ripped apart by the stewards and fed to the beadles.

Olivia forced herself to concentrate on the science problem in front of her. The beadles were offspring of the creature, but they needed more than just suffering, she realized. They were carnivorous. Based on the teeth around the giant thing's mouth, it needed meat, too. Like a Venus flytrap, Olivia realized.

The tentacles felt cold and leathery around her. She shivered, wondering how much longer the thing trapping her would obey whatever command had told it to remain motionless. The ones that held them were larger than the others, so Olivia assumed they were older. Older dogs usually obeyed commands better than puppies. Was it the same for the beadles? Olivia's heart beat faster as she wondered when the pheromones, sonar or telepathic signal would spread the feeding frenzy to the beadles holding them.

Olivia screamed as the beadle holding Maggie jerked. Their time was up. But the beadle's tentacles snapped open. Maggie's arms were loose, and she stabbed and slashed the tentacles with the hunting knife from her belt. In another second, she twisted loose and stood on the floor. She spun and sunk the knife into the beadle over and over until it was on the ground. And then she stabbed it through the back of the head. Twice.

Olivia felt the tentacles around her own neck squeeze a little tighter. Something wet dripped down her face. With a sickening shudder, Olivia realized the beadle was drooling. She knew she didn't have much time.

"Uncle Max!" Maggie screamed when a steward made a grab for the biker, but Max caught it by the throat, lifted it off its feet and smashed it into the ground. While stomping it into paste with his boots, Max pulled his goggles up onto his helmet and squinted. "Maggie? How did you get here?" He tilted his head. "You look different."

Olivia couldn't have processed Max's words, even if she didn't feel dozens of razor teeth scraping gently down her head. Maggie turned and pointed at her, screaming to Max, "Help them! Get them out!"

The confused look that had tied up Max's lips turned into a furious sneer. He charged. The last thing Olivia saw before the beadle's mouth closed over her face was the sheriff running, as much as his bulk would let him, toward the Noumenon.

Olivia felt cold wetness inside the thing's mouth. The rotten, fishy stench would have made her vomit, but spongy tissue covered her mouth and nose, cutting off her air. Its teeth were around her neck. She knew she was dead. She waited for the bite that would decapitate her, or for hidden mouthparts to start burrowing into her brain. She was afraid of the pain, and her heart ached for her parents. The wet mass on her face stifled her last sob.

Wind blew over her cheeks. Gasping for air and spitting out the thing's oily saliva, she blinked away the goo until she recognized Maggie, standing in front of her with her knife, stabbing and slashing the beadle's tentacles. They recoiled away from Olivia. She fell to her knees, coughing and heaving onto the stones.

"Move!" Maggie barked. Olivia saw the huge bulk of the beadle falling toward her. She rolled out of the way and it fell on its face. Its back and head were full of gashes and holes where Maggie had perforated it.

Still on her hands and knees, Olivia noticed the sheriff, right in front of her, reaching for the snow globe. Olivia sprang and grabbed his wrist. She regretted biting him as her mouth filled with a slimy saltiness and the taste of rotten meat.

She spat as he snarled and punched at her face. Ducking, Olivia felt his hand brush over her hair. His wild swing sent his bulk off balance. Shoving him, he toppled to his side.

Olivia grabbed the Noumenon as the sheriff drew his pistol. Olivia tensed, waiting for the pain to explode in her chest. She jerked when she heard him fire. It took her a moment to realize that the whistling that had gone by her face was a bullet.

Opening her eyes, she saw Maggie's knife sticking out of the side of the sheriff's chest. Maggie jumped for the snow globe, snatched it off the pillow and sprinted. Another shot rang out, and a chunk of the wall disintegrated next to her as she ducked out the door.

The beadle holding Alison dropped her and shambled after Maggie. Olivia ran to help Alison up, but turned when she heard a dull, wet thwack. Max landed on his feet, holding a dented folding chair. The tentacles on the last beadle recoiled, and Michael rolled to his feet. Max beat the beadle to the ground with the dented chair. When it stopped flailing, Max charged the sheriff.

Olivia jumped when another shot rang out. The chair spun out of Max's hands and clattered to the floor. Olivia's heart pounded. She was shaking.

"Nice shot, man," Max called wryly. For a guy who just got shot at in the middle of this insane nightmare, Max didn't seem rattled.

The handle of the knife still protruded from the sheriff's side. The blade must have been blocking an artery, Olivia figured. There wasn't any blood.

The sheriff hauled himself to his feet. His eyes narrowed cruelly, and he leveled his pistol at Max. The sheriff made a crooked smile. "I was aiming for your head."

The next shot rang off the ceiling. The sheriff staggered and sank to his knees. Michael stood over him with a chair. He swung again and brought the chair down squarely onto the sheriff's head. When he fell to his face on the stones, Michael gave him the finger, his face a triumphant grin. "That's for the ticket!"

"Far out." Grinning in his wild goatee, Max nodded to Michael. "Thanks, kid."

Without a word, Michael ran into the doorway after the beadle that had gone after Maggie. Some rational part of Olivia's brain told her it had only been a few seconds, but alone with a beadle it was an eternity. Her stomach balled itself up with fear and horror.

"Y'all got company!" Olivia looked over to where Maggie's grandfather called from the harp pedestal. He shot another beadle. Another steward. Another beadle. And then he knelt next to the pedestal. Olivia was too far away to see the details, but he was doing something with a small, silver box and a nest of wires. Sabotage, Olivia guessed.

At least thirty more beadles and stewards surged up from the beach, into the cathedral. Some ran after the fleeing Enlightened, but most wheeled toward Olivia and the others. What got her heart racing wasn't the stampede of the alien nightmares. She was getting used to those. There were at least a dozen feelers from the towering monster's neck, each bigger than a telephone pole. They writhed like giant snakes across the floor, wrapping people and hauling them up shrieking and begging toward the giant maw at the top of the thing's head. The monstrosity closed in, blotting out the sky.

Olivia snatched two oil lamps from their shelves and smashed them onto the ground between themselves and the creatures closing around them. The beadles stopped, their tentacles waving like they were testing the fiery air. A few stewards crossed the fire line and went up in plumes of foul smoke. They staggered around, igniting others who also staggered around and torched still more. Alison grabbed two more lamps and threw them into the stewards. The wind off the beach fanned the flames. The inferno drove back the beadles. For a second, Olivia thought they might have had a chance.

The army of beadles and stewards found a way around the flaming mess. Some came through the fire, ignoring the blaze. Others circled through the smashed rows of chairs. From the fire in front and down from the cathedral out to their left, the horde closed on them. There were no more lamps nearby to throw. With a chair, his boots and his fists, Max, choking in the smoke and dust, beat back the first wave, some still in flames. Olivia and Alison held chairs, too, waiting for the things to close in the cathedral. But there were just so many. Olivia tried to slow her breathing, to stop the constant shaking in her hands.

Maggie's grandfather stood up from the silver box and the tangle of wires he'd wrapped around the pedestal. "Hold onto yer britches! I'm about to exfluncticate the wormhole!"

Turning to run from the pedestal, he tripped and fell. A gigantic feeler from the big monster lifted him by the ankle and closed around his waist and chest.

Under his motorcycle helmet, the old man's face flushed red. He got off a single blast from the shotgun. The tentacle jerked, but didn't let go. The shotgun clattered to the stones along with a small, metallic box like the one he'd attached to the pedestal. His black boots flailed in the air.

Olivia turned at the sounds coming from the door. Michael backed out of the doorway and snatched up a chair. Screaming for Maggie, he swung at the beadle lumbering after him. It swatted the chair aside, and it clattered to the stones.

Maggie appeared, leaning against the doorframe. A huge, bloody gash stained her torn robe. Olivia winced, feeling the beadle's toothed suckers and the hot needles of venom all over again.

Propping herself up in the doorway, Maggie threw the Noumenon and then she slid down the wall and collapsed onto the stones. The dark ball tumbled through the air. The beadle grasped for it, but the squirming tentacles flailed the air. The Noumenon made it through without getting touched.

Michael jumped and caught it. "ALISON!" Landing, he pivoted on one foot and tossed the Noumenon to Alison, but the beadle grabbed him around the chest and jerked him back. Michael's face became a pale mask of pain. The snow globe flew wide of Alison, rolling into a group of beadles and stewards.

The sheriff crawled forward on his hands and knees. His mouth hung open. His mirrored glasses were gone, and he seemed to stare straight at the Noumenon with eyes as white as pus.

Olivia thought of her parents. How devastated they were going to be. They would have to act nice to each other at the funeral. That made Olivia laugh inside. And then she thought of how much this was going to hurt. But she didn't let herself think about that for long. She dove into the crowd of monsters. A million hot needles blistered her arms, legs and back. Her ankle exploded as a steward crushed it in its grip and lifted her half upside down. But she had the snow globe in her fingertips. Her jaw ached from clenching, and her gut felt as if she'd done a thousand sit-ups, but she refused to let them make her scream.

Something cracked in her spine, and she flicked the Noumenon out to Alison. It was agony when she twisted her neck up to see whether Alison had the stupid Noumenon so that at least she wasn't dying for nothing. She would have been happy just to see Alison, but she could only see bare, crusty feet. Belly buttons the size of fists. Pale, blubbery tentacles. Olivia did not want that to be the last thing she saw before she died, but hot and wet agony erupted in her hip and she gave herself over to the blackness.

55 NOUMENON

Panic fluttered through Alison as she lost sight of Olivia under the tangle of scabbed corpse limbs and flailing tentacles. She heard those awful crunching sounds. Carmine and Frankie, legs and arms, all came flashing back to her. Alison's heart felt like a hot gash. The Noumenon rolled across the floor and stopped at her feet. She choked down a sob.

She picked it up, but it still just looked like a weird snow globe. Everything inside her fell away; she had no more hope. Beadles thrashed over Maggie and Michael. Max had wrapped a broken chair leg in cloth torn from a robe and made a torch with lamp oil, but he was surrounded. A beadle pulled him down. Maggie's grandfather was being dragged away. And the sheriff lumbered toward her, staring hungrily with his white eyes and nubby smile. He waved the knife that had killed Olga.

Alison wanted rage. She wanted hate. She wanted horror, but all she felt was pity. Pity that everyone she loved died for nothing. Pity that her parents would never even know what happened. Pity that this misguided man who called himself a sheriff caused so much hurt for the sake of an alien he could not have possibly understood. And she felt a deep, agonizing sorrow that they had all given everything and still failed.

The swirling inside her stopped. She felt still and calm. Olivia had been right. It was impossibly hard to do the right thing. It made her laugh, and that pulled the sheriff up short. He paused, bulk swaying as he panted like an animal, pointing at her with his knife.

Alison looked hard into the Noumenon. She had learned what the sea monster statue was. It was attacking the cathedral. That lesson had cost her everything. But what about the white whale? What had the old woman said? The Noumenon had called Alison. Why it chose her, Alison could not imagine. She wasn't special. Olivia was special. Alison was just smart enough to get out of trouble.

The snow globe was frustratingly dark, and she hated it more than she hated the sheriff or the monsters. "This is what you wanted, right? You wanted me?" Her anger woke up. "Well now you have me, stupid! You have me, and you took away everything else!" The sheriff was three steps away, waving the knife and pawing toward the snow globe.

Alison looked down into the dark ball. She clenched her teeth and shook it. "You better help me!" The thing in her hand rumbled and vibrated. It startled her, and she would have dropped it, but the Noumenon's magnetic pull held her, just like it had at The Mansion. A pinhole of pink light sparked deep inside it. Alison looked up. Everything around her stopped, as if time itself had frozen, but then the pink light erupted like a supernova, sending out pink shockwaves of energy that knocked the sheriff back, smashing him through the podium and the tables. The pulses of light swept the beadles against the walls of the cathedral where they withered, quivering in big piles.

The Noumenon allowed Alison to feel the atoms that made up the universe. Energy flowed all around her, in and through everything. The stones, the people, the ocean, it was all flowing. Vibrating, like everything was humming a tune. Laughing as the stewards staggered toward her, groping with their scabby hands, she understood. It wasn't that the Noumenon wouldn't work on stewards. She just had to shift the vibrations to match theirs. The Noumenon helped her feel it. All it took was a nudge of mental energy and the pink light flared out, engulfing them in pink flames. In seconds, they were all incinerated.

Alison felt the pull of the Noumenon and followed it, out of the cathedral and onto the beach. The monstrosity towered above her, its feelers waving. In one of them, Maggie's grandfather thrashed, crying out. The Noumenon stopped pulsing out shockwaves. The pink energy still swirled inside the ball. The monster swung its massive feelers down at her, but Alison wasn't afraid. The Noumenon blazed out a swirl of pink light, and the feelers bounced off harmlessly.

Maggie's grandfather was just above her. Alison could see him gasping and struggling, his face almost purple. Alison concentrated on him and pointed the Noumenon. A single beam of pink light shot out and wrapped the feeler that held him. Alison felt the pull of the feelers in her own arms. The pink light became an extension of her own body. Through the energy of the Noumenon, she felt the tentacle struggling to hold onto its prey. Alison closed her eyes and gritted her teeth and pulled hard. The tentacle unwound. Maggie's grandfather tumbled down. A second pink tendril shot out, caught him and plopped him into the sand where he crawled to his feet, coughing and gasping.

Alison had one thought. She had to destroy this creature. Not because she hated it, but to protect her world. She raised the Noumenon. It went dark, but she had expected that. She was learning. It was teaching her. She knew what it would do because she asked it. She knew what to do because it told her.

The energy inside gathered, and a single, narrow beam of pink light shot like a laser into the monstrosity's gigantic head, scattering into a web of pink lighting. The ground shook as its enormous tentacles writhed and the monster staggered. Alison willed a second pink tendril to tighten around the creature's flailing tentacles. She kept both beams going by stubbornly concentrating. She could feel the pink light smash through the monster's head. She felt its insides fry. Through the pink light, she felt its pain and its fear. It made her sick, but she would not stop until the thing toppled into the ocean and its massive white head disappeared under the churning water. An enormous wave swelled up where the creature had fallen, and rushed toward the beach. Alison held the Noumenon in front of her, creating a shield of pink light. In her hands she felt a slight push as the tsunami crashed around her and the water settled.

She stared down into the Noumenon. The pink light swirled and condensed into darker shades, and distantly, she heard Maggie's grandfather beside her. "Much—*cough*—obliged, li'l lady. Now what say we skedaddle so's I can finish what I started."

Alison saw Olga lying at her feet. A painful shock jolted her heart. She held out the Noumenon. The pink light swirled, but didn't go out into Olga. She concentrated and willed the light to heal, but Olga didn't move. She understood. She was too late. Olga was dead.

With bat wings of panic fluttering inside her, Alison ran into the cathedral. She spotted Maggie slumped in the doorway, her face white and limp, her body torn and bloody. Alison felt sharp teeth bite her heart. She felt another bite when she saw Michael, flat on his back with a huge hole in his belly. She was glad she couldn't see his face. She felt a choking sob and couldn't breathe. Everything in her was collapsing. Her whole body shook, and she felt so cold when she turned to where Olivia lay on the stone floor, her body bent at impossible angles, lifeless eyes stared at Alison like glass marbles.

Alison opened her mouth, but she couldn't scream. Her heart tore. She dropped to her knees. It had been too late for Olga, but not for them. Not for Olivia. Clenching her teeth, she looked down into the little glass ball in her hand. "I don't know who you are or what you want from me! I don't know why I'm here, but you need to fix this! Take me instead! It can't be Olivia! Please! Take me instead. FIX HER! Fix them all! Please take me instead! Just take me!"

She heard a shriek. It frightened her until she realized it had come from her, and then it terrified her. She squeezed the ball until the pink light started swirling. Staring into it, it spun faster and glowed brighter. She knew it would take all her life and give it to Olivia, Michael and Maggie. She could trade. She felt a surge of energy and strength until the pink light became so bright she had to close her eyes. Even then it was like staring at the sun. A thousand rubber bands snapped over every inch of her body, and a moment later, she didn't even have the strength to stand. She knew the snow globe had listened to her. She had traded her life for theirs. That made her smile as everything else slipped away.

56 SPACETIME

Olivia remembered the dry, scaly hands on her skin. Tearing at her. She felt a cracking feeling, like a million sprains, as her joints popped. She had been dead, but she didn't remember anything about what that was like. There were no tunnels of light. She did not see herself floating above her body. Maybe she hadn't been dead long enough. Or maybe she just hadn't been dead enough. It was possible she was still dead.

These thoughts flitted around in her mind as she lay with her eyes closed. Gradually, she became aware of her body. She felt good and sore, like after a particularly rough practice or a long tournament. But she was lying on cold stones. She screamed when she felt hands grabbing her. But these hands were soft and gentle.

"It's okay," Maggie's face came into focus. Her eyebrows were sunk with worry. "It's just me. We have to go."

Olivia looked around at the wreckage. The beadles were shriveled up against the walls, and the only trace of the stewards was the oily film of ash that seemed to have settled over everything. There was no sign of the monster on the beach. "What happened?"

Maggie shrugged. "I think this was all Alison. She must have used the Noumenon."

Olivia felt weak as Maggie helped her to her feet, but then Maggie wobbled and Olivia had to steady her. "Are you okay?"

Maggie chuckled and winced. "About like you I guess. Coming back from the dead really takes it out of you."

Olivia's heart skipped. "Were we dead?"

Maggie smiled and shrugged. "Who knows?"

Her skipping heart raced almost painfully. "Where's Alison?" Her breath caught when she saw her lying on the stones. Michael lifted her like a rag doll. Olivia took a few wobbly steps and then she willed herself to run, no matter how much it hurt. "Is she…"

Michael looked up sadly. His eyes looked frightened. "She's breathing and her heart is beating." Michael shrugged helplessly.

"Alison!" Olivia screamed. She slapped her face.

"Hey!" Michael snapped.

Olivia ignored him. "Allie!" Olivia could breathe again when Alison opened one eye and moaned, "Liv?" She smiled weakly, and her eyes fluttered shut.

Olivia could breathe again. "She's out of it, but she's alive." She jumped when the motorcycle engine thundered off the stones. Max skidded to a stop next to Michael. "Give her here!"

"Why?" Michael turned his body slightly, like he was sheltering Alison.

"Because the professor is gonna fry this place." Max patted his shiny, black gas tank. "Time to saddle up, man."

Alison moaned a little as Michael placed her across the motorcycle's broad gas tank. Max cradled her like a child. "You, too, Gidget." he commanded Olivia.

"My name is Olivia." Wherever Alison was going, Olivia was going, too. She snatched the Noumenon from the ground and climbed on.

Michael and Maggie were already running up the ramp.

Olivia felt a thwunk as Max put his bike in gear, and she wrapped her arms around Max's chest as far as she could make them go. He felt like an oversized bronze statue. Max accelerated toward the ramp, plowing over the chairs and bodies that littered the floor. It made Olivia feel more sick and dizzy than she already did.

At the bottom of the ramp, Max paused and turned. "Now, Professor! We're clear."

The professor ran toward the ramp with his silver box. Behind him, Olivia saw the sheriff stand up. He teetered on his feet for a moment, and then scuttled toward the pedestal. He started pulling at the wires, but must have realized he was out of time because he bolted back, snatched up the harp and ran out onto the sand as much as his bulk would let him. She watched him getting smaller across the sand.

The professor reached the bike. "Why'd you stop here?"

Max shrugged his big, leather shoulders. "In case you needed me, Professor."

"MOVE!" The professor pushed a black button in the middle of his little box while running up the ramp. Max gunned the motor and took off.

Olivia felt her neck snap as she was thrown against the backrest. She squeezed Max's leather jacket with one hand and the Noumenon with the other.

In a few seconds, the motorcycle burst into the downpour outside the boathouse and tore up the path, passing Maggie and Michael. Just before it turned the corner around The Mansion, Olivia saw the professor clear the dolmen and sprint up the path.

The air around them turned blue. Streaks of lightning ripped across the sky like the claws of an angry god. Trees fell in the yard, crushing the cars still parked there. Behind them, Olivia heard a grinding, howling wind and strange electronic-sounding whistles and deep booms.

Max weaved through the blockade of abandoned vehicles and dropped the kickstand by the front steps.

Olivia felt a pang of remorse and longing as Max stepped over their bicycles, still lying there from their ride, back when the world was simple.

In their room, Max lay Alison gently in bed. She moaned quietly. Olivia sat beside her. Alison's head was hot, but she opened her eyes.

"Liv?" Her voice cracked, but she smiled. "You're okay?"

Olivia cried and hugged Alison to her chest. "Are you?"

Alison smiled and closed her eyes.

The room suddenly went dark, and Olivia wondered why Max would shut off the lights. But then she remembered that it was still daytime. Out the window, Olivia saw that the afternoon had turned to black midnight.

"You don't see that every day," Max said. "Far out."

His blonde goatee glowed in the flickering blue light that started to flash outside the window. She would not leave Alison, but craning her neck, Olivia saw the vortex of blue lightning swirl above the lighthouse. The moaning roar, thunder and sizzling, electric static made it hard for Olivia to hear, even inside The Mansion.

Michael, Maggie and the professor appeared at the door.

Alison moaned; it reminded Olivia of the way Maggie had moaned on the morning they met her.

"Is she okay?" Michael asked.

"She's alive," was all Olivia could say. Her breath came in quick gulps as the lighthouse cracked, torn apart from the inside by blue lightning. Huge chunks fell off and tumbled into the churning ocean. The Mansion shook with an earthquake. A great, rippling wave of blue lightning surged down the jetty, cracking it, and the middle of the jetty collapsed on itself. The ocean rushed in and Olivia knew the cathedral was buried and flooded. The wormhole was gone. No one would ever study it.

The room started to get lighter. Blue streaks parted the night, but Olivia saw that it was just the normal blue of the afternoon sky. In another few moments, the sun was shining and the ocean was calm. The dolmen creaked loudly, and the stones toppled over.

"Jumpin' Jimminy Christmas! I'd say we showed them bushwhackers once and for all!" The professor slapped his knee.

Olivia ran her hand across Alison's hot forehead. It felt like it might have been getting even hotter. She moaned quietly, and her eyelids fluttered.

Maggie walked up to the big biker slowly with a faraway look on her face like she was in a delicate dream that might end at any moment.

"You're...you're back?" Maggie threw her arms around Max's neck, and then she threw herself into his big chest, laughing and crying at the same time.

She wiped away her tears and looked at them. "Grampa? Where have you been?"

The professor scratched his bushy, white hair. "That's the bear of it, darlin'. Something must have gone wrong in my calculations because I didn't account we'd end up back at The Mansion. I think when the CNE went and switched on the wormhole, it warped spacetime more than I anticipated. Heck, I didn't even know I could get back here from there." He clapped his hands and rubbed them together. "Like the man says, all's well that ends well. Now how 'bout we go rustle up some grub." He chuckled and took a cigar out of his breast pocket.

"You can't smoke that in here," Olivia said. It was the one and only clear thought she could put together. Everything felt like it was zooming past her.

The professor looked puzzled for a moment, his bushy moustache twitching like a living thing. "No, I suppose it would not be beneficial to our young patient here." He crossed and looked down at Alison. "I don't know what she did nor how she did it, but that gal was magnificent."

"I know," Olivia said quietly. She wished more than anything that Alison would wake up.

"What was that little ball she had?" Max pantomimed holding the Noumenon and waving it around. "That thing really kicked ass."

"She sure saved our bacon with it, I tell you that," the professor said, gesturing with his unlit cigar.

"I wish we'd had it the whole time," Max said. "Would have made our job a lot easier."

"The Noumenon." Michael sounded so confident. Olivia imagined he must have been proud of himself for getting the name right. Too bad Alison didn't hear it.

"STOP!" Maggie's eyes narrowed suspiciously at the two men. "Not another word until you tell me where you've been." Maggie shot each syllable like a bullet.

Max shrugged. "It's a little complicated, but the professor here, he figured out a way to destroy the CNE's wormhole, only he had to do it from the ass end. So, he built a little machine that made a tiny wormhole, just big enough for me to ride him through on my bike, see? I know I'm not explaining it right. Anyway, we rode through to the other side and set the charges. Then we were supposed to open the wormhole enough to ride back to this side, finish setting the charges and then blow the whole thing sky high, man." Max nodded and looked satisfied as he stared out the window. "Far out."

"I knew they'd try to open it eventually," the professor said. "An' when they did, I'd be ready to use their own energy against them. I can't get into the technicals just now, but suffice to say…kablooey!" The professor grinned and chewed on the end of his cigar. "They just went and upped the timeline on me is what happened."

Maggie closed her eyes. "You knew about all this? About the wormhole and the monsters?"

"Talk to the boss," Max said, poking a thick thumb at the professor.

"Not all the what-have-yous and wherefores, mind, just the big picture." He took a deep, satisfied breath. "I been studying on them for years." He sighed and looked out the window. Olivia noticed a sadness that made his pert features sag. "It's been my life's work ever since your parents passed."

Maggie cried and sat on the edge of the bed. "Why didn't you ever tell anybody?"

"I warned you that if you ever found a door open under that jetty, it was the beginning of the end."

"You never said that!" Maggie said.

The professor shrugged. "Not exactly, no. You got me there. To be above boards with you, I didn't exactly know myself what would happen when the CNE accessed the wormhole. I knew they needed the harp to control it and that the stones were sort of like rechargeable batteries. Beyond that, I didn't have much in the way of specifics. But I did tell you to be on the lookout for it."

"That was years ago! I hardly saw you after that!" Maggie was crying, but her eyebrows gathered like angry storm clouds.

"Your Aunt Penny didn't want me filling you with ideas she thought were adding to your sickness. It's what them headshrinkers up at the hospital told her to do. Much as it pained me to leave you out of the loop, I obliged." The professor sighed and looked out the window. "Your Aunt Penny thought I had one boot in the loony bin and the other on a banana peel, so I had to mind my P's and Q's. I kept my investigations more or less to myself. Shucks, I only let Max in on it a couple-three days ago because I needed him to ride me in on his motorbike." The professor's bushy eyebrows and moustache drooped sadly as he turned to face Maggie. "Honestly, the less you knew, the safer you were."

"For the record, Professor, you didn't mention anything about monsters," Max added.

"I didn't know about them!" the professor snapped. "My studies were limited to the science of their wormhole. I didn't concern myself with no critters."

"For ten years you let me think that I was crazy!" Maggie's eyes were red and angry. "That my parents were crazy! How could you do that?"

The professor held up his hands. "I told you, you're safer not knowing."

"No, we weren't!" Maggie pointed at Olivia, Michael and Alison. "Do they look safe? Did you see those things down there? That sheriff?"

The professor chuckled weakly. "I didn't know how far the tentacles' reach was—pardon my pun."

Maggie's face condensed into anger that Olivia thought might have hidden real hate. "Pun? You're making a pun? They killed Olga and her whole family!"

The professor's face stiffened. "Olga?"

"Yeah." Maggie's voice was ragged. "They kill people. I think they killed us. If Alison didn't have the Noumenon…"

The professor rubbed his moustache. "The Noumenon…I think there's a lot we can learn if I—"

"NO!" Maggie screamed, pointing at her grandfather. "You stay away from her! And stay away from me."

The professor sighed. His eyes looked sad under his huge eyebrows. "Mags, I been keeping clear of y'all for too long as it is. Now I might have made some mistakes, but you and me…we're kin."

Maggie sighed heavily. "Why didn't you tell us how dangerous this place was? You think Aunt Penny would have stayed here? Or let tourists come down here to get killed by those monsters and kidnapped by those church fanatics?"

"When did they get Olga?" The professor looked sad and far away.

"Down there! In the cathedral you just blew up. They killed them to open the wormhole and then you came in."

The professor faced the window again. "I warned her that we were up against something big. I said that if'n I didn't come back, she should warn Penny and everybody should clear out of the Cape. But I told her I could fix it. Tarnation! I did fix it. Their gateway is gone. We won, see? This here was supposed to be a jubilation, not a funeral. Daggum! Olga. I sure am gonna miss that ol' girl." The professor hid his eyes under his hand. "I just talked to her. She believed in what I was tryin' to do. Might have been the only one keeping the faith about Cape November. Wanted to make things good again, y'know? Like old times?"

Olivia was struggling to make sense of the professor's story. Something wasn't lining up.

"When?" Maggie demanded. "When did you talk to Olga?"

The professor shrugged. "Today. Before Max and I lit out on his motorbike to make hay."

Maggie walked up to the old man and grabbed his shoulders. "You've been gone for two years!" Maggie sobbed.

Max looked puzzled. "Two years?" He looked at the large watch on his wrist. "No. We've only been gone a couple of hours."

Maggie stepped up to him and took both his huge hands in hers. "No, Uncle Max. You've been gone for two years."

The silence sat heavy on the room until the professor broke it. "Well, navigating through the fabric of spacetime can be a mite dicey." He turned abruptly. "Max, we better go find Penny. Sounds like you have a lot of explaining to do."

"Me?" Max's face darkened, and Olivia was afraid of what would follow.

The professor looked down sheepishly and kicked dejectedly at the floor. "Okay. I got some explaining to do."

Maggie turned to Olivia and Michael. "Take care of Alison. Please. I'll be back to check on her as soon as I can, but… my family needs me right now."

"Do what you have to do," Michael said, "We'll be okay."

At the door, Maggie stopped and ran back into the room. She stood up on her toes and kissed Michael's lips. Feeling like she was intruding, Olivia looked down at Alison.

"Thank you, Michael," Maggie said. "For everything."

She pulled away and headed for the door, but she paused again and called over her shoulder. "I bet you're never going to forget this first date." She laughed a little as she left.

Michael came over to the bed and put his hand on Alison's forehead. She moaned, and her eyes fluttered open, but just for a moment. "Hey, she's burning up."

"I know," Olivia said.

"She needs a doctor," Michael said.

Olivia felt frustrated and sad. "Good luck finding one."

"Is she going to be okay?" he asked. It caught Olivia a little off guard to see him look so worried, but then, he was Alison's only brother.

"Help me get her into the tub," Olivia said. "We need to get her fever down."

57 REALITY

"Alison?" Olivia sounded like she was standing in a tunnel. Alison kept her eyes closed, feeling the softness of the mattress under her back. She wondered why Olivia might be calling her from a tunnel, but Alison felt so comfortable, more comfortable than she had ever remembered feeling. She couldn't think about why Olivia might be in a tunnel. Or down a hole. Or in a grave. Alison's eyes popped open, and she jerked herself up, gasping for breath. Pain ripped through her whole body.

Olivia was leaning over her, stroking her hair. Her beautiful eyes had all their usual sparkle. Alison remembered them as dead as glass. Alison shook with fear as Olivia lowered her gently back to the softest pillow in the world.

Olivia squeezed Alison's hand. Even that hurt, but Alison would not have let her go if her hand were on fire. Fire. Something had been on fire. Something awful and terrifying. But Alison couldn't get it.

"Where am I?" Alison barely recognized her own hoarse voice. Her throat felt like she'd swallowed hot metal shavings.

"In bed," Olivia whispered.

"Is there any water?" Alison closed her eyes and settled deeper into the cloud she rested on.

Something plastic probed her lips. A straw. She sipped, letting the cool water wash around her mouth and her throat. She felt it run in a tiny stream all the way down into her stomach.

Weren't they supposed to be going on vacation? Why was she still in bed? They were going someplace new. Cape November.

Alison's eyes popped open again, and sickening waves of fear made the water in her stomach gurgle. "We can't go, Liv. There's something bad down there. Bad things are going to happen to us."

"I don't know, Tommy, I think we should get a doctor. She's delusional." It hurt to move her eyes, but there was Mom. A vague memory flashed across her mind. Mom was gone. Fear grabbed her, but it passed when Mom gently pressed the back of her hand to Alison's cheek, just like she'd always done when Alison was sick. Mom's eyebrows lifted; that meant she was thinking. "At least her fever broke. She's cool as a cucumber now, but if she's having hallucinations..."

Dad's face appeared over Mom's shoulder. "How're you feeling, Sweetie?"

It felt good to hear him call her that. For a second, Alison couldn't remember how old she was. She had another vague memory of fear. Terrible fear. And grief. Her heart had broken and she was alone. But that had just been a nightmare. A fever. Chunks of memories crashed back. Alison's arms ached and she felt the wet crunch of an old man's head. A fiery wave of dazzling pink light.

Blinking back tears she couldn't have explained, Alison looked around the room. It wasn't her own room, but she knew it. A wardrobe. A door to a bathroom. Windows. Terrible, terrifying things came to that window. They were called beadles because they worked for a church. The Church of New Enlightenment. Alison gasped for breath and shook with fear. New tears burned her eyes.

"She's coming around now." That voice came a little clearer. It was Maggie. Maggie from Maggie's Haunted Mansion. It wasn't just a gimmick. The Mansion hid terrifying things. A flash of white tentacles. Blood.

Alison felt like everything was new and strange to her. Nothing made any sense. She remembered Maggie. Hot chocolate. Crepes. Bicycles. But Maggie's face was pale, and her body was limp and bloody in a dark cave. No. Not a cave. A cathedral.

It was like Alison had an itch that she couldn't scratch. Her mind itched. There were things she knew, things she should remember, but they stayed just out of her reach, rustling like wild animals in the night, afraid to come too close to a campfire.

Her bones hurt. Her eyes and head throbbed. Every time her heart beat, her pulse felt like tiny hammers pounded every inch of her. Her throat burned. Her skin itched. She felt like a giant, rashy bruise. She had a vision of an army of naked, scabby people reaching for her. She gasped and tried to sit up again. To escape the nightmare.

"Whoa, hang on, Al." Michael was there. He wasn't dead. But a monster had chewed a hole in his belly and eaten his insides. No. That must have been a nightmare. The fever.

Lifting her head again gave Alison a new appreciation for pain. But she had to see if her brother was really there. "Have I been sick?"

"Oh yeah," Michael said. "You've been really out of it since yesterday afternoon."

"Is it morning now?" Alison forced her eyes to stay open no matter how much the sun in the windows hurt her eyes. She needed answers. Olivia's face was more angelic than ever with golden light streaming around her. Her hair falling in brown and blonde curls. "Liv?" Alison felt tears choking her. "You're alive!" Alison didn't care how much it hurt, she threw her arms around Olivia's neck, just to feel the reality of her.

Olivia leaned Alison back against the pillow and stroked her hair. "It's going to be okay now."

"Michael? Maggie?" Alison felt panic rising.

"We're all here with you, Al." Alison had never been happier to see her brother. Michael and Maggie smiled down at her, hugging her tight. Alison didn't mind the pins and needles it sent shooting through her.

Alison closed her eyes again. The tears hurt, and crying made her whole head throb. She kept her eyes closed. She felt so relieved that all the scary things floating around in her head had all been a dream.

"You're still at The Mansion," Maggie said.

"We couldn't take you home yet. You can't travel in your condition," Mom said.

"You've been here the whole time, right?"

"We're here now, Sweetie," Dad said.

Alison's eyes popped painfully open. Mom and Dad were at the foot of the bed. Dad had his arm around Mom's shoulders. They each came around and hugged Alison. She kept squeezing them. She refused to let go no matter how much it hurt.

Alison had to figure out what had been real and what was still real. "Were you ever not here?"

"Sweetie, you just woke up. We can talk when you're rested."

"I'm fine." Alison winced and closed her eyes. She wasn't fine.

"We would have called," Mom said, "but the phones were out."

"What happened to you? Did they get you?" Alison demanded. Her head throbbed with every beat of her heart.

"Who?" Dad asked.

"The Enlightened? The monsters?" Alison remembered people on a table. Webs of mucus like a cocoon. A tube. Something white under the water. Or had that been only a nightmare. She shivered.

Mom and Dad traded worried looks. Mom put her hand on Alison's forehead. "Is there a hospital nearby, Maggie? I'm starting to worry. Her fever was so high. What if she has brain damage?"

"Sara, come on!" Dad put his hand on Alison's forehead.

"How could you tell?" Michael added.

"Mikey!" Dad scowled at Michael.

It hurt to laugh, but Alison was so relieved to have anything happen that felt normal.

Olivia sat on the edge of the bed and stuck a thermometer in Alison's mouth. "She never went above 103, Mrs. Nunios, I promise." Olivia was so good at convincing her parents that nothing was wrong. "That's on the high side for someone her age, but brain damage isn't a factor until you get up to around 105 or 6." Olivia looked so serious.

Dad smiled wryly at her. "What're you, a doctor now?"

Sheepishly, Olivia grinned up at him through the tops of her eyes. "Not yet, but last summer I went to a medical program at Mossell University."

"Not as fun as this, right?" Michael muttered.

"Be quiet, you," Mom smacked his arm playfully.

Dad nodded. He was satisfied. "She's going to be fine, Sara. She's a tough kid." That made Alison smile.

"Is her fever really down?" Mom asked. "I can't imagine what happened to her. When we came home last night and found her so sick…"

Dad shrugged and put his arm gently around Mom. "She got sick, Sara. People get sick. Probably just a virus or something. Right, Doc?"

Olivia smiled and held up the thermometer for Mom's inspection. "Totally normal now."

"See? She had a rough night, but after everything that happened, the kids should be more worried about us."

Alison was sure that she was still hallucinating when Mom turned and pecked Dad on the lips. "I think that what happened to us is just wonderful."

Dad laughed. "Oh yeah, spending the night stuck on the highway is great fun."

Mom wrapped her arms around Dad's neck. "You know you had fun. It was a real adventure."

Alison's head swam. "What happened? Where were you? Did the church get you?" She felt herself slipping away again. She couldn't figure out what had been real.

"See, why does she keep talking about a church?" Mom sounded worried and her eyebrows furrowed.

"She had a high fever, Sara," Dad sounded so confident. "That messes with your dreams. She's just a little out if it, right, Sweetie?"

Olivia stroked her head. "Alison, your parents are fine."

Alison looked hard at her parents. For a second, she had a clawing feeling that they were imposters. The church had done something to them. To all of them. "Where's the Noumenon?"

Mom and Dad looked at each other.

Dad scrutinized Olivia. "What's she talking about?"

"Okay, we need to get her to a hospital," Mom said.

Michael picked up the snow globe from the nightstand and handed it to her. "She just wants this thing. I guess she named it."

"Oh. The shot put. What did she name it?" Dad's head was tilted, and his eyebrows crunched. "Newman?"

"You know kids," Mom said. Alison caught the worried edge in her voice.

Feeling the smooth, solid weight of the Noumenon, Newman, made Alison feel more grounded. She had a clear memory of a pink light. She felt it flowing through her like a warm fire. Like lightning. It made her feel so tired to think of it, but it made her feel stronger too. She hugged the sphere to her chest. It was almost cold against her skin. She noticed that she was naked. The clammy dampness of the sheets brought up a memory of a scary, bald man with white eyes. It made her shiver.

Mom noticed and her lips tightened with worry. "We're definitely getting her checked by a doctor as soon as we get home."

"Just tell me where you were, Mom." It hurt Alison's head to speak, but she had to know what had happened. She needed the story to fit. She had to know what was real and what had come out of her fever dreams.

Mom laughed. "It really is kind of funny."

"Yeah." Dad sounded annoyed. "Hysterical." More like his old self. That felt like a piece of solid ground.

"You weren't complaining last night." Alison caught the mischievous sparkle in Mom's eyes.

Dad broke into a wide smile. He put his arm back around Mom, squeezing her gently. Alison wondered for a moment whether she ended up in an alternate universe where Mom and Dad got along great. Alternate universe? She looked at the snow globe again. The sea monster inside scared her. It had been huge. Terrifying.

Mom started her story, snapping Alison back to the bedroom. "What happened was, we were in Friendly Point. Dad lied about Nelson and his girlfriend." Mom's face was beaming. Nothing made any sense. Why were they in Friendly Point? Alison could not land on what was real.

Dad chuckled. "Originally, I told Mom we were meeting Nelson and his girlfriend. Remember the night we got here, Al?" Dad asked.

Alison did remember that. Clearly. They had arrived at The Mansion in the pouring rain. She and Dad had a big fight about it.

"But that wasn't true. I never planned on meeting Nelson and his girlfriend. I don't even think she came down with him." Dad's eyes shifted back and forth like some spy in a bad movie. "Nelson was in on my cover story, but it was going to be a date, just me and Mom. I wanted to surprise her, so I made a reservation at La Maison Des Calmars."

"I didn't realize you went there." Maggie sounded impressed. "That's a Michelin two-star restaurant."

"Yeah," Dad said, scowling. "It wasn't cheap."

"Oh, Tommy!" Mom slapped his arm playfully.

Dad's scowl softened into a big grin. "Worth every penny."

"He had flowers waiting for me at the table and everything," Mom gushed. "I have them in our room. They're beautiful." Mom's face blossomed with her idea. "I should bring them in here to brighten the room for our patient."

"Later, Mom." It only throbbed a little when she said it, so Alison pressed on. "Finish the story." Alison was thrilled to hear that her parents had gone on a date, but that didn't explain what had happened.

"You remember I was all ticked off and Mom and I had a big fight at breakfast, right? Because I was going golfing?"

"We remember, Pop," Michael said.

"Yeah, yeah, I was acting stupid, but I was trying to keep a secret and you know I'm no good at that stuff. I really did want to get in one quick game while I was down here. There's a course here that's on the PGA tour, see, and Nelson knows a guy—"

Mom cut him off. "The point is that after he golfed, he found me, and we had a good long talk." She looked at Dad, and a small tear formed in Mom's eye. "It was a talk we should have had years ago." Mom wiped her eye and stiffened. "Anyway, he told me about La Maison Des Calmars. I mean, I've been telling Dad for years that I wanted to go there, but I never thought we would. It's so fancy."

"And expensive," Dad grumbled.

Mom ignored that. "Of course, Dad had packed a suit, but since he never told me, I didn't pack anything to wear to a place like that, so I told Dad we had to go to the outlet mall, since it's on the way to Friendly Point."

"Mom!" A sharp pain stabbed through her head, and Alison winced. "Just tell me what happened! Where were you?"

"I see somebody's feeling better." Mom started to laugh. "Can you believe that after a wonderful date like that, the stupid car broke down on the way home!" Mom and Dad both laughed hard. "It was like a nightmare." Alison jumped at the word.

"Nobody's phones worked, so we couldn't call you guys or The Mansion or even a tow truck." Dad shook his head. "We did leave you a note, but we knew you guys would worry—Alison would worry. But what could we do? We just sat there in the middle of nowhere in the middle of the night on the side of the road. You'd think a car or a truck would pass. Something." Dad said.

Alison kept waiting for something else. Something sinister or terrible, something that matched the bad feelings that swirled in her gut and the awful visions that flashed in her head. She looked at Olivia, but she just sat there smiling and nodding like she was listening to the story. "So what did you do?"

Mom smiled wistfully. "We talked more. A lot more. For once, we only talked about us. Not you, or the house, or work, or the bills." She looked at Dad warmly. "Just about the two of us."

Dad looked happy, too, just to be looking at Mom. "I tell you, kids, I felt like we were twenty years old again. In the dark, in the back of a car—except this was a minivan with folding seats." Dad took Mom's hand and kissed it, bobbing his eyebrows suggestively.

"Okay, let's not traumatize her any more," Michael groaned. "What happens in the minivan stays in the minivan."

"Shaddup, Mikey," Dad growled playfully. He and Mom kissed.

Alison felt little butterflies in her stomach…the good kind.

Alison looked at Michael, but he didn't seem to have any reaction. He just stood there holding hands with Maggie.

"It was like we were getting to know each other all over again." Dad said it distantly. He and Mom shared a little look between them like they both knew a secret.

For a moment, Alison wondered if she were dreaming. "How did you get back here?"

"The next morning, we still couldn't get a phone to work. We figured the only way we were getting back is if we walked," Dad said.

"There were more cars on the road," Mom added. "Dad wanted to flag somebody down to see if they were coming down the Cape, but I wouldn't let him. Might end up in the car with some axe-murderer."

The words chilled Alison. She had a clear memory of her brother, cutting people up with an axe. No. Not people. She remembered the stewards. The beadles. The wormhole. Every horrible memory exploded clearly in her head. Fear overwhelmed her as everything came rushing back to her.

"You okay, sweetie?" Mom said. "You don't look so good again."

"She got kind of pale all of a sudden," Dad observed quietly. He placed his hand gently on the side of Alison's face.

Olivia squeezed her hand tightly. Alison looked up at her. She narrowed her eyes and shook her head so slightly that Alison almost missed it. She knew her parents would not have noticed the look.

"I'm fine," Alison said. She closed her eyes and forced herself to smile. "Just tired. Still getting over this bug, probably."

"You should rest," Mom said. "Let's clear out and give her some space."

"How did you get back?" Alison insisted. "What happened?"

"That can wait," Mom said.

"No. Tell me." Alison felt so tight, like she could explode at any moment.

Dad chuckled. "It was starting to rain, I mean it was really coming down, and we were getting soaked. And get this! We saw a whole swarm of those big flies, the ones that got me and Michael on the way down—"

"Oh, they were disgusting. I've never been so scared."

"They were all over something on the ground. Big, dead bird I think. Anyway, we're getting ready to run for it when, all of a sudden, this little car pulls up next to us and somebody's yelling for us to get in."

Alison shivered.

"It was Penny!" Mom laughed. "She was driving back from her trip, and she saw us walking on the side of the road."

"But then we get back here and there's cars all over the place." Dad's face looked puzzled. "Penny thought she had a lot of customers suddenly, but there was nobody checked in. Only get this, her boyfriend? The guy she was talking about who left before he fixed anything? He's back now out of the blue with Penny's father. Good news, but, I mean, it's crazy, right?"

Alison looked at Maggie. She was crying, but trying not to show it.

If Dad noticed, he didn't say anything. "Then we come up here and you're sick in bed. Your fever was coming down, and Olivia and Maggie were taking care of you so we went to bed."

"We didn't get a lot of sleep in the van." Mom giggled.

"I woke up at like...three to take a leak. I came to check on you. It felt like your fever was down and you and Olivia were both out. I mean, you were dead."

Alison felt queasy. The memory of Olivia's glassy eyes still stared up at her. Olivia squeezed her hand.

Dad must not have noticed. "Down at breakfast is when Penny tells us Max and her father are back. I don't know what the story is there. Maggie, you were talking to them, right? I don't want to speak out of turn about your family. Oh, but get this, there was a huge fire at Olga's. I hate to say this... the place is wiped out. Nobody can find Olga and her family, but it doesn't look good. They were probably in there. They're saying it was a kitchen fire. The pizza ovens or something." Dad sighed heavily. "Can you believe it? We were just there."

Alison sobbed.

"Oh, Sweetie, I know. It's such a shame," Mom said. "They seemed like such nice people."

"And then," Dad said, "something happened down on the jetty, too. It's half-collapsed and the lighthouse is gone. Fell right into the ocean. Nobody can figure that one out. I'm thinking it had to be an earthquake or something, right? What a shame. Historic building like that." Dad sighed and shook his head. "We're gone for one night, and the whole world falls apart."

Mom turned to Maggie, "This must be a very emotional time for you and your family. As soon as Alison is up for it, we're going to get out of your hair." She pulled Dad toward the door. "And she'll never get better if she doesn't rest. Everybody out."

"No!" Pain shot through Alison's head. She took a deep breath. "Olivia has to stay."

Mom laughed and kissed Alison's forehead again. "Of course she's staying. It's her room, too. Just don't stay up gossiping. Rest."

Michael and Maggie held hands by the side of Alison's bed. Michael looked over his shoulder as Mom and Dad left. As soon as Alison heard Mom and Dad's door close, Michael leaned down and whispered, "They have no clue about what happened. It's probably best if we don't tell them anything."

Alison felt like the room was spinning away. "Did it happen? The church? The wormhole?"

Half his mouth turned up in something like a sad smile. She felt a little pop of surprise when Michael kissed her forehead. "You saved our lives with that thing," he nodded at the Noumenon on her chest. "And you almost died doing it."

"What happened after that?" She remembered everything up until she was surrounded by pink light. "Were you really..."

"Dead?" Michael shrugged. "I don't like thinking about it. Besides, Olivia can explain everything better than I can. She's the genius." Michael held his fist up. Olivia smiled and returned the bump. Maggie and Michael left, still holding hands.

When they were alone, Olivia lay on top of the sheets next to Alison. The solid weight of Olivia's body next to her felt so real and comforting. Olivia gently took the Noumenon from Alison and held it in the sunlight streaming in from the windows. The statuettes floated around, whale and sea monster, each going their own way, apparently immune to the laws of gravity or inertia. Alison wondered what the Noumenon really was and where it could have come from.

Trying to solve that made her head start to hurt, so Alison was glad when Olivia set it on the nightstand where it was just a snow globe, another curious trinket, like the antique oil lamp beside it.

Olivia found Alison's hand again under the cover and held it to her own chest. Alison could feel Olivia's strong, steady heartbeat.

"Your mom's right. You should rest now," she said.

"I can't." It was the first time that talking didn't send shooting pains across Alison's chest. And it only hurt a little when she propped herself up on her elbow to look at Olivia. She must have showered at some point. Her skin glowed, and her amazingly perfect hair cascaded across the pillow. "I need to know what happened after I used the Noumenon. How did it end?"

Olivia laughed slightly and Alison's hand rode up and down with her body. "I don't know if it really did."

Alison was too tired for games. If Olivia started, she would not have even played anagrams. "Just tell me what happened."

Under her hand, Alison felt the rise and fall of Olivia's chest as she took a deep breath. "It's kind of a long story."

Alison leaned her head against Olivia's shoulder and closed her eyes. "We have nothing but time."

ACKNOWLEDGEMENTS

Writers walk a lonesome road, but they don't work in isolation. This book would not be here if not for these people.

Antonio and Rita Favetta: As if bringing me into this world and then bringing me up in it weren't enough, you patiently gave me notes on my first remarkably awful draft of this novel.

Amy Favetta: Thanks for always telling the truth, even when it hurts.

Ed and Judy Horowitz: Thanks for inspiring me to be patient and professional with my craft—and for bringing Julie into the world.

Gary and Melissa Margolin: Thanks for taking this seriously, and more importantly, making me take it seriously too (but not too seriously).

Matt McGrath and Julie Peters: Thanks for believing, and more importantly, making me believe too.

Karen Hodges Miller: Your patience and guidance have been invaluable.

April Pratt: The circle is now complete. When you left me, you were but the learner. Now you are the master.

Khalid Uddin: Thanks for nudging me in the right direction.

Frank Verga: Thanks for keeping it real and not letting me get too hippy-dippy.

The Writers Circle—South Orange, NJ: Thanks for helping me untangle this story.

My Colleagues: Thanks for being so incredibly supportive.

My Students: Thanks for teaching me so many wonderful things.

ABOUT THE AUTHOR

When he isn't writing books, Tonio Favetta is a high school English teacher, writing mostly during the summer. This is one reason why it takes him a long time to finish things. The other reason is that he's lazy. He started teaching in 1990, but he started writing way back in the '80s when he was growing up in Jersey City, New Jersey. He loves New Jersey, so he still lives there, just a stone's throw from Newark, along with his wife, his daughters and a deranged labradoodle.

As a younger reader, he loved Tolkien (and still does!), and he devoured *Conan the Barbarian* novels and *The Sword of Shannara* series along with any other fantasy he could find. He still loves reading fantasy, especially Neil Gaiman, and science fiction, especially HP Lovecraft and Philip K Dick. He also loves *Moby Dick*, *The Odyssey* and *A Confederacy of Dunces*.

Tonio enjoys hanging out with friends and family, playing the guitar, riding his motorcycle, pig roasts, Bruce Springsteen concerts and all things Star Wars, Star Trek, Batman, Marvel and Coen Brothers. Not necessarily in that order.

www.ingramcontent.com/pod-product-compliance
Lightning Source LLC
Chambersburg PA
CBHW020244200626
46816CB00001BA/129